KATE KINSEY

KENSINGTON PUBLISHING CORP.
www.kensingtonbooks.com

KENSINGTON BOOKS are published by

Kensington Publishing Corp.
119 West 40th Street
New York, NY 10018

All Kensington titles, imprints, and distributed lines are available at special quantity discounts for bulk purchases for sales promotions, premiums, fund-raising, educational, or institutional use. Special book excerpts or customized printings can also be created to fit specific needs. For details, write or phone the office of the Kensington special sales manager: Kensington Publishing Corp., 119 West 40th Street, New York, NY 10018, attn: Special Sales Department; phone 1-800-221-2647.

PUBLISHER'S NOTE
This book is a work of fiction. Names, characters, businesses, organizations, places, events, and incidents either are the product of the author's imagination or are used fictitiously. Any resemblance to actual persons, living or dead, events, or locales is entirely coincidental.

ISBN-13: 978-1-60183-057-9
ISBN-10: 1-60183-057-2

First electronic edition: November 2012

ISBN-13: 978-1-60183-196-5
ISBN-10: 1-60183-196-X

Printed in the United States of America

For Sir, who made all my fantasies come true

Chapter 1

"If you will but fall down and worship Me . . ."
Worship with my suffering
offered up in tears and blood.
Worship with my body,
the least of His price.
  i fell. i soared.
    i answered with joy baptized in tears:
    "Yes, my God.
        My Dark Lord.
        My Fallen Angel...
        Yes . . ."
                                —"Waiting for God"

The desire had always been there. A yearning for dark, shadowed things that could not be spoken of, could hardly be put into words even if she dared.

Before she knew what sex was, it had been a craving for consuming intimacy. To be known. To belong to someone. To be utterly lost in another's soul.

And so she formed intense attachments to *bestfriendsforever*. But her singular devotion overwhelmed each in her turn, and their failure to comprehend and reciprocate cut her to the core.

Even as she built up a wall against that hurt, still she yearned.

She burned to be desired so intensely that savage conquest was the only course. The tender, tentative fumblings of first boyfriends only ignited dreams of passionate violence.

Then came the furtive, half-ashamed masturbation under the sheets, breath stopped for fear her parents on the other side of the wall might know, somehow, what she was doing. Know not just what her fingers did with increasing skill, but what dark thoughts pushed her to orgasm.

Fantasies of strong hands holding her down, binding her, using her, hurting her. Not because she deserved it, but because she wanted it.

She wanted to offer up her body and mind and soul in devotion and pain and suffering so sweet it denied all attempts to define, describe, quantify.

She learned what others called it. *Sadomasochism.* But it was inadequate, not the right word at all. *Perversion* was worse in its cruelty, its judgment.

But nothing could stop the want.

When she found him, it seemed as if he'd always been there.

He saw right through her, took all the dark yearnings, and gave them back to her, fulfilled beyond her wildest imaginings.

She was his, and only death could tear her from him.

Chapter 2

Wives, submit to your husbands as to the Lord.
—EPHESIANS 5:22

They called it a glory hole, but there was nothing glo-
rious about the dim little booths in the rear of the
adult bookstore. The plywood was hastily slapped with
black paint, and the concrete floors, sticky from God-
only-knew what, sucked at her high heels. The only light
came from the washed-out flicker of porn on the small
screen in the booth with her.

The air held the faint smell of mold, sweat, and jism under the cheap industrial deodorizer.

Yes, jism. Man-juice. Cum. Semen. The smell was unmistakable. After all, that was the point of this lurid little
alley of closets where men came to shoot their load, alone
with only video flesh and moans bought for a token.

She had never been here alone. She had come with him
once, of course. That time he had merely taken her into
one of the booths and used her. (Funny how his fingers
curled into the hair at the nape of her neck could cause all
bone and muscle in her legs to dissolve, even when the last
thing she wanted was contact with that floor. By the time
he had yanked her to her feet, pushed her against the wall,
and shoved his cock into her ass, she would have licked
the floor if he'd asked her to.)

Today he was testing her, and she was a little disappointed. It was her birthday after all, and she had hoped he would come with her.

"Imagine the fear," he had whispered through the phone line. "Imagine how your heart will beat. How your pulse will race. Walking into the back of that bookstore all alone. Feeling the eyes of the clerk following you. He'll think you're a whore. And he won't be wrong, will he?"

Her heart jerked in her chest as she argued with herself.

You don't have to get naked, the voice of reason whispered slyly in her head. *He won't know if you did or not. He won't know if you actually did what he told you or not.*

But he would know. She couldn't lie to him.

She took off her dress and then slipped out of her panties and bra. The thigh-high stockings and stiletto heels, she kept on. Not just because he had told her to, but because she liked the way she felt wearing them.

She folded the dress into a neat square and positioned it on the floor in front of the hole in the wall. She drew in a deep breath, equal parts fear and arousal, knelt on her clothes, and waited.

It wasn't really a hole, either. The crotch-high rectangle cut in the plywood was big enough for her whole head to fit through. Big enough for someone's hands to reach in . . .

She heard a door open. Steps in the hall outside. She could not breathe, waiting to see if some stranger's cock was going to appear through the hole.

Instead, she heard the sounds of tokens being dropped into a video machine somewhere farther down.

She waited and wondered if a cop might show up instead. What would she do if she got arrested?

Oh, God . . . Once more, she could hear feet outside in the hall, but no one came into the booth on the other side. Then all she could hear were the video moans and grunts over tinny porn music.

She brought her hands to her heavy breasts, stroking her

nipples to distract herself. She craned her neck upward and back to see the threesome fucking on the screen. Two men had a third impaled on their cocks, one in his mouth, the other up his ass. The sight of it sent a gush of her own juices down her thigh. Why was the sight of three men fucking such a turn-on?

She didn't hear him come in. He was just suddenly there.

But not on the other side of the hole.

In the booth. With her.

Oh, Christ, she hadn't locked the door . . . How could she have been so stupid?

She watched his thick fingers turn the latch and heard the dull click.

She had a glimpse of dark, intense eyes looking down at her through a black ski mask . . . And then a cock jutting through the khaki of his trousers as two hands came down on her shoulders.

Panic flared, but she clamped down on it. She could manage this. Just suck his cock and be done with it. That was all he wanted. If he didn't leave, she'd start screaming. Cops be damned.

She bent her mouth toward him, but his knees and hands were forcing her backward.

"No," he snarled abruptly. "I don't want your filthy mouth on me, whore."

The words both stung and inflamed her. How dare he? And yet, she was a whore, wasn't she? Her clit tightened, beginning to ache.

He reached down and grasped both nipples, twisting and pulling, even as he pushed her over onto her back. An outraged cry died on her lips when he spoke again.

"Man, you got some big titties on you." His words came in a rasp, and she lapped up his excitement, drawing it into her like a succubus growing drunk on his lust.

Large rough hands pawed, squeezing her breasts as carelessly as he might scratch his own balls. The very authority in his touch made something inside her melt as he groped and plundered.

He was sitting astride her now. His long, thin penis slid against her breasts and down into the valley between them. Even the weight of his body, pinning her to the concrete, drove her mad with excitement.

"Yesssss," he breathed. He held one breast, tightening his grip until the areola bulged over his fingers, and brought the other palm down in a sharp slap. "Big, soft titties. Just the kind made for titty-fuckin'."

She moaned and instantly regretted it.

"Oh?" The whiteness of his teeth shone in a grin. "Little whore likes this, does she?"

He slapped her breasts again and her brain reeled.

This man was using her body, pushing her breasts together until they formed a substitute cunt around his erection. But she couldn't deny the wetness between her legs. Even the phrase he'd uttered—"titty-fucking"—aroused her and kept circling in her head. So deliciously dirty . . .

His hands cupped around the outer curve of each heavy mound, fingers curling into the soft flesh even as his thumbs found her nipples. The tips were so hard now they ached, sensitive even to the breath he exhaled in soft guttural grunts.

He spit on her, spraying tits and cock with saliva. Humiliation battled desire; she loved the slick feel of it as he grew ever harder against her softness. He spit again, and again, until the cleft was as wet as her cunt.

When the swollen head of his cock peeked from between her breasts, her tongue flicked out like a starving thing.

"No, goddamn it." He slapped her left check, then reached around behind him, brought something flimsy and pink to her lips, and shoved it into her mouth.

Her panties, she realized. The satin gave up a musky she-juice as it settled against her tongue.

"Yes," he breathed again, low and thick. He was rocking back and forth now, squeezing her harder, working toward his own satisfaction with a single-minded drive that would have offended most other women. Most. Not her, though. For her, it was ecstasy.

"Oh, baby, that's it . . . That's it . . . Love those fuckin' tits—"

He was riding her, riding her titty-cunt. Harder, faster . . . Her breasts were just his tools, a temporary orifice fashioned for his pleasure.

The first spurt of cum hit her chin, and he groaned with release as the rest of his load shot onto her chest. The thin white semen oozed down around her collarbone and a final squirt landed on her throat. She could feel its warmth slithering over her flesh.

He pulled the mask from his head, looked down at her, and grinned. Oh, he was marvelous; he looked like an impish boy when he grinned like that.

Hadn't she really known it was him from the first, or had there been real fear? She didn't know for sure. The only thing that mattered was that he had, once again, made one of her fantasies come true.

"You said you wanted a pearl necklace for your birthday," he whispered. "And I knew you didn't mean jewelry."

She began to giggle, trailing her fingers in his cum and lifting them to her mouth.

"Oh, Roger," she whispered, beaming up at him. "It was the perfect gift. Thank you."

When she had dressed again, she slipped into the bathroom (almost as disgusting as the booths) to tidy up as best she could.

"Honey, you've got that just-fucked glow," Roger whispered in her ear as he walked her to the car. "Makes me wanna do you again right here in the parking lot."

Roger's phone began to beep.

"You'll just have to wait till you get home tonight," Marla said, but her smile faded as Roger's brow furrowed. He was staring at his phone, and she knew without asking whose number was on the caller ID.

"Aren't you going to answer it?" Marla asked.

"No," he frowned. "I'll call her back later."

"She's just a kid—" Marla said softly, stroking his back.

"She's a giant pain in my ass right now." Then he brightened and pinched her butt. "Speaking of asses—"

She giggled, then kissed him quickly on the lips before sliding into the driver's seat of the Accord.

"Don't be late," she teased. "Or I'll have to give you a spanking, bad boy."

Roger threw his head back and laughed.

"That'll be the day!"

"I love you, you big old pervert."

"You love me *because* I'm a pervert."

She pulled out of the lot, waggling her fingers out the window.

It was the last time she ever saw him alive.

Chapter 3

The imagination is the spur of delights . . . all depends
upon it, it is the mainspring of everything; now, is it not
by means of the imagination one knows joy? Is it not of
the imagination that the sharpest pleasures arise?

—MARQUIS DE SADE

Something woke her.

She had no idea what it was, only that something
yanked her up from the depths of fitful sleep and left her
lying there, completely awake, staring into the darkness.
Something made her heart thud heavily, suddenly out of
sync.

Something was such a big word. A scary word that held
the possibility of every conceivable horror and a vast,
yawning uncertainty that could swallow her whole.

She could not move, only lie frozen there and hope that
the *something* would go away. That if she held very, very
still, it would not see her. Would not smell her. Would not
find her.

When she was little, she would sometimes wake in the
dead of night like this, with an absolute certainty that
someone—*something*—was in the room with her. Her
mother said she had too much imagination.

"It's all those horror movies you kids like so much," her
mother always said.

Only now she was twenty-six years old, with a job and
an apartment and bills to pay. She knew that there were no
monsters under the bed or in the closet . . .

At least, not the kind of monsters she had feared as a
child. No vampires, no werewolves, no Freddy Kruger.

But there were monsters of another sort out there. She had the bruises to prove it.

If only she could sleep. In daylight she felt fuzzy and out of focus; at night, she was wound tight as a bowstring. She was going to lose her job if she didn't get this under control. Maybe Marla was right and she should see somebody.

She lay there, listening hard and hearing only the faint electric whir of the air conditioner and the static burst of crickets outside. Her eyes strained, seeing nothing but the usual dim outlines of furniture, window, and door.

Cherry didn't see how she could ever tell. They would only say it had been her fault. That she had—literally— been asking for it.

A dark shape moved, and the bed bounced on its springs. She yelped, springing upright—

"Oh, Jesus, Gunther! Oh, shit, you scared me half to death, you stupid cat!"

The big gray tabby pressed his head against her forehead, then sniffed at her face.

She lay back down, and Gunther settled on her chest.

Everything is all right. Breathe . . . just breathe . . .

The doors are locked and bolted. He doesn't know where I am now . . . I'm safe.

He had seemed so perfect in the beginning. His e-mails and phone calls, always saying the things she'd dreamed of hearing. She had wanted so much to be his.

Until the first time she screamed, "Red!" and he didn't stop.

Chapter 4

Tragedy delights by affording a shadow
of the pleasure which exists in pain.
— PERCY BYSSHE SHELLY

Tom Hanson and his partner, John Griggs, arrived on the scene just after six a.m. Both were still working on their first cup of Starbucks. Hanson couldn't decide what to do with his coffee; he didn't want to take the cup over to the body, but he didn't want to leave in the car, either. He needed every ounce of the caffeine.

"Jesus," Griggs grumbled, tossing his cup into the backseat of the unmarked car. "You'd think dead bodies could wait for a decent hour to be found. It's not like they're going anywhere."

"That cup had better be empty," Hanson said, leaving his cup in the console and getting out of the car. Bad enough that Griggs didn't know how to use a trash can, but Hanson would be damned if he'd clean up spilled coffee along with the fast-food wrappers and empty soda bottles.

"Of course it was empty," Griggs said, straightening and smoothing his awful tie. "I pay five bucks for a cup of coffee, I'm gonna drink every damned drop."

Hanson was nearly forty-two, of a respectable height and slender build. His best features—so women told him—were his soulful, puppy-dog brown eyes, and a head full of shaggy brown hair that promised he would escape the humiliation of balding as he grew older. Women were drawn to him, as often to mother him as to seduce him.

The harsh overhead lights of the parking garage gave a surreal edge to the great, looping arcs of cast-off blood spattering the grimy cinderblock walls and the oily black pools spreading from the body.

Hanson was relieved to see his preferred medical examiner, Miles, hunkered over the victim. It was way too early in the morning to deal with Creepy Carl, who never seemed to wash his hair and always reeked of morgue chemicals. Or Tyna, who was just too damned perky for both the job and the hour.

He fished a pair of gloves from his coat pocket. He had none of the little paper booties to place over his shoes—he could see the black pools sucking at the ones on Miles's feet—but decided to just try to stay out of the blood.

Griggs stood with his hands on his hips, squinting down at the body. He was forty-seven, and still looked a bit like a pit bull in his expensive suit and necktie of questionable taste. Today's specimen was a nightmare of red, purple, and orange stripes.

At least, Hanson thought, Griggs's tie was nowhere near as ugly as the body in front of him.

"Damn," Griggs said. "What the hell happened to this guy?"

"BFT," Miles said. "Baseball bat, maybe. Maybe a tire iron."

BFT: blunt force trauma. No shit, Hanson thought.

Hanson had seen dead bodies, but this one catapulted easily into his top five of all-time bloody messes. He and Griggs stayed back: Hanson out of respect for the evidence splattered all over the place, Griggs no doubt in fear for his Italian tasseled loafers.

More blood streaked the car. A handprint was clearly visible, as if someone had groped for purchase and found none. Some of the pooled blood had been stepped in, smeared across the concrete, evidence of a struggle.

The crime scene techs were gonna have a field day with this one, and Hanson didn't want to listen to Louise Fortner bitch about them having stepped all over *her* evidence.

"Found these under the body." Miles held out a set of keys.

"Bet one of those keys fits this Lexus," Hanson said, taking them with two fingers, careful to grasp the chain from the key fob.

Building security had found the body around five a.m. and had shut down that end of the parking garage. Hanson gave silent thanks that the rent-a-cops had had the sense not to fuck things up.

The Lexus was the only car within a hundred feet. A few business-types stared over at the little party as they waited for the elevator to open. Hanson wondered if they were curious or just pissed that they hadn't been able to nab one of the prime parking spaces inside the crime scene tape.

"Can't even tell what color his tie is." Griggs straightened up abruptly and turned away. "Aw, Christ, I don't wanna see that . . ."

Hanson was about to break his balls for being squeamish, but when he saw where Griggs was looking, his own bile rose.

The corpse's fly was open. Something ragged and bloody lay there like the product of a sausage grinder.

He studied the keys rather than dwell on what might or might not have happened to the victim's equipment.

Six, no seven keys on a ring with some kind of round metal tag. There was something on the tag; initials, maybe? He couldn't tell for the blood. But he could make out the Lexus logo on one of the keys.

"Yep, it's his car. Check the glove box for the registration, will ya, Griggs?"

Hanson dropped the bloody keys into a paper bag and turned back to Miles.

"He still got his wallet?"

"Yeah." Miles grimaced at Hanson's ancient Thom Mc-Cann's. "Let me hand it to you."

Hanson opened the wallet and took out the driver's license.

"Roger Andrew Banks," he read, passing it to Griggs.

"Hazelwood Lane." Griggs whistled. "Nice neighborhood."

Hanson flipped through the cards: American Express, MasterCard, a Blockbuster card, and a discount coffee bar card.

"So, he's leaving the building, late, after everybody else has gone home." Griggs was thinking aloud. "He's at the car, he's got his keys out . . ."

The coffee bar card had four little holes punched in it; Roger only needed one more. Poor bastard was never gonna get that free cappuccino now.

"So it wasn't a robbery." Griggs was eyeing the cash and cards.

"Muggers don't usually beat the hell out of someone like this." *Or filet their dicks, either.*

"Maybe a homo thing gone bad?" Griggs asked as he took out a notebook and began to write. "I mean, the pants being unzipped and all—"

Hanson sighed. Gina had once called Griggs "a knuckle-dragging, equal-opportunity bigot." He wasn't a bad cop, just an asshole. Still, Griggs was his partner now and Gina was history.

"Possible, I guess. We're looking at a perp with a hell of an anger management problem. Strong, too."

"Yeah," Griggs agreed, then grimaced. "Not your usual hundred-and-forty-pound faggot, anyway."

Roger had a bit of a beer gut, but he must have been close to six feet, 250 pounds easy.

"The killer hit him a good one to the head," Hanson said. "Doesn't look like Roger ever made it to his feet after going down the first time."

"Yeah, all the blood smears on the door. Either the killer snuck up on him, or it was somebody he knew."

"Possible." Hanson shrugged. "But the perp had to be carrying a fairly large weapon. If my own mother came up to me in a parking garage at night, carrying a tire iron, I wouldn't turn my back on her. Would you?"

"My mom or your mom?" Griggs snorted. "I wouldn't turn my back on my mom if she was holding a box of animal crackers. Your mom, I dunno the woman."

He squatted, grunted, reached under the car, and came up with a briefcase.

"Musta gotten kicked under here. Don't see any blood on it." Griggs carefully snapped the case open and peered inside. "Papers and shit."

"We verify that he works in this building yet?"

"Yeah, he works up on twelve. Wilmer, Banks, and Cohen," came a thin, male voice. "I mean, uh . . . I can't say a hundred percent if it's him, but that's Mr. Banks's car and his parking space."

They turned to look at a thin black male in a gray security uniform. He was in his early twenties and smelled slightly of vomit.

"Antone?" Hanson read his nametag. "You found the body?"

"Uh-huh. And it's An-to-NEE. Not AN-tone."

"Jesus," Griggs muttered. "Like it's our fault you people can't spell your own names right."

Antone gave Griggs a sullen eye roll, then looked back at Hanson.

It turned out that Antone had come on at four forty-five to open up. There was no night security, just a couple of cameras aimed at the doors. Griggs went off to find the tapes, but Hanson doubted they'd find any joy on them. The Lexus was too far from either the lobby door or the elevators, but maybe it had caught something or somebody worth checking out.

"I saw Mr. Banks's car still there," Antone went on. "Thought maybe his wife had picked him up or something. People sometimes leave their car here overnight."

Antone was losing some of his ashy pallor as he warmed to his subject.

"But then I saw the blood. First, I thought it was oil, you know? Didn't look like blood, it looked *black*. But I thought, that's too much oil for a leak. Even if somebody had changed their oil in here—you wouldn't believe the shit people will do—it was still too much—"

"Did you touch anything? Step in anything?"

"Hell, no!" Antone looked offended. "You think I'm stupid or something? I didn't want to get close enough to touch *nothing*. I just called nine-one-one and sat my ass back in the office 'til you guys showed up."

"Where'd you throw up?"

Antone looked at his feet.

"I made it 'round the corner," he admitted.

"Okay," Hanson said. "You did good. Thanks, Antone."

The crime scene unit had arrived. Lenny was taking pictures, and Hanson was happy he could leave his shitty camera in the car. Fortner was walking slowly around the Lexus, no doubt deciding where to dust for fingerprints first.

Griggs came back with a brown bag, and opened it to reveal a stack of videotapes inside.

"Probably taped over the same ones a hundred times," Hanson said with a grimace. "The picture will be shit."

"What gets me," Griggs said, "is that the perp must have

been spattered pretty good with blood, too. But I don't see any trail. Did he just walk out of here? Jump in his car? Either way, it's gotta help us find him."

"We can hope."

They took the elevator up to the twelfth-floor lobby to have a little talk with Wilmer, Banks, and Cohen, Attorneys at Law.

By the time they got to the morgue, Miles had already undressed and washed the body. Roger looked worse, if that were possible.

"That was fast," Hanson said as he approached the table.

"Slow day," Miles said. "I'm probably not even going to need the bone saw to get the brain out. His skull is fractured all over the place."

The face didn't look much like the one on the driver's license in Roger's wallet. The skin hung loose on his left temple, exposing bone underneath. The nose had actually slipped to the left, as if Roger had turned his head too fast and left his nose pointing in the wrong direction.

"One blow here." Miles pointed to a gash in the top rear of the skull. "Linear fracture. Over here, diastatic fracture along the suture lines, but then it looks like another blow to the same area caused a depressed fracture—"

"Crushed like a walnut," Griggs volunteered, crowding in for a better look.

"Definitely going to be a closed casket," Miles said grimly.

"Skull fractures what killed him?" Hanson asked.

"Nope."

"No?" Both of the detectives looked at Miles with raised eyebrows.

"Oh, he probably would have died from one or all of them, especially the depressed fracture, but I don't think he lived long enough."

"So what killed him?"

Hanson couldn't handle looking at the corpse's face any longer, so he glanced at the rest of the body. The story it told wasn't pretty. Roger's heart had been pumping long enough for angry blossoms to have already begun spreading over his fishy-white flesh.

"He's got a broken collarbone, at least three broken ribs, both kneecaps dislocated, and both arms broken—"

"Jesus." Hanson closed his eyes. Griggs whistled through his teeth.

Both kneecaps? So the perp had taken Roger down with the first blow to the head, then stood over him and busted both kneecaps. Or maybe he'd done the knees while Roger was still going down, trying to hold on to the car. No one could run with two dislocated kneecaps.

So the perp had specifically wanted him incapacitated, on the ground. The arms had been broken as Roger tried to shield himself.

"He was hit in the larynx, too. There's some swelling, so it happened early in the attack."

"Keep him from screaming for help," Griggs said, a statement rather than a question.

Miles nodded.

"It's not final, but what I'm seeing is consistent with a baseball bat. But here's where it gets *really* nasty."

Here we go, Hanson thought, steeling himself. The genital mutilation.

The man's pride and joy had been cut into strips of meat. It hung loosely together by gristle, and something that looked . . . well, spongy.

Hanson felt his balls shrink up into his body, as if trying to hide.

"Oh, not that," Miles said dismissively. "I was saving that for last. No, look here—"

Miles pried the corpse's mouth open.

Roger's tongue was missing.

"Perimortum," Miles said.

"You mean he was still alive?" Hanson asked.

Miles nodded, and whatever professional gleam might have been in his eyes faded.

"So, what's our cause of death?" Griggs asked.

"I'm still working," Miles said. "But if I had to give you a COD now, I'd say massive blood loss. He's practically dry."

Jesus. Someone had beaten the hell out of him, cut out his tongue and shredded his penis . . . And then left him, barely alive, to bleed to death.

It was enough to make a guy wanna get drunk.

But first somebody had to go tell Roger's wife that her husband wasn't coming home.

Chapter 5

Given the choice between the experience of pain and nothing, I would choose pain.
—WILLIAM FAULKNER

Hanson hated this part of his job.

Secondary victims of a crime all had the same look when he first met them. They might be confused and polite (a middle-class soccer mom), or pissed and suspicious (the lower rungs of the socioeconomic ladder who have no reason to trust a badge), but there was always hope and a question in their eyes. He knew that the words about to come out of his mouth would change everything, forever. As soon as he spoke the words, that flicker of hope was snuffed out like a candle.

Marla Banks had answered the door like she'd known something was wrong. Car accident, that was most likely what she thought. No one ever expected murder, certainly not this well-dressed woman in a pricey gated community.

She simply sat down on the sofa as if her legs could no longer hold her upright. She blinked first at Hanson, then at Griggs.

Hanson had to repeat it twice before some comprehension came into her eyes.

"Are you sure?" she asked in a childlike voice.

They always asked that. *Please, please, it's a mistake. It's got to be a mistake.*

"I knew something was wrong," she said, still in that

tiny, thin voice. "He called around six thirty and said he probably wouldn't make it home for dinner."

"Does that happen a lot?" Hanson asked.

"But then it got later and later," she went on. "I kept trying to think of all kinds of reasons. Like, maybe a client had taken him to dinner or they had gone for a drink after work . . ."

"Mrs. Banks, did Roger work late a lot?" Hanson repeated.

She didn't respond, just stared at the book of Georgia O'Keeffe paintings on the coffee table.

He didn't mind her silence. It was better than what would come next.

"What happened?" she asked finally. "Was he robbed? Was it a mugging?"

Hanson wondered how much she could handle right now. It was better that she heard the details from him than from the six o'clock news.

"It doesn't look like a mugging. He still had his wallet, and his cash and credit cards were still in it."

"I called the police last night," she said hurriedly, as if fearing what he might say next. "They told me Roger had to be missing for at least forty-eight hours before I could file a report."

"Yes, ma'am. That's standard procedure."

"Was it a car-jacking?" she continued. "Were they after the car?"

"No, ma'am," Hanson explained. "His car is still in the parking garage where we found him."

"Did you call him when he didn't come home?" Griggs asked.

"I called the office around nine," she said, turning to stare at Griggs, "but I just got the answering machine. I called his cell, but it went to voice mail. I must have called him a dozen times, every hour."

The tears started, just a slow ooze from the corners of her eyes.

"When did you last see your husband?" Hanson asked.

She looked up at him blankly.

"What?"

Hanson repeated the question.

"At lunch," she said, wiping at her eyes. "It was my birthday . . ."

Christ. More birthdays will come, Hanson thought, but he doubted she'd ever celebrate another one.

"Where was that?"

She blinked and hesitated.

"Where did you and your husband have lunch?"

Hanson hated this part, too. Looking at a widow and wondering if she had done it. He doubted it, just from the violence of the attack, but she could have hired someone.

"Caesars."

He nodded, making a note. Trendy little Italian place downtown, a few blocks from Roger's office.

"And he seemed okay? Nothing bothering him?"

"He was fine." She started to say something else, but then covered her face with her hands and began crying in earnest.

"Is there someone we can call for you?"

She shook her head. The two detectives stood there until she looked up again, drawing in a great hiccupping breath.

"What happened?" she asked, stronger this time, almost angry. "Will you just tell me what happened to Roger?"

"It looks like someone was waiting for him in the garage. They attacked him with something, most likely a baseball bat—"

"Oh, my God—" Marla was on her feet, hand over her mouth, rushing from the room.

Hanson could hear her retching just down the hall. He looked over at Griggs, who just shrugged.

"Nice house," Griggs said softly, eyeing the flat-screen and stereo system; the family portrait above the fireplace; the Oriental rug on the hardwood floor.

Hanson looked around the room as well, trying to get a feel for Roger Banks's life. Tidy, prosperous, comfortable.

"She's a nice-looking woman, too." Griggs squinted at a photograph on the mantel. "I mean, she's probably attractive when she's not, you know. Crying and all."

"For Christ's sake," Hanson groaned softly.

"Hey, I'm a guy, I can't help it," Griggs whispered. "She's a little on the plump side, but nice curves, if you know what I mean."

Hanson knew exactly what he meant. Griggs was a self-confessed "tit man," and Marla Banks did have a generous bosom.

"Oh, excuse me," Griggs grumbled low. "I forgot, she ain't your type. No, you like 'em with long legs, red hair, and handcuffs—"

"Shut the fuck up."

Griggs had become his partner after Gina left the force, and Hanson had spent the first two weeks listening to his adolescent bullshit with gritted teeth and throbbing temples. Finally, Griggs had brought up her name (her tits, actually) one too many times and Hanson had punched him in the face.

After that, Griggs had kept his mouth shut, mostly. But every now and then, he just had to get in a little dig. He never mentioned her name again, though. No one ever mentioned her name, not to Hanson.

Marla came back into the room. She steadied herself on a chair as she made her way to the sofa.

"I'm sorry," she said.

"No apology necessary," Hanson said.

"Did your husband have any enemies?" Griggs asked. "Anybody that had it in for him?"

"Of course not," Marla said, looking amazed.

"He was a lawyer, right?" Griggs continued. "Maybe a client got pissed off? A nasty divorce case, maybe?"

She went still for a moment, and Tom thought she was about to say something. But she just shook her head.

"Roger didn't handle divorces. He's in corporate law . . ." She caught herself. "He was, I mean. Everybody *loved* Roger."

Hanson had to ask, and he hated that, too.

"What about you? Were you and your husband getting along?"

"Oh, my God—" Marla looked at him with the anguished eyes of the lost. Then her voice broke, and she sobbed. "Yes. Oh, my God, you have no idea how much I loved that man."

Chapter 6

There are moments when, whatever the position of the
body, the soul is on its knees.

—Victor Hugo

Business associates, his paralegal, his neighbors . . . all
agreed Roger Banks was a decent guy. More than decent. He was a church deacon who coached Little League
baseball and gave money to animal shelters and AIDS hos-
pices.

"He could still be a bastard," Griggs said, leaning back
in his chair and shoving a handful of Cheetos into his
mouth. "Churches are full of them. And don't even get
me started on what working with *kids* could mean."

"He and his wife serve turkey at the local homeless shelter on Thanksgiving," Hanson said, without looking up.
"They've done it for the past nine years."

"So?"

"So, generally speaking, assholes don't go that far just to
look good to the neighbors. You know what those guys at
the shelter smell like."

"So they're freakin' Ozzie and Harriet." Griggs crunched
another handful of curls. "Not a damned hint of anything
hinky."

Griggs reached for a manila folder on Hanson's desk.

"Oh, for Christ's sake! Don't get that orange crap all
over everything, all right?"

Frustration made Hanson irritable. Apparently it just
made Griggs hungry.

Griggs wiped his hand on the papers spread on his own desk and raised his palms to his partner as if to say, *Look, Ma!* before grinning and pulling the file off of Hanson's.

"You find anything on the kids?" he asked. "A boy and a girl, right?"

"Yeah. The girl just got married. She's an ophthalmologist—"

"A what?" Griggs asked, his eyebrows drawing into a single ridge.

"An eye doctor."

"I thought that was an optometrist?"

"It's a different kind of eye doctor," Hanson explained, pawing through the piles of paper in search of a highlighter.

"So they both sell glasses. What's the difference?"

"An ophthalmologist makes more money. That's why they get the extra letters."

The daughter was living in Memphis with her new husband, who was also an ophthalmologist. The son was a senior at the University of Georgia, pre-law, on the dean's list.

Roger's bank accounts were neat and tidy as well, with surprisingly little credit card debt. His credit rating was as solid and respectable as the man himself seemed to be.

It was damned annoying. They couldn't find anybody with a less than kind word to say about Roger Banks.

Griggs was flipping through Roger's phone records—the local usage details—for the twentieth time.

"Looking at his LUDs, all I can tell is that Roger was paying a fortune in overage charges," Griggs said. "He needed a better calling plan."

"This guy knew practically everybody," Hanson grumbled. "He's even got calls from the governor."

"Shit," Griggs grunted. "That's all we need. A VIP murder victim."

"Christ, between his home phone, his office, and cell, we could spend weeks tracking them all down." Hanson dragged a hand through his hair.

They had already spent three days slogging through his voice mail. Roger's cell was programmed to automatically save voice mails for thirty days. That was a *lot* of messages.

Most were from his wife, messages like: "What do you want for dinner?" "How late are you going to be?" "Can you bring home a loaf of bread?" *Yada yada yada.*

Another twenty or so were from clients and business associates, a mind-numbing litany of meetings, appointments, reschedulings, and tee times.

But there were four messages they couldn't explain, all from the same person, all nearly identical.

"Lemme hear that last one again," Griggs said.

Hanson pulled it up on the computer.

"Roger, sir?" It was a female voice, relatively young but uncertain, anxious. "It's Cherry. I'm sorry to bother you, but please call me back as soon as you can. Okay?"

"She doesn't leave a number," Griggs said. "Is it in his phone book?"

"Yep. Saved under Cherry, no last name or other information." Hanson called out the number 555-471-6696.

"And no leads on the number because it's a prepaid cell," Griggs sighed. He leaned back and threw his pencil into the ceiling tile. The pencil just hung there, and he sat staring at it.

Hanson sighed. Sometimes working with Griggs was like being back in middle school.

"So far, we've only got three things anywhere near a lead." Griggs began ticking them off on his right hand. "One, Marla lied about having lunch with her husband the day he was killed—"

"That's got to be a simple mistake. You heard those messages."

The last eight messages on Roger Banks's phone were from Marla on the night he died. They were painful to listen to, moving from mildly concerned to frantic. If Marla was lying, then she could give Meryl Streep a run for the money.

"Whatever," Griggs grunted. Another finger. "Two, we got a couple of long, light brown hairs."

"Probably his wife's. The color matches."

"We still gotta get a sample to check." Griggs held up a third finger. "Three, we got this Cherry chickie."

"Shit." Hanson sighed. "Let's go back to Marla Banks's house and get this over with."

Chapter 7

I, with a deeper instinct, choose a man who compels my
strength, who makes enormous demands on me, who
does not doubt my courage or my toughness, who does
not believe me naive or innocent, who has the courage
to treat me like a woman.

—ANAIS NIN

Cherry couldn't stop crying. It was humiliating, being
out of control like this.

"Cherry, baby, look at me," Paul said. "Please, just look
at me."

She lifted her head from the pillow and blinked at him.
She could only imagine how awful she looked, all red-
eyed and snot-nosed . . .

"It's okay, baby-girl," he said, rubbing her back. "It's really okay."

"You m-m-ust be so disappointed in me," she croaked,
burrowing into the pillow again. "I'm s-so sorry . . ."

She had come to Paul looking for comfort, for the only
thing that ever made the wheels in her head stop turning.
Sex kept her completely, utterly in the moment. No fu-
ture, no past. Just that single moment.

"No, baby, no!" He pulled her to him. "I mean, I am disappointed that I got the room for nothing, but it's okay—"

"I really, really wanted to." She wiped her nose on the
corner of the pillowcase. "I want so much to enjoy it
again, all of it—"

She hadn't been sure she was ready; in fact, just the
idea of someone touching her made her feel a little
queasy. But she was getting desperate. She had hoped, if
not for pleasure, then just for a cathartic release of stress

that might let her sleep. For a connection to some other person. For reassurance that Kerberos hadn't ruined her completely.

She trusted Paul, she really did. But the first tiny swat of his hand on her ass—hardly more than a pat, really—set panic galloping through her body. She couldn't breathe.

Next thing she knew, she was curled up in a fetal position, wailing like a crazy woman.

She could hardly stand for him to touch her now. All she wanted was to get her clothes on and get out of this crappy little hotel room.

"Please forgive me, sir," she murmured, getting up.

Paul sighed and stretched out on the bed, his cock still semi-rigid.

"I *told* you it's okay. I'm not mad at you."

Suddenly she wanted to throw something at him. He wasn't mad at *her*? Then why was he whining about the wasted expense of the room?

She was mad at Paul, mad at herself, but especially mad at *him*. He had ruined everything. It had been hard enough getting her own head around the things she wanted, but now she was confused again. She felt guilty and ashamed.

She grabbed her bra from the floor, looking around for the rest of her clothes. Where were her panties, damn it?

He was flipping through static on the television mounted on the wall. Suddenly, the sounds of moans and sweaty flesh slapping together filled the room.

"Want a cookie?" He held out an Oreo without tearing his eyes from the screen.

She shook her head. She gave up looking for the panties and simply stepped into her jeans.

"Come on, baby-girl," Paul coaxed. "The sugar will do you good. Have a few cookies, a soda . . . and maybe a little blow job—"

"I don't want a fuckin' cookie," she snapped, pulling on her blouse. "And I don't want to blow you, either."

Paul blinked at her, still chewing.

"Hey, I just thought it might be less stressful for you, help you loosen up," he mumbled through a mouthful of cookies. "Jesus, Cherry! I can't help if I still have a hard-on—"

She grabbed her bag and opened the door.

He was already dialing the phone before the door slammed behind her.

"Robyn, baby-girl?" he said into the phone. "Today is your lucky day."

What was it about rope, Robyn thought, that even the loose slip of it over her bare skin made her nipples hard?

Even as a kid, she'd liked being tied up. When the neighborhood kids played cowboys and Indians, she always made sure she was an Indian.

She sure as hell was an Indian, now. She almost giggled at the thought, but the ropes pulled tighter, and her breath caught in her throat.

"You all right?" he whispered, lips brushing her ear.

"A little tighter. Please."

The ropes grew taut again, pulling wrists and ankles tight against the mattress.

The blindfold—cool, slick satin—blocked out everything but the sound of his voice and the feeling of his hands on her body.

Paul's gentle fingertips traced from cheek to throat to the first curve of her breasts, lightly brushing her hard little nipples.

She moaned and arched her back. Wanting his fingers to linger, but knowing that the teasing had just begun. He knew her so well, the location of every nerve ending wired directly to her cunt.

She was already wet, but when his lips followed the trail left by his fingertips, her cunt flooded with moisture.

"My sweet, sweet little pet," he whispered. "All mine for the taking."

She felt something new now, not flesh, but something sharp and prickling, run across her skin. For a moment, she was confused, even a little frightened. Then she nearly laughed.

It was the rose he had brought her. He said he'd had to look in three florist shops to find one that still had its long, sharp thorns.

He ran the stem up and down her body, lightly in some spots, and harder in others. How much of her young life had she already wasted, not knowing that flesh was capable of so many sensations?

He switched from the stem to the bud itself. Such softness, tickling over her breasts, her stomach. He slapped her breasts lightly with the rose petals.

"Maybe I should turn you over. Spank you with this rose. Would you like that?"

She nodded, smiling widely.

Instead, his tongue flicked against one nipple, then the other, then back again. When his teeth nipped ever so gently, she felt her clit swell and harden into an ache.

She was panting now, wanting to writhe but unable to twitch even a single muscle. Being tied down like this, it was heaven and hell together. Being eagle-spread, arms and legs stretched taut, seemed to take all the growing tension in her body and drive it mercilessly down between her legs. Focusing it all into a tiny, shining bullet of need.

His fingers dipped between her thighs, rubbing her pussy lips, then spreading them wide.

Oh, God! His tongue slid across her clit and the dizzying rush of wanting arched her back again, this time violently enough to make the ropes cut into her wrists.

"Not yet, pet," he whispered again, this time with a hint of glee. "I don't think you really want it yet."

"I do, I do," she insisted hoarsely. "Please . . ."

His tongue moved down to the place on her hip where the skin was still tender.

"Does it still hurt, precious?" he cooed. "Your pretty little tattoo?"

"Yes, sir," she breathed. "Thank you, sir."

She had wanted to have his initials branded into her, but Paul had convinced her that branding was something she had yet to earn.

Instead, he had taken her to Ace's Ink and held her hand as the emblem, small and perfect in simple black, was pricked into the meat of her left hip.

"It's beautiful. You are beautiful. Let me kiss it better."

His lips pressed against the sore spot as his hands caressed her thighs.

Then she felt the bed bounce, and his tongue was moving between her toes. This time she jerked, only to have the ropes hold her fast. Helpless. Vulnerable.

"Oh, oh—that tickles! Please, no—"

The giggles left her panting, breathless.

But *no* was not a safeword. *No* was not stop. *Red* was stop. And she was nowhere near *red*.

Her squirming only made the ropes tighter. Her cunt wetter. Her need spiked like a flame in gasoline.

"Please . . ." She was begging now. "Please, sir . . ."

"I know, I know. You want to cum, don't you? Naughty little girl."

His fingers slid easily into her, soft at first, then deeper, harder.

"Yes, please—Finger-fuck me! Finger-fuck me like the dirty little girl I am!"

"You *are* a nasty little girl. Your pussy is so hot, so wet."

Fingers retreated, just enough to spread her lips wide.

He knew how she liked it. She loved how his palms held her hips hard down on the bed.

His mouth was on her now, sucking and licking her juices. His tongue danced around her clit in teasing, torturing circles.

"*Please—*" Nearly a wail now. Desperation rising.

"Tell me you want it," he said, voice muffled. Even the vibration of his lips drove her mad.

"I want to cum, please . . . Please let me cum!"

"Let you cum? Don't you mean *make* you cum?"

"Yes . . . *Please!*"

She was so close, teetering on the brink of it, trying to hold back. Tears ran down her cheeks, she wanted it so badly.

"Wait."

Fingers now massaged her clit, driving her closer to the abyss. She felt herself slipping, unable to stop.

"*Please!* Oh, God, sir, please, *please make me cum!*"

He drove his fingers hard into her again as he sucked on her clit. She was blind with pleasure so sharp and sweet it cut her in two.

"Cum, then. Cum for me, pet."

Finally, finally! The blazing surrender to it, to him. The orgasm rolled over her, and over her again. And just when she thought she could go no higher, her body straining against the rope, again it came.

She was crying, laughing. Hysterical with the release. Giddy as he unfastened the ropes and drew her to his chest.

"That's my good girl," he whispered.

This was completion. This made her whole. His arms around her, his lips on hers, gently, as he smoothed her wild hair with fingers that smelled of her musk. She nuzzled against his chest, running her tongue through the hair that curled there.

Now, it was her turn to worship him.

And she would do it eagerly, with desire and gratitude and a love so enormous she felt she would burst with it.

He opened another six-pack of Oreos, and fed them to her, one by one.

"No, no more," Robyn said, turning her head from the last cookie.

"Come on. Do it for me. I want to make sure your blood sugar doesn't drop. You had a big afternoon."

She sighed like a reluctant child, then smiled dutifully and took the cookie into her mouth. She sat crunching, cross-legged and naked, on the bed.

"What about you?" she mumbled, still chewing. "Don't tops need aftercare, too?"

"*You* are my aftercare. Just seeing you smile like this." He grinned. "Besides, I'm stopping at the nearest drive-thru on my way home. I'm talking super-sized combo meal. I'm starving after the workout you put me through."

"Me?" she squealed, rising to her knees only to fall on top of him with kittenish slaps. "You ravished me!"

"And you loved it!"

"Yes. I did. I did. I'm so glad you called."

"I'm glad my meeting got canceled. You know I wish I could spend more time with you . . . and that sweet ass of yours."

She giggled.

"I gotta run." He kissed her lightly on the forehead. "Don't forget to put away the rope properly. No stuffing it in your bag."

She nodded. He'd shown her how to weave it into a thick braid that kept it from tangling, and also made it easy to uncoil.

"Just drop the key at the front desk. I'll call you in a couple of hours to check on you."

"Yes, sir."

She tried to put the brakes on her heart, to stop the drop she felt as he said good-bye . . . and went back to his wife.

Chapter 8

To the uneducated, being a Dominant or Master
sounds like an excuse for getting your own way in a
relationship. But that's not the case at all. A true
Dominant understands his or her responsibilities: to
protect, to nurture, to cherish that which belongs to
him. It is very much like the ancient concept of chivalry.
—JACK LEVINSON, *The True Dominant*

Marla had taken two Valium with a glass of Merlot to numb herself enough to get through the visitation, but obviously it hadn't been enough. When she spied the woman in the royal blue dress, outrage broke through the haze, the grief, the agonizing emptiness that she'd been dragging around since Roger's death.

The gall of that woman. The goddamned, utter gall—

She told the kids that she was going to the ladies' room, then circled back to the foyer of the funeral home to approach the woman from the rear. She simply had to hope no one saw her.

"What do you think you're doing here?" Marla asked through gritted teeth.

"Marla, honey!" Cassandra Lee gave Marla a sad little smile and stepped toward her with open arms.

"You can't be here," Marla whispered, stepping back. "My children and my family—"

Cassandra was somewhere in her fifties, a petite woman with soft, round curves. In her too-tight satin dress, she made Marla think of a well-upholstered chair. Her face, doughy and pale, bore too much makeup, though it was carefully applied. Her blond hair was pulled back from her face with some sort of gaudy, jeweled clip, and then fell in a wild explosion of over-processed frizz passing for curls.

"How could I not come and pay my respects?" Cassandra's voice was wounded and her eyes blinked back tears.

Marla knew the crocodile tears as well as she knew the tacky jangle of the half-dozen bracelets on each of Cassandra's wrists.

"I appreciate your sympathy." Marla bit down hard on her fury; to confront Cassandra would only be asking for it. Cassandra *thrived* on drama.

"I just wanted you to know," Cassandra's lips quivered, "if there's anything I can do for you—"

"Thank you. But it's not the time or place—"

"Well, you haven't returned any of my phone calls or e-mails." Cassandra straightened her shoulders. "I thought you of all people wouldn't turn your back on me."

Oh, Christ, here it comes. Her husband was dead, and all this woman could think about was her own petty problems. Marla didn't trust herself to speak, but Cassandra didn't notice.

"I understand loss more than most people," Cassandra whispered confidentially, putting her arm around Marla's waist. "I lost my husband and my club, and all those people I thought were my friends—"

"Yes, Cassandra," Marla murmured grimly, stepping away from Cassandra's embrace. The woman's touch made her skin crawl. "I know you've had a hard time."

She saw her daughter looking at her from the other side of the room, and wondered how she would explain this pathetic, out-of-place stranger. She had to get Cassandra out of here.

"I really hate to bring this up now," Cassandra said, drawing close again and patting Marla's arm. "But I do need to talk to you about, well, our *arrangement.*"

"What?" Marla blinked, genuinely bewildered.

"Roger and I talked last week. Didn't he tell you?"

"I have no idea what you're talking about."

"Well, Roger was going to lend me a little money," Cassandra whispered. Then she smiled, this time almost flirtatiously. "Enough to get my club going again—"

Marla felt her blood pounding in her ears, and for a moment she didn't know if she was going to faint or punch Cassandra in the face.

She no longer cared about creating a scene. She grabbed Cassandra by the upper arm, fiercely enjoying the feel of her nails biting into the woman's flesh, and marched her toward the door.

"I knew you were a lying, manipulative bitch—" Marla hissed. "But to come here now and try to get money from me—"

"Owww, Marla, you're hurting me!"

"To pretend that Roger promised you anything! That even you could stoop so low—"

Cassandra stumbled as Marla shoved her through the double doors into the parking lot.

"But you've got to help me!" Cassandra whispered urgently. Tears stood in her eyes, and her cheeks were splotched a sickly red. "After all I've done for you and this community! I've sacrificed everything!"

"You didn't sacrifice shit," Marla snarled. "Your slut-hound husband left you because you are fuckin' *insane*, and you lost the club because you mismanaged funds and *shit* on everybody—"

"No! It wasn't my fault! All I've ever done is try to keep the community together and help—"

Cassandra was approaching hysteria, as she did whenever someone confronted her with reality. How many times had Marla listened to her bullshit?

"Leave now." Marla's voice was icy, but her hands were shaking. "Or I will call the police."

"I've lost everything! My husband, my club—everything!" Cassandra was babbling now. "I've even lost my best client to that bitch!"

Suddenly, Marla wanted to laugh. So Cassandra had lost her trust fund baby, had she? He had been Cassandra's pride and joy, the one she had said would set her up in a new club, one that would put the Inferno to shame.

If another dominatrix had him now, more power to her, Marla thought. Even cute little rich boys deserved a better mistress than Cassandra Lee.

She watched as Cassandra tottered to her battered Volvo. She watched as the woman sat there, head bowed and dabbing at her eyes with a tissue, before starting it up.

Marla knew it was all part of her act. Cassandra played the victim so well.

I hope she burns in hell, Marla thought.

Then she began to cry.

Chapter 9

Thou art to me a delicious torment.
—RALPH WALDO EMERSON

H anson tried not to think about baseball bats, but another bloody, beaten body so soon on the heels of Roger Banks was pretty damned coincidental.

"Check-out was noon," Griggs said. "They rang the room, got no answer. Housekeeping banged on the door. When they still got no answer, the manager used the master and found this."

"Looks like Roger Banks all over again."

"She don't look like a hooker." Griggs stared down at the body on the bed. "Crack head, either."

The Madison Inn didn't rent by the hour (that would be the Airways, over on the other side of town), but it was a dump that offered free twenty-four-hour porn. Most of the Madison's clientele checked in with no luggage.

The manager, a small Pakistani man who spoke in heavily accented English, would not come into the room. He stood wringing his hands in the doorway, insisting that nothing like this had ever happened at his motel before.

"She's in rigor," Miles volunteered. "Anal temp is eighty-six degrees."

"Can't you just say body temp?" Hanson asked sourly. It was bad enough that someone should die so violently; he didn't like thinking about Miles shoving a thermometer up the victim's dead ass.

Griggs was going through a purse on the sad little dresser.

"Still got her wallet." He pulled the driver's license out. "Robyn Ann Macy."

"What time did she check in?"

"Mr. Patel here says he never saw her check in. Says a man rented the room, paid cash—"

"Let me guess. John Smith?"

"Nah. George Harrison." Griggs grinned. "Mr. Harrison checked in around three p.m. yesterday afternoon."

"So she died sometime between . . ." Hanson hesitated, hoping Miles would jump in and do the math for him.

"She's been dead at least four hours," Miles said. "It could have been much earlier. Lividity is no help, because it looks like there's very little blood left in her."

So much blood. The mattress literally *squished* as Miles removed his knee from its edge.

They would have to get Mr. Patel together with a sketch artist. Talk to housekeeping and other guests—assuming they could be found. He wondered if her car was in the lot.

"Well, lookee here!" Griggs pulled a neatly braided length of rope from a small duffel bag. "She musta been here for a little of the nasty if she was carrying this much rope around."

"Sure the bag is hers? Maybe the killer left it behind?"

"Of course, it's hers." Griggs turned the bag around so Hanson could see the HELLO KITTY logo.

It didn't make sense. The rope was here, but the killer hadn't used it?

"Ligature marks?" Hanson glanced over at Miles.

Miles shrugged.

"Only a slight abrasion on one wrist. Something that could be a rope burn under one breast. If she was tied up at some point, she wasn't when she died."

The rope was pristine, without a drop of rusty red, unlike the body on the bed. The dead girl was staring through blackening, half-closed eyes at the ceiling. Her matted hair seemed to be blond. She was naked, and what appeared to be a T-shirt, jeans, bra, and pink satin bikinis were scattered on the floor and bed. All were ripped and torn.

"What's this? A tattoo?"

With the tip of a gloved finger, Hanson wiped a small bit of blood away for a better look.

The small circular emblem looked a little like a yin and yang symbol, but with three curving divisions instead of just two. It looked vaguely familiar.

"Was she raped?" he asked.

Miles grimaced. "Too messy to tell."

"Aww, shit." Hanson rubbed his eyes. "And her tongue?"

"Gone."

Chapter 10

But you wished to be my plaything, my slave! You found the highest pleasure in feeling the foot, the whip of an arrogant, cruel woman. What do you want now?
—LEOPOLD VON SACHER-MASOCH, *Venus in Furs*

"That's my good boy, ooh, isn't him my precious widdle baby?"

Lady Cassandra sat back in the faded Victorian sofa, one of the Pekingese cradled in her arms, scratching the animal behind the ears.

"Mmmmf." The voice behind the ball gag came out in a muffled whine, not all that different from the rest of Lady Cassandra's dogs, which were now scratching at the other side of the door.

"Shut up, Randall. You were late. You know what the punishment for that is."

The punishment was being made to wait in the corner, with the ball gag firmly in his mouth. That, and the shoes. Five-inch heels that barely fit his big feet. Pink shoes.

It wasn't the pain he minded; he was a hard masochist—that was why he adored his Lady Cassandra. But he was not into sissification. That was a hard limit and she damned well knew it.

Still, he didn't have the balls to call *Red*. He needed to please her too badly. Other mistresses had all cut him loose, for reasons that were never clear to him.

But not Lady Cassandra. For that, he would suffer the shoes, the stockings she sometimes made him wear—even the pink ribbons braided around his prick.

So he wobbled on the heels, legs trembling, with hands clasped behind his back.

He was disappointed that he was not even allowed to look at her while he waited. She was wearing that lovely blue kimono again.

She was on the phone, talking as if he were just another piece of furniture.

"You listen to me," came Lady's voice. "I never promised you that."

Her voice had turned deep and deadly. It made the hair on Randall's neck stand up. He knew where her anger would go as soon as she hung up the phone.

"Those photos don't matter because there will always be new ones. Apparently, you can't keep a leash on him any better than I could."

There was a pause, and then she laughed.

"I wouldn't care if you were God himself. Your ass is on the line here, not mine. You just remember that."

He heard the sofa creak and the sound of her heels crossing the floor.

"Go to the bench and bend over. You know the position. Hurry up!"

The vinyl padding was cool against his stomach as he stretched his cuffed arms and ankles toward the legs of the bench.

She took a crop off the wall and swung it a few times. He could hear it cut through the air. The anticipation made his prick twitch.

Thwap!

She brought the crop down on his ass and he gasped. She was swinging hard, right out of the gate.

"No warm-up for a piece of shit like you," she said.

Thwap, thwap, thwap!

"Pathetic bastard, making me . . . wait . . . for . . . you!"

The crop punctuated the last four words. He swayed

on the high heels, feeling the heat spread along his backside.

She moved around in front of him and grabbed his hair. She yanked his head up and stared into his eyes.

"Fuckin' piss-ant cocksucker."

She let go of him and walked over to the wall of toys.

"MMmfff," he grunted, watching her with miserable eagerness. *Oh, please, Mistress,* he wanted to beg . . . *Please, the big wooden paddle!*

"I don't give a shit what you want, asshole. You'll take what I give you and be thankful for it."

Yes, Ma'm! Yes, Ma'am, always . . .

She grabbed his balls, stretching them away from his body, and then he felt the excruciating pressure of the metal clamps biting into his scrotum.

"Don't you dare move your filthy hands off the legs of that bench. Move and I'll chain your ass down and leave you there all night."

The leather flapper of the crop flickered back and forth against his ass cheeks, then down to his balls. Softly at first, a tease that made him squirm and moan.

"Look at you." She laughed. "Pushing your ass out, just like a whore."

She moved the crop faster now: back and forth, back and forth, the edge of it grazing his balls until they began to sting.

"Dance, fucker. Dance for me."

He couldn't help it, torn between the desire to twist away from the pain and the need to take it, to take it all and more. He heard the clamps jangle against each other, and with every tinkle, their teeth pulled sharply.

He didn't think he could bear it a moment longer. God, it was sweet, that mother-fucking sting!

She left his balls and hit him a few more times on the fleshy buttocks.

She walked away again. He lay there panting, waiting. Sweat made his stomach stick to the vinyl padding.

Thwap! Thwap! Thwap!

Oh, Christ, the paddle! The paddle! He almost wept with gratitude.

The weight of it pushed him against the bench, made the legs screech against the wooden floor.

She was swinging with both hands now, slower but harder. The shock wave of every mighty *thwap!* made the clamps jingle.

Then, he felt her nails trail lightly over his burning ass. The cool, sharp prickle sent shivers through him, made his legs weak with yearning.

"Mmmgg," he moaned. The drool was running from the corners of his mouth.

"Christ, look at you! You're a fuckin' mess. Get on your knees."

He dropped hard, feeling his kneecaps scream as they hit the floor. Then the pointed toe of her dainty blue kitten-heels crashed into his groin.

He screamed and fell forward, barely catching himself in time to keep his face from smashing into the floor.

"Up, on your knees, you sorry bastard," she hissed at him.

He struggled up onto his knees before her.

She opened the kimono to reveal the plastic eight-inch cock jutting out in front of her.

She grabbed his head and roughly unbuckled the gag, taking some of his hair out at the root.

"Oh, Mistress—"

But she was shoving the plastic cock into his mouth. Once she had it between his lips, she grabbed his hair with both hands to hold his head firmly in place.

"Shut up and suck my dick. Suck it, bitch."

The dildo hit the back of his throat, and he did his best

not to gag. The taste of the silicone was terrible, almost acidic. The head of it caught the roof of his mouth and he tasted his own blood.

"You're my bitch, aren't you? Take every goddamned inch of it, you cocksucker."

She thrust her hips, driving her "prick" so deep that he did gag.

She grabbed his nose between two fingers and pinched his nostrils shut. He made terrible gurgling sounds as he struggled to catch a breath between her strokes.

"Ugg," he choked. "Uugggr . . ."

The need for oxygen burned in his chest. He was just on the edge of panic as she released his nose and granted him air once more.

His scalp stung as she once again held his hair by both hands.

"You like being face-fucked? Having your . . . throat . . . raped?"

Abruptly she shoved him away.

"Please, Mistress," he croaked. "Fuck my slut mouth some more . . ."

He groveled, bending his head to lick her shoe.

"Get your nasty tongue off me! Get up, over there. On the cross."

He scrambled to the St. Andrew's, nearly twisting an ankle on the damned shoes.

"No, you moron, face me!"

He turned and she pinned him hard against the wood with the full weight of her body.

"You disgust me," she said, driving her knee up into his balls.

He nearly bent in two, panting raggedly.

"Stand up!"

When she removed the first clamp, he screamed, high

and shrill. The pain was razor sharp and blinding. He was still howling when she pulled the second off.

"Shut up!"

She slapped him hard in the face. He felt his teeth cut into his inner cheek.

"One more sound out of you, the gag goes back in."

She snapped his wrist cuffs to the top eyebolts in the cross, then leaned down. She grabbed his left foot.

"Move it," she growled. "Spread those fucking legs for me."

When she had his ankles cuffed in place, she stood and regarded him with hard eyes.

"Ah, here's a good place!"

She grabbed his nipple and caught the tip of it in the clamp's teeth.

He whimpered, tears rolling down his face. He pressed his lips together against a desperate urge to shriek.

She added the second clamp to the other nipple, but not before giving it a vicious twist between two fingers.

"Oooh, God!" he gasped, unable to stop himself.

She slapped him again, so hard that his vision blackened as spots of white danced before his eyes.

She bent to snatch the ball gag off the floor.

"Open your mouth," she demanded, shoving the ball gag against his lips. "Open it!"

He tried to turn his head away at the dog hair clinging to the wet ball, but she just forced it between his teeth.

She reached around his head to buckle the leather strap, pulling sharply to bring it so tight into his stretched, raw mouth that he could not move it at all with his tongue.

She stood back, looking at him, a smile on her thin lips.

All he could do was gaze longingly into her eyes.

Then his eyes grew wider as the door behind her opened.

Chapter 11

Beat me, beat me, o dear Masetto
Beat your poor Zerlina.
I'll stand here meek as a lamb
And bear the blows you lay on me.
You can tear my hair out, put out my eyes,
Yet your dear hands I'll gladly kiss.
—LORENZO DA PONTE, *Don Giovanni*
    (music by Wolfgang Amadeus Mozart)

Roger Banks's murder had made the news, but so far they had managed to keep any mention of the mutilations out. They were holding that in reserve to weed out crackpot confessions.

And now, seven days later, Robyn Ann Macy: a twenty-six-year-old bank teller who still lived with her parents.

There was no semen in the vaginal vault, just some lube. The two used condoms in the wastebasket yielded DNA, but results weren't back yet. DNA didn't mean squat unless they had something to match it to.

Robyn's fingerprints were on one of the Coke cans and the lube; the fingerprints on the other can, the wrapper from the Oreos, and on the tube of lube, had not come up in IAFIS.

They were coming out of the Macys' tidy little ranch house for the second time. Their first visit, on the afternoon of the body's discovery, had ended with Mrs. Macy having to be sedated; Mr. Macy had been too shaken to provide much information. Two days later, the conversation had been better, but still yielded little of use.

Hanson felt as if someone had slipped twenty-pound weights into his pockets. Nice people always made him feel this way.

Bad people—the ones always bumping up against the law in one way or another—had an attitude of resignation, as if they had known violent death was coming sooner or later. The nice ones—the ones whose experience with police went no further than traffic stops—were merely lost, unbelieving, always asking: *How did this happen to us?*

"Yeah, her folks thought she was their little shining star," Griggs said, flicking at some dust on his jacket. "But she was a dirty girl who liked to party. Probably with some married guy since they were in a no-tell motel and the guy paid with cash. No credit card bill for the little woman to find."

"You speaking from experience?" Hanson's voice was carefully flat. He didn't like Griggs's callous glee at the dead girl's sex habits, but that was Griggs.

He, on the other hand, couldn't stop seeing those dull blank eyes staring at the ceiling. He got into the driver's seat and put the key into the ignition.

"Nah." Griggs grinned, sliding in beside him. "I only fuck the ones with their own apartment."

"Is that a policy since the first divorce or the second?"

"The second. I'm a slow learner. You think the boyfriend is the doer?"

Hanson sighed. If you hear hoofbeats, think horses, not zebras, so they said. But there was something wrong with these hoofbeats.

"It doesn't feel right," he said. "Have you got the rope report over there?"

"It won't make any more sense the twelfth time than it did the first." But Griggs pulled it out and read it aloud anyway. " 'Traces of spermicidal lubricant consistent with several popular commercial condoms. Human sweat from two sources: one male, one female.' "

"So it was used at some point, even though it and everything else was put away. As if playtime was over and done."

"Maybe she and lover-boy had done the deed, all lovey-dovey, and *then* she said something that set him off," Griggs suggested. "I mean, she was dressed when she was killed, too. Looks like she was on her way out the door."

The door had a loose mortise plate and some splintering on the jamb. But it was impossible to tell if the damage had happened the day of the crime or weeks before.

And fingerprints? A motel room wasn't even worth printing.

The techies had found hairs everywhere, all different colors and textures. The long blond ones were probably Robyn's, but Hanson wouldn't be surprised to find the sheets hadn't been changed since the last time the room was rented. The hairs could even be transfer from the spread or, hell, the carpet.

"What's he do about his clothes?" Griggs looked at Hanson. "Strip naked before he kills? Bring a change of clothes and take the old ones with him?"

"Damned if I know," Hanson said. Lenny had taken photos of what looked like bloody boot prints all over the carpet. "Big damned shoes, though. Thirteen's, maybe."

When they arrived back at the station, they headed for the morgue.

"Have you got the report on Macy finished?" Hanson asked.

Miles didn't answer. He was too engrossed in digging around the chest cavity of the nameless dead man on his table with a pair of long tweezers.

"Can you at least tell me if it was the same weapon? Baseball bat?" Hanson did not approach the table. This wasn't his body, and he didn't want to see it.

"Didn't you read the final report on Banks?" Miles asked, annoyed enough to finally look up. "Whatever it is, it's not a baseball bat. The impact impressions are similar, but much smaller. Definitely has a rounded end, though."

"But you think it's the same weapon?"

"Yep. It's probably made of wood, though I didn't find any traces in the wounds." Miles lifted a lead slug from the dead man's chest and dropped it into a bowl.

"Then what makes you think it's wood?" Hanson asked.

"Because I found flakes of polyurethane. Like the stuff used to finish furniture."

"So, we got polyurethane." Griggs shrugged. "On both bodies?"

Miles nodded and went back to probing the open chest.

"Hit in the throat, too?"

"Yep."

"So you're almost done?" Hanson asked. "With the final report, I mean?"

Miles looked up again, just long enough to glare.

"You'll get the report when you get it," he said. "Now let me do my job."

Hanson followed Griggs back upstairs, but his spirits sank with every step upward. The media was gonna love this. Even without the details of Roger's diced penis and missing tongue, the case had already attracted a lot of head shaking from both the mayor and the chief of police. And now they had another victim. A very young, very pretty woman.

"I need coffee," Griggs muttered, stepping into the break room and reaching for the coffeepot. "Grab a filter out of the cabinet, would ya?"

But Hanson ignored him. He was staring at the television mounted on the wall.

"It's a terrible, *terrible* thing when a decent, upstanding member of the community falls prey to a *violent* crime," Milton Daubs, police chief, told Channel Six.

"Christ," Griggs groaned. "Bastard almost sounds sincere."

Griggs was right and wrong, Hanson thought. Daubs

was a bastard. But he was also sincere. That was what made him so dangerous: his self-righteous sincerity.

And his sincere foot was gonna land up their asses as soon as the media got wind of Robyn Macy's murder.

The only question was: who was going to say it first? Daubs or the press?

Griggs said it first.

"Well, buddy boy, I think we got a serial killer on our hands."

"What in the *blazes* did you *say* to her?"

Milton Daubs always seemed to be wound tight as a jack-in-the-box just before it sprang, but today he was in rare form. He wasn't a particularly big man, but his lungs were gigantic—and when he yelled, walls vibrated.

Hanson looked not at Daubs, but at the big damned warning on the wall behind his head: *Fear God and give glory to Him, for the hour of His Judgment is come.*

The cross-stitched Bible verse held a place of honor in the middle of Daubs's vanity wall, surrounded by plaques, awards, and photographs of the chief shaking hands with important people. After all, they lived in the buckle of the Bible Belt, and the separation of church and state was only an ugly rumor started by communists and liberals.

Staring at the wall was preferable to looking at the chief's face, growing an ugly, splotchy red. A vein in his left temple, just under his receding hairline, was throbbing.

"Look, we had to check it out." Griggs jammed his hands in his pockets. "She lied to us about having lunch with her husband that day, and we had those hairs—"

"Roger Banks and I went to college together," Daubs thundered. "We played golf together. We were *fraternity* brothers!"

Hanson nodded, all the while sending desperate tele-pathic messages to Griggs to shut up.

"I sent him a *Christmas* card every year for the last twenty years! That means he wasn't just a friend of mine, he was an *old* friend of mine, do you get that?"

"Yes, sir," Hanson said quietly. "And we're very sorry for your loss."

"Don't be a smart-ass with me! I don't need your sym-pathy, I *need* you to find the bastard who killed him."

It was a measure of Milton Daubs's sincere outrage that he'd used profanity. For Daubs, swearing belonged in the gutter with the criminals. He'd actually passed out memos asking everyone to watch their language in the squad room.

"Yes, sir, I understand—"

"What I *don't* need is you two asking his wife stupid questions that will only *upset* her." Daubs fell heavily into his chair behind the desk.

Hanson wondered if Daubs knew that they mimicked him behind his back, the way he seemed to talk in italics. It wasn't just when he was *pissed off*; he talked this way *all* the time.

"Marla is *devastated. Just devastated*. Roger was her *world*." Daubs spoke in a more reasonable tone now, but Hanson knew better than to relax. "Now, tell me what you said to send her into hysterics."

"Hysterics" was an exaggeration. Sure, she'd been up-set. People usually were when they were caught in a lie. Even a little one. Especially when it was an embarrassingly personal one.

"She said she had lunch with her husband at Caesars on the day he was killed," Hanson explained. "The reserva-tion book said they'd had lunch there on Monday, not that Thursday."

The waiter had remembered them, too. Roger and Marla were good tippers who ate there often.

"So? I can't tell you what *I* ate for lunch *yesterday*! She'd just learned that her husband was dead, for Pete's sake!"

"Yes, sir, it's an understandable mistake," Hanson agreed. "But we wouldn't have been doing our job if we hadn't followed up on it."

That was always the best defense with Daubs. Bring up duty. Honor. The American Way.

"All right," Daubs said with a sigh. "You're *right*. But what difference would it make whether she had lunch *that* day with him or not?"

Hanson exchanged a quick glance with Griggs and saw his partner's eyes roll. Was Daubs serious? What *anybody* had been doing in the twenty-four hours prior to being murdered was important.

"Well, if it had just been whether or not they'd had lunch together, it might not matter." Hanson knew he would have to be very careful here. Daubs wasn't just sincere, he was a sincere prude. "There were also the hairs we found."

"What *hairs*?"

"We found three long brown hairs wrapped around the dead guy's dick," Griggs said.

Hanson resisted the urge to punch him.

"The poor man is *dead*!" Daubs roared. "Show some *respect,* do you understand me?"

"Sorry. But we found three long brown hairs wrapped around Mr. Banks's *penis*. What was left of it."

Daubs paled, his face tensing for a millisecond in what Hanson assumed was shock at such a graphic image. How long it had been, he wondered, since Daubs had actually seen a dead body?

"We found another hair, the same type, snagged in his watch band," Hanson said, plunging forward to prevent

Griggs from speaking again. "We had to make sure it didn't come from the killer. That's all."

"Did they?" Daubs asked.

"No, sir. Based upon the sample we took from Mrs. Banks, the hair was hers."

"Turns out she *did* have lunch with her husband that day," Griggs grinned. "Only food wasn't on the menu. That's why she lied."

For a moment, Daubs didn't say anything. Maybe it took him a minute to put the pieces together. Maybe he was too embarrassed to speak.

"Thank God, it was *Marla's* hair," he said finally, pushing papers around his desk.

"Yes, sir."

Hanson was glad to say no more about it. He didn't relish telling Daubs that Roger and Marla had been playing sex games at the local porn shop. Personally, he thought it was sweet, an old married couple getting kinky together.

"Anything *else*?" Daubs asked.

"Just a handful of unexplained phone calls." Hanson was eager to give Daubs proof of their due diligence, but he knew Daubs wouldn't like the implication. "He had voice mails from a woman who identifies herself as Cherry—"

"Cherry?" Daubs blinked. "What kind of name is *that*?"

"Sounds like a stripper to me," Griggs said.

Daubs glared and the throb in his temple flared again. Hanson threw himself into the breach before the other man could speak.

"The number comes back as a prepaid phone."

"So you traced it?" Daubs demanded.

Another glance at Griggs, who was equally dumbfounded. Jesus, Hanson thought. You'd think the man at least watched *Law & Order*. An episode was playing every time you turned on the damned TV.

"Prepaid phones are almost impossible to trace," Hanson explained, hoping like hell he didn't sound as annoyed as he felt. "People just walk into a store, pay cash; they don't have to sign anything or even give them a credit card."

"Yeah, they're popular with drug dealers and terrorists," Griggs said. "And people with lousy credit."

"So who *is* this *Cherry* person?" Daubs asked. "I *assume* you asked Marla?"

"Sure, we asked," Griggs said, shrugging. "She says she never heard of anybody named Cherry. So maybe she is a stripper—"

"You—" Daubs pointed a finger at Griggs. "Not another *word* out of *you*."

Griggs mimed zipping his lips and looked at the ceiling.

Marla's reaction to the question about Cherry did bother Hanson, though he saw no need to tell Daubs. Most wives, even the ones who trusted their husbands, would be at least a little annoyed to find a strange woman had been leaving messages on their husband's cell phone.

Not Marla. She had simply shrugged and said the woman must be someone he knew through work. A paralegal or secretary, perhaps.

The chief turned his scowl back to Hanson.

"What about this *new* girl two days ago? Is it the same guy?"

"We think so. Same weapon. Some kind of blunt object with a rounded end, probably wooden. Same kind of small blade, very sharp."

"Same mutilation?"

"Afraid so."

"Any connection at *all* between—what was her name? Robyn *Macy*? And Roger?"

"None that we can find. Not personally, not professionally. Nothing. They didn't even use the same bank. We're still waiting on the LUDs from Robyn Macy's phone to compare them against Banks's."

"That's *it*?" Daubs asked.

"Well, there was one thing," Griggs said, hands still in his pockets, rocking slightly. "That symbol. The one on his key chain and her ass."

"What *kind* of symbol?" Daubs asked, suddenly suspicious.

"Roger Banks had a key chain with a round tag on it." Hanson circled his finger and thumb to show the size of it, about an inch and a half in diameter. "It has a symbol, some kind of emblem on it. Robyn Macy had the same design as a tattoo."

He pulled the photo of the key chain from his coat pocket where he'd been carrying it around for two days, showing it to everybody with no luck.

"Any idea what this is? I don't suppose it's any kind of fraternity symbol?"

Daubs squinted, pulled the paper closer, and shook his head.

"I have *no* idea. *Marla* didn't know?"

"Mrs. Banks says she has no idea where it came from."

Hanson thought he'd seen something odd flicker across Marla's face when they'd asked about the key chain. She'd been just a little too eager in suggesting that it was probably just some promotional giveaway. Roger was always picking up stuff like that, she had said.

Griggs hadn't liked it, either. When they'd left Marla, he had snorted. "Who gives away something without their name on it?"

But this was something else he saw no point in confusing Daubs with. The man was beginning to breathe hard again.

"And the girl had a *tattoo*?" Daubs demanded.

"We found the artist who did the tat. But she claims Robyn Macy brought in the design and that she has no idea what it is."

Hanson had spent a couple of hours on the Web, but it was damned hard to know what to search for when all you had was a symbol that couldn't be typed into Google. Astrological, Celtic, Egyptian, mathematical, chemical, Hindu, Christian. Entire websites devoted to that Da Vinci Code crap. Don't even ask about witchcraft and Satanic symbols. A guy could go blind.

"Nearest thing we can find is a symbol for Okinawan Karate." Griggs laughed sourly. "And the U.S. Department of Transportation."

"That doesn't make *any* sense," Daubs frowned. "I never knew Roger to be involved in any martial art or *anything* with the DOT."

"Neither does anybody else," Hanson said, wiping a hand over his mouth, just in case he lost the fight not to smile. "Robyn Macy's mother didn't even know she had a tattoo. One of her friends at the bank where she worked said, yeah, Robyn had been talking about getting some ink, but not whether she actually went through with it. The tattoo was only a couple of days old."

His gut told him the tattoo artist knew more than she was telling, but he didn't tell Daubs that. Neither did he tell Daubs that he couldn't shake the feeling that he'd seen that symbol before.

"And the *boyfriend*?" Daubs asked.

"We don't know who he is. Friends and family didn't know she was dating anybody, so I figure he's married. We got fingerprints and DNA, but nothing hit."

"That just means he doesn't have a *criminal* record."

Daubs was stating the obvious, apparently to remind them that he was a real cop, and not just a bureaucratic suit.

"I don't think he's the killer," Hanson said. "Right now he's just a person of interest."

"Keep on it. And keep *me* informed. *Daily*. You understand? You get a *lead,* I want to *know* about it."

The press had already given the killer a stupid name: the West Side Basher. Never mind that Robyn Macy had died on the south side of the city. Roger Banks had first dibs.

God help them, Hanson thought, if they got another body before they got a lead.

Chapter 12

Why I tie about thy wrist,
Julia, this silken twist,
For what other reason is't
But to show thee how, in part,
Thou my pretty captive art?
But thy bond slave is my heart.
'Tis but silk that bindeth thee,
Knap the thread and thou art free,
But 'tis otherwise with me:
I am bound and fast bound so
That from thee I cannot go;
If I could I would not so.
—ROBERT HERRICK,
"The Bracelet (to Julia)"

The package sat on the welcome mat at her front door. Cherry stared at it, then looked around. She didn't see anybody or anything else, just the package, wrapped in shiny paper decorated in pink and red hearts, tied with a bow.

She lifted it gingerly and wondered if she should hold it to her ear to see if it ticked.

Don't be so paranoid.

It was probably a mistake, something meant for the previous tenant. She had only moved in here almost three weeks ago. Maybe a housewarming gift from a friend?

Except none of her friends knew where she had moved. None except Roger and Marla.

She took it inside and laid it on the kitchen counter. Gunther jumped up and rubbed against her shoulder.

"Hello, stupid cat," she said, running a hand down his back as she looked at the package.

The wrapping was pretty, but not extravagant, and the

bow was taped on a little crooked. It looked ordinary enough, but its very presence was odd, and these days, odd made her uneasy. It hadn't come through the mail or FedEx; someone had delivered it to the door.

She could carry it down to the complex office; they might be able to forward it to the proper person. Then again, knowing the manager, he would probably keep it for himself or throw it in the trash. She hated the idea that someone had gone to all the trouble to deliver a gift that wouldn't reach its intended recipient. The recipient might never know someone had remembered his or her birthday.

She thought there might be a card inside.

"Should I just stand here looking at it?" she asked the cat. "Or go ahead and open it?"

The cat blinked at her and then mewed.

She pulled the wide red ribbon off, then slid a finger carefully under the paper so she could tape it back up if necessary.

The box was ordinary white, cheap and flimsy, about six inches square, not very deep.

Whatever it was, it was wrapped in newspaper. She pushed it aside.

Inside the box lay a collar. Not an ordinary collar like you would put on a dog, but a sleek metal band with a locking clasp.

It was the kind of collar a slave would wear. An expensive one that she recognized from the Stock Room's website, back when a collar from her master was the thing she most desired.

Now the sight of it made her feel sick.

A card lay inside the circle made by the metal collar. Just a white card without an envelope, printed in neat block letters.

"MINE" was all it said.

Then a headline from the newspaper caught her eye.

Local attorney found dead, beside a grainy photo of Roger Banks.

"I know, honey, I know," Marla said on the phone. "But you've got to get a hold of yourself—"

"He left the damn thing on my doorstep!" Cherry was getting all leaky again. She was sick from crying.

"I know it's upsetting. But if he'd wanted to hurt you, he wouldn't have just left the box. It was a gift, not a dead animal or something. He probably thinks he's wooing you, for heaven's sake."

"But the newspaper . . ." Cherry took a deep breath. "You don't think he was the one who . . . who hurt Roger, do you?"

"No," Marla said curtly. "If I thought that, I'd have told the police. It's just a stupid coincidence. He's got no reason to hurt Roger!"

"No," Cherry said uncertainly. "But—"

"Whoever killed Roger was an animal. This Kerberos guy may be crazy, but cowards like him just beat up on women. They don't have the balls to pick on someone their own size."

"I guess you're right," Cherry said softly.

"Besides, you stopped talking to him before you ever came to me and Roger, right? If he was going to hurt someone just to get at you, it'd be more likely he'd go after Paul, wouldn't it?"

That was true. She wondered if she should warn Paul. Kerberos knew that Cherry had been seeing Paul on and off, even though he wasn't really her dom.

She had been afraid to go to Roger's funeral, though it was unlikely that any of their kink friends would show up. Roger and Marla were too deeply in the closet, and their Lifestyle friends wouldn't want to cause them any potential embarrassment. If you saw someone from the club at the grocery store, you didn't even say hello; they might be with vanilla friends or family. You just never knew.

"You haven't told anybody else, have you?"

"No! I mean . . ." Cherry felt her stomach churn. "I told Robyn. About you and Roger. But I didn't tell her where I'd moved. I haven't even given her my new phone number."

Her phone had been the first thing she'd gotten rid of, even before she moved. She couldn't afford another iPhone, so she'd just gotten one of those pre-paid disposable cells. She didn't want any more calls from Kerberos or ranting messages on her voice mail.

"You deleted all your old e-mail accounts, right? Alt and CollarMe and FetLife? What about the club's discussion group?"

"You think I should? None of that has any personal information that could be traced back to me—"

"Honey, I don't know enough about that computer stuff, but I'd rather you be careful. After all, you met this nut online."

It was bad enough that she couldn't go to the club or the munches; without e-mail and chat rooms, she'd be completely cut off from the community. She couldn't bear that. She didn't even have any vanilla friends anymore.

She had blocked her FetLife account from Kerberos; surely that would be enough. She was safe online, as long as she didn't post her real name, address, or phone number. Right?

"You didn't tell the police anything about me, did you?" Cherry asked.

"No, honey. I promised you I wouldn't, and there's no reason for me to. Roger would want me to take care of you. We both cared about you very much. I still do."

"You've been so good to me. I'm so sorry."

"Where are you now? You'll feel safer if you get out of that apartment."

"I can't afford to move again," Cherry said, more tears threatening.

"Come by my office in the morning. I'll give you the keys to the lake house—"

"Oh, no, Marla, I couldn't—"

"You can and you will. I'd ask you to come stay with me, but my daughter's still here and I don't know how I'd explain it to her."

"Are you sure it's no trouble?"

"No, honey. No trouble at all. It's just sitting there empty."

"Thank you, ma'am."

"You just take care of yourself. But try to keep Gunther out of my potted plants, okay?"

Chapter 13

On her, my treasure, all joy dependeth,
Life hath no pleasure, but that she sendeth,
Sorrows that grieve her, torture my heart,
E'en when she sigheth, my sighs awaken,
And joy it dieth, by her forsaken;
Oh, worst of torments, from her to part!
—Lorenzo Da Ponte, *Don Giovanni*
(music by Wolfgang Amadeus Mozart)

The bedroom was dark but for the candles. At least a dozen flickered on the dresser, their number doubled in the mirror. Another, long and white, stood on the nightstand beside the bed.

She was straddling him, naked but for the silver chain and medallion around her throat. The candlelight danced along her curves, all golden light and shadow.

"Do you trust me? I know you trust me every day, out on the job. But do you trust me here and now?"

She leaned over him, lips soft against his ear. Her teeth pulled at his earlobe with the soft little bites that always made his cock rise to attention.

"Yes."

He curled his fist into her hair, pulling her head down to his.

In one swift move, she grabbed him by the wrists and pinned him to the mattress.

"How does that make you feel?" she whispered.

She was surprisingly strong. He was afraid to use the force necessary to break her hold. Instead, he looked up at her, into those amazing eyes.

"It makes me feel . . . interested." A small electric thrill started in his guts, shooting down into his balls.

Her breasts hung above him. His tongue flicked out toward one nipple, puckered hard as a bullet. He wanted it in his mouth, stiff against his tongue. But she shifted her body and denied him even a taste.

"Uhn-uhn-uhn," she whispered softly. "I'll say when you get to suck my tits."

Out in the real world, she had an ordinary voice that was flat and cool. But, here, in the bedroom, she could make her voice silky and husky at the same time. A cigarettes-and-sex kind of voice.

She let go of his wrists, but for some reason he made no move. He only watched as she opened the drawer of the nightstand and brought out two of the padded leather restraints that the EMTs used.

"Never use handcuffs. Handcuffs are uncomfortable as hell . . . not to mention a terrible cliché. Especially for us."

She put the first cuff on his wrist and then clipped it with a carabiner to an eyebolt mounted on the headboard.

"I'm not sure I'm exactly comfortable now," he said, watching as she put on the second cuff.

"But you are turned on, aren't you?"

Yes, he was turned on, but also uneasy as she snapped the carabiner into the other eyebolt. Something about being stretched out like this—and unable to do a damned thing about it—made him excited and uneasy at the same time.

When she moved to the bottom of the bed with yet another set of restraints, he pulled his foot away from her.

"I thought you said you trusted me? Haven't you ever fantasized about being tied up and ravished by a beautiful woman?"

Hasn't every man, at least once? he thought.

She pulled at his legs, stretching them out taut, to snap the last carabiners in place.

"Does that make you feel . . . vulnerable?"

"Yes." Looking down at his erection, he felt *exposed*.

She reached down and used a single long red fingernail to trace a vein in his cock. It twitched violently at her touch, just like the single-minded little bastard it was.

"It may be that you like the bottom. And I don't mind being on top."

She climbed onto him once more, her thighs pressed against his hips. She leaned forward, and the small medallion swung before his eyes in a glisten of silver.

Her warm, soft tongue explored his mouth slowly, thoroughly. He thrust his tongue into her greedily, but she caught it and sucked on it, hard, until he made a sound of pain.

She let go and pulled back, tossing her loose hair over his face. He was lost in a sea of golden red curls. She was teasing him with the hair he loved to gather into his hands; now, he could do nothing but inhale the faint scent of warm vanilla.

Her tongue flickered along his throat, then into his ear. Her teeth nipped his earlobe, not softly this time, but hard enough to ignite a flash of pain as sweet as it was disturbing.

Her hands moved down his body, not the light teasing touch this time, but the firm command of ownership. Over his throat, down his shoulders, along the subtle definition of chest muscles.

"Right here, right now," she whispered in his ear. "Your body belongs to me."

Her wet mouth fastened on one of his nipples. It puckered as she traced circles around the tight nub of flesh with the tip of her tongue. She pressed her mouth to his chest and suckled.

He had never known a man's nipples could be so sensitive before she proved it to him. She sucked, nibbled, and sucked some more, alternating between them, her mouth and teeth getting harder each time. His nipples seemed to be attached directly to his cock. That swollen muscle was so hard, it ached.

She sat up, licking her lips. He looked down and saw his cock jutting up between her thighs and his, as if it belonged to both of them.

She reached for the white candle.

"There's a fine line between pleasure and pain . . ."

"I'm not so sure about this—"

"Oh, don't whine. Men should beg, but never whine."

Her naked flesh glowed as she leaned backward, thrusting her breasts forward. He watched, fascinated, as she tipped the candle and allowed several drops of wax to spatter onto her skin.

At the contact of the wax, her back arched and she made a little noise deep in her throat.

Then she rolled her hips, grinding her pussy lips against his cock.

"Untie me." His voice came out just a little breathless and it pissed him off. "Untie me, Gee. Let me fuck you."

"You want to fuck me, baby?" She smiled coyly, her voice lilting like some porno movie sex kitten. But then it dropped again into that deep husky silk. Raw, hungry, dirty. She spat out the words.

"You want to slam your hard cock into my hot, wet little cunt and fuck it, do you?"

He jerked against the restraints, but only managed to rattle the carabiners.

"Goddamn it, you know I do."

The hand not holding the candle was toying with his cock.

"Tell me, baby." She reached down to his balls and squeezed. "Tell me how bad you want to fuck me."

"I wanna fuck you—"

He wanted to impale her with his cock, fuck her into the goddamned mattress, fuck her until he split her in two—

"No," she said coolly.

She ran a finger across the head of his aching cock, catching the glistening drop of pre-cum and raising it to her lips. Her tongue flicked out; then the finger slid in and out of her mouth.

"Tonight, *I* fuck you. I'm going to ride your cock like you're a dog put out to stud . . . but not yet."

She tipped the candle over him. The first drip of wax hit the middle of his chest.

"Shit!" It wasn't exactly pain, but the heat of it against his flesh was too foreign. "What the fuck are you doing?"

"It's called wax play."

"I know what it's called—Ah, *shit!*"

The candle moved closer, and the next drop was hotter. "Fuck, fuck, *fuck!*"

He felt his balls draw up, tighten. It was confusing, the way his mind said *this is fucked up,* but his cock was screaming *yes, yes, yes.*

The wax ran slowly, warmly, into his belly button, sending shivers down into his toes. The carabiners rattled louder this time.

He stared up at her, into those deep emerald eyes, and there was something more than simple playfulness in them. More than simple enjoyment. Something complicated and maybe even dangerous . . .

"Christ!" The word came out a moan. "You sick bitch, you're enjoying this."

"So are you," she whispered, smiling that Mona Lisa smile. "Admit it."

More wax spattered down onto his chest. His body spasmed, but her weight on his thighs kept him from bucking her off.

Christ!

She laughed softly and ground her cunt against his thighs. She was slippery with her juices. He could smell her sex, the sweet musk of her warm, wet snatch—

"You like being used, dog?"

She lifted herself up on her knees, wiggled forward and came down hard on his cock. It slid into her heat like a knife through butter, and then her cunt muscles clamped down on him.

"*Oh, fuck, yes . . .*" he panted in gratitude.

More wax, just quick dribbles in a line across his chest. His back arched as much as her body weight and the restraints would allow.

"That's the wonderful thing about bondage," she whispered into his ear. He could feel that medallion dance coldly across his throat. "All that energy with no place to go but into your cock."

She must have put down the candle, but he was hardly aware of anything except the feel of her cunt swallowing his cock, the impossible ache of his balls.

She rocked, slowly at first. He opened his eyes to see her watching him.

"Yes, baby. Look at me. Watch me fuck you."

Her fingers pinched one of his nipples. He moaned out loud.

She was really riding him now, working his prick with her cunt muscles. He was so deep inside her that her wetness was grinding against his balls, making a wet slapping sound.

She reached down and began rubbing her clit with two fingers.

"But don't you dare cum, nasty boy," she commanded, a little breathless now. "Don't you dare shoot that filthy load of cum into me unless I tell you to."

"Goddamnit!" He felt pressure prickling behind his eyes.

Christ, his cum was boiling upward, and he wanted to cry like a little boy. He wouldn't do it. He would not beg her.

"Do you want to cum, baby?" she panted, rubbing harder as she rode him. Her tits, small but high and round, bounced. The medallion between them swung wildly. "Does my little doggie want to shoot his wad?"

"Oh, damn you, Gina!" He thrashed against the restraints. To hell with her, he wouldn't cum for her, either. He wasn't some performing monkey. "You fucking *bitch*!"

"Yes, I'm a bitch." She pushed the fingers that had been stroking her clit into his mouth. "Suck them. Suck my fingers like you'd suck a dick for me right now if I told you to."

He thought about biting her, but the taste of her juice was intoxicating. He wanted it. He sucked and licked, drawing her fingers deep into his mouth.

The motion of her body against his grew faster and he could feel his cock twitching, straining, trying to get as deep into her body as it could.

She took her fingers from his mouth.

"Please . . ." The words were out before he could stop them.

But she was off him. The cool air hit his cock, which was suddenly jutting up into emptiness. He let loose a sound, not even a moan, but just a desperate cry of loss.

He heard her laughing, and then, miraculously, felt her breath on his cock.

"You didn't think I was gonna let you cum so soon, did you?"

Fucking torture, that's what this was. Her tongue ran

over his balls, around and around, lapping roughly into every curve.

"Goddamnit!"

"I bet I could make you cum right now with just one little stroke of my tongue."

"Then do it, bitch!"

She squeezed his balls, hard this time. But it barely registered as pain; it only made his cock dance more pathetically.

"Please, Gina, fuck, I'm begging if that's what you want—"

"Say, 'Please, Mistress,' " she whispered gleefully, wickedly. " 'Please let me shoot my filthy load into your sweet mouth.' "

"Please, Mistress," he moaned, abandoning all pride. *"Please let me shoot my filthy load into your sweet mouth—"*

Then her mouth—her sweet, mother-fucking, cock-sucking whore of a mouth!—was on his prick, swallowing it whole, her tongue lashing the swollen head, her hands squeezing the base of his cock as if she would force the cum out of him—

The orgasm was blinding. Atomic. Shattering. He could actually feel the cum shooting through the head like a hot bullet.

He lay there, panting, eyes unfocused, feeling unreal.

Then her mouth was on his. He felt her lips open, her tongue forcing its way in, and a warm unfamiliar taste flooding his mouth.

"Do you like the taste of your own cum," she whispered, "as much as I do?"

Hanson opened his eyes to early morning sunlight. There were no candles, no cuffs . . . and no Gina. Just a dream from memory, and a wet spot on the mattress. Yet he still had a hard-on and needed to piss like a mother-fucker.

He was loosing a stream of urine into the toilet when realization destroyed his aim.

Fuck! That was why that symbol had looked so familiar.

Suddenly a piece of the puzzle clicked into place. Roger and Marla's little afternoon delight; Robyn Macy and her rope . . .

He looked down and saw that his cock, having wilted just enough to take a piss, was standing at attention again.

He grabbed the hand lotion and a sock off the bathroom floor, and headed back to the bed. The day could wait another ten minutes.

Chapter 14

Haven't I always been honest with you? Haven't I
warned you more than once? Didn't I love you with all
my heart, even passionately, and did I conceal the fact
from you, that it was dangerous to give yourself into my
power, to abase yourself before me, and that I want to
be dominated?
—LEOPOLD VON SACHER-MASOCH, *Venus in Furs*

Gina Larsen had been his partner for seven years, his
lover for three of those, and his best friend for all of
them. He thought he knew her completely—until the
night she was led from a downtown hotel in handcuffs.

Vice hadn't been after her; they hadn't even known her
name until it was too late. She was just a minnow caught
in a net cast for a much bigger fish: a whale named Howard
Tunney, Republican candidate for governor.

The governor's race that year was a mud-spattered
cluster-fuck. Tunney accused the incumbent of awarding
DOT contracts to friends, and he had leaked documents
to the press.

Then, two weeks before the election, when polls were
showing the incumbent behind, the vice squad got an
anonymous tip about an escort ring operating outcalls in
the very upscale Union Hotel. The source even supplied
a room number.

The anonymous source was probably the Honorable
William R. Denton, incumbent governor, but no one was
ever able or willing to prove that. Insiders also knew that
Milton Daubs, chief of police, was deeply in Denton's
pockets, as only the son-in-law of Denton's sole daughter
could be. Daubs had personal and professional reasons to

give this anonymous tip his full attention via his pet vice squad.

Daubs had been appointed after a campaign of heated rhetoric about corruption and immorality, endorsed by the most powerful coalition in any Bible-Belt Southern state: the Christian Right. In a city like theirs, with a church on every corner and many with membership in the thousands, morality was still in the majority, at least in public.

As soon as Daubs had taken office, he began a righteous crackdown on every strip club, massage spa, adult bookstore, and nightclub in town. Even cops were taking their bachelor parties over the county line for fear of getting caught up in some sting.

Daubs must have been tickled pink at catching Howard Tunney not just with a call girl, but a genuine leather-clad dominatrix.

That is, until the dominatrix turned out to be an off-duty homicide detective named Gina Larsen.

All charges were dismissed the next morning. No one cared about Gina since the primary objective, the political ruin of Howard Tunney, had been satisfactorily accomplished as soon as the press had a photo of him being led away in handcuffs.

But that photo ruined Gina's life. That photo changed everything.

One side of Tunney's face was barely visible; he had both hands up and appeared to be hiding behind the woman between him and the photographer. The woman, also in cuffs, was good-looking with a mane of reddish curls. She stared coldly and unapologetically into the camera. She was wearing a long trench coat, but her shapely legs in seamed black stockings and high heels were clearly visible, caught in swift, strong strides.

There was no escort ring and no prostitution, either.

Only professional domination, a gray area that rarely got much police attention because there was little of it in their conservative, smallish city, and because it was difficult to prosecute without proof of actual sex taking place.

Professional dominatrixes were careful to walk that line. Some of them never even touched their clients.

Gina claimed she wasn't a serious professional; that she sometimes did it "just for fun" and that she'd only been doing it that night as a favor for a friend who was Tunney's regular playmate. Even Tunney said he'd never met Gina before that night, when his regular called and said she was sending a substitute instead.

Neither ever named the "friend." No one ever admitted to tipping off the press, either.

The press loved Gina from the start, but when they discovered she had a badge as well as a whip, the story exploded. Gina was still getting ink and YouTube hits weeks after Howard Tunney was forgotten.

She wasn't exactly beautiful, but the total package came together in a way that made men stare after her, even if women claimed they couldn't quite see the attraction. Hanson thought they could see it, all right; they just didn't like Gina, for reasons he couldn't fathom. Whenever Gina stepped into the break room for coffee, the roomful of secretaries would lift their heads and sniff the air, as if catching a whiff of a predator.

She was tall, with long legs, and a surprisingly muscular body softened by modest but more than adequate breasts. She had full, wide lips—almost too wide for beauty—and a nose that was a bit too sharp. Her shoulder-length hair was a natural auburn that burned brilliantly in the sun. But it was her eyes that had rendered him speechless the very first time they met.

Her eyes were enormous, and slightly tilted, like a Siamese cat, and just as inscrutable, reflecting everything but giving nothing away. They seemed to change color, depending on the light and whatever emotion lurked behind them. Pale sea green in sunlight, a deeper shade of hazel under fluorescents; a cool gray-green when she was angry.

With Milton Daubs at the helm, nobody doubted that Gina would lose her shield eventually. Daubs was furious—*rabid* even—that this victory for his father-in-law had shot his own department in the foot.

Hanson himself had been dumbstruck. Their affair had been over for nearly two years by then. Things had been strained between them for a couple of months after they stopped sleeping together, when it became clear to Hanson that he could not give her what she wanted. Hanson had been far more wounded than he ever let her know—how could he, when they still had to work together? Things had gradually gotten better, though there was still a big hole left in his life and a frequent ache that could not be remedied.

He had known that Gina was kinky, of course; that was one of the unspoken things that had come between them. But to take money for beating a stranger in a rented hotel room? That was a whole other level of kink, one that he couldn't quite get his head around.

The woman he'd bailed out of jail that April night was someone he didn't know. She didn't seem to be able to speak for the tight clench of her jaw, and she wouldn't look him in the eye. Neither of them spoke until they reached the privacy of the elevator.

"Tell me what the fuck you were doing there," he had hissed, frustrated by her stony silence. "Do you know what everybody is saying?"

"I can imagine," she had said flatly.

He didn't think she could. He could hardly believe the conversations he'd overheard in the hallway of the courthouse, in the squad room. Fellow officers, some of whom he knew, had been laughing, talking about her with the ferocious joy of men talking about a woman they wanted to fuck but who wouldn't fuck them.

Then the elevator opened, and the two of them had to walk through a gauntlet of their fellow detectives. Men who had worked with Gina for seven years, Hanson thought, and respected her competence as a fellow officer.

But as he and Gina edged past and walked down the corridor, their words struck him as hard as if they'd thrown actual punches.

"Do you got a law enforcement discount, Gee?" Bingham had called. "Do I hafta wear handcuffs to get a blow job? I cum in your mouth, does that cost extra?"

Gina had not looked at them; did not, in fact, seem to be aware of them at all. She seemed to move in some impenetrable bubble, while his own skin grew hot and moist.

"Nah, Bingham," Griggs had called out. "Swallowing is probably standard. I'll bet those golden showers cost plenty, though."

"Hey, Gee," Mercer had joined in. "What does piss taste like, anyway?"

Gina just kept walking, and Hanson simply followed her, hoping they made it out of the building before the itch to draw his gun began to seem like a good idea. How could they? *How dare they?*

"Hanson, you get a discount, or does she make you pay full price?"

He had Bingham up against the wall before he knew he was doing it, his right arm shoved hard up against the man's windpipe.

Griggs had been the one to pull him off.

"Just a joke, man, just a joke." Griggs grinned, slapping his shoulder.

Bingham stood there coughing and glaring, rubbing his

throat. Hanson had stared at him a long moment before turning on his heel just in time to see Gina disappear through the door to the parking lot.

He drove her home, and still she wouldn't say anything until he pulled the car to the curb, and then it was only to tell him not to bother getting out.

She was out of the car before it came to a complete stop. Hanson had no choice but to follow her across the lawn.

"Why won't you talk to me, damnit?" he shouted, grabbing her arm. "Don't you have anything at all to say?"

She had stopped, turned, and looked at him with an expression that made him drop her arm.

"I don't owe anybody anything," she said. "Not even you."

Her gaze had drilled into him, until he looked away.

"This isn't like you! I know you, Gina—"

"This is *exactly* like me. There are things you don't know about me, things you didn't want to know then—"

And he knew she was talking about two years earlier, when he had stalked out of her bedroom, confused and heartsick—

"—and you don't want to know now, either."

Then she was gone.

He had stood there in the yard for some time, watching the light come on in her bedroom window. He wondered, idiotically, about the sheets on her bed. Did she still have the pale lavender ones, or had they been replaced by now? The lavender set had been his favorite, the oldest and softest, infused by her scent through years of use.

Hanson spent two hours the next morning with a knot in his gut, waiting for Gina to emerge from Daubs's office.

"Did he ask for your badge?" Hanson asked when she reappeared.

"The charges have been dropped," she told him. "But I'm on desk duty until . . ."

Her voice trailed off as she picked up some papers from her desk and started to file them.

"Until what?"

"Until he finds a way to make me quit," she said without looking up.

In the days that followed, Hanson was paired up with John Griggs, while Gina was held hostage inside a department bent on breaking her.

Someone scribbled "Pig Whore" on her locker with a permanent marker. A dildo was left on the front seat of her car; pictures cut from S&M magazines were taped to the mirrors in the ladies' room.

One day she found a used condom, still sticky, in her desk drawer.

She stormed into the men's locker room and flung the condom at Bingham.

"This yours?"

The condom hit him in the face. He flailed at it, then roared as the men nearby started laughing. Bingham charged her, slamming her into the row of lockers.

No one moved to stop either of them. Everyone just watched, slack-jawed, as the laughter died and something much uglier took the stage.

Hanson watched. The rage radiating from her scared the hell out of him, and the violent unreality of it all kept him from moving.

Bingham had a handful of her hair, one fist cocked back. Woman or not, he was going to punch her. She kneed him and he bent double. Before he could recover, she grabbed a nightstick from an open locker and brought it down on his left knee.

"Fuckin' cunt!" Bingham screamed, writhing on the floor. "You busted my kneecap!"

"You lay a hand on me again," Gina panted, staring

down at him with wild eyes, "I'll cut your fuckin' dick off. Swear to God, I'll castrate you."

It was Griggs who grabbed her and pushed her to the door. Whether it was to save Bingham's dick or Gina's ass, Hanson wasn't sure.

"Are you all right?" he asked when he caught up with her.

Even asking felt like a lie. Did he care, really? If he was honest with himself, he was relieved not to be partnered with her anymore. He could hardly bear to look at her. And she knew it.

"Don't worry about it," she said.

Reporters and "fans" stalked her, went through her garbage, snapped photos on their cell phones at the grocery store.

When she picked up the phone at her desk, she got heavy breathing, death threats, offers of money for her story, her photos, her services, her underwear.

Hanson saw it all, felt himself pulling away from her, and wondered what that said about him. He knew he should reach out to her and find a way to backfill the gulch he felt opening between them. But then he heard the snickers of the clerks as she passed, and saw their eyes slide over to him with curiosity, as if he were somehow suspect, too.

Bad went to worse when two new—and obviously professional—photos of the "Dominatrix Detective" appeared in national magazines.

The first photo, in a supermarket tabloid, was a portrait: a tasteful black-and-white of Gina in a black leather corset and a long velvet skirt. She just happened to be holding a riding crop, looking like every naughty boy's wet dream. She stood in front of a weathered stone wall, staring straight into the camera with the slightest twist of her lips.

The second photo showed up in *Playboy*. It, too, was black-and-white, photographed from the side. It showed Gina on her knees with her hands wrapped in chains. She was nude, but only the side swell of one breast was visible, along with the line of her back curving into a lovely ass, the graceful profile with eyes closed and long curls spilling over her shoulders and back.

When those photos hit the stands, a church group began protesting outside the station, demanding that Jezebel be thrown to the dogs.

Hanson bought copies of both magazines, tearing out the photos and taping them up on his living room wall. Then he got the bottle of Jack Daniel's out from under the sink and drank until he began to talk to her images, then to shout, and finally to cry.

He woke the next morning, hung-over and eyes raw, and found the photos torn into pieces, strewn over the carpet like confetti.

When he reported for duty, the lieutenant called him into his office.

"You look like shit, Hanson."

"I think I've got a touch of the flu," Hanson mumbled.

"Sure you do." The lieu sighed. "You should know, she's gone."

"Gone?" Hanson blinked at him.

"She turned in her gun and her badge yesterday. She's gone and I still need you. So pull your shit together."

Hanson nodded, numbly, his head pounding.

"Don't do anything stupid." The lieu put a fatherly hand on his shoulder as he opened the door for him. "You're gonna have a rough time distancing yourself from this mess as it is."

Hanson thought that the lieutenant needn't have bothered with the warning. For nearly a year, the thought of

Gina made him sick to his stomach, so he pushed those thoughts into a small dark corner.

For the next year, he couldn't stop thinking about her, or what a shit he'd been. She had been his partner, and he hadn't had her back.

Hanson wasn't looking forward to staring into those eyes again. He had no idea what she would say to him, if she would even talk to him.

But he had to see her now. She was the only person he knew who could answer the questions bouncing around in his brain. Gina Larsen could be the difference between stopping a killer or seeing another body in the morgue.

Or was all that just an excuse to see her again?

Chapter 15

There is no more lively sensation than that of pain; its impressions are certain and dependable, they never deceive as may those of the pleasure women perpetually feign and almost never experience.

—MARQUIS DE SADE

Gina still lived in the little bungalow over on the East Side. The neighborhood had become trendy, full of vegans and artists who recycled. Hanson had driven by dozens of times, telling himself he was only curious about the renovations. They had never moved in together—that had been impossible because of the job, even if they'd wanted to—but he had enjoyed helping her transform the old house.

He was spared having to knock on the door. She was on her knees in the front yard, planting orange flowers along the stone path they'd laid one hot summer Sunday. For a moment, he could only stare at her back, wondering what in the hell he should say.

"Hey, Gee."

She twisted to look up at him, squinting in the sun.

Her lips tightened, their fullness pulled taut. She turned back to the flowers.

"Place is looking good." He felt like the biggest idiot in the world. "I like the yellow molding. It's nice."

"It's not yellow." She shoved the trowel into the dirt again. "It's ochre."

Hanson hunkered down, elbows on his knees, and picked up one of the waiting flowers and offered it to her.

"Don't touch my fucking zinnias." There was no anger in her voice, just a dead flatness that made his chest ache.

He set the little pot back on the ground.

"I know you aren't exactly happy to see me."

She snorted, grabbing up the plant he'd just offered her.

"Why are you here?" She yanked the flower out of its pot.

"To apologize, for starters—"

"Sorry. Two years too late. Try again."

"Okay." Christ, he thought; she wasn't going to make this easy. "I've got a case I need to ask you about."

She slammed the plant into the hole and began scooping dirt over the roots.

"They crucified me," Gina said flatly. "And you just stood by and watched."

He considered a dozen lies, all pathetic, and shoved his hands into his pockets. He watched as she began digging another hole, stabbing the rich black dirt.

"You said you didn't want an apology."

"I said it was too late for one. Not the same thing."

"I'm sorry. I didn't handle it well."

"You didn't handle it at all. You turned tail and ran."

She shoved the trowel into the dirt and stood up, meeting his gaze for the first time. The morning light fell across her incredible eyes and made the wisps of hair escaping from her ponytail glow red.

Looking at her made it hard to think, hard to breathe. The desire to draw her close and bury his face in her hair rushed over him.

"I didn't know what else to do—"

"You were afraid they'd think you were some kind of freak. Just like me."

She turned her back to him and walked toward the house.

He had spent much of the last two years wondering why her arrest had surprised—and hurt and disgusted—him so.

Their partnership had quickly developed into a genuine friendship. Eventually they talked about the people they dated, and even the occasional one-night stands, though their jobs left little time or energy for a personal life.

There had been nothing coy or flirtatious in her conversation when they spoke about sex; he had been cautious at first—the department had regular in-services about sexual harassment—but she talked about sex like a man, with a matter-of-fact nonchalance, though without the embellishment and posturing a man would feel compelled to add.

Shots had been fired during the takedown of a meth dealer who'd killed a couple of rivals. Afterward, they had gone out for drinks, to celebrate being alive and unscathed, and the adrenaline rush had made them both horny and a little stupid.

They had ended up in her bed, and the flicker of attraction he'd always felt for her flamed into a conflagration that threatened to devour him.

She liked it rough; she liked him to call her names while he held her down. She bit and scratched, urging him on with the kind of dirty talk he'd only dreamed of hearing from a woman's mouth.

They spent the next couple of years fucking like wildfire. He couldn't seem to get enough of her. Passionate, adventurous, she was the most uninhibited woman he'd ever known, the kind of woman men wrote letters to *Penthouse* about. She was always pushing him further down paths he'd never dared before.

On a trip to Macy's, she pulled him into the dressing room to watch her masturbate in the triple mirrors. Afterward, she had gotten on her knees and sucked his cock until he had to bite his hand not to cry out.

She took him to a swing club, where he watched her eat the pussy of a sexy blond trophy wife while Hanson and the woman's husband beat off, shooting cum all over their asses and tits.

She had shown him how to tie her up, and then convinced him to switch places. He had liked it. He had liked it a lot.

But then one night, when his cock was deep inside her, her hips grinding and her nails raking down his back, he'd looked down at her. Her eyes had gone emerald green, slightly glazed with that lost look of someone gone so deep she couldn't say—even remember—her own name.

"Hit me," she whispered, her voice hoarse, desperate. "Please, please . . . Hit me."

His cock had gone soft, shriveling until it fell out of her.

Hanson had known three things at that moment: that he loved her beyond reason; that he could never give her what she really wanted; and that their relationship was over. There had to be something wrong with her for wanting . . . well, what she wanted.

She had seen it in his eyes, just as he saw the flicker of disappointment in hers. And there was something else there, a hint of pain and shame, even as she tried to explain it to him.

"Erotic pain turns me on," she had said, shrugging. "I don't think anything is wrong with that, if I'm asking for it from a consensual partner."

But he was already putting on his clothes.

"I don't think I'm that consensual," he'd said. "I just . . . can't."

"You know me, Hanson." She gave a laugh that sounded forced. "You know damned well I'm not a doormat looking for abuse. I know who and what I am, and I don't take shit off anybody. I'm not crazy. This is just the way I'm wired."

Hanson didn't think he was a prude. He liked it when she pretended to resist, liked the rush of testosterone that flooded his cock when he held her down and felt her body writhing under his. He could deal with the rope and the spanking, even a timid slap or two.

But she wanted more, and he couldn't give it to her. He felt dirty and confused by the fact that she asked for it, and that some part of him hated himself for not being able to give it to her.

And now she was walking away from him, across the newly mown grass, without so much as a backward glance.

"I know I fucked up," he said, following her up the front steps. "Scream at me, hell, take a swing at me if you want. But I need to talk to you."

"I can't think of one damned thing I could possibly need to talk to you about." She stopped on the top step and faced him. "Get off my porch and go home to whatever little 'nilla wafer you're screwing these days—"

"Gee, we got a serial killer."

"Lucky you. I'm not a cop anymore, remember?"

"Do you still wear that little silver medallion? The one with that symbol on it?"

She stopped and stared at him.

"Yeah. So?" Her eyes were dark with suspicion.

"Can I see it?"

She frowned, but reached into her T-shirt and pulled out a shiny chain. The silver medallion swung back and forth.

"We've got two victims. Both had that symbol on them."

She stood there a moment, her eyes drifting past him to the street beyond before closing as she sighed deeply.

"Ah, shit."

Chapter 16

The only antidote to mental suffering is physical pain.
—KARL MARX

She handed him a beer and sat down on the sofa, leaning over to get a better look at the photos on the coffee table.

"Jesus. I heard about these on the news, but *fuck*."

"Yeah, I know. Worst I've ever seen. In person, at least."

Hanson pulled the photos of Roger's key chain and Robyn's tattoo from the pile.

"We've got nothing, no leads going anywhere at all. The vics didn't seem to have any common ground, it was looking totally random—"

"Until you put these together." She nodded. "It's the BDSM emblem. Just like the one I wear."

Gina had worn that medallion for years. He'd asked her once what it was. She just said the necklace had been a gift from a friend.

"BDSM?"

"We perverts call it BDSM," she said wryly. "What you vanillas call S&M."

"I get the S and M part. What's the B and D stand for?"

"Christ." She sighed, taking a long pull of her own beer. "You should have let me teach you all this stuff years ago, and I wouldn't have to go through Kink one-oh-one now."

He took a gulp of beer to hide his discomfort at the dig.

"So tell me now."

"BDSM. Bondage. Discipline. Some say the D and the S stand for dominance and submission. The S and M, that's sadomasochism. It's a blanket acronym that covers a whole range of kink. Perversions to you."

Another dig, Hanson thought. But at least she was talking to him.

"And you—the people who do this stuff?—call it BDSM?"

"Yep." She was studying the photos of Roger Banks. "Some people call it the Lifestyle, or the Leather Lifestyle, just to differentiate it from the swingers who also call what *they* do 'the Lifestyle.' Some people just call it kink, or fetish, or WIITWD."

"WI— What the hell does that stand for?"

"What It Is That We Do." Gina laughed, then sobered. "Jesus, I can't get over these pictures. So much blood. CSU must have shit themselves."

"So the symbol—"

"The emblem," she corrected, now studying the photo of Robyn Macy. "Some people wear American flags, ribbons, peace signs . . . We wear this."

She waved a photo of Robyn Macy's tattoo in the air.

"Nice tat. New, too. Still a little inflamed."

"She got it two days before she was killed."

"You find the shop?"

They had fallen back into the old routine, almost as if no time had passed. Hanson was sure it was a cop thing, being able to drop personal baggage and focus on the case.

"Yeah, little place called Ace's Ink. The artist's name, a girl—shit, I got it written down somewhere—"

"April something?"

"Yeah," he said, surprised. "You know her?"

"I know her work. She does a lot of the local community's ink."

"So she would know exactly what this symbol means, right? I thought she knew more than she was telling."

"Like she's gonna tell you," Gee snorted.

"So it's some big secret? This emblem?"

Gina shrugged.

"Not secret so much as . . . discreet. Like an inside joke. I'm sure Roger Banks didn't want his wife to know about his kinky proclivities."

"I think the wife knows. The day he was killed, she and her husband had a quickie down at the Purple Onion."

"Glory-holing?" Gina smiled a little. "Go, Roger, you perverted bastard . . ."

"But you don't know either of them?"

Gina glared at him over the top of her bottle, taking a swig before she answered.

"We don't all know each other. It's not like we register for a license or something. Some people never come out to the clubs or parties—"

"But the ones who come out to play, most of them know each other? Right?"

"Most of them. Some people lose interest, drop out for a while, maybe they come back. New people come in. But basically, it's a small population."

"So, if you didn't know Roger or Robyn, they were probably not into the local community, right?"

Gina shrugged again.

"I'm not exactly in with the cool kids anymore. They could be new, I wouldn't know."

"You mean, you're not—into it—anymore?"

He was afraid she'd see the hope reach his eyes.

"You and the department weren't the only ones who abandoned me." Her face tightened once more. "After I was busted, I was not made to feel particularly welcome there."

"Why not?"

"Because we're in the buckle of the fuckin' Bible Belt, Hanson! In New York, California—not so much of a big deal. But around here? Most people are scared shitless that their family or their neighbors or their bosses will find out what they're into. Some of them are professionals who could lose their licenses over something like that coming out. Some could lose custody of their kids. And some are just plain assholes who think they're a lot more important than they are."

She took another sip of beer.

"So here I am, with my name and face all over the place as the Disgraced Dominatrix Detective, reporters all over me, people recognizing me—friends in the lifestyle didn't want me anywhere *near* them."

"I'm sorry," he said, looking at the photos so he didn't have to look at her. "I didn't know."

"Of course not. You never bothered to find out. This case is the only reason I even let you in my house."

They sipped their beers in silence.

"You want to know about the case, then?" Hanson said finally.

Hanson talked, and she asked a few questions. He realized then that the real injustice was that Gina was and always would be a cop at heart. He could see just how much she'd missed the job.

She paused over one photo in particular.

"You gotta be kidding me."

She turned the photo around toward Hanson. It was the shot of the dresser in Robyn Macy's motel room, showing the empty Coke cans and the cookie wrappers.

Then she picked up another photo—this one of the rope—and held it up alongside the first.

"I think I know who Robyn Macy was with."

"You said you didn't know her."

"I don't. But I know the Oreos and the rope."

"I'm not following."

"Don't pout. You didn't miss anything. But I know—used to know—a guy who always gave his good little girls Oreo cookies after playtime. And he had this thing about storing his rope braided this way. Separately, could be co-incidence. But together, I'd bet it's the same guy."

"Don't tell me. Did he give you cookies, too?"

Gina looked at him, as if trying to decide whether he was being an asshole. She shrugged.

"Paul likes to score all the newbies, the fresh meat. I'd be willing to bet that he's done half of the women in the local community, at least when they first started out and didn't know any better."

"What's his last name?"

"Don't know. Paul may not even be his real name."

"Where can I find him?"

"No idea."

"Shit!" Hanson had thought finding a link in the murders was going to help, but it was looking more like he was stepping into quicksand.

"Don't get your panties in a wad," Gina said. "Look, most people use scene names, or their screen names from the Internet."

"But you fucked him."

"Yes, I fucked him," she shot back. "You know the last name of everybody you ever fucked?"

Hanson frowned and shoved his hands into his pockets. The phone on her belt erupted into a familiar ringtone, a song he knew but for a moment could not place. Then it came to him. Rick James. "Superfreak." He almost smiled. Gina always liked irony.

She held the phone up, looking at the screen. Her lips tightened, but she said nothing as she returned the phone to her hip.

"You need to answer that?" Hanson asked.

"Later."

"So how do I find this Paul?"

"The kinky community—the ones that socialize—is pretty small. People that hang around long enough come to know most of the same people, even though they might not ever know their real names. But there is one place you can find them all."

She stood up, and Hanson followed her down the hall to the tiny room she used as an office. She sat down at the desk, touched the mouse, and the screen sprang to life.

"What's this?" he asked, watching over her shoulder as she typed rapidly.

"It's a computer."

The screen came up black and gray—

"I know that," he said. "Smart ass. What's this site?"

"It's FetLife. It's like Facebook or MySpace for perverts."

She was navigating so fast it was hard for Hanson to keep up.

"There's also Alt.com, Collarme.com—those are the biggest. Those sites have memberships in the hundreds of thousands."

"You're shitting me."

"I shit you not," she said. "In the olden days, people had to use personal ads in adult magazines. Now we've got the Internet, and you're never more than a few clicks away from talking to other perverts."

"So, Paul has a profile here?"

"Under his screen name, yes. If he hasn't deleted it yet. If he's heard about Robyn's death, he may have panicked and trashed everything—"

"Then just give me his screen name, I'll call the site and get his—"

She hit a key and the screen went dark. She spun around in her chair and looked up at him.

"If I do this for you, you have to promise not to go Big Brother on these people."

"He could be a murderer, for Christ's sake!"

"Paul's not a killer." She waved a hand dismissively. "He's an oversexed little shit who lives in fear of his wife—"

"Then he's a party of interest, possibly a witness."

"And he's more likely to cooperate if you don't go charging in with both barrels blazing."

He said nothing for a long minute, considering.

"I'm serious, Hanson. I wanna help you catch this guy, but I also want to protect my own people—"

"*Your* people?"

She sighed.

"Well . . . Yes. My people. Promise me."

"All right, I promise to try it your way first. Is that good enough?"

She shrugged and turned back to the computer.

"It may take a day for him to read this and e-mail me back."

"Superfreak" rang out again. This time she didn't even look at her phone, just ignored it completely.

"You're still connected to . . . them?"

"I mostly lurk these days. I haven't gone to the club in over a year."

"But you're still doing pro work? Is that why your phone keeps ringing?"

"Yes." She stared at him. "You want to bust me for it?"

"That's not what I meant—"

What *did* he mean? He wasn't sure. Looking at her confused him and he wondered if coming here was a massive mistake.

"I don't fuck my clients." She looked at him steadily, her chin jutting forward as her left eyebrow arched ever so slightly. "I dominate them. For money, yes. I provide a valuable service. And since I don't particularly want to wait tables or do data processing for minimum wage, I do it for a living now."

"It's still illegal."

Actually, sexual domination's legal status was a little fuzzy, but Hanson was suddenly feeling pissy.

"Fuck you. So is anal sex in some states, but you didn't have any problem with breaking that law."

He knew he couldn't find Paul without her, and he probably wasn't going to get anybody else in that community to talk to him, even if he could find them.

"If you work this case with me," Hanson said, "it's got to be totally as an informant—"

"Informant? No way. Consultant, maybe—"

"And I gotta let my partner in on this. You know that, right?"

"Shit." She made a face. "It would have to be Griggs."

The problem of how to bring Gina into the investigation became entirely academic when the phone rang; not Rick James this time, but the familiar beeps of Hanson's T-Mobile.

They had another body.

Chapter 17

I am your spaniel; and, Demetrius,
The more you beat me, I will fawn on you:
Use me but as your spaniel, spurn me, strike me,
Neglect me, lose me; only give me leave,
Unworthy as I am, to follow you.
What worse place can I beg in your love,—
And yet a place of high respect with me,—
Than to be used as you use your dog?
                    —WILLIAM SHAKESPEARE,
                    A Midsummer Night's Dream

The house was a run-down ranch in a middle-class neighborhood sliding downhill. A couple of patrolmen were standing in the street, keeping a few gawking neighbors behind the tape.

Hanson saw Griggs on the edge of the lawn. He was staring over the shoulder of one of the CSU techs. Hanson didn't recognize the tech, but he could see that she was making a mold of a shoe impression in a patch of dirt.

"Bet it belongs to the fuckin' neighbor who called it in," Griggs said.

Hanson waved him away from the tech. Griggs gave him a quizzical look.

"We need to bring Gina in on this," he said. "She identified the key chain and the tattoo—"

"You're jerking my dick, right?" He looked around at Gina, who was making her way toward them, and his tone was jubilant. "I knew this was a sex thing! I *knew* it!"

"We need her help. Try not to be as big an asshole as you are. I'm begging you."

"Hey, you're hurting my feelings," Griggs said with

mock pain. "But you know we could both get fucked over this, bringing her in. She's not a cop anymore. She's a civilian."

"She's a resource. Just play nice, all right?"

"I'll be as sweet as a sixteen-year-old pussy." Griggs leered, then turned toward Gina, calling out in a jolly voice. "Gee, you picked a hell of a day to drop in! Sure you're up for this? It's a doozy!"

"Fuck you, Griggs." She nodded toward the truck parked at the curb. "What's with Animal Control?"

"Well." Griggs scratched his head, doing his bad Columbo impersonation. "We couldn't figure out how to bag and tag the little fuckers."

He handed them both a pair of booties.

"You're gonna need these. And this."

He tossed a small bottle of wintergreen oil at Hanson, who managed to catch it against his shirtfront.

"Come on," Hanson groaned. "I didn't know you even had this stuff—"

"I borrowed it from Creepy," Griggs said. "Believe me, you're gonna need it."

Hanson threw it back to him. Real cops didn't need that stuff.

"Fine, have it your way," Griggs grunted.

Hanson and Gina slipped the booties over their shoes, though Hanson thought, as always, Gina performed the maneuver with much more grace. He fished gloves out of his pocket and put them on as well.

"You got an extra pair?" Gina asked.

"Whoa, you ain't touching nothing," Griggs said. "You shouldn't even be here."

High-pitched barking—and the most God-awful stench—grew as they approached the front door. Hanson raised a hand to his nose and tried not to gag.

"What the *fuck*? What *is* that? It's not just decomp—"

He'd had a body once, left for three days in a car trunk in summer heat, that didn't stink this bad.

Human decomposition is the worst smell in the known universe, almost beyond description: like raw meat gone rancid; a hot, cloying smell of sour rot. But this smell was more and worse.

"Christ," Gina croaked, looking a little green. "Do I smell dog shit?"

"Dog piss, too." Griggs smirked. "You want the wintergreen now?"

"Yes," Gina and Hanson said at the same time.

"If you're gonna puke, go 'round the side of the house," Griggs said, handing over the bottle. "That's where everybody else tossed their cookies. Everybody but Creepy."

Hanson was nearly knocked over by a guy in an Animal Control uniform.

"Close the door! Don't—Aw, shit, stop him!" the uniform shouted. "Catch that little bastard!"

He ran after a small mop of matted fur that darted between Hanson's legs and then shot down the driveway.

"No way to contain a scene this fucked-up," Griggs said. "So don't bust my balls over the dogs."

Hanson tried to avoid a mostly shredded plastic bag spilling garbage just inside the front door, and stepped in a wet pyramid of feces instead. The wintergreen helped the smell a little, but it did nothing about the flies buzzing everywhere.

"Jesus Christ," Gina gasped quietly, sidestepping another pile of dog shit.

An ACU officer was attempting to lower a wriggling, yelping dog into a cage. Two other dogs, carbon copies of dirty reddish hair, were already in one cage, barking their ugly little heads off.

"Fuckin' Pekingese," ACU growled. "I *hate* fuckin' Pekingese."

"Yeah, we got five of these little ankle-biters," Griggs said. "I think it's five, we mighta missed one. I'm not even sure, are they evidence? Are they witnesses? Or accomplices? What do you think, Gee?"

"Accomplices?" Gina asked, waving a fly from her face.

They threaded past another pile of garbage: empty pizza boxes, used take-out containers, wadded-up clothing, soda cans and bottles . . .

"I don't think our vic was much into housekeeping," Griggs said. "Some of this is from the dogs playing in the bags of garbage, but most of it is just . . . well, shit."

Another dog charged into the room, jumping frantically against Hanson's legs and yapping. He grabbed it, while trying to keep its sharp little teeth out of his wrist. But as the dog wriggled in his arms, he noticed that the matted hair was moist.

"This is blood," Hanson said suddenly, dropping the dog. "The dogs have been into the blood."

"That ain't all they been into," Griggs said. "They freakin' *chewed* on both victims."

"Both?" Gina asked.

"Yeah. We got two bodies this time."

The next-door neighbor had smelled something really, *really* bad.

"I thought maybe a skunk or something had crawled under the house and died, you know?" Mrs. Hernandez told the police. "It smelled so *bad.*"

Mrs. Hernandez, unable to locate the odor, had knocked on her neighbor's door and realized right away that the smell was coming from inside.

"I don't know her so well," she said, shrugging. "I went in her house once and it was nasty. Something wrong with that woman, if you ask me. Who lives like that? But this smell was so much worse than ever before. And the dogs, always barking! Yap-yap-yap!"

"You didn't hear anything else? Screams, shouting?"

"I always hear stuff from over there. Loud music, mostly, sometimes screams," Mrs. Hernandez said, shrugging. "I call the police the first couple of times, but they just tell me it's her TV too loud. Then they tell me not to call no more."

Griggs led Hanson and Gina to the back of the house, where Creepy Carl was a white ghost in coveralls, booties, and mask. His gloves were already smeared with blood.

"Does that mask help at all?" Hanson asked him.

Carl's perpetually bloodshot eyes blinked once, like an owl, and he shrugged.

"Keeps the flies out," he said in his usual monotone.

Hanson couldn't say anything. He just stared, trying not to breathe through his nose and waving the flies away.

The room wasn't very big, maybe ten by twelve at the most, but the odd mixture of furniture made it feel like a closet. All of it was old, antique perhaps, but shabby.

The walls of the room were paneling painted over—badly—in a shockingly bright primary blue. One wall held a large piece of pegboard—also blue—on which hung a variety of instruments, only some of which he recognized. Rope. A feather duster. Leather cuffs. Two whips.

Someone had pulled back the heavy drapes to open the windows, and dusty shafts of sunlight fell onto a male body.

At first, the naked man seemed to be standing upright with his eyes open. The effect was unsettling until Hanson realized the body was cuffed ankles and wrists to a big wooden X. He wasn't standing so much as just . . . sagging. Like a sack of meat gone bad, complete with squirming maggots in his eyes.

He was completely naked but for the pink stripper shoes crammed onto his feet, two metal clamps dangling from his nipples, and a red rubber ball gag in his mouth. Blood had dried in streaks down his chest from a deep slash in his throat.

The other victim, a woman, was lying on the floor. Her blue satin kimono was open, revealing deep cuts in both breasts in addition to the mess the killer had made of her genitalia.

Gina squatted near the body, studying the corpse's face.

"Aw, shit," she breathed softly. "This is *not* good."

"What? Do you know her?"

"Yep." Gina straightened up and ran a hand through her hair. "This is Lady Cassandra."

"What's that mean to us?" Griggs wanted to know.

"It means, boys," Gina grimaced, "that the proverbial shit is about to hit the fan."

Another Pekingese ran into the room and went straight for his mistress.

"No, no!" Gina shooed the dog away. "Aw, shit. Have they really been *eating* her?"

Hanson looked down at Lady Cassandra's left leg, which indeed showed signs of chewing.

"You'd think they'd be put off by the maggots," Griggs said. "But I guess protein is protein."

Hanson felt his stomach drop and suddenly Gina was gesturing wildly at the door.

"Take it outside!"

Hanson didn't think he would make it to the door, so he stumbled to the open window. He punched out the screen and hung his head out just in time for a second look at his breakfast.

"It looks like they've been dead four, maybe five days," Creepy Carl said. "I guess the poor dogs got hungry."

The three of them turned to stare at Carl, then glanced at each other.

"Miles is gonna be so pissed he didn't catch this one," Griggs mumbled.

"*I'm* pissed that Miles didn't catch this one," Hanson grumbled.

"The dogs have stopped barking," Gina said. "They must have finally gotten them all in the truck. Thank God."

In the end, Miles was called in anyway, along with four more CSU. They all crowded into the little house.

"I don't even know where to start," Louise Fortner said, one hand rubbing across her mouth. "With all this clutter and garbage, I can't tell what's important and what's just crap."

Hanson was digging through the piles on the kitchen counters. Newspapers from yesterday . . . the day before . . . Magazines, junk mail, receipts, scribbled notes . . .

"Grocery list," he said, reading: "Dog food, milk, tuna, Preparation H—"

"Oh, I so did *not* want to know that," Griggs groaned. "I got six carry-out menus from the same Chinese place. Didn't this bitch throw anything away?"

"This is interesting," Hanson said, pulling a scrap of paper from underneath a magnet on the fridge.

"What? Another Taco Bell wrapper?" Gina asked.

"I got some Mickey D's over here if you wanna start a collection," Griggs said.

"It's a phone number," Hanson said. "Important enough that she put it somewhere she couldn't lose it. And the initials *MD*."

Griggs snatched it from Hanson's hand and squinted at it.

"Could be her doctor," he said.

"Could be."

Hanson took the cell from his pocket and dialed the number: 555-7286. Then he hit the button for speaker-phone, and held it away from his ear.

"This is Milton Daubs," said the familiar voice. "I'm not available to take your call but if you—"

"Damn." Hanson clicked off, and lowered his voice. "What's she doing with the chief's private cell phone number?"

"Holy shit," Griggs said. "You think he's one of her customers?"

Gina laughed loudly.

"What?" Griggs demanded.

"He's not a customer," Gina said, rubbing her eyes. "She's a snitch."

"Huh?" Griggs said.

"I'll explain to you over dinner," Gina said. "I need to eat something."

Two hours ago, Hanson hadn't thought he'd ever eat again, but now his stomach was demanding to be fed.

"There's no way we can go into a restaurant with this stink on us," he said. "Even Waffle House would throw us out."

"Why don't you two go home," Gina said. "Shower six or seven times, then come over to my place. I'll feed you if you'll let me talk this one out with you."

Griggs gave her a hard look.

"You're not a detective anymore, Gee."

"No shit," Gina said. "But you need me, like it or not."

"I'm too fuckin' tired to argue with you," Griggs said. "Man, I'm gonna have to burn this suit."

Gina's hip started playing "Superfreak" again.

Griggs burst into laughter.

"Nice ring tone, Gee!"

This time, she answered the phone as she walked out of earshot.

Chapter 18

The true man wants two things: danger and play. For that reason he wants woman, as the most dangerous plaything.

—FRIEDRICH NIETZSCHE

Hanson felt better after scrubbing until the hot water ran out, but he could still smell it. The stink was up his nose, in his mouth.

Griggs was sitting in his car outside of Gina's house. Hanson tapped on the window and was rewarded with a start from Griggs, then a finger.

"You afraid to go in without me?"

"Who knows what that twisted bitch might try," Griggs grunted, getting out of the car.

Hanson couldn't help laughing.

"I ain't just whistling Dixie, Hanson. Have you considered that maybe Gee is a little too close to this case?"

"What are you talking about?"

"Hell, I got nothing against a little kinky sex, but Gee was into some seriously rough trade. More than a few swats with a Ping-Pong paddle, if you know what I mean—"

"No, I don't know what you mean," Hanson said coldly. "What do you know about it?"

"I did some checking up on her, you know?" Griggs lowered his voice, glancing at the house as if he feared being overheard. "She showed up at the ER one night with a black eye, split lip, and vaginal bleeding. *Vaginal bleeding*, Hanson. I mean, Christ! How do you think something like that happens?"

"You pulled her medical records? How the hell did you get them? And why?"

"Because fuckin' Daubs told me to! When she got busted, he wanted all the dirt on her—"

"You investigated my partner?" He was getting angrier by the minute. "You got some secret line into the pervert community, too?"

"No, but I got a friend in vice who knew some guy she was involved with. Supposed to be this hard-ass sadist. They questioned him on rape charges a while back."

"Questioned? Did they charge him?"

"Nah. Supposedly he set up some fantasy kidnapping gang-bang for this chick who got a little more than she bargained for. She dropped the charges, though, when she realized all her dirty laundry would get hung out in court."

"Sounds like this mystery man is somebody we need to check out. Why didn't you mention him before now?"

"I only remembered him when you brought Gina into the case," Griggs said testily. "And by then we were knee-deep in blood and dog shit."

"So Gee's twisted. That doesn't prove anything."

"Proves she's not exactly what I would call stable."

"You're full of shit," Hanson said, starting to walk away.

"Listen to me." Griggs laid a hand on his arm. "Gee's always been a hard-ass, but toward the end of all that shit, she got downright scary."

"You would have gotten a little bent out of shape, too, if everybody fucked you over—"

"She broke the law and she made us all look like assholes! You don't shit on your fellow officers!" Griggs's face was getting red. "Most of the crap she got, she had it coming. But the thing with Bingham, man—"

"Oh, not that again—"

"She busted his kneecap, Hanson! Then she told him if he ever touched her again, she'd *cut his fucking dick off.*"

Hanson looked at him for a long moment.

"Doesn't mean anything," he said. "People say shit all the time. Women are always threatening to Bobbitt somebody when they get pissed."

"Sure." Griggs sounded unconvinced. "But I think we oughta see if our murder weapon might be a night stick."

Gina fed them a meal of pasta Alfredo and chicken, with a big salad and garlic bread. Knowing Gee, Hanson thought, the sauce was probably Prego, the chicken was precooked from the deli, and the salad out of a bag, but it was good and filling.

"I didn't figure anybody was up for tomato sauce," she said.

Hanson realized he was staring at her again, so he looked at his plate, then at the red striped curtains over the sink. It was both unsettling and deeply comforting to be back in her kitchen, to see her sitting on the other side of the table.

"So this Lady Cassandra," Griggs finally said, "how well did you know her?"

"We used to be friends, sort of." Gina sighed and took a swig of beer. "She's the one who got me busted."

"You're shitting me." Griggs stared. "You mean Lady Cassandra was the mystery friend? The one doing Tunney?"

"That explains why she had Daubs's phone number," Hanson said.

"Bingo." Gina grimaced. "I didn't do pro work back then, but Cassandra called me begging for a favor. And stupid me, I agreed to fill in for her."

"And the client turned out to be Howard Tunney," Hanson said. "She set you up."

"Why'd she wanna do that?" Griggs asked, cramming the last of a second helping into his mouth.

Gina shrugged.

"Probably because I was fucking her husband."

Hanson stared at her, and she simply shrugged again.

"It was before," she said in a flat voice. "And after."

Before him. And after him. That was what she meant.

Suddenly Hanson understood a great deal. There had been a period of nearly two years when Gina had gone silent about her personal life, and Hanson had wondered if the guy was married, maybe even someone in the department or the DA's office; why else wouldn't she talk about him? Then came a period of moody distraction, and he had known the relationship was over.

That had been right before they began fucking like proverbial rabbits.

"He's the one who gave you that necklace, isn't he?" Hanson asked, not sure he wanted to know the answer.

"Yes."

Their eyes locked. Hanson looked away first. Suddenly the pasta sat heavy on his stomach. He pushed away from the table and got another beer out of the fridge.

"I don't think it was just about setting me up because of Quinn," Gina said. "Daubs was the one who shut her club down."

"What club?" Griggs asked.

"A dungeon," Gina explained. "A members-only private club where the community came out to play. It was a dump, honestly, but it was the only game in town."

"Until Daubs closed it."

"Yep." Gina took another sip of beer. "She let Daubs think she was setting Tunney up for the governor to trade favors, and Daubs was so eager to prove himself to his father-in-law, he took the bait hook, line and sinker. But when she made sure I was arrested, too — "

"The whole thing was a great big fuck-you to Daubs," Griggs grinned. "She made him look like a total asshole."

Hanson knew he should be paying closer attention, but he was thinking about Cassandra Lee's husband. What kind of man married a professional dominatrix?

"Yep." Gina actually grinned. "She is—I mean, *was*—one vindictive bitch."

"Why does she still have his number?" Griggs asked. "She calling him at three a.m. and hanging up just to piss him off?"

"I don't know." Gina shrugged. "But there have been rumors . . ."

She nibbled at the edges of a thick slab of garlic bread while Hanson and Griggs waited for her to go on. But she said nothing.

"Spit it out, for Christ's sake," Griggs said irritably.

Gina sighed.

"She's been telling her faithful followers—amazingly, she actually has a few, but generally they're just people she hasn't fucked over yet—that she had something on Daubs, and that's why he was going to let her reopen."

"You think she was telling the truth?" Hanson asked.

Gina's shoulders rose and fell again.

"Who knows? Cassandra lied like most people breathe. Now there's another dungeon where she's not even welcome as a guest."

"Are you sure Daubs wasn't one of her clients?" Griggs said. "I can sorta picture ol' Milt in one of them gimp suits."

Hanson frowned at him, but Gina merely waved her hand dismissively.

"Milton Daubs can't find his own dick with both hands," Gina said. "Trust me, I'd know if he was kinky."

"Well, something was still going on between them," Hanson said. *Is there still something going on between you and Cassandra Lee's husband?*

"Maybe Daubs offed her." Griggs grinned.

"That's not funny." A new anxiety hit Hanson between the eyes. "Oh, shit."

"What?" Gina looked up sharply.

"Do we put finding Daubs's phone number in the report?" Hanson asked. "Or do we leave it out?"

"Hell, no!" Griggs said. "Are you kidding?"

"I'd vote no," Gina said. "But I'd love to see his face when he finds out she's dead. That would tell us something."

"Christ, I hate this shit," Hanson grumbled, rubbing his hands over his mouth. "What if it comes back to bite us on the ass?"

"I *do* think he was doing favors for her." Gina stood up and moved around the table to the fridge. "Her neighbors have been complaining about her for years, but whenever they called the cops, they were told to mind their own business."

"Daubs would never let someone like her keep operating, not out of a private house," Griggs said. "Unless she had something on him."

Griggs ogled Gina's ass as she bent over to pluck a bottle from the lower shelf, and Hanson kicked him under the table. Griggs just grinned at him.

"I told you, she was a vindictive bitch," Gina said, closing the fridge and sitting down again. "Look at what she did to me."

"So you'd have a motive to kill her," Griggs said.

Gina's gaze nailed him to the wall. Hanson had seen those amazing eyes drill through a hundred suspects in the interrogation room.

"If I had killed her, there'd be a stake through her heart," she said coldly. "If you're looking for motive, I can name at least fifty people who won't be shedding tears over her or her stupid dogs."

"All in the community?" Hanson asked.

"The majority of them," Gina said. "But I don't think our perp is one of us."

"The pervert community, you mean?" Griggs laughed. "Oh, you gotta be kidding me. This thing has pervert psycho written all over it!"

"This thing has *rage* written all over it," Gina said. "This is personal, not some sicko just getting his jollies."

"What makes you say that?" Hanson asked.

"I'm not saying we don't attract a few lunatics." Gina tipped back in her chair, in that faintly masculine way of hers. "But so does the Republican Party and the Catholic Church. The Leather community has its own rules—"

"But you said not everybody comes out to play," Hanson said.

"I'm not saying he couldn't be someone who stays in the shadows—"

"He?" Hanson asked. "You're certain our perp is male?"

"Don't be a moron," Griggs said. "A woman wouldn't have the strength to beat Roger Banks to death."

Damn Griggs, Hanson thought; he was *baiting* her. As if she were a suspect.

"Thanks," Gina said sourly. "A woman could have taken him down, if she surprised him."

"Snuck up on him, maybe." Griggs shrugged. "Got him down on the ground with a couple of busted kneecaps. That the way you'd do it, Gee?"

"You know as well as I do," Gina said flatly. "Ninety percent of all serial killers are male."

"True." Griggs shrugged.

"What I *meant*," she continued, "is that our guy isn't a *legitimate* member of the community. We're pretty damn good at weeding out the wannabes and assholes who think that BDSM is gonna get them a hot little sex slave, or that beating his wife makes him a dominant."

"Damn!" Griggs slapped his hand on the table dramatically. "I always wanted a sex slave in black leather!"

"Stop fucking around," Hanson snapped.

"All those wacko survivalists shopping the Army-Navy surplus stores may try to enlist," Gina said, "but the military doesn't tolerate guys who want to bomb the IRS any more than the BDSM community tolerates serial killers."

"You really don't think it could be somebody inside?"

"The community has a standard called safe, sane, and consensual," Gina explained. "You don't toe the party line, you're ostracized. We don't let you play our reindeer games. For the most part."

"For the most part?"

"We don't have time for me to educate you in all the nuances. A sociopath may be attracted to BDSM, but real kinksters are all about consent. A serial killer isn't. I just don't think we're looking for someone inside the community. The perverts I know are more like Roger Banks than Jeffrey Dahmer.

"Look at the two victims today," she said. "He didn't beat or mutilate the male, even though he was all wrapped up like a Christmas present from Sadistic Santa. The killer just slit his throat, quickly and relatively painlessly."

"Lady Cassandra got all his attention," Hanson agreed. "But we know he's not just into women, because he killed Roger Banks."

"Exactly."

"Serials usually go for strangers," Griggs argued. "Not a hit list of people who pissed them off."

"So maybe he's not your typical serial," Hanson said. "But it sure looks like he's got a definite shopping list, and the guy on the cross wasn't on it."

The guy on the cross—Randall Heeler—had been identified by his wallet, found in the bathroom along with his clothes. It seemed Randall had just been in the wrong place at the wrong time.

"Have you checked your e-mail, Gee?" Hanson asked.

"What e-mail?"

Hanson filled Griggs in on Mr. Oreo.

"Don't get excited," Gina said. "I got one of those delivery errors. No such e-mail account."

"Shit," Griggs groaned.

"He's probably heard about Robyn's murder by now—"

"Assuming he's not the perp," Griggs said.

"Either way, he's freaked. First thing he would have done is delete all his e-mail accounts, his profiles. He probably scrubbed his whole computer, if he's smart."

"Is he smart?" Hanson asked.

"Not particularly." Gina shrugged.

"Then we get a court order to get at the e-mail accounts of everybody who belongs to that online group—"

"No." Gina shook her head. "It's a gross invasion of privacy—"

"What the fuck?" Griggs exploded. "Are you kidding me?"

"Look, getting a court order would take days that we don't have," Gina said. "I wasn't kidding when I said the shit was gonna hit the fan. I don't know what will happen as soon as word gets around about Cassandra."

"What do you mean?"

"You see what Paul did. I doubt anybody has put two and two together yet with Roger Banks and Robyn Macy. Right now, they're just two random victims. But Cassandra? Even people who don't know her, know who she is. She's completely out of the closet."

"You saying the entire community is gonna start dumping their computers 'cause they think the killer is after them?" Hanson asked.

"They won't be worried about a killer targeting them," Gina said. "They're terrified of being found out as perverts. They will scatter in a million directions and we may never find them."

"So what the hell do we do?" Griggs wanted to know.

"I'll work on the computer angle," Gina said. "Listen to the chatter, e-mail a few people—"

"Well, tomorrow morning we go talk to Cassandra Lee's husband," Hanson said. He watched her face for a reaction, hating himself.

"Her ex, you mean." Gina stood up and began gathering dishes. "Good luck with that."

"I gotta take a piss," Griggs announced. "Where's the john?"

"Down the hall, first door on the right," Hanson said.

Griggs flashed a grin at him—*that's right, you know your way around here, don't you?*—before hiking up his pants and walking away.

Hanson stood up and moved to the sink, trying to see the face she kept carefully angled away.

"I thought you'd like to go with us."

"You and Griggs are big boys," she said, scraping plates into the sink. "You don't need me along for the ride."

"He may tell you things he wouldn't tell us."

"I doubt it," she said, still not looking at him.

"Are you still seeing him?"

"Fuck you," Gina said tiredly, shoving a plate into the dishwasher.

"We'll pick you up at nine," Hanson said, and walked out of the room.

Hanson didn't sleep much that night. He couldn't stop thinking about Gina.

There had been plenty of women in his life. He had even been married once, right out of the academy, but it only lasted three years. Anna, like so many women, decided she didn't like being a cop's wife. He didn't blame her.

His connection with Gina had gone much deeper because she was his partner as well as his lover; that was two counts of intimacy rolled up into one convenient package. With Gina, there were no broken dates or missed dinners because of a case, no complaints that he didn't spend enough time with her.

He'd been dating a woman on and off for a couple of months when he'd started the affair with Gina. When he'd told her he thought it would be better if they didn't see each other anymore, she had guessed the truth immediately.

"You're fucking your partner, aren't you?" She hadn't shouted or cried, just looked at him with something like pity and annoyance. "How convenient."

"I'm not—"

"Hey, I'm not mad," she had continued. "It might actually work for you. Fucking Gina is almost like fucking yourself, isn't it? She *understands* you. Understands the *job*. 'Cause it's always about the damned job, isn't it?"

Hanson had to admit she was right. Cops, he thought, were just different from most people. Cops were the good guys, the criminals were the bad guys, and everybody else was just a civilian.

Cops could talk to civilians—lovers, friends, family—about what they did, but the civilians didn't really get it. There were plenty of other reasons for not taking the job home; no one wanted to carry the unimaginable cruelties people practiced on each other home to the dinner table. You didn't want that stuff crawling into bed with you at night while you watched Letterman. Cops, he thought, ended up with a crappy little fence around a big part of their lives.

Now he realized that Gina had another crappy little

fence inside that crappy little fence, and until now, he'd only half understood what was on the other side of it. She'd invited him in, but he couldn't live there. He just couldn't.

He'd been miserable when the affair ended, miserable the first few weeks of seeing her leave at the end of their shift, not knowing where she might be going, or who she might be seeing. The idea of never touching her again, never waking up beside her again, made him feel as if his heart was caught in a vise.

He'd thought about seeing a shrink, except that no cop wanted that kind of thing on his record. He had gotten through it, somehow, perhaps because of the daily proximity that made it so painful in the first few months. She was still his partner, and he still had a part of her.

But when she was gone completely, he had drunk a little too much, fucked around a little too much, and thought about eating his gun once or twice.

Which made him almost as crazy as her.

Chapter 19

The art of life lies in taking pleasures as they pass, and
the keenest pleasures are not intellectual, nor are they
always moral.

—ARISTIPPUS OF CYRENE

"You're telling me that Roger Banks was some kind
of *pervert*?" Milton Daubs sat behind his desk with
his fingers steepled and a seriously pissed-off expression on
his face.

"No, sir," Gina said. "We're telling you that Roger Banks
and the other three victims were all engaged in an alterna-
tive lifestyle. If you consider those people perverts, that's
clearly your own judgment call."

"I wasn't speaking to *you, Ms. Larsen,*" Daubs said. "*You*
shouldn't be *here* at all."

"We need her," Hanson said.

"Didn't you get enough free publicity *last* time around?"
Daubs asked, staring at Gina. "Do you want to drag this
department through the *mud* one more time?

"Do you realize," Daubs said, turning his gaze to Hanson, "what the press will do if they find out she's involved
with this case?"

"She has connections in that community—"

"*Community?*" Daubs barked scornfully. "I don't want
her anywhere *near* this case, do you understand me?

"If I see *you* in this building again," he said, pointing a
finger at Gina, "I will have you *arrested.*"

"You can't do that!" Hanson insisted.

"Aw, come on, Chief!" Even Griggs sounded outraged.

"I *can,* and will!" Daubs shouted.

"Sir, I believe I can help—"

"Leave *now.* Or do I have to get someone to *escort* you out?"

Gina stared at the chief, then left the room without a backward glance.

Hanson shoved his fists into his pockets to keep from jumping over the desk and hitting Daubs. Not just for his stupidity, but for the way he had looked at her.

"Two more victims yesterday! Do you *realize* that the ASPCA is *screaming* about those darned *dogs?*"

Hanson stole a sideways glance at his partner, who looked just as confused.

"They found out we're going to put them *down,*" Daubs said. "And they are *pissed.*"

"Shit, Chief," Griggs said. "They ate two people—"

"Shut up." Daubs pointed his stubby sausage finger at Griggs. "I don't want to hear another word out of you. I'm talking to your *partner.*"

Hanson felt his stomach constrict. Considering that the case now had a great big land mine in the middle of it— Daubs's connection to Lady Cassandra—it was probably a good idea that Griggs kept his mouth shut. But now he had to tap dance along the high wire all alone.

"You could always turn them over to a local shelter," Hanson said. "Ask them if they can find people willing to adopt an animal that ate its last owner."

"Do *you* think that's *funny,* Hanson?"

"No, sir, I don't." He crossed his arms over his chest. "But it's lucky that so far the lead on the morning news is about the dogs, and not about a dead man chained to a cross."

"I don't want a word of this—this—*deviant* rubbish getting out. I will not *stand* for Roger's reputation to be *smeared* by this."

Hanson counted to five before he spoke.

"We had a lot of people in and out of the crime scene yesterday—"

"That's *why* you need to close this case *quickly*! This Lee woman was *obviously* a prostitute *and* a pervert— Did *Larsen* know this woman?"

"Yes, she did. I believe you did, too."

Daubs went completely still.

"What the hell do you mean by *that*?"

Hanson didn't enjoy the look on his face half as much as he'd thought he would. There was fear, yes, but something else. Something that made Hanson wonder if he'd played this card too soon.

"She used to run a private club. The Lair. You closed it down in a vice sweep three years ago."

Daubs swallowed so hard that his Adam's apple bobbed visibly.

"Yes, that's *right*. And if her *record* comes out in the media, we can be sure to *remind* them of that. But let's hope that's not *necessary*."

"Yes, sir," Hanson said.

"So what *have* you got?"

Bastard! Hanson thought it was just like the chief to tie their hands and then chew their asses.

"We've got trace from the new scene. But between the garbage and the decomp and the dogs, we may have nothing at all."

"I heard it was a *terrible* mess." Daubs's nostrils pinched and he made a face. "They said the smell was unbelievable."

Hanson wondered who "they" were. Daubs had informants all over the department.

"It was like those apartments when some old guy drops dead," Griggs piped up. "You know, they have to break down the door and there's all these piles of newspapers and garbage—"

Daubs looked at him. Griggs shut up.

"You've got nothing else? Nothing at *all*?"

"This guy is either smart or lucky," Hanson said. "He's not leaving us a lot of clues."

"The boyfriend from the motel? Still no ID on him?"

"We're working on it."

"Just find one of these *perverts* who knew Lady Cassandra and arrest them. What more evidence do you need besides that they're a deviant?"

"Are you serious?" Hanson was so stunned he dropped his careful deference.

"You want us just to arrest someone because they're into this S&M stuff?" Griggs asked just as suddenly.

Daubs glared. "What *difference* does it make? They're guilty of *something*. I want an *arrest* and I want it *fast*."

In the hallway, Hanson leaned close as they walked to the elevator.

"Did you notice, he didn't refer to her as Cassandra Lee?" he asked.

"He called her *Lady Cassandra*," Griggs finished for him. "I noticed."

Gina was waiting for them at the car.

"So?" she said.

"Get in," Hanson said.

"Are you driving me home?"

"No." Hanson felt Griggs's eyes and turned to him. "You got a problem with that?"

"Me?" Griggs shook his head, getting into the passenger seat. "Naw, boss-man. I'm not even allowed to talk, remember?"

"I shouldn't have gone to the crime scene," Gina said. "I'm sorry."

"We needed you at the crime scene. I'll deal with Daubs. Don't worry about it."

"You could just as easily talk to Quinn without me," she said.

Gina crossed her arms over her chest. When Hanson looked at her in the rearview, she met his eyes for a moment and then looked out the window.

"Yesterday you were fightin' to take over the whole damned case," Griggs said impatiently. "Today, you don't wanna go. You on the rag, or what?"

"You don't need me to find Cassandra's ex-husband," Gina said tersely.

"He knows you, Gee," Hanson said. He didn't want to question his own motives, this perverse desire to see Gina in the same room with another old lover. "It will throw him off guard, maybe get him to open up."

"Maybe she just don't want to go see an old flame," Griggs said. "Eh, Gee? You still carrying a torch for this Quinn Lee?"

Gina said nothing. Not even a *fuck you.*

"Come on," Griggs whined, turning to look at Gina over the seat. "What's the story? He into foot worship, spankings, all that sissy shit? Did you shove household objects up his Hershey highway?"

Gina let loose a bark of laughter.

"You're such an asshole, Griggs!" She shook her head. "What makes you assume Quinn is a submissive?"

"What? His wife was a dominatrix, you're a dominatrix—what else would he be?"

"I happen to be a switch, Griggs." Hanson caught the sly little gleam in her eyes in the rearview mirror. "I go both ways."

"You know what a submissive is?" Hanson asked Griggs, surprised.

"Of course, I do," Griggs said, annoyed. "I look at porn as much as the next guy."

"Probably more," Hanson said sourly.

"Hey, maybe Griggs here is a closet pervert," Gina said.

"I like looking at half-naked women in leather! Ain't nothing wrong with that."

Gina giggled, then stopped, then lost it again.

"What? You think I'm just some vanilla schmuck who only does it with the lights out?" Griggs growled. "I ain't no prude, you know. I can rock your world any day of the week, honeybuns."

"Stop," Gina gasped, leaning back against the seat, one hand to her stomach. "Oh, please, stop, before you make me pee in my panties."

"What the hell is wrong with her?" Griggs demanded, looking at Hanson.

"I think it was hearing you use 'vanilla' in the proper context," Hanson replied.

"Fuck you both," Griggs said.

"Sorry," Gina said, wiping her eyes. "I just forget how mainstream kink is these days. But for the record, Quinn is not a submissive. He's not even a switch."

"So he's a dominant." Hanson shrugged, eyes in the rearview again. "He was *your* dominant."

"Not just my dominant," Gina said quietly, retreating again. "He was my master."

"You mean, like sex slave and all that?" Griggs grinned. "Shit, this just gets better all the time."

Suddenly it occurred to Hanson that the mystery sadist who'd sent her to the emergency room and Quinn Lee were the same person.

And he didn't like that at all.

The sign out front read: LEE'S CAMERAS and underneath, in gold script: QUINN LEE STUDIOS.

"This guy?" Griggs whispered. "You're shitting me."

Quinn Lee was not what Hanson had imagined, either. He was about five-ten, and almost effeminately slender.

More than anything, he looked like an aging hippie, with bald head, jet-black goatee, single gold earring, and John Lennon glasses. He wore fashionably faded jeans, a well-starched blue Oxford shirt, and a thick pewter chain around his neck.

But Hanson only had to watch him for a couple of minutes to know he was definitely a predator. Quinn was standing in front of the counter, leaning very close to a pretty young woman with a camera in her hands.

"Now, you can scroll to look at the photos you've taken," he was saying, dropping an arm easily around her shoulders to press a button. "And just delete the shots you don't want to keep."

His arm did not withdraw. The hand landed on the girl's shoulder, and she made no move to shrug it off.

"I don't know." She sighed, her eyes giving Quinn a coy sidelong glance. "My boyfriend says digital is just a fad. He says real photographers still use film."

"No offense, but your boyfriend is an idiot." Quinn Lee smiled, bringing his face within inches of hers. "Especially for letting a lady as lovely as you go shopping all alone."

The girl dimpled up at him, then ducked her head as if both embarrassed and flattered.

Hanson had the distinct feeling that Quinn had been aware of their eyes on him from the moment they'd walked into the shop, and wondered if part of this little flirtation was for their benefit. Quinn looked up as they approached, and his eyes widened as teeth appeared in his close-cropped beard.

Looking full into Quinn's direct gaze, Hanson had an uncomfortable glimpse into the man's charisma. The power of that gaze—direct, uncompromising, with a trace of amusement—was unmistakable, as if the man was seeing deeper than the skin.

"Lisa, my dear, I'm going to get Maggie over here to

show you a couple of other models." He motioned to the clerk behind the counter. "But I will be back. I promise."

He gave the girl's shoulder a squeeze, and she dimpled up at him again.

Hanson already hated the smug little bastard.

Quinn Lee stepped toward them and reached for Gina's hand.

"This is quite a surprise." He raised her hand to his lips without taking his eyes from hers. "*Rosso,* my *bella rosso . . .* how nice to see you."

Gina removed her hand, as if she had touched a hot stove.

"Save it for the little girl." Gina jerked her head in the direction of Quinn's pretty customer. "I haven't been your *bella rosso* for a very long time."

"Bella what?" Griggs asked. "That Spanish or something?"

"It's Italian," Quinn said, still gazing at Gina with that touch of amusement even as she turned away. "It means 'beautiful red.' A pet name for a lovely redheaded pet. Once upon a time."

He gave Hanson and Griggs a blatant up-and-down. A slight twist to his lips said he wasn't impressed.

"So, Gina, are you going to introduce me to your . . . friends?" Quinn asked.

Hanson pulled out his badge and enjoyed seeing Quinn's eyes narrow.

"I'm Detective Tom Hanson. This is my partner, John Griggs. And you obviously know Ms. Larsen."

"So this is an official call?" Quinn turned back to Gina, retreating once more behind a cool smile, his eyes guarded now. "I didn't know you were back with the police."

"I'm not," Gina said stiffly.

"Ms. Larsen is a consultant," Hanson said. "Is there some place private we can talk?"

Quinn inclined his head, almost bowed in a courtly manner, and pointed them to a door.

"My apartment is upstairs," Quinn said, leading them through a supply room. "I suppose you know that already, but I'm not letting you into my home without a warrant. We can talk in my studio."

"That's pretty paranoid," Hanson said. "What makes you think we want to see your apartment?"

He ignored the question completely, nodding toward a leather sofa and chair.

"Have a seat, if you like."

Griggs let out a low whistle. Hanson followed his partner's stare.

The far wall was lined with several huge blowups, presumably the work of Quinn Lee. They were all portraits of women in various stages of dress and undress.

And there, in all her naked glory, was Gina.

In the photo, she was standing against a brick wall. Her arms were spread horizontally, straight out to the sides, as if she were nailed there. One leg was slightly lifted, knee bent. Her head was tilted back, chin lifted, eyes closed.

It was a crucifixion without the cross. Everything was crisp black and white except for two trails of bright red drops coming from the upturned palms of her hands, like stigmata.

"Do you like it?" Quinn's teeth shone between his mustache and goatee. "It's some of my best work, I think."

That was why he had brought them into his studio, Hanson thought. Quinn knew who he was, knew about his relationship with Gina, and he wanted Hanson to see this. The man was a sadist, after all.

He couldn't stand to look at the photograph, and yet he couldn't drag his eyes away.

It was all there: beauty and violence; sex and seduction. The vulnerability of her outstretched arms, opened to embrace the torturer behind the camera. The graceful white throat exposed, the prey seducing its predator. The fringe of eyelashes making a dark crescent above a single, glistening tear . . .

Beautiful and obscenely intimate. The photograph offered up her body like some kind of perverted sacrifice.

The photograph said it all. It told Hanson everything about the greatest passion of Gina's life. Quinn Lee. Not him. Not ever him.

"Well, all these ladies are lookers," Griggs said, running a hand over his mouth. "But damn, Gina! That's hot!"

Hanson glanced at Gina, only to find her somehow smaller and tighter, as if drawing into herself.

He realized something else: Quinn Lee was the one who'd sold her photos to the press.

"Did you do something to her tits?" Griggs asked, turning to Quinn. " 'Cause they look bigger somehow."

"No need to alter perfection," Quinn said.

Hanson felt anger rising and clamped down on it. He had to treat this like any other interrogation, and could not afford to let Quinn keep the upper hand.

"So you do erotic photography," he asked in as neutral a tone as he could muster, "as well as—?"

"As well as weddings and people with their dogs? Yes. A photographer has to pay the rent."

The photo was having an uncomfortable effect on Hanson's head and other parts of his anatomy. This was a woman he had loved. But somehow he felt like a dirty little boy sneaking a peek at his mother's underclothes.

"Your customers aren't put off?" Hanson snuck another glance at the photograph and realized Gina wasn't *entirely* naked. She was wearing that damned medallion. "They aren't offended by having these kinds of photos here?"

"If they are, then they're in the wrong studio." Quinn sat down in the largest chair in the room, crossed his legs, and leaned back. "Don't worry. I don't let the kiddies in here. I don't do children. Not even with a camera."

"Seems like kiddie shots would be where the money is." Griggs sat down opposite Quinn on the sofa, and Hanson sat beside him.

Gina walked around behind Quinn and leaned against the wall. She often did this to intimidate suspects, but Hanson thought the maneuver was also calculated to avoid the man's laser gaze.

"I dislike children," Quinn said. "I hope that's not why you're here. I have full twenty-two-fifty-seven documentation and releases on all my models—"

"We're not here to bust you for dirty photos," Griggs said. "We wanna talk to you about your ex-wife."

Something hard came into his face.

"What now?" His voice was dull. "I'm no longer responsible for her debts, parking tickets, or any of the twenty-seven voices in her head—"

"She's dead," Hanson said, intentionally cruel. "Someone murdered her."

"Ah." He scratched his beard, then looked at the floor for a long moment.

"You seem all broken up about it," Griggs said.

Quinn squinted at him and sighed.

"Cassandra and I have been divorced for more than a year. Our marriage was nine years of nonstop drama. I'd be lying if I said I was sorry or even particularly surprised."

"You're not surprised?"

"Cassandra had a lot of enemies," Quinn said, shoulders rising and falling. "Gina can attest to that."

"I told them there wouldn't be a shortage of suspects," Gina said tersely.

An ordinary person would be uncomfortable having someone stand behind them, but Quinn didn't bat an eyelash. Nor did he give in to the temptation to turn around.

"Since we divorced, Cassandra's been doing a lot more pro work," Quinn went on. "She was never particularly smart about picking clients."

"So you think a client killed her?" Hanson asked.

"It's just the first thing that occurred to me," Quinn said. "What was it, a botched burglary? Pretty unlucky thief, if that was the case."

"Why do you say that?" Griggs asked, leaning forward with his elbows on his knees.

"Because Cassandra didn't have a pot to piss in, to use the vulgar vernacular. How was she killed?"

"Someone beat her to death," Gina said.

Quinn grimaced.

"So you came to talk to me." Quinn didn't take his eyes from Hanson's face, even though Griggs was the one asking the questions. "You think I killed her."

"Dunno," Griggs said, scratching his ear. "Did you?"

"I made it through nine years of hell with that woman without ever striking her in anger," Quinn said in the same weary voice. "If I was ever going to kill her, it wouldn't be now when I was finally free of her. And I wouldn't have beaten her to death. She might actually have enjoyed that."

"That's cold." Griggs shook his head. "Even for a sadistic bastard ex-husband."

"Is that what this is about? Not because I'm the ex-husband, but because I'm a sadist?"

"Well, there was that little gang-bang of yours that went bad a few years back." Griggs smiled. Hanson realized he had put two-and-two together as well. "Yeah, we know about that."

Quinn didn't look as surprised as Hanson had hoped.

"That was a carefully negotiated and orchestrated role play," Quinn said as coolly as if discussing a photography client. "The young lady requested it—begged for it, in fact. I set it up because I was afraid she would find some-one else who would just fuck it up."

"Sounds like you didn't exactly knock it outta the ball park," Griggs said.

"It's an unfortunate fact," Quinn said with a little mock-ing frown, "that some people find the reality doesn't live up to the fantasy."

"She accused you of rape," Hanson said.

His lips tightened, and Hanson was thrilled to see him annoyed at last.

"She eventually came to terms with it. That's why she dropped the charges. You have no idea how many scenes like that I've arranged that produced deliriously happy re-sults."

"We'll have to take your word for it," Griggs said. "Those gang-bang kidnappings, they sometimes get a lit-tle rough? You *are* a sadist, aren't you? You admit that?"

"Sadism *with* consent is entirely different from sadism *without* consent," Quinn said. "You people think we're all serial killers and child molesters—"

The man's eyes lost all traces of that mocking amuse-ment, and Hanson glimpsed the iron under the kid gloves.

"We're not interested in a witch hunt," Hanson said quickly, even managing a friendly smile, as if to say, *I don't need you to explain the game to me, you smug little bastard.* "That's why we brought Ms. Larsen with us."

"So *bella* is here as your guide to the kink community?" Quinn showed his teeth this time. "I suppose that makes sense, seeing as she's been on both sides of the badge."

"We just need to know where you were last Friday."

They had been able to pin down a more definite time of death for Lady Cassandra and Randall Heeler; Heeler's sister had seen him leaving the little garage apartment he rented from her on Friday morning, but he had never come home.

"Just Friday?" Quinn raised his eyebrows and twisted his lips. "That's a rather wide time frame."

"Where were you?" Griggs asked.

Quinn sighed, as if suddenly wearied by their little games, when in truth, he seemed to be enjoying himself immensely. Hanson had seen it before in other sociopaths.

"From eight a.m. until six p.m., I was here. At six, Maggie and I closed the shop and went to dinner—we had Mexican, if you're interested."

"And after that?"

"Then we went to a photo club meeting until around nine thirty. Then we came home and fucked for a while. Do you want to know the particulars of position and orifices?"

"No," Hanson said. "And after that?"

"Then I fell asleep watching Conan."

"So you were with Maggie the whole time?" Griggs asked.

"Yes," Quinn said, then reconsidered. "Oh, wait. I did go out at lunchtime to meet a lady at Starbucks around the corner. I'm sure I have a receipt somewhere. She had a latte, and I had a Chai tea."

Gina snorted, then shook her head. But she said nothing.

"No, I didn't bring her back to the studio," Quinn said pleasantly, answering the unspoken question, tipping his head slightly toward Gina behind him. "I was a little off my game."

"Look, Mr. Lee," Hanson said, "we brought Gina in on this because we think there may be a connection between BDSM and the murders."

"Murders?" Quinn's eyebrows shot up. "You mean there's more than just Cassandra?"

Real surprise? Or fake? He was damned hard to read through that superior veneer.

"We have four dead bodies." Hanson pulled photos from his coat pocket. "Do you know any of these people?"

Quinn took the photos and looked at them.

"Oh, my." He held up the photo of Roger Banks, taken from his driver's license. "Grey Dragon? He's dead?"

"You didn't see it in the news?" Griggs asked. "His real name was Roger Banks."

"And Kitty, too?" Quinn was looking at the photo of Robyn Macy, a picture from her college ID. "I heard about the murders, of course. But I never put it together with people I actually knew."

Quinn handed the photos back, but the corner of his mouth twitched, as if in some private amusement.

"Terrible." Quinn sighed. "How awful for Dragon's wife."

Hanson opened his mouth, then shut it again quickly. Quinn had known both Roger and Robyn immediately . . . It seemed odd that Gina hadn't recognized them.

Or at least claimed she hadn't. Was that why Quinn was looking so smug?

"You knew Marla Banks as well?" Hanson asked instead.

"Yes, of course. Lovely woman, a very devoted submissive."

"What kind of relationship did you have with Roger Banks?" Griggs asked. "You were friends?"

"Do you mean, did we go bowling together? Hardly. We moved in the same circles, that's all. Dragon suffered from White Knight Syndrome, something diametrically opposed to my own philosophies."

"What's that mean, that syndrome thing?" Griggs asked.

"Dragon believed that submissives—female submissives—had to be protected and sheltered," Quinn said, leaning back regally once more. "Defenseless little things who can't defend themselves from the big bad wolves."

"And you disagreed?" Hanson asked.

"I believe that being submissive doesn't excuse you from taking responsibility for your actions, or what happens to you—"

"He means that if a woman can't stand up for herself," Gina interrupted, "she has no business playing around with BDSM."

"Absolutely right, *bella*." Quinn grinned, again without turning, just that slight incline of his head and the roll of eyes in her direction. "What we do is powerful magic. It's not for the weak of mind or spirit."

"Besides, Dragon's views were sexist," Quinn added. "He felt no similar need to protect male submissives from predators like my former wife."

"You think she was a predator?" Hanson asked.

"I know she was," Quinn said, his weary tone edged with a hint of real bitterness, the only sincere notes Hanson trusted. "Ask anyone she ever got her hooks into."

"Anybody particular you have in mind?" Griggs asked. "Someone we should talk to?"

Quinn shrugged.

"I'm afraid I haven't been privy to Cassandra's dramas for some time. She was always prowling for submissives with deep pockets, or influence. But she never kept them very long. Have you heard any rumors, lately, *bella*?"

Gina's face was stone.

"I don't put much stock in rumors," she said. "Or anything that came out of Cassandra's mouth."

"What about Robyn Macy?" Hanson asked. "We think she was at the motel with a guy named Paul—"

Quinn surprised him by laughing.

"How predictable! Paul's been sniffing after Kitty for the last couple of years, and she's been collared to just about every other dom in a four-county radius."

He leaned forward and lowered his voice, confidentially.

"I'm sorry, I should explain 'dom' is short for dominant. I wouldn't want you to be confused."

"I got it," Hanson said, giving him a sour smile. "Thanks."

"I'm surprised he got to her before you did," Gina said.

"Who says he got there first?" Quinn smiled slyly, still not turning around. "Kitty's old news, *bella*. Old news. I don't collar *all* my fucks."

Hanson's gut clenched with another urge to smash the man's face in, but Gina betrayed no reaction at all.

"You say she was collared?" Griggs asked. "You mean, like wearing a dog collar?"

Griggs was doing his Columbo again. Act stupid, keep them talking. It worked particularly well with Quinn's superiority complex.

"Collared, as a slave or submissive." Quinn smiled. "Some do use dog collars, some use chains or even expensive jewelry . . . It's a personal preference. But a collar is a symbol of ownership. To collar someone is to take ownership of them."

Hanson tried not to look at Gina's necklace. Was it a collar? Had Quinn owned her?

Did he still own her?

"You know where we might find this Paul?" Hanson asked. "Do you know his last name?"

Quinn shook his head.

"We're not exactly friends. I run into him at the club every once in a while; that's about it."

"Sounds like you don't have many friends, Mr. Lee," Griggs said.

"Most of my friends happen to be female," Quinn said pleasantly. "I have quite a few of those."

"What about the other guy?" Hanson asked. "Randall Heeler?"

Quinn studied the last photo and sighed.

"Randall. Known as Randy or 'subgeek' online. A total waste of oxygen, if you ask me, but it takes all kinds."

"He wasn't a popular guy?" Griggs asked.

"Randy is one of those poor bastards no one wants to play with," Quinn said. "Poor social skills. And bad hygiene."

"Probably why he ended up dead with your ex-wife," Griggs said. "Not much of a housekeeper, was she? That could have been enough to drive a guy crazy."

"I had no reason to kill her," Quinn said. "Gina had just as much motive as I did. Maybe more. Have you questioned her?"

"I'm well aware of Ms. Larsen's relationship with your ex-wife," Hanson said. "And with *you*. So you can drop the bullshit, all right, and just answer the questions."

Quinn looked at him appraisingly, then smiled a little.

"Ask away, Detective Hanson," he said, spreading open palms.

"Do you know anyone named Cherry?"

"Is that a real name? Or a scene name?"

"Does it matter?" Hanson asked. "Either."

"I know lots of women *online* named Cherry. Usually it's 'Cherry-one-two-three' or 'slavecherry' or some variation."

"Because 'cherry' sounds sexy, huh?" Griggs asked.

"Exactly. Because of the sexual connotations. Just as there are dozens of Kitties, Cats, Angels, and Slaves."

"So you're saying you don't know her?" Hanson asked.

"But there *was* a Cherry around a while back," Gina said slowly, rousing a little. "A red-haired newbie, rather pretty, now that I think of it. You must remember her. You have a thing for redheads, after all."

She smiled at the back of Quinn's head, but the smile had a nasty edge to it.

"There have been so many. I don't recall."

"Oh, *I* do," Gina said. "At one of the charity slave auctions. She put you down as her only limit."

Quinn's jaw tightened.

Hanson looked at Gina questioningly.

"The club has a slave auction once a year," she explained. "People auction themselves off—"

"You mean for sex?" Griggs asked, a little too eagerly.

"No," Quinn interjected as if talking to a toddler. "That would be *illegal*."

"Not for sex," Gina said. "For scenes, for playing. Submissives list what they like to do, and what their limits are—the things they won't do."

"And this girl, Cherry," Hanson said, beginning to smile. "She said she was willing to do anything but *you*?"

"Ouch," Griggs exclaimed. "Man, that's cold!"

"She was afraid I might get through to those deep dark places she wanted to go, but didn't have the nerve to explore." Quinn shrugged. "It's one of the drawbacks of my big bad reputation."

"But you don't know where she is now?"

"No."

Hanson glanced at Gina. She only shook her head.

"We'll need to confirm your alibi with Maggie," Hanson said, getting to his feet. "And I would like that Starbucks' receipt and the name of the woman you met with."

"Is that *really* necessary?" Quinn asked, standing also and literally showing them the door.

"Yes, it is," Hanson said, passing back through the supply room and into the showroom once more.

"I'll have to go check my pockets upstairs."

"We'll wait," Hanson said.

They watched Quinn step through another narrow door, glimpsing stairs beyond.

"I'll go have a little talk with Maggie," Griggs said quietly, moving toward the counter.

Hanson pushed the victim photos at Gina.

"Why didn't you tell me you knew them?" he said into her ear. "Damn it, you lied to me!"

"You never showed me *these* photos." Gina pushed them back at him. "All I saw were the crime scene photos. Their own mothers wouldn't have recognized them."

"And you never connected the names?"

"Christ, Hanson! I told you people go by scene names, just like I did before I got outted. And I haven't seen these people in a couple of years—"

"What about this Cherry? You just suddenly remembered her?"

"Yes, I did." She stabbed his chest with a finger. "Seeing him made me think of it."

"It doesn't look good, Gee. Griggs already thinks you're wound just a little too tight—"

Did you check out her alibi? Griggs had asked. She could have taken Roger out, if she got the drop on him. You said it yourself, this perp is one angry fuck, and Gina Larsen is pissed at the world . . .

"I don't give a damn what he thinks."

"Well, maybe you should. He's a good cop."

He could hardly look at her without seeing that damned photograph. *Bella Rosso Crucified.*

"Are you actually looking at me for these murders?" Her eyes narrowed. "Are you out of your mind, or just stupid?"

Hanson rubbed a hand over his face and took a deep breath.

"Just stupid, I guess . . . So, this Maggie. She's his slave?"

"Slave or sub." Gina shrugged. "He's probably got one or two more. He likes his harem. Many doms do."

"Do you know her?"

Gina looked over at Maggie, who didn't seem to be enjoying her talk with Griggs. She was moderately attractive, a little on the heavy side, but dressed in a low-cut blouse that showed generous cleavage, and a short skirt.

Maggie kept looking over at Gina, her big brown eyes narrowing with every glance.

"No," Gina said. "Please tell me he's not hitting on her."

"If she can handle Quinn, she can handle Griggs."

Gina snorted.

Her phone chose that moment to blare "Superfreak."

"Go ahead and answer the damned thing," Hanson said, watching her read something on the screen.

"Maybe I don't want to answer it," she said, tucking it back into her belt holster.

"Can we trust an alibi from her?" Hanson asked, jerking his head toward Maggie. "Would she lie for him?"

"People lie all the time."

"But if she's his slave—"

"Christ, Hanson." Gina sighed. "Slave is just a word; it doesn't really mean anything. It's not like it's legally binding in a court of law."

"You mean it's like voodoo? It only works if you believe in it? Maybe Maggie does."

Gina shrugged. All the fire was gone from her. She was flat and empty.

"The relationship between slave and master can be a very strong, intimate bond," she said softly. "It's frightening, really . . ."

Hanson waited, but she said nothing else.

"What is?"

"The things you'll do for someone," she said, staring out the window. "The things you'll let them do to you."

Quinn reappeared and held out an envelope.

"Inside you'll find my Starbucks receipt, the one from

the Mexican restaurant, and a receipt from when we got gas on the way home. Do you want the three condoms I used that night, too?"

"You forgot the name of your coffee date," Hanson said, not smiling.

"No, it's in there. The name she gave me, at least, and her phone number. Please do try to be discreet."

"If you think of anything else that might be helpful—" Hanson handed him his card.

"Of course," Quinn said. "Now if you don't mind, I have a pretty wannabe photographer on the hook."

He moved toward the counter, then abruptly turned back.

"I read in the paper that the killer used some kind of wooden object. It wasn't a baseball bat, was it?"

It wasn't a question, but a statement.

"The details of the case are confidential," Hanson said.

"Ah," Quinn said, smiling. "So you don't know what it is, do you?"

Bastard.

"Never mind." Quinn shrugged. "I understand. But it occurred to me that the weapon might be a tire thumper."

"A what?" Griggs asked, stepping in.

"A tire thumper," Quinn said. "Gina can tell you about it."

He winked at them and walked away.

"Man, he's a real piece of work," Griggs said.

Hanson kept his eyes on the road, then glanced at the speedometer and realized he was doing 50 in a 35 zone. He eased his foot off the gas.

"So, Gee," Griggs said into the silence. "What's a tire thumper?"

"It's what truckers use to check the pressure in their tires," Gina said flatly, eyes focused on the scenery flashing by. "It's like a miniature baseball bat, or a billy club. Filled with lead shot."

"Shit," Griggs said. "That could do some real damage. That could be it."

"Could be," Hanson said cautiously, glancing at Gina in the rearview. "But why would he tell us about it?"

"Especially if he's right," Griggs said. "I mean, what the fuck? Does he *want* us to think he's guilty?"

"Quinn likes to play games," Gina said. "He's just fucking with us."

"He guessed we didn't know the weapon yet," Hanson said. "And the bastard wanted us to *know* he knew. It was just a lucky guess—"

"Lucky guess?" Griggs asked. "I didn't even know there was such a thing—"

"Well, Quinn does," Gina said. "He has one in his toy bag."

"Holy shit," Griggs cried. "He hits people with that thing?"

"No, of course not," Gina said tiredly. "You'd break bones with that."

"Then what does he do with it?" Griggs asked.

Hanson didn't want to know.

"He inserts it," Gina said.

"Oh, shit," Griggs said. "What, a dildo ain't enough?"

"Sometimes," Gina said, "it's not."

Griggs whistled low, but didn't say anything else. They drove along in silence until Hanson pulled up to Gee's house.

"Call me if you get something," she said as she got out. "I'm gonna check the computer, see what I can find there."

Maybe she just needed to check the messages piling up on her cell phone, Hanson thought, watching the swing of her hips as she mounted the front steps. Who the hell kept calling her? Some needy client, an old pervert who needed a spanking?

Quinn?

"Seriously, *is* she on the rag?" Griggs asked.

"Shut up," Hanson said, pulling away from the curb.

"Did you check out that sales clerk, what was her name? Maggie?" Griggs grunted. "She was cute. A little plump, but I like a little meat on the bones."

"You were supposed to be getting a statement, not trying to pick her up."

"You know, it hurts my feelings that you think so little of my detecting skills," Griggs said. "You were too busy eyeing Quinn's jugular to notice, but if looks could kill, Gee would be dead meat."

"What are you talking about?"

"That Maggie. She recognized Gee the minute we walked through the door, and she didn't like it one bit."

"She's his submissive. Or slave. Whatever."

"Well, duh," Griggs grunted. "I knew he was fuckin' her even before he volunteered the information. You could tell just by the way she kept looking at him.

"And because you can tell just by lookin' at him, he's a slut-hound," Griggs continued when Hanson didn't respond. "I don't get it though, he ain't exactly Brad Pitt. And he talks like a goddamned professor or something. So what now, kemosabe? We go check up on Mr. Lee's alibi?"

"Hell, yes," Hanson said. "I don't trust that little fuck."

Chapter 20

Everything in the world is about sex except sex. Sex is about power.

—OSCAR WILDE

Unfortunately, Quinn Lee's alibi checked out in every detail.

The local camera club met at the YMCA, where there was a wall of their work and a bulletin board full of photographers' business cards. The first two Hanson called had not been at the meeting that night, but the third and fourth verified that Quinn had attended.

"He and Maggie even stayed a little late," Sarah Spivey volunteered eagerly. She sounded at least sixty. "He was helping me decide on what glass I should get next."

"Glass?"

"Lenses," she explained.

Angela Sabatta, the latte lady, was not happy to get his phone call, but agreed to meet them in the cafeteria of the hospital where she worked.

"This is so embarrassing," she whispered. "We just had coffee. That's it."

"Where did you meet Mr. Lee?" Griggs asked.

Angela, in her pink scrubs, shifted in her seat. She was a registered nurse in her forties, and very uncomfortable.

"Starbucks. I told you that already."

"I mean, before you met for coffee. How did you first come in contact with him?"

"Oh. Umm. On the Internet, okay? It's not illegal . . . Is it?"

"You're not in any trouble, Angela," Hanson assured her. "We're just trying to verify his whereabouts that day—"

"Is he in trouble? My husband *cannot* find out about this—"

Hanson thanked her for her time without making any promises.

CSU operated in the basement, and to Hanson the crew down there always seemed a little pale and squinty, like cave dwellers unused to daylight.

"I've ID'd the weapon." Fortner grinned upon seeing them. "I've been testing and measuring, trying to match the wound dimensions—"

"It's a tire thumper," Hanson said wearily.

"How did you know?" she asked. "Damnit!"

"Lucky guess," Griggs grunted.

"It's a little like a police baton, or nightstick," she explained, handing Griggs a printout from a website. "Truckers use them—"

"I know what it is." Hanson looked at Griggs. "Quinn was right. How'd he know?"

In the photo, it looked like a sawed-off baseball bat. Hanson read the ad copy over his partner's shoulder:

> This high quality Tire Thumper is made here in the USA! Crafted out of a solid piece of cedar that is turned on a wood lathe to give it the proper contours down the body.

"Well, at least he's buying American," Griggs commented, handing the sheet back to Fortner.

"Sure." Fortner laughed. "I found a lot of them advertised online in trucking and RV equipment, but this one had the right measurements. And it's being advertised on this website as a *self-defense* item."

The tire thumper measured nineteen inches long and roughly two inches at the tip. The compact size made it easier to hide than a baseball bat or tire iron.

"That must be why it says right on the club 'Use only as a Tire Thumper,' " Hanson murmured.

"Says it has a 'light gloss coating,' " Griggs muttered. "Miles said he found polyurethane trace in the wounds."

"So this is a match to all the cases?" Hanson asked.

"Roger Banks and Robyn Macy are matches so far," Fortner said. "I did an Internet search, and there are cases now of people being arrested for carrying tire thumpers as 'lethal weapons' even when they haven't used them on anything but their tires."

"Hell, anything can be lethal if you use it right," Griggs said. "I could throw my cell phone at somebody, hit 'em in just the right spot, they drop dead. We gonna arrest people for carrying cell phones, too?"

"We gotta go back to Quinn," Hanson said. "I want *his* tire thumper."

"What if he won't give it to us?"

"Then we get a fuckin' warrant."

Quinn handed over his "toy" without hesitation.

"Do I get a receipt for this? I would like it back. For sentimental reasons."

Hanson had known he would give it to them. Gina was right; he was playing games. He didn't even bother to hide his amusement.

"That was fast," Fortner said when Hanson handed her the sealed plastic bag.

"Hey, we're professionals." Griggs grinned.

"Well, wood is difficult to get completely clean," she said. "Blood gets down in the grain. Unless someone completely submerged it in bleach, we should be able to find something."

"It's clean," Hanson said. "It's gotta be or the bastard wouldn't have given it up so easy."

She got out a tape measure.

"Measurements are in the ball park. I think this is the same model as the advertisement. Got the same warning stamped on it."

"How fast will you know something?"

"I'll get to it as fast as I can," Fortner said, annoyed. "But do you have any idea how far behind we are? The lab was already backed up before this case—"

"Yada yada yada," Griggs said, rolling his eyes and making yakking motions with his hand. "You're breaking my heart."

"Oh, blow me," Fortner snapped.

Hanson glared at Griggs, then turned back to Fortner.

"I promise to beat the crap out of him at the first opportunity," he told her. "Please, do what you can. We really need your help—"

"Yada, yada, yada," Fortner said, mimicking Griggs's talking hand. "Get out of my lab."

"Jesus, you're not even housebroken," Hanson groaned in the hallway. He punched Griggs's shoulder.

"He still could have done it," Hanson said, scooping out more guacamole with a chip.

"Come on," Griggs said. "I don't like the guy, either, but unless Maggie is flat out lying, or he drugged her and snuck out in the middle of the night, I don't see how he could've found the time."

They were having dinner at the Mexican place Quinn had mentioned, and, Hanson had to admit, his chimichanga was excellent.

They not only had Quinn's receipt, but the manager and a waiter remembered the couple.

"You're sure you remember them?" Griggs asked. "Both of them?"

"She has lovely . . ." The manager hesitated, then cupped his hands in front of his chest and gave them an embarrassed smile. "And Mr. Quinn, he always requests extra hot, and . . . Well . . ."

"And well what?" Griggs asked.

"I always have to make sure I put them in Jose's station," he said reluctantly, lowering his voice. "Rita, my waitress, she don't like to wait on Mr. Quinn."

"Why is that? Does he treat her badly?" Hanson imagined Quinn pawing the waitress's ass as she leaned over the table with more salsa.

"No, it is not like that," the manager said. "He always gave her very big tips. She just doesn't like the way he look at her. Like she has no clothes on."

Hanson thanked the manager, and the man gave a slight bow before turning away.

"We didn't ask Quinn where he was for the other two murders," Hanson said.

"Come on," Griggs said, wiping his mouth. "If he didn't do his wife, why bother with the other two?"

Gina appeared around the corner. She slid into the booth beside Hanson.

"So you got my message," Hanson said.

"Good timing." She reached for the chips. "I was hungry."

The waiter came over, and Gina ordered a Number Six and a Margarita on the rocks.

"Quinn's alibi is looking good," Griggs said in between bites of a soggy fajita.

They filled her in on the afternoon's events. When

Hanson told her they'd taken Quinn's thumper to the lab, she didn't seem surprised.

"You know it's not the murder weapon, right?" she asked.

"I know." Hanson took a swig of beer. "Right type of weapon, but not the right one. Any luck on the computer?"

"There are only twenty-two women on FetLife in this part of the state using some version of 'Cherry' as their screen name," Gina said. "Another fifty-seven on Collarme and eighty-six on Alt."

"Shit," Griggs said.

"No kidding. Almost none of them have photos—showing their faces, I mean. Half don't even include a physical description in their profile."

"I'll bet half aren't even women," Griggs said. "Just a guy in his basement named Chuck."

"Personal experience?" Gina asked.

"Fuck you," Griggs said.

"I sent e-mails to all of them, but I'm not holding my breath. For all we know, this girl's real name is Cherry and her screen name is something else entirely . . . Or she's got another scene name—"

"Why would she need more than one?" Griggs asked.

"How many e-mail accounts do you have?" Gina countered, forking a slice of steak from his plate.

"I dunno," he mumbled defensively.

"I have six different profiles spread out on Fet, Alt, and Collarme," Gina said. "One on each as a fem-domme, but they aren't all under the same name.

"I didn't do it that way on purpose," she continued. "Lady Gee was already taken on Fet, so there I'm Lady-G2U—"

She pulled out a pen and wrote it on the place mat.

"On Alt, I am DominaG499; and on Collarme, I'm LdyGina—"

"Right." Griggs nodded. "I tried to get Goodcop4sex on Yahoo! but it was already taken."

"What did you end up with?"

The waiter set down her combo plate.

"Cuffs762."

"What about the one on AdultFriendFinder.com?" Gina smiled around a forkful of rice.

"How do you know I have a profile on there?" Griggs asked, looking surprised and guilty.

"Every guy like you has a profile on there. Did you post a photo of your cock, too?"

Hanson laughed.

"He did, didn't he?" Gina chortled. "Oh, my God—"

"It's not funny." Griggs shook his fork at Hanson. "Shut up or I'll tell her about that eHarmony crap you signed up for."

"You said six profiles?" Hanson interrupted.

"I also have one on each site as a submissive. Again, three different names. That's in addition to my regular e-mail accounts, including my old AOL addy that I can't even remember the password to.

"My point is that even vanillas have half a dozen different personas online," she continued. "With kinky folks, the number is usually double."

"Even if we ran down all the Pauls." Hanson sighed. "We probably wouldn't find him."

"Some lifestyle folk are completely out, they've got their kinky pseudonyms right on their Facebook profiles," Gina said. "But most are more careful. Don't underestimate just how paranoid these people can be."

Hanson's phone chirped, and he held it to his ear, listening.

"No surprise there," he said, his lips curving downward. "Yeah . . . Yeah . . . Hey, do me a favor? Get someone to deliver it back to Quinn Lee at Lee's Cameras. And hey, make sure you send a guy . . . Just because. Thanks."

"That was Fortner," Hanson said, tucking the phone back into his pocket. "Quinn's thumper is clean."

"Well, we knew that," Griggs said. "But why did you bother asking her to get it back to the asshole so fast?"

"Because I wanted him to know we're moving fast on this," Hanson said. He didn't want to say his real reason out loud: that he didn't want Quinn to have any reason to come asking for it as an excuse to "run into" him or Gina. Neither did he want to risk Quinn asking Gina to bring it back to him personally.

And mostly, because he just didn't want to see the damned thing again.

"I told you he was just fucking with us," Gina said.

"So what do we do now?" Griggs asked.

"First, we finish our dinner," Gina said. "Then we go talk to Marla Banks again."

Hanson realized he should have thought of that. He had no idea how Marla Banks would react to seeing Gina, but he hoped it would shake loose anything she might be holding back.

"It's getting pretty late," Hanson said. "Let's do it first thing in the morning."

"Fine," Gina said. "Order me another margarita."

Marla took one look at Gina and burst into tears.

"Oh, God," she choked out. "I was so afraid of this—"

"Marla, it's all right," Gina said, taking the woman in her arms. "It's gonna be okay, don't cry."

Marla hung on to her for a moment, then stepped back and wiped at her eyes.

"I need a tissue. And a drink."

"Is anybody here with you?" Hanson asked.

"No, thank God."

Marla plucked a tissue from a box on the coffee table and blew her nose into it. She dropped it into a little wicker basket already half full of wadded tissue.

"I have to carry a box around the house with me," Marla said weakly. "I seem to cry at the drop of a hat these days."

She moved to the sideboard and poured two fingers of Jack Daniel's into a cut-crystal glass.

"My daughter is still in town, but I made her go shopping with some friends. I'm tired of her hovering. I don't suppose I should offer you a drink?"

"No, thank you," Hanson said before Griggs could say anything. It was barely noon, but he figured Marla had a right to drink herself into a stupor if she wanted.

"I was sorry to hear about Dragon," Gina said. "How are you holding up?"

Marla took a sip, then another.

"Give me a minute," she said, shaking her head. "This is too strange, having you here in my house—"

"I know," Gina said. "And I'm sorry for that, too."

"It's like worlds colliding," Marla said with a weak little chuckle. "But it doesn't change anything, really."

"We think it might," Hanson said. "That's why Ms. Larsen is working with us on this case."

"Good Lord." Marla took a deep breath, then offered Gina a hesitant smile. "It's been a long time, Gina. I was always so sorry about what happened . . . you know."

"I know. And I know that you wanted to protect Roger's reputation, but now there's no reason not to be completely honest."

"But I have been! Except for that one little fib about our lunch, but that was our private business, and it had *nothing* to do with this."

"Sometimes the smallest detail can help," Hanson said. "Maybe there's something else you haven't told us?"

"If there was anything I thought would help catch the bastard who killed Roger, don't you think I'd have already told you?"

"You don't think it's strange that four people in the community have died in the past three weeks?" Gina asked.

"What?" Marla looked confused. She clutched the glass to her chest and stared at Gina. "What do you mean?"

"You haven't been reading the papers?" Griggs asked. He sat on the arm of a Queen Anne chair. "Watching the news?"

"My daughter keeps hiding the newspapers from me," Marla said shakily, sinking down onto the sofa. "She's afraid the articles about Roger will upset me."

"Robyn Macy—you may have known her as Kitty," Hanson began. "She was found murdered in a motel room a week after Roger was killed—"

"Oh, no! No, no!" The glass slipped from Marla's hands. "Kitty? That can't be—"

Hanson moved to retrieve the glass. Gina disappeared and came back with a kitchen towel, which she offered to Marla.

When Marla simply sat there, her hands to her mouth, Gina knelt and dabbed at the wet spot in the carpet.

"Poor Kitty." Marla began to cry softly. "Oh, poor, poor Kitty . . .

"You don't think—" She looked up at Hanson with enormous eyes. "You don't think it was the same person—Not the same way—Oh, my God!"

Marla was sobbing now, great hitching breaths between wails.

It took about ten minutes for her to calm down enough

to talk. Gina pressed a cool washcloth on Marla's forehead. Griggs got her another drink.

"There's a bottle of Valium on the table," Hanson whispered to Gina. "Should we give her one?"

"Not with the Jack Daniel's," Gina whispered back.

"Marla, did you know Robyn—Kitty, I mean—did you know her well?" Hanson asked.

Marla shook her head.

"Not well, really. Just to say hello to, when we saw her at the club. She was always so sweet. And she was so *young*."

Marla blew her nose again.

"You think the same person killed her?" Marla closed her eyes and shuddered. "It's just too horrible to think about."

"It was the same person," Griggs said. "We don't think it was the guy she was at the motel with, though."

"Who was she with?" Marla's eyebrows rose.

"We think it was Paul," Gina said. "But we haven't been able to find him."

"Paul?" She pursed her lips. "I shouldn't be surprised."

"Do you happen to know Paul's last name?"

Marla shook her head.

"I'm over fifty," she said. "For men like Paul, I don't even exist. I never liked him much anyway."

"You have no idea where we might find him? Any idea where he lives, or where he works?"

"I have no idea." Marla sniffled. "We really never had much to do with him. We'd just run into him at the club now and then."

"So Roger wouldn't have known him well, either?" Griggs asked.

"Roger?" Marla stiffened. "No! Roger thought he was pond scum, same as I did. *Paul cheats on his wife!*"

"And you both disapproved of that?" Hanson asked.

"Of course we did!" Marla bristled. "We may be into BDSM, but we're very moral people! I teach Sunday school, for God's sake!"

Gina, sitting beside her on the sofa, took Marla's hand and squeezed it. Hanson thought, not for the first time, how easily Gina switched gears when it was called for. In general, she was not a touchy-feely kind of woman, but when comforting witnesses, she was golden. *How many faces, exactly, did Gina have?*

"He didn't mean to upset you," Gina said. "We just have to ask these things if we are going to find out who did this to Roger and Kitty."

"And Cassandra Lee and Randall Heeler," Griggs added.

"Cassandra?" Marla looked dumbstruck. "Lady Cassandra?"

"Yes," Hanson said. "Her body—and that of Randall Heeler—was found in her home yesterday morning."

"Oh, my God," Marla whispered. "Oh, God forgive me, I wished the woman dead so many times."

"You ain't the only one," Griggs said. "Doesn't sound like she was a very nice person."

"She was horrible," Marla said, taking another sip from her glass. "No, she was *evil*."

"Can you think of anyone in particular who might have wanted her dead?" Hanson asked.

"Easier to ask who didn't," Marla mumbled into her glass. She looked over at Gina. "You know, she still hated you with a passion."

"She hated everybody who wouldn't let her have her own way," Gina said. "But was there anybody specific she was arguing with in the last month or so?"

Marla sighed.

"She kept pestering everybody for money. She even had the nerve to come to the funeral home to ask for a loan."

"To reopen her club?" Gina asked.

"What else? She completely ignored the fact that there's a new club where everybody is deliriously happy to be rid of her."

"Who owns the new club?" Hanson asked.

"Actually," Marla said, "it's owned and operated by the community itself. We elect a board of directors every two years. It was set up that way to keep Cassandra and Quinn out of it."

"So Quinn's not welcome there, either?" Griggs asked.

"Oh, Quinn's a member. But one of the terms of his membership was that he would not run for the board."

"The community blackmailed him, in other words," Gina said.

Was she defending him, bristling on his behalf?

"That's such a nasty word," Marla said. "You know how it works, Gina. The club is no different from the Ladies Junior League, or my church board, come to think of it."

"I know," Gina said. "Get three people in a room, sooner or later, two of them will gang up on the third . . . But nothing else? No other gossip recently?"

"Oh, there's always gossip. This couple broke up, somebody posted a snide comment on the discussion group, this person is now seeing that person . . . but nothing serious."

"Are you sure?" Hanson asked. "You told us you didn't know anyone named Cherry."

Marla looked back at Hanson cautiously, shifted in her seat, and looked down at the Georgia O'Keeffe book on the coffee table.

"I remember a newbie named Cherry a couple of years ago," Gina said. "Pretty, red-haired girl. The one who listed Quinn as her only limit."

"She's got nothing to do with this!" Marla said. "Honestly, you can't think she's involved in some way!"

"We don't know anything at this point," Hanson told her. "But we need to talk to her. Why was she leaving messages for your husband?"

Marla heaved a deep breath and looked at Gina.

"Roger and I had her under protection. She's a very dear girl."

"Protection?" Griggs asked. "From what?"

"It's a BDSM status thing," Gina explained. "A dominant will place someone under his or her 'protection'—usually a newbie or an unattached submissive—just to help fend off unwanted attention."

"Sort of like a big brother?" Hanson asked.

"Exactly. A sub will have 'under the protection of so-and-so' in his or her profile. That lets other dominants know they have to go through the protector if they want to talk to the sub."

"Yes, that's it," Marla said. "Cherry was having a hard time with this dom she met online—"

"What exactly do you mean, 'a hard time'?" Gina asked.

"They had been talking for a while," Marla said. "Just online. She was crazy about him, said he sounded wonderful."

"Until she met him face to face," Gina said.

"You know how it is." Marla sighed. "There are a lot of creeps out there, and unfortunately, this guy turned out to be one of them."

"Was he married or something?" Griggs asked. "Or are we talking about a *serious* creep?"

"Serious creep." Marla paused. "He violated her safeword."

"She said stop and he didn't, you mean?" Hanson asked.

Marla nodded. "He raped her."

"I think you'd better tell us how to get in touch with her," Gina said.

Chapter 21

Being your slave, what should I do but tend
Upon the hours and times of your desire?
I have no precious time at all to spend,
Nor services to do, till you require.
Nor dare I chide the world-without-end hour
Whilst I, my sovereign, watch the clock for you,
Nor think the bitterness of absence sour
When you have bid your servant once adieu;
Nor dare I question with my jealous thought
Where you may be, or your affairs suppose,
But, like a sad slave, stay and think of nought
Save, where you are how happy you make those.
So true a fool is love that in your will,
Though you do any thing, he thinks no ill.
—WILLIAM SHAKESPEARE, *Sonnet 57*

After Cherry moved into the lake house, she left it only to go to work. She was glad it was summer, so that she could get back to the little house at the end of the long graveled road before darkness settled in.

The lake house was so quiet; it seemed like some other planet. There was no traffic noise, no stereos playing too loudly, no car doors slamming. She was used to living in apartments with walls so thin she could hear her neighbors' phone ring, hear the kids next door screeching with laughter, and the Chihuahua over her head that barked and barked and barked.

She had hated the sound of that ugly little dog. Now she missed his noise. *Yap, yap, yap* meant everything was just as it should be.

But here at Marla's lake house, there was nothing but the occasional click of the HVAC unit coming to life. Even that noise, so pathetically small, was loud enough in the silence to make her jump. She had tried leaving the radio or television on, but then she was afraid of not hearing the sounds she kept listening for: tires crunching the gravel drive, the rattle of a locked door, or the sound of breaking glass.

The first night she had taken a beer out onto the deck, thinking it would be comforting to hear the cicadas drone as she stared out at the water. But the lake was an enormous swath of black with a silver swizzle of reflected moon, and the lights on the more thickly inhabited opposite shore seemed a million miles away. She felt too lonely and too exposed; she went back into the house and checked all the doors one more time.

The very first night there had been a metallic banging on the roof that sent her diving into a closet. Her hands were shaking so badly that it took several tries before she managed to dial Marla's number on her cell phone.

"It's the fireplace damper," Marla assured her. "It does that whenever the wind kicks up."

"I can't sleep," Cherry said. "Either I can't go to sleep, or I wake up from a bad dream and can't get back to sleep."

"Check the medicine cabinet in the master bath. I think there's some of Roger's Ambien. That should help."

The Ambien was there, all right, but Cherry was afraid to take it. What if he broke in and she didn't wake up?

That was the dream that drenched her in sweat every night. The dream of waking up in the dead black of night, unable to see anything. But hearing his breathing, feeling his weight pressing down on her . . . his hands squeezing tight around her throat . . .

Hard fists, hitting her again and again.

On the third night, she'd heard a heavy thud outside at the back of the house. She could see nothing moving outside the bedroom window. Then she heard it again, a rustling of dry leaves and another thud.

She ran on bare feet to the living room and grabbed the iron poker from the hearth. Holding it to her chest, she padded to the kitchen. She had to stand on tiptoe to peer through the blinds over the sink.

Later, she would wonder why she'd done that. That was what stupid people did in horror movies: they heard a noise and went to investigate. But she understood, now, why they did it.

People were accustomed to a lifetime of safety, of things that made sense. When something went bump in the night, threatening the usual order of things, they went not to find something, but to find nothing. They went to prove to themselves that there was no burglar, no peeping tom in the bushes, no psycho with a chainsaw. Because how else could you go on to the next moment, and the next, without knowing for certain? Not looking would leave you permanently paralyzed, afraid to take even one more breath.

Even now, afraid as she was, some part of her believed nothing was out there. There couldn't be. Things like this just didn't happen, and she *needed* to know it wasn't happening now. If she didn't prove to herself that nothing was out there, she would start screaming and never stop.

A shadow moved around the corner of the house. For a moment, she couldn't breathe, could only stare into the darkness.

Was he out there? How had he found her?

Then the automatic light came on, flooding the back-yard with glaring brightness. A large possum raised his head, his eyes catching red in the light, then resumed his pillaging through the overturned garbage cans.

Gunther wasn't helping. He didn't like the new sur-roundings and prowled from room to room, yowling.

But after the third day, she couldn't go back to work.

She had thought she was safe at the office. No one

could get past the security desk on the first floor without a badge.

Then the switchboard had buzzed her desk.

"You have a delivery up front," the receptionist said.

"Is it your birthday?" Al, the security guard, asked as she neared the front desk.

A dozen red blooms in a vase, tied with a large bow, sat waiting. Their scent was overwhelming, sickeningly sweet. She saw the red roses and could only think: *Red means stop . . . red means stop.*

"No," she said dully. "It's not my birthday."

She reached for the card.

"Mine" was all it said.

"Wait, you don't want these?" Al called after her.

"No, keep them. Throw them away. I don't care!"

How had he found out where she worked? He hadn't even known her real name, yet he'd found out where she lived and then where she had moved. Now he'd tracked her to work.

She made up a lie for her supervisor, a bad one about a forgotten dentist's appointment.

She drove around for an hour, watching her rearview mirror rather than the road ahead of her until she narrowly missed rear-ending the Hyundai in front of her.

When a white car followed her through three traffic lights, she made a left. When the white car continued straight, she began to cry in sheer relief.

Finally she passed a police station. She pulled into the parking lot and sat there for half an hour.

What are you going to tell them? a voice in her head asked. *That you found him online, told him you wanted to be his slave, that you wanted to be used for his pleasure . . . And then you met this stranger at a hotel and changed your mind?*

You don't even know his real name.

She started the car and drove back to the little house at the lake. She didn't leave it again.

On Thursday, her supervisor had called and said that if she didn't come back to work the next day, she would be fired.

She no longer cared. Even in broad daylight, she couldn't bring herself to step farther than the welcome mat.

It was those damned bushes, she thought. The big ones on either side of the front porch. She couldn't see beyond them. She could only imagine *him,* waiting there for her to come outside.

Then last night she'd fallen asleep in front of the television, a half-eaten Lean Cuisine on a tray in front of her.

She woke up to find Gunther licking the congealed chicken Parmesan while the ten o'clock news rolled.

"Police have identified the owner of the house as Cassandra Lee," Cynthia Jenkins told the camera. "The other victim's identity is being withheld pending notification of the next of kin."

Cherry stared.

"Lee made local news in 2007, when the adult club she operated was closed down by Metro police," the anchor continued. "Police will not confirm whether her death was related to the previous charges of prostitution."

The scene switched to a balding man with a red-cheeked face. The caption underneath read "Chief Milton Daubs."

"We do *not* believe her death had *anything* to do with her illegal activities," the man said. "At this time, it *appears* that she is merely another *random* victim of the same person or persons responsible for two other *vicious* killings—"

Two photos flashed on the screen: Roger Banks and Robyn Macy.

Cherry began to sob.

★   ★   ★

Cherry's real name was actually Cheryl Ann Gavin.

"But everybody calls me Cherry," she said. "Even my parents."

"When was the first time you communicated with him?" Gina asked.

The big leather chair seemed to swallow the girl. The circles under her eyes were so dark they looked bruised, and she twisted her hands as she spoke.

"He messaged me on Collarme.com. I guess it was about two months ago."

"And the name he used was Kerberos?"

Hanson had decided to let Gina take the lead; Cherry was obviously more comfortable talking to her.

"Yes. He never told me his real name, and I never pushed him. I mean, I didn't want to tell him my real name, either—"

Cherry broke off and shook her finger at the cat, who was climbing onto Griggs's lap.

"Gunther, don't bother him! Get down!"

Hanson watched with amusement as the cat settled comfortably in the crook of his partner's arm.

"It's okay," Griggs said, rubbing the cat's belly. He caught the look on Hanson's face and scowled. "I happen to like . . . cats."

Hanson knew he'd been about to say *pussy*.

"But you talked a lot after that?" Gina asked the girl.

"Every day. Sometimes two or three times a day. Real letters, not just little messages. That was what I liked so much about him. We really talked."

"About what?"

She shrugged.

"Everything. What kinds of movies we liked, our favorite foods, what music we listened to . . ."

"And you talked about your fantasies." Gina looked into Cherry's face. "Right?"

"Yes. I feel so stupid."

Cherry blushed. Hanson hadn't actually seen a woman blush in years.

"Don't," Gina said softly. "We all need to share ourselves with someone."

Again, Gina was the gentle friend, almost motherly. Not someone you could imagine shattering a coworker's kneecap. Hanson had to remind himself to focus on Cherry's reactions, not Gina's.

"For so long, I thought something was wrong with me, you know?" She brushed her copper hair from her eyes. "I thought, How could I want these awful things? I'm not from a broken home, my dad didn't molest me, and my mom didn't beat me with coat hangers."

"Me, either." Gina smiled. "But we can't control the things that turn us on. No one knows why some of us are aroused by bondage, or pain, or licking someone's shoes. We're just wired this way."

Griggs shot a look at Hanson and rolled his eyes.

"I know that now. Or I thought I did. It really helped when I found the local community, you know? I went to the first munch scared to death, and then I met all these people who looked so . . . well, normal."

"Have you had other doms? Even as casual play partners?" Gina asked.

"A few. I was never collared, though. I played mostly with people at the club. I thought it was safer that way, with other people around."

"Did you ever meet anybody else the way you met Kerberos?"

"Oh, I got a lot of messages, most of them jerks. But I only met two of them. One of them, I just had coffee with and it never went any further. He was much older, and there just wasn't that connection, you know?"

"No chemistry," Gina said.

"Right."

"The other?"

Cherry frowned.

"He was a little pushy. Told me that if I were a real submissive I'd . . . I'd give him a blow job in the parking lot. I didn't like him at all."

"I know the type," Gina said.

"Everybody tells you how dangerous it is to meet people online," Cherry said. "But everybody does it. Most of the time, it works out just fine. I know lots of people who met their doms or subs on the Internet."

"How long did you and Kerberos talk online?"

"About a month. He sounded so exactly right for me, you know? He seemed smart—"

"What made you think he was smart?" Hanson interrupted.

"Just the stuff we talked about." Cherry chewed her lip. "Like, he said *Ulysses* was one of his favorite books. I was an English major, and I could never get past the first chapter."

"Did he ever say if he'd lived anywhere else? Did he grow up in this area?"

"I don't think so. He talked about places he had visited—San Francisco, Chicago—but he was probably lying."

"Why do you say that?"

"Well, he lied about just about everything else," Cherry said bitterly. "He *said* he was a 'true' dominant. He *said* he would respect my limits."

"You said his profile didn't have a photo," Gina said. "Did he ever send you one privately?"

"No!" Cherry covered her face with both hands. "I'm not even sure I could recognize him again! That's what's so scary about this. He could walk right by me and I might not even know him!"

Hanson felt for Cherry, but he also wanted to shake her until her teeth rattled. She was an attractive, educated twenty-something who seemed to be relatively intelligent. But she had gone to a hotel to meet a total stranger.

Not just to meet him . . . She had followed his instructions to the letter.

"He told me which hotel. It was a very nice one. I remember thinking an ax murderer wouldn't pick such a nice hotel, would he? Then I was supposed to text him the room number.

"He wanted me to have the lights off, and to light the candles I brought with me. I had wine—red wine, that's what he told me to get—chilling in the ice bucket. And Enigma on the portable CD player."

Jesus, Hanson thought. This guy made plenty of demands, and poor Cherry had been so eager to please him. No wonder she hadn't wanted to file a report.

"He said to take off everything except my bra and panties—and he told me I should wear something sexy, something red or pink if I had them. I was supposed to leave the door unlocked and wait for him on my hands and knees, with my forehead against the floor."

"I see how you're looking at me," Cherry said, hiding behind her hands again. "I know how stupid it was! But at the time, it sounded so exciting and romantic even . . ."

Cherry had waited as instructed, until someone entered the room. All she saw were shiny black shoes, when a male voice, with no particular accent, told her to lick them.

As she licked and kissed his shoes, he began hitting her with a leather belt.

"I think it was a belt. Things began to happen so fast, and I never got a good look at his face or what he was hitting me with—"

"I tried so hard not to scream. I was still trying to be a good submissive, but I must have tried to crawl away from the belt. That's when he grabbed me by my hair."

He had pulled her to her feet, then lifted her and thrown her on the bed. She realized that this was all wrong, but she was afraid to do anything except what he told her to do.

"He—he put his— his penis in my mouth. I tried to— tried to do what he wanted, but he said I wasn't taking it deep enough."

He had forced her head down until she vomited.

"I tried to say I was sorry," Cherry cried softly. "But that was when he started hitting me. In my face, in my stomach . . . just all over."

That was when Cherry realized this was not what she'd signed up for, not the erotic fantasy she'd been promised. She'd started to scream.

"At first, I just kept shouting, 'Red'! Over and over! But he didn't stop! He just shoved a rubber gag in my mouth and hit me harder."

He had ripped off her bra and panties as she'd lain there sobbing, begging him through the awful taste of the gag to *please stop, just please, please don't hurt me anymore.*

"My nose was bleeding and I couldn't breathe . . ."

"And then he raped you?" Gina asked quietly.

Cherry nodded miserably.

"Did he say anything to you this whole time?"

"Just—just that I was his now, and he could do anything he wanted to with me."

She had pulled her bare feet up under her and curled her arms around her knees, as if she could make herself small enough to escape the memory.

"How did you get away from him?"

Cherry was silent, looking up at Gina with agonized eyes.

"I can't—" She was choking on her tears now, her voice a croak. "I just can't tell you, I'm so . . . so ashamed."

When the beating stopped, when he was done with her, she had been too terrified to move. She had lain facedown on the bed where he left her and she had felt his weight lift from the mattress. She heard him go into the bathroom and the sound of water running.

She realized now it wasn't just fear that pinned her to that bed, it was shock. She had begun trembling all over, suddenly cold as if the temperature in the room had dropped twenty degrees. It had made her even more afraid, afraid that he would see her shaking and it would make him angry again.

She had felt his weight on the bed again and tensed, waiting for the next blow.

But it never came. Instead, she had felt a hand stroking her hair. Tenderly.

"I'm proud of you," he had whispered.

She couldn't have heard him correctly. He was *proud* of her?

"I am disappointed that I had to gag you," he had continued, still stroking her hair. It had taken all her strength not to flinch away from his touch. "But you'll do better next time.

"I have so much to teach you, but that's to be expected. You are mine now, to mold into a perfect vessel for my pleasure."

Cherry shuddered with the memory, realizing that she could try to explain for hours, but that no words could capture the horror of that final realization: he was crazy. He had to be. This wasn't the way it was supposed to be. It couldn't be. She had called RED. She had screamed it, over and over. He was supposed to stop.

"I had told him in the e-mails that I didn't think I was into pain," Cherry said, getting a little more control over herself and sipping the water Gina pressed on her. "He had said that was okay, that he was more into domination and control. I said that was what I wanted."

Cherry gave a pathetic half-laugh, half-sob.

"Serious pain scared the hell out of me," she said. "I thought people who wanted to be hurt were *sick*. How fucked up is that?"

"D/S and sadomasochism are two different things," Gina said. "Unfortunately, too many people don't get that."

"Yeah, well, I know that now," Cherry said wearily. "Roger and Marla explained that to me. They explained a lot of things that no one bothered to tell me before. They made me go to some classes at the Inferno and made me read a lot of books."

"So this guy," Hanson said, "he just left you there in the hotel room?"

Cherry nodded.

"He told me to take a shower, clean myself up. He said I could take a nap if I wanted." She laughed, a bitter sound this time. "And then I should go home and begin my assignments."

"Assignments?" Griggs asked. The cat was asleep in his lap now, and he was still rubbing the feline's belly.

"I was supposed to start an online journal 'processing' my experiences." Cherry blushed again, but there was nothing pretty or coy about it. Just two hectic blotches on her cheeks. "And I was supposed to get a dildo and practice . . . Practice how to—"

"It's okay," Gina said. "Did you do what he asked?"

"Are you kidding?" Cherry asked, almost angrily.

As soon as she'd been able to get to her feet, she had gotten in the shower and scrubbed herself until the hot water turned cold.

She had looked at herself in the mirror and begun crying again. She had been terrified that he would come back. She had wanted out of that room, but couldn't find the nerve to walk out through the lobby where people would see her. They would take one look at her and know what had happened.

Her clothes would hide most of the welts and bruises, but one eye was turning black, and she had a shallow cut running down the other side of her face. Her lip was split in two places. Her nose had stopped bleeding, but more blood kept trickling from her anus. She had thought about going to the emergency room, but how could she explain it? They would call the police. They might even call her parents.

The idea of her parents finding out had made her vomit in the sink.

"I finally sneaked out one of the fire exits," Cherry explained.

And then she burst into full sobs of such pain that Hanson wanted to put his hands over his ears.

The two men waited in the kitchen while Gina talked Cherry down from her crying jag.

"She's a mess," Gina said, coming into the kitchen. "I'm going to make her some tea."

"So, we have an online profile," Griggs griped, "but no real name, no photo—only a fuckin' vague physical description that could be anybody—"

He flipped back through his notebook.

"Mid to late thirties," he read. "Average height and weight. Brownish hair, *she thinks,* but it could be dark blond. Are people really this stupid?"

"Keep your voice down," Gina whispered. "She took a dumb risk, but that doesn't make this her fault."

"You think this Kerberos could be our guy?" Hanson asked.

Gina was filling the kettle.

"He could be. He's certainly violent, attracted to the Lifestyle but not really a part of it—"

"Whaddaya mean, not a part of it?" Griggs demanded. "Oh, come on!"

"He's a sociopath who hides behind BDSM because he thinks it legitimizes what he wants to do anyway. But he's the kind of person we do our best to keep out.

"If this guy has approached the community, he's probably been shut out, or just hangs around the edges. He probably hasn't got the social skills to deal with people face to face, that's why he runs his game online."

"But why would he kill the others?" Hanson asked. "Cherry said she had already stopped communicating with him before Roger put her under his whatchacallit— protection."

"He could have found out," Griggs said. "It pissed him off; he snaps and kills Roger."

"He did send her that newspaper clipping with the collar," Gina said. "That's pretty creepy."

"And Robyn?" Hanson asked. "Why kill her?"

"Robyn and Cherry were friends." Gina shrugged. "He might have seen her as a threat, someone coming between him and Cherry."

"Could be he started out the same way with Robyn," Hanson said. "He lost control and went further than just beating and raping her."

"You're talking like this guy has to make sense," Griggs said. "He's a nut job, plain and simple."

"Whoever the killer is," Gina said, "he's been smart enough not to leave us shit for trace."

"If it *is* this Kerberos," Hanson said, "we need to find Paul as soon as possible. He could be at risk."

"Marla Banks, too," Griggs said, pulling out his phone. "I'm gonna get some guys over to her house."

"I don't think Cherry should be here alone," Gina said,

pouring water into a mug. "Even if we post a couple of guys outside, she needs somebody with her."

"Maybe Marla will let Cherry stay with her?" Hanson asked. "Kill two birds?"

"Maybe. But Marla sent Cherry here. She's probably worried how to explain Cherry to her family and friends."

Gina moved toward the door with the mug of tea. Hanson put a hand on her arm.

"She's the same redhead you remembered, right?"

"Yeah, why?"

"So she knows Quinn, right? She would know if he was the one using an alias to get to her?"

Gina just looked at him, then went on into the living room.

But she hadn't said it was a crazy idea.

Chapter 22

A woman should learn in quietness and full submission.
I do not permit a woman to teach or to assume
authority over a man; she must be quiet—
—1 TIMOTHY 2:11–12

They spent an hour or so reading the e-mails Cherry had saved from Kerberos. By the time they left, Hanson knew more about Cherry than he knew about his ex-wife. She loved *24* and *House*; her favorite book was *Pride and Prejudice*; and her favorite ice cream was Chunky Monkey.

He still didn't know anything about Kerberos, though, that would help them find him. His favorite book wasn't going to give them his address.

"I bet that's a lie, anyway," Gina said. "Nobody reads James Joyce without a gun to their head."

His profile picture on Collarme.com was just an icon of a whip, and a long, rambling "About Me" section:

> I am a True Dominant seeking a slave who will serve Me obediently; whose every thought is for My pleasure.
>
> This slave must know that her rightful and natural place is at My feet.
>
> I will be her Master, and she will be Mine. . . .

"Christ," Hanson muttered. "This guy just goes on and on about what he wants in a slave. Nothing about him personally."

"Except that he's a 'true' dominant," Gina said with a snort. "My first advice to newbies? If someone tells you they are a 'true' anything, run like hell."

"Listen to this, will you?" Hanson said. "This is the first e-mail he sent her after he raped her—

> You pleased me so much yesterday, my girl. But you will please me more when you learn to control your fear and accept what I choose to give you without resistance or hesitation . . .

"At least the bastard had a clue that it wasn't completely peachy for her," Gina snorted.

"Can you really rape someone and not know what you're doing?" Hanson asked, incredulous. "She's screaming—or trying to—and crying and bleeding, and he doesn't get it?"

Gina shrugged and looked at him with weary eyes.

"You know I told you about the unofficial motto: safe, sane, and consensual?" Gina asked. "This is what the 'sane' part is about. Knowing the difference between fantasy and reality."

"Either this guy doesn't know the difference," Hanson said, "or he doesn't care."

"It almost sounds like he's trying too hard to play the part of what he thinks a dominant should be." Gina sounded thoughtful. "Everything he says, it's a stereotype, almost like he copied it from someone else."

"So?"

"So, I'm thinking he may be even more of a babe in the woods than Cherry. No, hear me out! I'm not saying he's not a monster, but I honestly think he has no idea what BDSM is supposed to be, only what he's read in some bad S&M online porn."

"He's a fuckin' nutcase, is what he is," Griggs interjected.

"I told you we were looking for someone outside the community," Gina insisted.

Hopefully, Hanson thought, the techno geeks would be able to track him down through his e-mails. Griggs was making the necessary phone calls to start the ball rolling with a warrant for Collarme.com.

"Collarme.com isn't going to lead anywhere," Gina said. "It's a free site; you don't have to give them anything but a valid e-mail to sign up."

"Then we'll just have to track *that* e-mail address," Hanson said.

The geeks were also having a look at Cassandra's computer, as well as Robyn's, in case Kerberos had made online contact with either of them. The techs had already gone over them once, but now they had something specific to look for.

Cherry had left the package with the collar at her apartment. They collected it and took it to the lab for fingerprinting.

"It would be nice if we got lucky," Gina said. "But I'm not holding my breath."

"Kerberos," Griggs said. "What kind of name is that, anyway?"

Gina typed K–E–R–B–E–R–O–S into Google.

"It's the Greek word for Cerebus. The three-headed dog from hell. Or it's the name of an authentication software."

"Or a science fiction series," Hanson read over her shoulder.

"I'm thinking he chose it because of the hell-dog thing," Griggs muttered, putting a hand over the mouthpiece of his cell. "Shit, I am still on hold with the D.A.'s office."

"Whichever reason he chose it," Gina said, "it's a great geeky name for a monster."

Cherry had also provided a phone number for Paul. She

didn't know his last name, either. Gina called the number and it went straight to voice mail.

"Let's see if he returns the message," Gina said. "If we haven't heard from him by tomorrow, we'll pull his phone records."

They placed a squad car outside of Marla's as well as the lake house. As Gina had suspected, Marla wasn't crazy about Cherry staying with her, and even Cherry fought the idea.

"Marla's already done so much for me," Cherry said. "Besides, with the police outside, I'll be okay here."

They had nothing else to do except wait. Wait for the tech guys to track down Kerberos's e-mail; wait for any further leads from trace still being processed back at the lab; wait for Paul to call them back.

The next day brought no joy, either.

Paul didn't call, but the phone number Cherry provided did yield an address. Google gave them details.

"Say what you want about the Internet"—Griggs grinned—"but it sure makes it easier and faster to get info on somebody."

Paul's last name was Carlson. He was married to Joanna nee Nader, and the father of two boys: Chip, age eight; and Michael, age six. He was the lead sales manager at a Kia dealership, and his credit rating was in the crapper.

The house was in one of the new subdivisions of postage stamp homes shoehorned into an older and desirable ZIP code. Hanson looked at the marigolds making little yellow-gold pillows along the flagstone path and wondered if Paul and the little woman had planted these together some weekend, or if they'd just paid someone to do it.

No one answered the front door, though there was a Forte Koup in the driveway.

"Doesn't look like anybody's here," Griggs said.

The neighbor on the right said she barely knew the Carlsons, but hadn't seen them in a few days. The little old lady on the left, however, was happy to tell them that Paul, Joanna, and the kids were on vacation.

"They asked me to get their mail and paper for them," she said.

"Did they say when they would be back?"

"No, I asked. Joanna said she wasn't sure, that the vacation was a last-minute thing and she was in a dreadful hurry."

"Son of a bitch is hiding from us," Griggs said as they walked back to the car.

"We're gonna have to trace his phone," Hanson said. "Why can't anything ever be simple?"

The florist that sent the roses to Cherry's office said the order was paid for in cash by a walk-in.

"Did he write the card himself?" Hanson asked.

"No, I did," said the florist, a middle-aged man named Davis. "He asked me to. Said I had a very neat handwriting."

It didn't matter. They didn't have the card anyway.

"I don't really remember what he looked like," Davis said. "Nothing stood out to make me remember him."

"White?" Hanson asked.

"Yeah," the man said.

"Tall or short?" Griggs asked, impatient.

"About average, I guess."

They gave him a card and left. Hanson was feeling like he lived in the damned car.

"I wish just once," Griggs said, "we could catch a murder done by a four-foot-tall hunchback with Papa Smurf tattooed on his forehead."

"Yeah, but then we'd probably have a dwarf hunchback Smurf convention in town." Hanson sighed. "Be careful what you wish for."

"Where's Gee today, anyway? She too good for the grunt work?"

"She's working."

"Well, we all got bills to pay, I guess. Ain't no rest for the wicked."

Griggs's phone began chirping.

"Uh-huh," he spoke into the phone. "Yeah? Shit. Okay, thanks."

"That didn't sound good," Hanson said.

"It wasn't." Griggs put the phone back in his pocket. "The only fingerprints on that collar belonged to Cherry."

Hanson's phone went off. It was Gina.

"You wanna take a field trip tonight?" she asked.

Chapter 23

So long as the laws remain such as they are today,
employ some discretion: loud opinion forces us to do so;
but in privacy and silence let us compensate ourselves
for that cruel chastity we are obliged to display in public.
—MARQUIS DE SADE

"Hot damn! We're going to a sex club."

"It's not a sex club, Griggs." Gina sighed. "Not in the way you mean it, anyway. The average city cab probably sees more actual fucking than the Inferno."

"Come on!" Griggs said. "You're telling me people come to this place to beat each other, but they don't have sex?"

"Yep. Very few actually fuck in public. I don't get it, either, but that's the way it is. At least in the het side of the BDSM community. Gay kinksters fuck like bunnies at their parties. It's enough to make me wish I had a dick."

"Are we going to have to look at fudge-packers?" Griggs asked with anxiety in his voice. "Oh, man, I don't wanna see that shit—"

"No, you knuckle-dragging bigot," Gina snapped. "This club is primarily straight. Gay men don't really like to share their playpens with us. Guys like you being the reason why."

"Okay, then," Griggs said, grinning once more. "No fags. That works for me."

"There is no way I can take him in there . . ." Gina said, looking at Hanson in desperation.

"Come on, Gee," Griggs wheedled. "I promise I'll be a

good boy. One night and I can store up a year's worth of free jerk-off material—"

"Asshole. If you were my slave, I'd have to keep a gag in your mouth all the time."

"I could be down for that." Griggs grinned. "If you were wearing some of that leather get-up."

Gina looked at Hanson, then back to Griggs.

"We *do* need to dress appropriately," she said without even a hint of a smile.

"What do you mean *appropriately*?" Hanson asked.

"I mean trying not to stand out. Blending in."

"Okay," Griggs said. "You wear the leather, I'll do a leash and a gag—"

Hanson burst out laughing. He couldn't help it.

"But I ain't wearing a gimp suit," Griggs continued. "Or showing my package to the world."

This, Hanson thought, just kept getting weirder.

The Inferno was located in a warehouse in one of the older industrial parks. There was no sign, just the street number stenciled above the front door of a cinderblock building painted a bland shade of beige.

But on a Saturday night, when the whole area was deserted, the parking lot was filled with a mix of vehicles, including three big, gleaming Harleys.

They walked toward the door and it struck Hanson as funny, somehow, that there was a handicapped ramp. Gina shot him a look when he laughed.

"Sorry," he said, sobering. "I'm a little nervous, I guess."

Griggs, on the other hand, was practically bouncing on his toes.

Hanson had nothing very edgy in his closet, so he was in black slacks and a plain black T-shirt that actually belonged to Gina. It was a little snug, but she said it made him look buff.

Over Gina's objections, he had added a black sport coat, to conceal his gun.

Griggs was in black jeans, with his handcuffs dangling from one belt loop. He had on a pair of engineer boots and a Metallica T-shirt.

"I thought they looked good," Griggs grumbled when Gina told him to lose the studded cuff and leather vest. Hanson had been stunned, never suspecting Griggs had such things in his wardrobe.

"Metallica?" Hanson asked. "Really?"

"You're trying to look average," Gina said. "And the leather vest has certain . . . connotations. For you to wear it would be insulting."

"What about my gun?" he asked, scowling. "Hanson's got his—"

"You don't need a gun," Gina said. "Stop whining or I'll make you flag yellow."

"Huh?"

"Look it up on the Internet," Gina said.

Gina was in a wine-colored velvet corset that pushed her breasts up and out, transforming them from merely lovely to astonishing. Her long silk skirt was slit nearly to her crotch, and the black leather boots reached her mid-thigh.

"Is what you're wearing *average*?" Hanson asked.

Hanson tried not to stare, but his penis kept twitching involuntarily. Griggs didn't bother to hide his admiration or the erection that strained at his jeans. In the four-inch stiletto heels, she was taller than either of them.

Gina's usual easy grace was transformed into untouchable perfection. She rarely wore much makeup, but tonight her skin was luminous, flawless; her eyes, ringed with impossibly long, deeply black lashes, threatened to suck his soul from his body.

"I have a professional image to uphold," she said without a touch of irony. "This is what they expect of me."

"Now I understand why some guys pay you to spank them." Griggs snickered. "If it means they get to look at you dressed like this."

Gina brought out a dog collar and buckled it around Griggs's throat.

"Hey," he said, fingering the collar as she snapped a leash to it. "Does this mean I'm your bitch?"

"It means that when you say something stupid, I'm gonna tug on this leash. When I tug, that means shut up."

"Or what?" Griggs grinned.

"Don't push me. I know ways to hurt you without leaving any marks."

Hanson watched a black van slow along the street. The van sped up and disappeared into the night.

"Probably newbies." She shrugged. "Some people get to the front door and lose their nerve."

"Surveillance?" Hanson nodded to the camera above the door. "Could we get anything useful off of it?"

"It doesn't record. Closed circuit only. People wouldn't come if they thought they were being photographed. It's purely for parking lot safety."

"And to see if the cops are at the door, I bet," Griggs said.

"This place is entirely legal. It's a private club, members only. Daubs used city codes to shut Cassandra down, but the Inferno even meets ADA standards. They were very careful about that."

Hanson half-expected someone to open the door and ask for a password, but Gina walked right in.

A large woman sat at a desk in a dim room. Rolls of flesh peeked over the top of her vinyl dress, but she smiled warmly.

"Lady Gee!" she squealed, jumping up to embrace Gina. "Oh, my God! It's been ages!"

Gina grimaced at Hanson over the woman's shoulder.

"Hello, Angel. Am I good for guests?"

"Of course!"

Angel asked them to sign in and explained that as guests, Hanson and Griggs would have to sign a waiver.

"It just means you know what goes on here." Angel giggled. "And that you're okay with that."

Hanson watched Griggs sign in as *Milton Daubs*.

"That's not funny," he said.

A few people milled around a table of chips and dip, crackers and cheese, and cheap cookies. Typical party food except for a cake shaped like a penis. Music thudded from behind another door.

"I want a drink," Griggs said, nodding at the Styrofoam cups.

"All they have is coffee and soda," Gina said.

"No beer? Not even wine?"

"Nope. Alcohol is not allowed."

"You're shitting me!"

"Would you let a drunk tie you up and beat you?"

"I couldn't let someone tie me up and beat me unless I *was* drunk." Griggs shrugged.

A drink sounded like a good idea to Hanson, feeling off-balance and edgy. It was more than just Gina and the way she looked, or the way other men were looking at her: this was the world she had invited him into, and the one he'd refused. What had he been so afraid of?

That he might like it. That he might fit in.

A man wearing a silk shirt of dancing flames approached. He had a powerful build except for a slight gut, a head full of curly, salt-and-pepper hair, and a matching beard. More curly hair peeked from his shirt collar.

"Lady Gee!" He enveloped her in a bear hug. "Good to see you."

"Hanson, Griggs; this is Dante. He's the current director of the Inferno."

"Appropriate," Hanson said, shaking the hand he extended.

"I started out as Crimson Dragon." He grinned. "But then I realized that every other dominant in the Lifestyle is named Dragon. New pet?" Dante nodded toward Griggs.

"Being considered," Gina said. "Just taking him out for a test drive."

"Didn't you tell me you had a friend named Grey Dragon?" Hanson said to Gina, hoping to cut off any comment from Griggs.

"Is that why you're here?" Dante's eyes narrowed. "Goddamn it. I thought you weren't a cop anymore?"

"I'm not. But they are."

Dante herded them into a corner.

"You brought cops into our house? That's a violation of confidentiality—"

"We've got a serial killer out there who seems to be targeting people in the community," Gina said. "Would you rather they'd come flashing badges?"

Dante groaned and ran a hand through his beard.

"People are pretty on edge about all this already. Attendance is way down tonight, and rumors are running wild."

"What kind of rumors?" Hanson asked.

"The ones about Cassandra's dogs seem to be the most popular. Did they really . . . *eat* her?"

"Afraid so," Gina said.

"Damn, that's fucked up. Even for Cassandra."

"You weren't a fan of Lady Cassandra's?" Hanson asked.

"She was a hard woman to like," Dante said. "But it's downright ghoulish how some people are enjoying this."

"How did people react to Grey Dragon's death?" Gina asked. "And Kitty's?"

"Shocked, sad. Dragon was very well-liked."

"And Kitty?"

"Oh, the ones who knew Kitty were upset, of course. But she'd been in and out a lot, so not everybody knew her. And as for Randy, the poor bastard. People always felt sorry for him, but none of them really considered him a friend."

"You know anybody might have wanted any of them dead?" Hanson asked.

"If it was just Cassandra, I'd say look at any of the people she used, backstabbed, or borrowed money from," Dante said. "But Dragon and Kitty? I can't think of anybody who'd want to hurt them."

"Have you had any problems here lately?" Gina asked.

Dante ran a hand through his wild hair.

"Nah, not really. I mean, hell, the Internet has changed everything. We get a lot of new folks. Some are sincere, some are just tourists."

"We had a guy who came in as a guest last weekend," Dante continued. "We had to throw him out because he was drunk."

"What about wannabes?" Gina asked.

"Just a couple of doormat subs." Dante shrugged. "Female."

"Doormat subs?" Hanson repeated.

"Broken or abused women who think that being smacked around is what they deserve, rather than what they want," Gina explained.

"We have to save them from themselves," Dante said. "Otherwise they become prey for a different kind of predator."

"I thought that you guys were all about consent,"

Griggs piped up. "Gina said you don't allow those kinds of predators here."

"We try not to," Dante said. "But what I consider a predator, someone else thinks is the perfect dominant."

Hanson didn't miss the look that passed between Gina and Dante.

"You talk to Quinn?" Dante asked.

"Yeah," Gina said flatly. "We talked to him yesterday."

"You consider Quinn a predator?" Hanson asked.

Dante hesitated, again glancing at Gina.

"Gina would know better than me. I don't think Quinn is dangerous in the way you mean. I just don't particularly like his style."

"Which is?" Hanson prodded.

"Quinn believes that some women need to be pushed a little—"

"Some women do go for the more aggressive alpha male types," Gina said coolly, but Hanson didn't like the idea that she was defending Quinn. Or was she merely defending herself?

"And you don't?" Griggs asked. "Think they need to be pushed a little, I mean?"

"I think it's too damned easy to cross the line when you play those kinds of games."

"We're looking for Paul, in particular," Gina said. "Is he here?"

"Paul? I haven't seen him. Why?"

"We think he was the last person to see Kitty alive," Gina said.

"Oh, God. You don't think *he's* a killer?"

"You don't think it's possible?" Hanson asked.

"Paul isn't even alpha enough to dom his own wife." Dante grunted. "And he's too lazy to work that hard."

Griggs laughed.

"Do you know Cherry?" Gina asked.

"Cherry? Cute little redhead, no bigger than a minute?" Gina nodded.

"Sure, I haven't seen her around in a while, but—"

Gina explained the situation to him, but Dante didn't know anyone using the name Kerberos, or anyone that had shown special interest in Cherry.

"You better find him before we do," Dante said quietly, his face suddenly thunderous. "I'll castrate the mother-fucker—"

"If you think of anything, anything out of the ordinary," Gina said, "call me, okay?"

"Look, talk to whoever you need to. Just be discreet, please?"

"We will. I promise." Gina made a cross over her heart. "Keep your eyes and ears open for me, will you?"

Gina led Hanson and Griggs through another door. She said she didn't feel welcome anymore, but Angel's reception at the front desk had been friendly enough. Hanson felt staring eyes, but he couldn't tell which stares were unfriendly and which were merely checking them out.

Or rather, checking Gina out. He was doing it, too, he couldn't help it. She'd be gorgeous in a potato sack, but tonight she didn't even belong on this planet. There was more than just beauty, though; it was the authority with which she moved and the imperious tilt of her head. Was it just the boots, or did she stand straighter dressed like this? Like a chameleon, she had transformed herself yet again.

"It's been two years," Gina said. "I don't know most of these people."

She had to lean close to his ear to be heard over the music, and Hanson was distracted by the thought of kissing her throat, her bare shoulders, the tops of her breasts . . .

This was never going to work, he thought. He couldn't

think straight with her standing so close to him, looking like that. He forced himself to study the room instead.

It was large, dimly lit by sleek modern sconces along the cinderblock walls and scattered spotlights aimed at various pieces of equipment. Hanson spotted several of the large X's they'd seen at Lady Cassandra's.

He was also aware of a half-naked young man, with a ponytail and rings in his nipples, who kept staring at Gina.

"They're called St. Andrew's crosses," Gina said, dipping close again. "Very popular, but boring. Most of what you see here is just flog, flog, flog. Yawn."

"What would you prefer to see?" Hanson asked.

"Something with real passion," Gina said, eyes roaming the room.

The youngster was suddenly on his knees before Gina.

"Mistress," he said, head bowed. "This slave is overjoyed to see you again—"

"Get up, Jason," Gina said in a voice beyond cool. It was frigid. "I did not give you permission to speak to me."

"Please forgive me," the boy murmured, looking miserably at Griggs on the end of the leash.

"Run along." Gina flicked her hand. "I'm busy."

"You just broke his heart," Hanson said, watching the youngster back away.

"His idea of protocol annoys the shit out of me," Gina snorted.

"Oh, man," Griggs said, twisting his head. "Tits and ass!"

A woman walked by wearing nothing but a leather collar and a smile. It wasn't until she'd passed that Hanson saw the bruises and welts on her back.

"Damn." Griggs winced.

"But see how happy she looks?" Gina said.

"I just don't get it," Griggs said. "I can understand a little butt-slapping, but how can anybody enjoy getting the shit beat out of them?"

"It's not all about pain. A lot of what we do is softer, more sensual. But even the pain is about sensation, and getting that endorphin rush."

"Endolphins?" Griggs asked.

"En*dor*phins," Gina corrected. "When the body is stressed, it produces hormones called endorphins. They produce a natural high."

"Seriously?" Griggs didn't look convinced.

But even amid the sounds of flesh being struck, and the shrieks and wails of pain, the unmistakable sounds of a woman's orgasm carried from the far end of the dungeon.

"Somebody's having a good time," Hanson said.

"How do they walk in those shoes?" Griggs stared at the five-inch stilettos being tongue-washed by a naked man on his knees.

The shoes in question were on the feet of an Amazon in a black latex nun's habit. She looked up at them with a haughty expression, but nodded slightly at Gina.

"You know her?" Hanson asked.

"Yes. I know him."

"Shit," Griggs said. "That's a him?"

"Used to be."

"So, he—she? Is queer?" Griggs asked, peering around.

"Listen asshole," Gina said, tugging Griggs's face close to her own and speaking slowly and deliberately, "the lady in the latex is transgendered, not queer, not a faggot, not even gay."

"Should we talk to him . . . or her?" Hanson asked. "The nun, I mean?"

"I think we should say hello to Marla," Gina said, nodding to a corner.

"I'll be damned," Griggs said.

As they approached, Marla's smile fixed stiffly on her lips.

"Hello, Siren." Gina leaned in to hug Marla, and Hanson heard her whisper something in Marla/Siren's ear. He tried to smile in reassurance.

"Didn't expect to see you out partying," Griggs said.

Gina tugged on the leash hard enough to make him sputter and clutch the collar. He glared at her.

"I'm sorry, he hasn't yet learned not to speak until spoken to."

An older woman sitting beside Marla/Siren laughed.

"Siren is here with her family," the woman said, patting Marla/Siren's shoulder. "She needs our company and support right now."

Griggs's eyes were focused on a naked girl being tied to a cross nearby. Gina tugged on the leash again until he turned back to her.

"Roger and I spent our happiest hours at the club," Marla/Siren said. "I feel closest to him here, with the people who really knew us."

The generous bosom that Griggs had admired on their first meeting was on display in a low-cut dress—black, like nearly everything in this damned place—but nothing flashy. Many wore quite ordinary street clothes. There were a few, however, in elaborate costumes, including the gorgeous doll of a young woman in a pink latex dress with ribbons in her pigtails.

Marla fairly vibrated with anxiety.

"This is Hanson," Gina said, speaking very deliberately. "You've never met before. Right, Hanson?"

"No, we've never met," Hanson agreed, looking Marla directly in the eye. "I'm brand new to all this."

Griggs grinned, but kept quiet.

"Nice to meet you, Hanson." Marla relaxed a bit.

"I'm Medusa," the older woman said, extending her hand to Hanson. "A pleasure to meet you."

Gina had told him not to worry about titles and protocol, that simple courtesy would do the job. Being a good
Southern boy, Hanson had no problem with that.

"The pleasure is all mine, ma'am."

"So you have a new plaything, Gee?" Medusa laughed
throatily. "Are you going to play him tonight? I always
loved watching you work."

Griggs looked so frightened that Hanson almost laughed.

"Probably not. Unless he provokes me by being very,
very naughty."

Someone screamed, louder and longer than any he'd yet
heard in a room full of moans and giggles and yelps. He
resisted the urge to look around.

"I'm looking for someone to beat tonight," Medusa
said, looking up into Hanson's eyes with an unsettling in-
tensity. "I don't suppose you're interested?"

"Hanson is strictly top." Gina smiled. "If he weren't,
he'd be wearing *my* collar."

Medusa and Gina both laughed, and Hanson felt
strangely thrilled at being discussed by two women as if he
weren't standing right there. Medusa was a good fifteen
years older than Gina, and not so provocatively dressed or
so classically beautiful. But there was still something won-
derfully confident and unabashedly sexual about her that
was very appealing.

But there *he* was again, standing in the shadow of a
nearby column.

"Your boy is still watching you," Hanson said into
Gina's ear. "Who is he?"

Gina didn't even glance his way.

"No one you need to worry about."

But he did. He couldn't stop himself.

Gina worked the room, while Hanson and Griggs
trailed after her. Aside from some of the clothes—or lack

of them—and the *twap, twap, twap* of paddles, it was not much different from a cocktail party or backyard barbecue. Hanson caught snippets of talk about football, computers, and poker. Three half-naked women were discussing their kids' day care problems.

"These people are so . . ." Hanson began.

"Normal?" Gina finished.

"See that guy over there in the Grateful Dead T-shirt?" Griggs asked, jerking his head to the left. "That's my fuck-in' *dentist!*"

"The one hanging the naked guy up by his ankles?" Hanson asked.

"Oh, shit," Griggs said, as if only just noticing. "Does that mean he's a fag, too?"

"Use that word one more time, and I will beat the shit out of you," Gina said, looking down haughtily at him. "Which bothers you more? That's he a dominant, or that he's gay?"

"Well, I knew the guy was a sadist." Griggs shrugged, still watching. He sucked in his breath abruptly and turned away, nearly shrinking into Gina's side. "Oh, fuck, what is that *thing* he's putting on the guy's dick?"

"Calm down." Gina sighed. "They're just clothespins strung together—"

"I gotta get a new dentist." Griggs shook his head. "Sadist, gay, all right, I can deal, but now I've seen him with another guy's *dick* in his hands . . ."

"There's a saying, Griggs," Gina said. " 'What you see here, what you hear here, stays here.' Understand?"

"Sure, I get it. It's like Vegas."

"Only the submissives get naked?" Hanson asked.

"Pretty much," Gina agreed.

"Some of them should keep their clothes on," Griggs muttered. He glared when she jerked the leash. "Seriously, Gee, there are some damned unattractive people here."

"You think only pretty people should have a good time?" She jerked the leash again. "This is the real world, not a porn site. And in the kink world, it's about *acceptance*."

"Why don't the dominants get naked?" Hanson asked, more to derail an argument between Griggs and Gina than out of real curiosity.

"Because it's hard to maintain a sense of authority when you're naked," Gina said.

"A real man isn't going to show his dick," Griggs said smugly.

"Except on the Internet, right?" Gina snapped.

There was no sign of Paul, nor had anyone they talked to heard of Kerberos. Gina was careful not to hint at the real reason she wanted information on someone named Kerberos; she explained that he had contacted her online, wanting her to 'mentor' him, and that she was merely checking his references.

"People do that?" Hanson asked. "Check references?"

"Only the smart ones," Gina said.

Gina kept moving through the room, pausing at random conversations, occasionally exchanging a few words.

"I saw it on the news yesterday," an elderly gentleman said. "They said her dogs *ate* her—"

"I hope they pumped the dogs' stomachs," quipped a slender bald man in a Zoot suit, provoking laughter.

"Ya'll are awful," protested a heavy girl covered in tattoos. "This maniac killed Dragon and Kitty!"

The laughter died except for a couple of nervous snickers.

"Do you think the killer was one of us?" Gina asked.

The little group looked at her.

"More likely it's somebody who hates us," the elderly gentleman said.

"I don't even want to think about it," the tattooed girl said.

The conversation turned to something else, and Gina moved away.

"Damn, my feet are killing me," Gina whispered.

"Then let's go sit down somewhere."

"I can't sit down in this thing." She frowned and motioned to the corset. "I can barely go to the toilet. *Damn.*"

"What?"

"Now I have to pee." She sighed. She handed Hanson the leash. "I'll meet you out front."

"Man, this is off the hook," Griggs whispered. "But I thought the women would be, you know, hotter."

Hanson eyed him with a frown.

"I mean, some of them are attractive, but it ain't like the porn on the Web."

"Nothing ever is," Hanson said.

"Gee left you two on your own?" Dante was standing behind them.

"Don't worry," Hanson said, smiling politely. "We'll try not to embarrass ourselves before she gets back."

Griggs craned his head to get a better look at two women chained face-to-face on a small platform.

"What is that he's hitting them with?" Griggs asked.

"That?" Dante chuckled. "That's a flogger."

"I thought you used whips?"

"Nah—" Dante shook his head. "Very few people actually use whips. They take a great deal of skill—and practice—to use properly. You can cut someone to the bone with a whip if you don't know what you're doing."

The two women were kissing each other as the man circled them, flogging each back in turn. Griggs yanked the leash out of Hanson's hand and took a step closer to the scene.

"You've known Gina a long time?" Hanson asked.

"About ten years, I guess," Dante said. "I felt bad when she was outted."

"She says you all abandoned her," Hanson said evenly, watching his reaction.

"People were scared. Myself included. I teach middle school. Do you know how fast I'd lose my job if anybody found out what my wife and I do here?"

"I can imagine. What's your real opinion on Quinn?"

"You mean, now that Gee's not around?" Dante flashed a grin, then sobered and shrugged. "He's a twisted fucker, I'll say that."

"But his relationship with Gee," Hanson said, trying to sound off hand when he really felt sick with jealousy just saying the man's name. "She was his slave, right?"

Dante slanted his eyes, as if weighing his words.

"Gina and Quinn were . . . legendary. Or notorious, depending on who you ask."

"How so?"

Dante smiled a little, almost wistfully.

"Everything in the dungeon would come to a complete stop whenever they played. People just watched them. You couldn't help it."

"Sure," Hanson said. "She's a knock-out."

"Yes, she is." Dante laughed. "But it was more than that. The two of them together. They danced on the edge."

"What does that mean?"

Dante shrugged.

"They played hard, at a level most people just don't."

Hanson didn't like the sound of that.

"You mean they did risky stuff? Isn't all this risky?"

"Hell, crossing the street is risky. Everything has some element of risk in it. But yeah, they pushed it further. Some people, they scared the shit out of. Other people admired them for doing what they didn't have the nerve to do."

Dante must have sensed his discomfort, or worried that he'd said too much. Though Hanson was sure the man had no way of knowing his relationship with Gina was anything more than professional.

"But I think it was also their chemistry. You could just feel the energy, the heat, between them." Dante laughed. "And Quinn is a natural showman. Very theatrical. It was something to see them play."

Hanson wished he hadn't asked. He looked around the room and imagined Gina, naked, bound to one of the crosses . . .

"What about Maggie?" He roused himself with difficulty. "Does he have the same heat when he plays with her?"

"No." Dante didn't even have to think about it.

"Would Maggie lie for him?"

Dante peered at him, eyebrows raised.

"Why are you asking? Is he a suspect?"

"Should he be?"

Dante said nothing for a moment.

"I just can't imagine anyone capable of that kind of violence. Goddess knows, Cassandra could drive anyone to it. But as far as I know, he'd never had a beef with Dragon, not really."

"What does 'not really' mean?"

"Dragon backed Cassandra's old club. Loans that Cassandra never repaid, of course."

"How would that affect Dragon's relationship with Quinn?"

"I don't know that it did. I'm just saying there was a lot of history. Cassandra didn't just mismanage her club; she almost cost Quinn his business. I think he was relieved, in a way, when the Lair closed. There was nothing else to keep him tied to her."

"Quinn ever have any issues with Robyn—I mean, Kitty?"

"Nah, he and Kitty patched it up a long time ago."

"Patched up what?"

Dante sighed and ran his hands through his hair.

"Oh, he helped set up this kidnapping thing for her a while back. It didn't go well, she got upset—"

"Kitty was *that* girl?"

"Yeah, but she eventually calmed down. A lot of newbies get what we call 'sub frenzy'—they want to do it all, right away. Kitty was going too far, too fast."

"Neither of them held a grudge?"

"No, I don't think so. They weren't exactly close anymore, but—speak of the devil."

Dante was staring at the door, and Hanson looked, too.

Quinn stood there with Maggie on his arm. He was wearing a pinstripe suit over a black shirt and red silk tie. Maggie was in a leather halter, miniskirt, and dangerous fuck-me shoes.

"Where's Griggs?" Gina demanded, suddenly appearing beside Hanson. "You were supposed to be keeping an eye on him—"

"Chill, mama," Griggs said, sauntering up. "I was just getting a closer look at something going on over there in the corner. Did you know you can get not one but two whole fists into a woman's—"

"Yes, I know." Gina frowned. She was staring at Quinn. "I think we've seen all there is to see here."

Hanson could feel the anxiety rolling off of her like waves. It suddenly made him angry. What kind of hold did Quinn have on her, that she reacted this way just at the sight of him?

"Are we really done or are you just afraid of watching Quinn with Maggie?"

She turned to glare at him, grabbing up Griggs's leash.

"Green is not a good color on you, Hanson."

She strode toward the door, pulling Griggs along behind her.

"Bella rosso," Quinn was purring as Hanson caught up. "You look positively ravishing. And good enough to eat."

He clicked his teeth together.

She didn't flinch.

"I'm not on your plate anymore."

"Ah, but *bella rosso . . .*" Quinn leaned in close to Gina, lowering his voice so that Hanson couldn't catch the words.

As he watched, Quinn reached out, trailing his fingertips lightly across Gina's bare collarbone, and picked up the medallion around her neck. The very sight of his fingertips so close to her skin made something in Hanson's head explode.

"You'd better enjoy your freedom while you still can," Hanson said, stepping between them. "There aren't any safewords in prison."

"I'm very hurt, Detective Hanson," Quinn said, putting a hand to his heart. "I don't think you like me."

"I think you're a pompous little shit. You may even be a murderer—"

"Hanson—" Gina put a hand on his arm, but he shook it off.

"Why would I kill anybody?" Quinn asked. "I'm a very selfish man. I don't do anything unless there's something in it for me."

"Maybe you killed Roger because you were afraid he was gonna give Cassandra money to reopen her club—"

"That's got nothing to do with me."

His smug little smile again.

"The old club was in both your names; she ruined you financially. You've been trying to distance yourself from any association with Cassandra to save your own reputation—"

"That may be true. But that's a pathetic motive for murder."

"So what about Robyn?" Hanson smiled nastily.

"Kitty, you mean? What about her?" Quinn looked at Gina. "I think your boy here is out of control, *bella.* Maybe he should be the one on the leash."

"Robyn was the one from that gangbang that went bad. I bet that really pissed you off, didn't it? Ruined your reputation?"

"Actually, it probably helped my reputation," Quinn said, as if sharing a confidence. "Air of danger and all that. But she dropped the charges."

"Maybe you still held a grudge."

"Half the people here saw us play a dozen times after that," Quinn said, finally showing some impatience. "*Bella,* call off your dog. This is getting tiresome."

Quinn took Maggie by the hand and led her off into the dungeon.

"What the hell is wrong with you?" Gina hissed.

"Me? What the hell is wrong with you?" Hanson shot back. "He's got half a dozen motives—"

"Hey, hey!" Griggs stepped between them. "If you two are gonna fight, can we take it outside? I'd like to get out of this freakin' collar. It chafes."

It was a silent drive except for Griggs's blabbering, but Hanson was still too angry to hear any of it. All he could hear was blood pounding through his ears. He didn't dare speak to Gina until they dropped Griggs at his apartment.

When he parked in front of her house, he still wasn't sure he could manage a conversation. He'd been in a state of constant tension since the moment he saw her again, and now realized his own stupidity in thinking he could handle this.

"What did you think you were gonna accomplish by provoking him like that?"

"*Him?* You mean Quinn? Funny how you don't like saying his name. Why is that?"

She got out of the car and slammed the door. Hanson got out and followed her.

"Are you still seeing him?" That was the question driving spikes into his guts. "Are you?"

He caught the door before she could close it and pushed his way in.

"No! Not that it's any of your business!"

"It *is* my business if you're screwing up my investigation!" He grabbed her arm.

"Fuck the investigation." Gina laughed bitterly, jerking away. "You've been pissed ever since you saw that damned photo—"

"I'll bet he took a lot more than just that one, too."

"Oh, he took plenty of photos! I have a whole box full. You want to see those, too?"

Suddenly Hanson could see the way she looked when he fucked her, recognized the surrender in that beautiful up-turned face; it was the same expression she wore in that photograph.

"He fucked me, too; before, during, and after that photo shoot," she said slyly. "The best fucking I ever had, no contest."

"Shut up." She was deliberately trying to hurt him now, another side of her he'd never seen.

"He enjoyed knowing that his cum was leaking out of me as I posed for him—"

"Stop it!"

"Oh, come on, baby." She chuckled darkly in her dirty

bedroom voice. Suddenly her long velvet skirt puddled around her feet. "You're just dying to know all about it, aren't you?"

She took a step closer and began unhooking the corset.

"You want to see the photos where his cock is halfway down my throat? Or the ones where he pissed all over me?"

"That's disgusting—" His voice was suddenly thick with longing.

She dropped the corset to the floor and stood before him, naked except for the medallion and her thigh-high boots.

"Sure, that's why you got a hard-on, just like you do now," Gina said. She spread her arms, putting herself on display. "Is this what you want? You think you're man enough to just take it?"

"Whore," he hissed.

She brought her hand smartly across his face.

He stood there, feeling the heat spread across his cheek. Without thinking, he had her by the shoulders.

"Get off me—"

She twisted but couldn't break away. She tried to bring her knee into his crotch, but he was already pushing her down.

"I make you angry, and suddenly you think you're man enough to fuck me?" She hit him again, this time a fist against his temple. "Stupid bastard, didn't momma tell you never to hit a girl?"

One of his hands grabbed at her hair, twisting it into a long rope around his fist, and forced her to the floor.

"You fucking bitch."

He climbed on top of her, felt his erection against her hip, and ground it against her in a savage dry hump.

"This how you want it?" he demanded. "This how he used to fuck you?"

He had been desperate to touch her. Now that he had his hands on her—all that naked flesh straining against him—he could not stop. Some beast had crawled out of the dark corner of his brain, and it was in control.

Her nails clawed at his arm, and the pain only fanned the lust flooding his veins. He used his body to hold her down and felt her struggling for breath under his weight. She was strong, but he outweighed her by fifty pounds. Every twitch of her body excited him.

"Bastard!"

Her tits were heaving. His hands plundered, squeezing soft flesh.

Goddamn her! Goddamn her for three years of wet dreams and jerking off to her memory! Goddamn her for making him feel weak and uncertain and inadequate—

He twisted one nipple viciously. When she cried out in pain, his cock went from merely hard to stone.

"You like that, whore? Is this what you always wanted from me?"

He brought his mouth down on hers, forcing his tongue inside until she bit him.

"Goddamn you!" He tasted blood and drew back.

"You don't have the balls to rape me, remember?" She spat into his face. "You're just a little momma's boy—"

He hit her. A hard open-palmed slap across her left cheek. She gasped, but then grunted a laugh of utter contempt.

"Bastard . . . you'll never get that . . . pathetic cock of yours . . . inside me . . ."

Her hand found his hair and yanked, until he grabbed both of her wrists in one hand. Her bones felt so small and fragile in his grip. He liked the way it felt: like he could break her if he wanted to.

She tried to scuttle away, crab-like, and her boot heel

scraped hard against his chest. It nearly knocked the wind out of him, but nothing would stop this blind urgency to take her, to have her, to impale her with his cock.

"Sick, fucking whore," he panted. "You're soaking wet."

And she was, oh, she was. The scent of her cunt hit his nostrils as he used his knees to force her legs open.

"Is this the way you want it?" he kept demanding.

But he didn't give a fuck what she wanted.

She was punching him with hard, balled fists. He grabbed her wrists once more, pinning her down. He slammed his cock into her, feeling the wet heat of her pussy suck him deeper as her back arched.

He imagined every thrust of his hips driving the head of his prick into her spine, splitting her in two. He couldn't fuck her hard enough or fast enough.

He buried his face in her tits as he fucked her like a machine. His teeth fastened on her nipple, chewing and biting, tasting copper on his tongue and not giving a damn.

She was moaning even as her hips rose to meet each thrust. He felt her teeth on his shoulder.

"Goddamned whore! Fight me, bite me, but you'll fuckin' take it . . . Take my fucking cock."

Suddenly she was no longer fighting him, only crying out in sharp little cat-cries of pain as he rode her. Her hips were jutting wildly now, grinding her cunt against him.

"Yessssss!"

Her head flew back, exposing her throat, and he wanted to put his hands around it. He was the predator now, taking his pleasure in this prey.

"Use me . . . Use my fuck-hole. *Please.* . . ."

He could feel her orgasm coming as intensely as his own. He felt the small shudders build up from deep inside her, then grow harder as her muscles clamped down on his cock.

"Oh, God! Yes! Yes!"

He slapped her again, because he could. Because he wanted to. Because he knew she wanted it.

She came, and then came again.

He pulled his aching cock out of her, and knee-walked up her body until his erection was poised over her face.

She looked up at him with unfocused eyes, but as soon as his cock touched her lips she was on it like a starving thing.

He grabbed her by the hair again, and held her head still.

"No, bitch." He pulled his cock from her mouth and began stroking it with his free hand. "You don't get to suck it . . ."

"Please . . ." She looked up at him, breathing hard. "Yes, please . . . cum on my face . . ."

He jerked harder, feeling his balls contract. It was sweet to use her like this, to force his will on her until she became this depraved slut eager for his cum.

Jism shot from the head of his cock and landed in heavy strands over her chin and mouth. He watched her tongue greedily lap it up, until there was no more, and he was left spent and panting.

Dear Christ, what had she done to him? What had he done to her?

He fell back onto his ass and looked down in horror as her body began to convulse in sobs. He thought he might puke. He began to scuttle away, but her hand landed on his ankle.

"Please," she said in a tiny voice. "Please . . ."

He didn't understand, just sat there looking at her helplessly, until she dragged herself toward him. She curled against his ribs, pulling his arm around her.

"Please. Just hold me."

He lay back down on the floor, afraid to touch her. Her arms were around him, her face rubbing against his shirt as her breathing began to slow.

When she finally looked up at him, her tear-stained smile took his breath away.

"That." She sighed. "That was just what I needed."

"I don't know what the hell came over me."

They were in her bed. Hanson marveled over the sensation of flesh against flesh. It had been so long since he'd held a woman in his arms like this.

She was as drowsy as a puppy, her lips moving blindly against his chest as she snuggled closer.

"Don't think too much," she mumbled. "Can I have another slice of cheese, please?"

He fed her another cracker with a sliver of Gouda. Starving after their violent lovemaking—if that was what he could call it—he'd carried the only food he could find into bed with them.

The most confusing part was that he felt so ridiculously tender toward her now. And he was pretty certain it wasn't just out of guilt for having raped her. He watched her nibble at the cracker between his fingers, and liked the way it felt to be feeding her like a pet.

"I was just so damned angry. I wanted to hurt you."

"And I got off on it." She smiled lazily.

"I didn't care whether you did or not. There's something wrong with that."

She sighed.

"You say you didn't care, but I don't think that's true. I don't think you're capable of that. We've pushed those limits before, and I was doing my damnedest to provoke you—"

"You were?"

She laughed, an easy sound.

"Do you really think I couldn't have stopped you if I'd wanted to?"

"No, I don't. I'm a man, and I'm bigger than you."

"Really?" She sat up and pushed her hair over her shoulder with a shrug. "Why do you think I took my clothes off and paraded around naked? I knew you'd never be able to get the damned corset off."

"You're trying to make me feel better. This can't be . . . It can't be . . ."

His voice trailed off, unsure how to say it. *This can't be right. It can't be normal.*

"I'm sorry, I was wrong," she said. All teasing was gone from her voice. "Wrong for doing it this way."

"This way? Is there a right way?"

"Yes. Absolutely." She looked him full in the face, her eyes holding his. "If I were playing by the rules, I should have sat you down and told you what I wanted. I should have explained that I needed to fight you, that I needed you to force me. I should have negotiated the scene with you."

"The scene? You make it sound like a play."

"It is, really. That's the downside of 'safe, sane, and consensual.' All these carefully orchestrated rules, they suck the magic out of it. It takes something wild and primitive, and turns it into something tame and careful. I didn't want tame and careful. But now I've dumped something on you that you weren't prepared for. And that's breaking a rule I do take seriously, pushing someone beyond their limits. Can you forgive me?"

She was watching him intently. He knew that whatever he said now might change everything. He could wipe out the last two years if he told her what she wanted—what she needed—to hear.

The thing was, what she needed to hear was what he needed to say. What had happened between them tonight had been wild and primitive and . . . magical. Wasn't that what Quinn had said? That BDSM was a powerful magic?

"If I gave you what you wanted and what you needed,"

he said, stroking the side of her face, "there's nothing to forgive."

"And you can forgive yourself?"

From the way she seemed to be almost holding her breath, he knew it was a test, and he smiled at her.

"Nothing to forgive there, either. Isn't that what you always tried to tell me? That I don't have to feel dirty and ashamed of making us both happy?"

"And it made you happy? Truly? I was cruel provoking you like that . . ."

Now it was his turn to peer into her face, asking his own question.

"Why were you trying to provoke me? Why now?"

She looked away.

"Because I was a fucking mess after seeing Quinn."

"Do you still love him that much?" He hated himself for asking, and wasn't sure he wanted to know the answer.

"No," she said flatly. "What I feel—what I felt—for Quinn was way more complicated than love."

"I don't get it," he said, stroking her back to soften his words. "What's more complicated than love?"

She was silent for so long that Hanson thought she wasn't going to answer the question. She rolled onto her side, snuggling her ass up against his hip, and he spooned against her back. He could feel each intake of breath, and the soft, slow release of it.

He thought she might have gone to sleep, but then she finally spoke.

"Complicated is knowing for most of your life that you're not quite the same as most other people," she said softly. "Having the darkest, most desperate desires that you can hardly admit to yourself, and wondering if you're somehow . . . damaged. Sick, in your mind and in your soul. And you don't dare tell anyone because then they'll know you're different, and they will never, ever love you if they know what you really are. They'll look at you the way you try so hard not to look at yourself—as something twisted and wrong."

She took the arm he draped over her shoulder and pulled it down closer around her, bringing his hand to her cheek and rubbing against it like a cat. He lay still against her, fearing any movement from him might stop her from continuing. He needed to hear this as much as he feared it.

"So you keep these dark secrets locked away for years and years," she went on, still in that same soft, somehow distant voice, "and all the while you're wanting those things—those dark, scary things—more and more, so much that it's like a physical ache."

He wished he could see her face, but realized that she had turned away precisely so he couldn't. Maybe she could only say these things without being seen.

"Normal sex is fine, it's wonderful, but it just isn't quite . . . *enough,* and you begin to wonder if you will ever feel anything as deeply, as passionately, as you so desperately want to. You feel as if everyone you have sex with—make love to—is only touching half of you.

"Imagine having sex for years without anyone ever kissing you. Don't laugh. Just try to imagine it. Imagine dreaming about being kissed all your life, but no one has ever pressed their lips against yours, never explored your mouth with their tongue, never pulled your tongue into their hot, wet mouth . . .

"They've stroked every inch of your body, fucked you, made you cum, eaten your pussy or sucked your cock, stuck their fingers inside you, wrapped their body around yours, but no one has ever kissed your mouth. Imagine that.

"That's what it's like. Having a part of you that no one has ever touched, or even thought about exploring. As if you didn't have a mouth or lips at all.

"And then one day, you meet someone who sees that you do have lips made to be kissed. Hot, slow kisses that go on and on, and hard, fast kisses that devour you.

"That's what it's like when someone recognizes that twisted desire in you. He sees it and calls to it, and for the first time in your life, you let that part of you out of the cage you've locked it in. For the first time in your life, someone is making love to all of you."

Her voice was so low he strained to hear her. He was afraid to breathe, lest the sound of it in his own ears swallow her words.

"And this man, he's even more twisted than you are, and instead of turning away from you in disgust, he says he loves you, not in *spite* of what you are, but *because* of what you are . . ."

He felt a tremble run through her, just once, and then it was gone.

"That," she said finally, sighing deeply, "is what's more complicated than love."

He thought again about how he'd taken her by force, and enjoyed it. Yes, that was certainly more complicated than love.

When he was certain she was done, he dared to ask.

"That's what Quinn is for you?"

She took a moment before she responded.

"What he was, maybe, for a time. You have to understand the nature of the submissive heart."

"I still don't see you as submissive. You're a hardcore bitch."

She laughed softly and rolled back into his arms again. She kissed his chin.

"That's because I fought against it all my life. I protected myself like crazy from anybody that got too close. I was afraid that if I fell, I'd fall damned hard. And I was right."

He pressed his lips against her eyelid, liking the soft, vulnerable flesh there.

"A submissive has this . . . I don't know . . . this tremendous capacity for devotion that borders on obsessive. You want nothing more in this world than to belong to someone who knows you in the most intimate detail. You don't just want to love someone, you want to worship someone.

"When I met Quinn, I'd read all the books. I knew all the theory behind dominance and submission. I thought he was my soul mate, my true Master. I thought I'd really grabbed the brass ring that all good little submissives hope and pray for. There was a time when I literally could not refuse him anything.

"I let him do things to me . . . Things that I could never have imagined letting anyone do to me . . ."

She fell silent, and he waited for her to continue. But she didn't.

"What changed?"

"One day I got a glimpse of the man behind the curtain. What had been an earth-shattering event for me was, after all, just a game for him. I was only one in a long, long line of 'true slaves' for Quinn . . ."

He felt warm wetness on his chest and realized, too late, that she was crying.

"Do you have any idea what it's like to tear down all of your walls, to stand completely naked in front of someone begging them to love you? Surrendering absolutely everything in your heart and soul, only to find it was all smoke and mirrors? A mind-fuck?"

He gathered her to him, felt her chest heave as hot tears slid across his chest.

"I hate the bastard," she whispered between hitches of

breath. "I hate him for making me feel all those things, for making all of my fantasies come true, then ripping them all away from me."

"I'm sorry, Gee," he whispered, kissing her on the forehead. "I'm so sorry . . ."

"And those pictures. Goddamn him!" She gripped his shoulder hard enough to hurt, as if he were a life preserver in a desperate ocean. "He sold me for thirty fucking pieces of silver . . ."

"Sssh," he whispered.

And he kept whispering until her crying became sniffles and she fell asleep in his arms.

He looked down at her tear-streaked face, and thought of what Quinn Lee had done to her.

He hated the bastard, too.

Chapter 24

Rhett Butler is definitely a dominant. If you don't believe me, read that chapter where he carries her up the stairs. That's hot stuff.
—FELICITY SPARKS, *S&M in Modern Culture*

"Where the fuck have you been?" Griggs's voice on the phone was impatient. "I've been leaving messages for two solid hours. Where are you?"

He was still in bed with Gina. He was disoriented to wake in this strange and yet familiar place, to the odd slant of the sun through the windows.

"What time is it?"

"It's almost noon. You're with Gee, aren't you? Goddamn it!"

"What do ya want, Griggs?"

He looked down at Gina, who was just beginning to stir. She opened one eye and smiled as she reached for his cock.

"We found Paul. You think you can make some time between fuck-fests to help me question him?"

"Where is he?"

"Dirt-bag is in Shelby at some cheapo water park."

"That's a two-hour drive there, and two hours back."

"Which means get your ass out of bed pronto, if you can walk."

"Gimme half an hour."

Hanson flipped the phone shut and relayed the information to Gina.

"Shit." Gina sighed, letting go of his half-erect cock and rising from the bed.

"You coming?" he asked.

"I'd like to, but I really can't. I have another job, re-member?"

He watched her naked ass sway to the bathroom. He stared at the large bruise on her hip and the finger marks on her shoulder. His finger marks. It took him a moment to re-alize what he was feeling. Not guilty, not ashamed. Satisfied.

He had marked her as *his*.

It was nearly five before they got to the hotel, and they waited another half hour for Paul and family to return from a day of fun. They saw a light blue Kia Sorento pull into the lot, and then a man matching Paul Carlson's de-scription climbing out of the driver's seat. He went around to the back of the car, taking out a cooler, as a woman and two small wet boys tumbled out.

"How you wanna play this?" Griggs asked, getting out of the car as they watched the Carlson family climb the metal stairs to the second floor. "Cheating Husband Cover Story Number Two?"

Paul's hair was a fine, pale brown, just beginning to re-cede, but he had a trim build in swim trunks and a blue plaid shirt unbuttoned down the front. He was probably considered attractive, Hanson thought, by women who didn't mind that he had the small, shifty eyes of a weasel.

"Why cover for him?" Hanson asked as they closed the distance.

"Because she looks like one of them soccer moms that does some kinda cardio-boxing shit," Griggs replied. "I don't wanna have to pull her off him."

Joanna Carlson, a wet-haired and sunburned woman wrapped in a terrycloth beach cover-up, looked thin but wiry, in a sort of Linda Hamilton *Terminator 2* kind of way. That, and an unmistakable aggressiveness about her, made Hanson think she did indeed wear the pants in the family.

She looked Hanson and Griggs over with sharp eyes as they showed their badges and introduced themselves.

"What's this about?"

"We're investigating a hit-and-run involving a car matching the description of your husband's Forte Koup," Hanson said.

"That's ridiculous," she said. "He didn't hit anything. His car is at home without a scratch on it."

"Honey, I'm sure this is nothing," Paul said. "They're just doing their jobs."

"Unless," she said, her face tightening even further, "you're saying his car was stolen out of our driveway?"

"Our car was stolen?" one of the boys asked. "Was it, Mom?"

"We don't know that anything has happened to your dad's car," Griggs told the boy. He looked at Paul. "But we need to talk to your dad about it."

"I have to pee," announced the younger boy.

"Why don't you and the kids clean up," Paul said to his wife, running his card key through the door and holding it open. "I'll be in as soon as I can."

With a hostile glare, Joanna herded the two boys into the room.

"Is this going to take long?" Joanna squinted. "We have reservations for dinner."

"We'll try to make it as quick as we can, ma'am," Hanson said.

The door slammed shut and Hanson heard Joanna yelling at the kids not to lie on the beds in their wet swimsuits.

"You've been a bad boy," Griggs said to Paul. "Let's talk down in the lobby. It's hotter than hell out here."

"I swear to God, I didn't hurt her—"

"But you're into all that, aren't you?" Griggs interrupted. "Spanky, spanky?"

"You know what I mean!" Paul lowered his voice to a frantic whisper. "I mean I didn't kill her!"

Paul's weasel eyes darted from one face to the other, but even that eye contact was fleeting. He might not be guilty of murder, Hanson thought, but the man sure as hell felt guilty about *something*.

"We don't think you killed her," Hanson said.

"What's this 'we' shit?" Griggs asked. "I haven't made up my mind yet."

"But you were the last person to see Robyn alive," Hanson continued. "Why'd you run? This wasn't a scheduled vacation, was it?"

"I saw it on the news," Paul said, sitting on the edge of the lobby's rock-hard sofa and chewing a cuticle. "It scared the hell out of me—"

"I'll bet," Hanson said.

"Kitty—Robyn, I mean—was fine when I left," Paul insisted. "She was getting dressed—"

"Maybe the game was over," Griggs said. "Ya'll ate your cookies, she packed her little Kitty bag . . . and then she said something that pissed you off? Is that what happened?"

"No! Kitty and I were friends! I'm sorry as hell that she's dead, I really am!"

"I can see you're all torn up about it," Griggs said. He turned to Hanson with a shrug. "Poor guy, up here drowning his troubles in water slides and cotton candy."

"Don't you get it?" Paul whispered urgently, leaning forward. "It must have happened right after I left. If I hadn't left when I did, I coulda been killed, too!"

"That's possible," Hanson said. "Of course, maybe if you'd stuck around long enough to walk Robyn to her car, she'd have been as lucky as you."

"Damnit." Paul wiped a hand over his mouth, and his small eyes disappeared into crescents as his face screwed up. Hanson wondered if the man was going to cry. "Don't you think I've thought about that, too? Don't you think I already feel like shit?"

Paul said he'd left Kitty in the room around 6:15. He was sure about the time because he knew he had to pick his oldest son up from soccer practice by 6:30, and meet his wife for dinner by 7.

"Your wife and kid can verify this?"

"Oh, shit." Paul's shoulders slumped, and he collapsed back on the sofa like a rag doll. "You can't tell her about this. She'll divorce me, if she doesn't kill me first—"

"Guess you should have thought of that sooner," Griggs said.

"Look, I'll do anything I can to help, but please, *please* don't tell my wife."

"She must be one mean bitch," Griggs said with a glance at Hanson. "He's about to pee his pants."

"You didn't see anybody hanging around?" Hanson asked. "No one paying a little too much attention when you checked in or when you left?"

Paul's face went blank, as if he were thinking hard, and then he shook his head.

"I didn't see anybody special. There were some cars in the lot, sure—"

"What's that mean, you didn't see anybody 'special'?"

"I dunno! There was a black couple going into a room down on the other end, I think. A woman and a kid getting into a car, and some maintenance guy—"

The Madison didn't seem like the kind of place to have a regular maintenance crew. Patel ran the office, and his wife and daughters did the housekeeping.

"He was wearing one of those coverall jumpsuits, you know? Like a mechanic or house painter. But he didn't even look at me, he was messing around with a broken window or something, like twenty or thirty feet away."

"What did he look like?"

"You mean besides the coveralls?" Paul squirmed. "I dunno! Average, I guess. Just a guy, all right? He was wearing a ball cap and carrying a toolbox."

"Was he white or black? How tall?"

"White, far as I could tell." Paul was beginning to whine. "Average height, I guess. He mighta had a mustache, I don't remember for sure."

"What color were the coveralls?"

"Dark. Blue, I think."

"Was there any kind of writing or name on them?"

"Not that I can remember."

Eyewitnesses were a pain in the ass, Hanson thought. Mr. Coveralls could be their perp, or he could be nobody. They'd have to go back to the Madison.

"Was Robyn seeing anybody else?" he asked. "Maybe someone she met online?"

"Robyn was always meeting people online. But as far as I know, she wasn't playing with anyone else. Hadn't been for a while."

"Why not?"

"She was just getting over a breakup with this dom about three months ago. She was bitching and moaning about having to FedEx the collar back to him in Canada—"

"You sure he dumped her? Not the other way around?"

"Yeah, I'm sure." Paul rolled his eyes. "She never even met him, it was strictly an online LDR."

"LDR?" Griggs asked.

"Long distance relationship," Paul explained.

"How in the hell can you do this stuff online?" Griggs asked. "Or long distance?"

Paul simply stared at Griggs with disdain. But when they questioned him about Lady Cassandra's death, he snickered.

"I didn't know you could kill the devil," he said. "I stayed as far away from that crazy bitch as possible."

"So you didn't like her?"

"No, but I sure as hell didn't kill her! I've never had that much to do with her, you know?"

"You know anybody named Cherry?"

"Yeah . . ." Paul looked confused and even more anxious. "I know Cherry. Why? Did something happen to her?"

"Someone raped her about a month ago."

"Oh, I know about *that*. But, she's okay now, right? She's not, you know . . . The guy who killed Kitty, he didn't hurt her, too?"

"No, she's all right," Hanson said. "For now."

"Shit, you scared me. I thought . . . shit!" Paul wiped a hand across his mouth and took a deep breath. "I'm glad she's okay."

"You knew about what happened to her before?" Hanson asked.

"About her and that crazy fuck from Collarme? Yeah, she told me about it. Me and Cherry are friends, have been for almost a year."

"You have any ideas about who this Kerberos is?"

"No. If I did, I'd tell you, because that crazy fuck needs to be locked up for what he did to her. It really messed her up. Not just physically. Mentally, too."

"Messed her up mentally, how exactly?"

"Last time we tried to play, she freaked out, started crying and shaking."

"When was this?"

"The same day—" Paul's mouth fell open. "Oh, shit, it was the same day I played with Kitty."

"The same day?" Griggs rolled his eyes and looked at Hanson. "Can you believe this guy?"

"A regular Don Juan," Hanson said.

"I took the room at the Madison for me and Cherry. But then she got upset and just wanted to go home. After she left, I called Kitty—"

"No sense letting a cheesy motel room go to waste, right?" Griggs asked with a smirk.

"It was already paid for, for Christ's sake!"

Griggs and Hanson exchanged glances over Paul's head.

"The perp mighta been following Cherry," Hanson said.

"And was pissed that he missed her, so he killed Robyn instead," Griggs said, nodding.

"Aw, shit!" Paul turned pale even under his sunburned cheeks. "I thought it was just some random thing. You think they were looking for us specifically?"

"It's possible," Hanson said. "We need to give you some police protection, just in case—"

"Oh, man! Oh, no, this can't be happening," Paul moaned. "Can't I just stay here until you catch this guy?"

"You're a shit, Paul." Hanson sighed. "I shouldn't just tell your wife, I should hold you down while she beats the crap out of you."

"I'm not a bad guy," Paul insisted. "I love my wife and my kids. I don't want to see them hurt. Can't you cut me some slack? Man-to-man?"

Griggs and Hanson exchanged looks. Griggs shrugged. Hanson sighed.

"You can waive police protection," Hanson said, taking Paul's elbow and pulling him to his feet. "We can stick with the story about the hit-and-run, for now. But if we found out you lied to us, we'll have to tell her everything."

Paul gushed his thanks pathetically, until he realized they were following him back to the room.

"We've got to confirm your alibi," Griggs said. "No way around it."

Joanna wasn't happy to see any of them. She listened to

their questions with steely eyes and both arms crossed over her chest.

"Of course I can vouch for his whereabouts." She bristled. "I'm sure Chip's soccer coach can verify it, too. The man has a real attitude problem about parents being late for pick-up.

"Now, if you don't mind," Joanna said, squaring her shoulders, "I need to finish getting ready and Paul needs to get in the shower."

Griggs waited until she turned her back and handed Paul his card.

"If you think of anything else, you call us. And if we call you, you better answer the phone, understand?"

"Thank you," Paul said in a low rush, as if he'd been holding his breath. "I will, I promise I will."

Paul shut the door so quickly it scuffed the back of Hanson's heel.

"What a piece of work," Griggs muttered as they went down the stairs. "He still coulda done her, but I don't think he's got the balls."

"We could try putting him with a sketch artist," Hanson said.

"Yeah, we'd get a picture of a ball cap," Griggs grunted wearily. "Maybe with a mustache or maybe not."

"Still, it's a lead. If you wanted to hang around someplace, pretending you were a maintenance guy would be a good way to do it."

"Everybody sees the suit, nobody thinks nothing," Griggs agreed.

"A jumpsuit would keep the blood off his clothes. He unzips and walks away, all nice and clean . . . You checked the parking garage's trash cans, right?"

"Yeah, asshole! This ain't my first rodeo. We didn't find anything but empty Starbucks cups and fast-food wrappers."

Hanson's phone beeped. It was Gina.

"Yeah, we talked to him, and his wife." Hanson filled her in on the important details.

"So we've got a lead at least," she said. "A shitty lead, but it's something."

"If the techno geeks don't call me with something tomorrow on Kerberos's e-mails," Hanson said, "I'm gonna go down there and kick their asses."

"Sounds like a plan," she said. "I've been trolling around online, but no bites."

"So . . ." Hanson glanced at Griggs, who wasn't even pretending not to eavesdrop, and bit the bullet. "You gonna be up for a while? I can come by . . ."

"I'm really beat, Hanson, and I've got an appointment early tomorrow—"

"Sure, I understand," he said quickly. *Damn it.* Was she having second thoughts about last night, or had it not really meant anything?

"Don't freak out," she said, as if reading his mind. "Seriously. I want to see you. Just not tonight, okay?"

"Okay." Hanson took a deep breath, held it a second, then released it. He didn't want to screw this up, and neither did he want to want to blow the case. Suddenly it seemed like they were one and the same.

Griggs looked at him as he put the phone away.

"She blew you off, didn't she?" he asked.

"Don't start."

"Hey, I don't blame you for wanting to hit that, Hanson. But don't go letting your dick do all your thinking."

"I'm supposed to take this advice from you?"

"God gave us two heads, man. I'm just saying, use both of 'em."

Chapter 25

The great art of life is sensation, to feel that we exist, even in pain.

—LORD BYRON

Cherry hadn't realized just how much her secret had been weighing her down until she'd told her story to the detectives. It was as if a heavy stone had been rolled off her back and her lungs could fully inflate for the first time in weeks.

The police car out front helped some, too. Whenever they changed shifts, two new officers would come to the door and introduce themselves.

But she still couldn't sleep more than a few hours at a time. She found herself wandering to the window without even being conscious of it, just to reassure herself they were still there. Sometimes she would stand there for several minutes, just looking, grateful for the presence of another soul.

Even last night, sometime just after three a.m., she had peered out the blinds and watched until she saw one of them move. She had been so afraid—so certain—they had fallen asleep.

Tonight it was Officers Bowers and Hill again. Bowers was in his forties, with thick iron-colored hair and a barrel-shaped body; his manner was businesslike almost to the point of brusqueness, and the way he looked at her made Cherry feel as if he were judging her. She wondered if he knew all the details of her situation. God, she hoped he didn't. She didn't mind his curtness, though; in a strange way, it made her feel safer, as if his mind were too completely absorbed with the job to spare any energy for pleasantries.

On the other hand, Officer Hill—Tony—was about her own age, and he seemed very sympathetic. She hoped he didn't know the whole story for a different set of reasons.

He had a shy, slow smile that started at one side of his mouth, almost a dimple but not quite, and spread to the other whenever he knocked on the door. She knew the difference in their knocks even before she peeked through the viewer: Tony's was three soft, almost tentative, raps, while Bowers's was a rapid staccato hard enough to make her jump.

Bowers never said anything beyond the bare bones: was she okay, did she need anything? But Tony—Officer Hill, she reminded herself—would sometimes comment on the weather outside, or the music she was listening to. Once or twice he lingered to pet Gunther and didn't even seem to mind the cat hair clinging to his dark pants.

She was pathetically happy when Tony knocked on the door and asked to use the bathroom. She didn't know if she was just desperate for company, or if she was actually attracted to him, but she took a deep breath and took a chance.

"There are some steaks in the freezer. Are you allowed to come in for dinner?"

"We're not supposed to," Tony Hill said. "Regulations, you know—"

His eyes met her gaze and held it long enough that Cherry felt the heat rise to her cheeks. Then his smile finally reached the other side of his mouth and shone fully in his eyes.

"Oh, I'm sorry, I didn't realize—" How could she be so

stupid? Of course they weren't allowed to just come in and hang out like regular people. What had she been thinking?

"No, it's okay," he said quickly, sensing her embarrassment. He looked down at his feet and shifted his weight. "It's real nice of you to offer. Nobody's ever asked me to dinner on the job before."

"Do you—I mean, have you—worked a lot of assignments like this? Protecting people like me?"

Again that slow, almost lazy smile.

"Naw," he admitted. "You're my first . . ."

He stopped, and this time it was his face that flushed with heat. She brought a hand to her mouth, but not in time to stop the nervous giggle from popping out.

"That didn't come out right," he said sheepishly.

"It's okay," she said. "But I could make some sandwiches and bring them out to you . . . Is that allowed?"

"Sure, I guess so. Be a whole lot better than the bag of pretzels I was gonna eat. Thanks a lot, Miss Gavin."

"Call me Cherry, please. If that's allowed, I mean."

He smiled again, and her heart fluttered.

"I reckon that can be our little secret," he said. And he winked.

She shut the door but kept her eye pressed to the viewer and watched as he walked back to the cruiser. Nice butt, she thought, then giggled as she realized that for five whole minutes, she had forgotten to be afraid.

Then Gunther came zooming into the room, past her feet, and out again in a furry blur. She jumped.

"Damn it, Gunther! You scared the bejesus out of me! Stop doing that!"

She went to the kitchen and opened the fridge. Marla had brought by enough food for an army the day before, including a smorgasbord of cold cuts and cheeses from Whole Foods. It must be nice, she thought, to have enough money to be able to shop at a place like that. She would make Tony the most awesome sandwich ever. And one for Officer Bowers, too, of course.

Having the police outside helped, but in a way, also made it worse. It made what was happening more real, somehow.

When she'd heard about Roger's murder, she had never dreamed it could possibly be connected to what had happened—what was still happening—to her. Even when the collar arrived with the newspaper clipping, she had wanted to believe Marla's reassurances: that it was merely a gruesome coincidence. She kept telling herself to stop being paranoid, that the whole world did not revolve around her and her problems. Things like this just didn't happen.

But now Kitty and Lady Cassandra—and Randy, someone she'd never even met—were dead, too. The detectives seemed to think Kerberos might be the one who'd killed them.

Not merely killed them. Beaten them to death. Butchered them.

Thinking of Kitty made her want to throw up. She hadn't even gone to Kitty's funeral. She knew Kitty's parents and would have been welcome—though, of course, Kitty's parents had no idea what their daughter had been into, and Cherry would have had to be careful to refer to her as Robyn, not Kitty. She had just been too afraid to go.

She had thought the rape and beating was the worst thing that could happen to her. Now she realized there was far worse lurking out there, maybe even looking for her right now.

Her nightmares had escalated. She hadn't thought that was possible. But before they had all been about the hotel room, in terrible detail: the feel of the carpet beneath her knees and the faint taste of shoe polish on her tongue as she licked Kerberos's shoe, just before that first explosive shock to her backside. Pain radiating everywhere, and the blows that just kept falling no matter how she twisted and begged. Feeling the hair pull from her scalp as he dragged her across the floor . . .

He had raped her anally, too; that was something she hadn't told the detectives, because she didn't see how it could possibly matter now. That had been the worst pain she'd ever known. Like being torn in two—no, worse, being *certain* that you were being torn in two, because surely nothing else could hurt so badly. Worse even than the blows to her face that made a static haze of stars dance across her darkening vision.

That was always how those dreams had ended: feeling the impossible hardness forcing its way into her body, tearing her flesh, making her scream even louder but to no avail because of the gag in her mouth, and the way he simply pushed her face into the pillows on the bed until she could barely breathe.

Now the dreams still held bits of the rape and the beating, but they were also full of things she couldn't quite remember, and somehow that scared her more. The only images she retained upon waking were blood that was dark and red; the flash of a knife; snapshots of familiar faces distorted and blurred; the sound of screams that were not her own.

She finished the sandwiches—four of them, just to be sure—and cut them into neat diagonals. She placed them on paper plates, added a couple of pickle spears and plenty of napkins, and loaded it all onto a silver tray she'd found in the cupboard.

She'd intended to take the tray right to the car, but as soon as she stepped onto the porch, she froze. It was so dark out there, even with the porch light and two security lights mounted on the side of the house, even with the light from the pole at the end of the driveway . . . She couldn't move. She just stood there. Even the moon was out tonight, full and bloated with light . . . but darkness was all she could see. Anything could be in that darkness.

By the time Officer Hill reached her, tears were rolling down her cheeks.

"Are you all right?" He took the tray from her, peering into her downcast face. "It's okay, Cherry. I'm right here."

"I'm sorry, I'm so stupid," she said shakily. "I just couldn't . . . I just—"

"You're not stupid," he said softly. "You're just scared. No one can blame you for that. It's all right."

She wiped at her eyes with the back of her hand and managed a weak laugh.

"I hope I didn't get your sandwich all soggy. Or that you're not a vegetarian. You're not, are you? I didn't even think about that—"

"I am *not* a vegetarian," he said as if he found the idea appalling. "And Joe will eat anything that doesn't eat him first."

She hiccupped a laugh and wished she could crawl into his arms. That would be the nicest thing in the world. Having safe arms to crawl into.

But she couldn't have done that, even if he wasn't holding a tray of sandwiches. Instead, she did the only thing she could do: she opened the screen door and stepped back inside as he thanked her again.

After she cleaned up the mess in the kitchen, she curled up on the sofa with her laptop. It had been a godsend, the only thing that kept her from going completely out of her mind. The lake house had no computer, but it was equipped with Wi-Fi, thank God. She spent a lot of time playing Mahjong, Bejeweled, Blitz, and Farm Town. The games were mindless, numbing, and comforting, full of small, defined tasks in an environment she could control.

She debated with herself, then logged onto FetLife.

She wanted to know what was going on in the world of people who could sleep a whole night through. She wanted to know what her friends in the community were up to, but the local group on FetLife was nothing but talk about the killings.

They rehashed the news and argued about what it meant. Someone was stalking the community; others said it was pure coincidence. Some argued that parties and munches should be canceled until the killer was caught; others refused to go into hiding from a rumored threat.

She even saw a post from someone named LadyG2U:

> The police are investigating the murders of four people with ties to this community. At this time, we are specifically looking for any information on a white male using the screen name KERBEROS on Collarme.com. If you have any information, please contact me privately. All information will be handled confidentially.
>
> At this time, we are urging you not to meet with anyone you do not know and trust absolutely. Please, go about your normal routines, but be alert, and aware of your surroundings. Report any suspicious activities or incidents . . .

She had to read it twice before she realized LadyG2U was the woman who'd been with the two detectives. Cherry had thought she was a detective, too.

LadyG2U's thread was filled with comments, some from people she knew:

> What are you doing to protect us?
> Why should we trust you?
> Do you know why they were killed?
> Whoever killed Lady Cassandra should get a
> medal—

She clicked off the thread. She didn't want to read any more.

Her incoming box on FetLife showed two messages waiting.

The first was from Dante:

> I don't know if you're still online, but those detectives were here asking questions, and they told me what you were going through. Don't worry, they didn't share this information with anyone else and neither will we.
>
> I just wanted you to know that Kat and I are here if you need us, and we're lighting a candle for you. Blessed be.

She felt the pressure of tears behind her eyes. She didn't know Dante and his wife that well, so their kindness touched her even more.

There were so many kind and wonderful people out there, and she needed to remember that. Kerberos was just one really rotten apple.

The second message was from a name she didn't recognize: Theonly14U.

> You've been a bad girl. I asked you to do something but you haven't. And you aren't wearing the collar I sent you.

"Oh, God," she moaned aloud.

She had deleted her Collarme.com and Alt.com pro-files, but had kept the FetLife because Kerberos had never contacted her there; he didn't even know the name she used on FetLife: *lillamb99.*

Her FetLife account had never had a recognizable photo—just a picture of her wrists, bound behind her back, that Paul had taken. She hadn't even listed an age, or a specific city location, just the state.

So how had he found her here?

Oh, shit. You idiot! Marla told you to stay off the computer and to get rid of all your profiles!

Then the meaning of the message hit her, and she felt lightheaded.

You aren't wearing the collar I sent you . . .

He was watching her.

Chapter 26

Lust's passion will be served;
it demands, it militates, it tyrannizes.
—MARQUIS DE SADE

The scene was beginning to feel a little too familiar. The surroundings were different, sure, and at least he wasn't stepping in dog shit this time. But the blood and the body looked pretty much the same.

Except that he'd seen this body alive less than forty-eight hours ago.

Quinn Lee didn't piss him off nearly so much this time. It was hard to hate a man missing a tongue and part of his penis.

"The woman who found him rolled him over," Miles said, looking up. "He was on his stomach."

"She thought he was still alive?" Griggs asked. "Talk about optimism. Where is she?"

"Paramedics took her to County. She's in serious shock."

"Shit," Hanson said. "Poor Maggie."

Poor Maggie, indeed. Hanson couldn't feel anything but the most distant pity for Quinn Lee now—and, just perhaps, the smallest flicker of satisfaction tinged with relief—but he did feel sorry for Maggie. He supposed she must have loved Quinn, even if in the same complicated way Gina had. Maybe Quinn's death was actually a lucky thing for Maggie; she would be spared the disillusionment that still lingered in Gina's system like a toxin.

"TOD?" Griggs asked. "Best guess?"

"Sometime between midnight and three a.m.," Miles said.

"What kind of photography studio is this, anyway?" Fortner was holding up a used condom with a pair of tweezers. "I've got three of these in the wastebasket."

"All fresh?" Griggs grinned down at Quinn's body. "Dude, you the man! Or I should say, you *were* the man . . ."

"Do you want me to test this stuff?" Fortner asked, staring in dismay at the assortment of sex toys and BDSM paraphernalia they found in one of the equipment cases. "All of it?"

"What in the hell do you do with this?" Griggs wanted to know, gingerly lifting a metal instrument with two gloved fingers.

"That's a speculum," Fortner offered. "A gynecologist uses it to open the vagina for—"

"Okay, okay!" Griggs dropped the speculum back into the open case. "Don't really wanna know."

"Yeah, sorry," Hanson told Fortner. "But you can skip that one."

Fortner was holding the tire thumper, still wrapped up inside the evidence bag it had been returned in.

"Gee, thanks, Hanson," Fortner snorted.

Hanson's cell phone began to vibrate. He fished it from his pocket and flipped it open.

"Yeah?"

"Where are you?" It was Gina, and Hanson's heart sank. How did he tell her Quinn was their latest victim? How would she even feel about it?

"Um . . . I'm kinda in the middle of something right now. What's up?"

"I got a call from Cherry. She got another e-mail last night."

"She okay?" He stared at Quinn's half-open eyes. The stupid little goatee was clotted with blood.

"She's upset, but she's okay. She wants me to come over, but since I'm not actually on the job, I thought you should come with me."

"Uh-huh." Hanson watched as Griggs went through Quinn's pockets: a couple of wadded receipts, some change, and breath mints . . .

Wallet? He mouthed at Griggs.

Griggs nodded.

Phone? He mouthed again.

Griggs shook his head.

"Are you listening?" Gina asked in his ear. "You sound funny."

Hanson sighed. He had never been any good at lying to Gina.

"I'm at Quinn Lee's studio. Maggie found him dead this morning."

Silence on the other end.

"Gee? You there?"

"Yeah. I'm here." A pause. "I'll wait for you in the morgue."

He didn't know what he expected from Gina. Hell, how was somebody supposed to react when an old lover was murdered?

He was relieved that she didn't come out to the scene. But once Miles had the body cleaned up and on the table, she insisted on being there for the autopsy.

"It's funny, isn't it?" she asked softly.

"What?"

"How empty they look. Somehow that's worse than the rest. That feeling that nobody's home."

Suddenly he felt a tickle along his spine. He'd seen lots of bodies, but now he tried to imagine looking at one so brutalized and remembering what it was like to hold *that* hand, to caress *those* shoulders . . . to kiss *that* mouth. To look into the eyes that you had gazed into a million times, only to see nothing at all looking back at you.

They said the body was merely a shell, but it wasn't, Hanson thought. It was the thing you held on to.

He took Gina's hand—shielded by the table, where Miles wouldn't see—and squeezed. She squeezed back, but did not look at him.

"Same weapon?" he asked Miles. "Just like the others?"

"It appears that way," Miles said shortly. "Something hinky about this one, though."

"Hinky?" Gina asked, suddenly alert.

"I don't know." Miles shrugged. "I could be completely off base, but it seems like there's more damage to the face, and look here—"

Miles pulled back the sheet to expose Quinn's groin.

"Not so many cuts to the penis," Miles concluded. "Or the rest of the body."

"More bashing, less cutting?" Griggs asked.

Miles nodded.

"Maybe Quinn struggled more than the others?" Hanson suggested.

"Maybe the perp was interrupted," Griggs offered. "Or he got spooked."

Gina bolted out the door with a hand over her mouth.

Gina spent a long time in the ladies' room, but when she came out, she was dry-eyed and professional.

"Autopsy finished?" she asked. "Anything new?"

Hanson nodded. She wasn't looking him in the eye, so he decided not to piss her off by asking if she was okay.

"Pretty much the same as the others," Griggs said. "Blood loss and BFT. Except that Miles thinks most of the cuts were postmortem."

Gina glanced at him with her eyebrows raised.

"We didn't find as much blood at this scene as the others." Griggs shrugged. "He died quick, lucky bastard."

"Maybe it was accidental," Gina said.

"You mean the perp lost control, killed him sooner than he meant to?" Griggs asked.

"It's possible," she said. "Could explain the lack of as many cuts. Maybe it wasn't as much fun for the perp once the victim was dead."

For a moment, none of them spoke. Then Hanson remembered there was work to be done.

"We need to go talk to Maggie. She's over at County."

"I tried to see if he was still alive," Maggie said. "I thought he could still be alive."

Maggie's voice was small and tight, but calm. They had given her a mild sedative after they'd gotten her blood pressure stabilized.

"Did Quinn use the studio a lot at night?" Hanson asked.

"It was his studio," she said hollowly. "He worked all kinds of hours."

"You sure it was just work?" Griggs said. "He use those eyebolts in the ceiling for . . . what? Hanging cameras?"

"He played there, too."

"With you?" Hanson asked.

"With me. With others."

"What time did you find him?" Hanson knew when she had called 911 and wanted to see if she slipped up with any unaccounted-for time.

"A little after seven, I think. I was in a rush because I knew I had to get the store open and there was an accident on I-440—"

"Hold on." Hanson held up a hand. "I thought you lived upstairs with Quinn?"

"I do." She closed her eyes and rubbed her forehead.

"But on Sunday nights I take my momma to church, and last night I just stayed over."

"Is this something you do a lot? Spend a night away?"

"Yes." She sighed and looked away. "Especially when he's got a date."

"A date?" Griggs asked, his eyebrows rising.

"Quinn is polyamorous," she said, tilting her chin defiantly. "That means accepting other lovers. It's all out in the open. No lies, no cheating."

Griggs grunted, and Hanson shot him a warning look.

"So you stayed away last night because you knew he had a date?"

"You agreed to this stuff?" Griggs shook his head. "Seriously?"

"Yes, I did," Maggie said sullenly. "You can love more than one person at a time. Quinn needed other partners, and I wanted him to be happy. But I spent the night at my mom's 'cause it's easier than sitting upstairs listening to him fuck somebody else. There, I said it, are you happy now?"

"I understand about poly," Gina said gently. "It's not easy, especially if you don't choose it. You had to accept it if you wanted to be with him."

Maggie didn't speak.

"You also didn't want to be there," Gina continued, "because sometimes he'd insist on bringing his other lovers to bed with him . . . and you."

Maggie nodded and brushed away a tear.

"Yeah, you know Quinn, all right." She laughed bitterly. "I'm supposed to be polyamorous, too, but I never wanted anybody but him.

"He was always pushing me to go out with other people. Sometimes I'd lie to him, say I had a date, just to make him feel better."

"Do you know who his date was with?" Hanson asked.

Maggie shook her head.

"Sometimes he tells me." Her fingers plucked at the edge of the blanket. "Sometimes he doesn't. I don't ask because I don't always want to know."

"Do you have any ideas about who it could have been?"

"No, except that it was probably some fresh meat." She sighed. "If it was somebody I already knew about, he would have said."

Gina's phone rang "Superfreak." She grabbed it from her hip and cut it off in mid-verse. She didn't look at it.

"Check his phone," Maggie said with another brittle little laugh. "He was always messaging or texting somebody."

Hanson glanced at Griggs.

"We didn't find his phone. Could he have left it upstairs?"

"No," Maggie said. "He couldn't live without the damned thing. He took it to the bathroom with him."

Chapter 27

Who though he existed in the form of God
did not regard equality with God
as something to be grasped,
but emptied himself
by taking on the form of a slave
by looking like other men,
and by sharing in human nature
He humbled himself,
by becoming obedient to the point of death
—even death on a cross!

—PHLLIPIANS 2:6

"You said Cherry called you?" Hanson asked Gina. "She got another e-mail from Kerberos?"

"She probably just needs some hand-holding, but I thought I'd go over there."

"You two do that," Griggs said gloomily. Hanson knew he got this way when a case dragged on with no new leads. "I'm gonna go talk to a couple of witnesses again. See if this maintenance guy rings any bells."

Hanson and Gina stopped by the tech department, where someone explained the situation with Kerberos's e-mails. The news wasn't good.

"I should have just taken her laptop away from her," Hanson said to Gina as he started the car.

"We made a copy of her hard drive. We didn't *need* the laptop."

"Well, we should have been monitoring her accounts."

"We still don't know that this is even related to our case. He could be just an asshole stalker. There are a lot more of those than there are serial killers."

"I don't like it." Hanson shook his head. "All these people around Cherry turning up dead? It's a hell of a coincidence."

He was afraid to ask, but he did it anyway.

"How are you doing?"

"Don't ask right now," she said, her lips tightening. "We've got work to do."

"All right. We gotta assume the killer took Quinn's phone. Either he knows there's something on it, or he thinks there might be."

"Or he just wanted an iPhone," Gina said.

"Quinn was straight, right?"

"Yeah. I mean, he would beat anyone, but sex?" Gina shook her head. "No, he didn't like any dick but his own."

"We found condoms in the trash. He was having sex with somebody last night. Either he had a date, the date left, and the killer got to him after, or . . ."

"Or the date was the killer." She shrugged. "It's possible."

"Possible, but not likely."

"Because a sweet little ol' girl just isn't strong enough?" Gina said in an exaggerated, sugarcoated accent. "Is that what you mean?"

"Don't bust my balls. Some women may have the strength, but women in general just don't kill this way."

"No, women use poison or guns," she said, staring out the window. "Or drive their kids into the lake in their minivans."

"Maybe we'll get lucky with the condoms. Otherwise we're gonna have to interview half the city to find whoever he fucked that night."

Cherry met them at the door in a T-shirt that looked as if she'd been wearing it for days.

"How could he have found my profile on Fet?" Cherry

cried, pacing the living room. "I haven't posted anything or sent e-mail to anybody—"

"Take it easy," Hanson told her.

"Just about everybody has multiple profiles," Gina said. "It wouldn't take a genius to guess you had a profile on FetLife, too."

"Who *did* know about your FetLife account?" Hanson asked.

"Well . . . just my friends. I mean, the ones I know in real time. I don't use Fet for hookups or anything."

"But you would have been listed as a friend on Kitty's page?"

Cherry collapsed on the sofa and hugged a cushion to her chest.

"Oh, God, I'm so stupid!"

Hanson watched over Gina's shoulder as she clicked the screen on Cherry's laptop. She brought up Cherry's profile—lillamb99—and clicked on the *Friends* link.

A page full of names—some with photos, some with icons—came up on the screen.

"There they are," Gina said. "If he found Kitty, Paul, or Roger—or all three—he could have cross-referenced the friends listed on their profile pages."

One of the photos caught Hanson's eye: *Jason, 21 M Slave.*

The buff boy with the piercings.

Gina clicked back to lillamb99's profile.

"He may have sent the same message to every one of their friends," Gina added. "In that case, he still has no idea which profile is yours."

"But he's been watching me! He knew I wasn't wearing his collar!"

Hanson wanted to shake her again, then remembered she was too scared to think straight.

"Come on, Cherry," Gina said. "Do you really think he expected you to?"

"Yes! He's that crazy! You didn't see the way he talked to me after—after. But you read the e-mails he sent! He thinks I belong to him!"

"I don't think he's watching you," Gina insisted. "He said that to scare you. He doesn't know where you are."

"Well, he did scare me!" Cherry's voice was becoming shrill. "Why haven't you found him yet? Can't you trace his e-mails or something?"

"We traced Kerberos's e-mail to a computer," Hanson said. "The problem is that we can't find the computer."

"How is that possible?" Cherry demanded.

"Tracing an e-mail only gives you the IP address it was sent from. His e-mails came from wireless Internet sites all over the city."

"Can't you find anything out from those?" Cherry deflated, looking like a bewildered child.

"He's been using Wi-Fi from places like Starbucks, McDonald's. Places where anybody can just walk in and use their laptop. We are checking security tapes to see if we spot anyone suspicious."

Gina glanced at Hanson over Cherry's head and Hanson shrugged. There was no use scaring her more by telling her just how long a shot it was that they would find anything.

One of the IP addresses belonged to a seventy-year-old retired schoolteacher. Kerberos had simply piggybacked onto her connection, just as he had several others.

They had people checking those neighborhoods, in case he lived nearby. But the locations were scattered all over. It seemed he was just driving around town, looking for access that couldn't be traced back to him. Smart bastard.

Cherry buried her face in her hands and said nothing.

"You said he seemed intelligent," Gina said. "Did he

ever say anything that might make you think he worked
with computers?"

Cherry sighed and raised her head.

"He told me how to get rid of cookies on my computer. I was complaining about the spam—"

"Give me your computer," Hanson said.

"You can't!" Cherry protested, beginning to cry. "I'm
completely cut off from everybody and everything!"

"Look, we don't know how smart he is," Hanson explained. "The last thing we want is him tracing you *here*."

Hanson and Gina got back in the car, where it had to
be at least 100 degrees.

"Was that really necessary?" Gina asked. "Taking her
laptop?"

"We know he's at least computer literate, and smart
enough to realize using Wi-Fi would be a dead-end to
anyone trying to trace him. It's safer just to remove any
temptation that she'll get back online and do something
stupid."

"So what now? Go verify Maggie's alibi for last night?"

"I'm gonna get Brigham or Mercer to run that down,"
Hanson said, rubbing his eyes. "I'm starving and you look
exhausted."

She didn't argue.

When Griggs called, Hanson told him to meet them at
a nearby twenty-four-hour chain restaurant where everything was sticky with maple syrup and grease.

"I hate this fuckin' place," he grumbled, sliding into the
booth beside Gina and lifting a French fry from her plate.

Gina didn't try to stab him with her fork. She'd hardly
touched her plate. Hanson wondered if she was more than
just tired and discouraged. If she was grieving, he could
forgive her that. Quinn was dead, after all.

Then he noticed that Griggs was grinning around a
mouthful of food.

"You found something?"

"I went to talk to the garage attendant who found Roger," he said, then looked up at the waitress who'd come to the table. "Coffee, black. Steak and eggs, well done. Hash browns, scrambled and smothered."

"Antone?"

"Antone doesn't remember seeing any kind of mainte-nance guy, but he *does* remember seeing a white van with the name of some kind of air-conditioning service on it."

"We didn't see that on any of the tapes."

"That's because the van wasn't in the garage," Griggs said, stealing another fry. "Van was on the street. Antone saw it pulling away from the curb when he drove into the garage."

Was it possible they'd gotten a real break? Hanson glanced at Gina, who still said nothing.

"Now, he don't remember the name of the company. Just that it said 'air-conditioning repair.' Said it looked pretty crappy, like the company wasn't doing too good."

"Maybe it's out-of-business," Gina said, staring out the window at nothing. "Our guy coulda picked it up used."

"Did Antone get a look at the driver?"

"All he saw was a baseball cap."

Hanson tried to resist that little surge of excitement a cop always gets when something finally shakes loose. It could still be nothing. There must be dozens of beat-up HVAC vans being driven by guys with baseball caps in the city. But only one had been in the right place at the right time.

Then Hanson remembered the van idling on the street in front of the Inferno.

Thank God, it had been black.

But he still didn't like it.

He liked it even less when he drove Gina back to her place.

"Fuck!" she said as soon as she opened the door.

The place was a shambles. Books had been pulled from shelves, furniture overturned, and the big ginger jar lamp shattered on the floor.

"Shit, shit, shit!" Gina stepped over more broken glass to right a chair. "Goddamn it!"

"Don't touch anything—"

"For Christ's sake, Hanson! My fingerprints are already everywhere."

"We still need to get CSU out here."

She put her hands to her face, looking around through splayed fingers.

"Probably just a burglary," Hanson said, rubbing her shoulders. He wasn't sure he believed that, but what else could he say? "I'll call. You see if anything's missing."

The techs dusted and photographed, while a uniform took down Gina's statement.

It took a while for Gina to realize what was missing.

"My iPod's gone, goddamn it!"

"You got insurance, right?"

"Insurance isn't going to give me back all the music that was on it! Fuck!"

There had been a twenty-dollar bill on top of her dresser; it was gone, and so were the contents of her jewelry box.

"All they got was the cheap shit I wear every day," Gina said, running her hands through her hair. "I keep the real stuff in the gun safe, and it hasn't been opened."

"You check the medicine cabinet? Sometimes junkies and teenagers break in just looking for drugs."

The back door had been clumsily jimmied open. Hanson tried not to think of Cassandra's back door, or the door to Robyn's motel room.

"Everything's still there," Gina called from the bathroom. "Even a half-full bottle of hydrocodone. No self-respecting druggie would have left that."

"So it was probably some kids," Hanson said. "They grabbed what they could stuff in their pockets."

"I'm still pissed about my iPod. And they broke my favorite mug, damn it."

When the crew finally left, Gina sat on the edge of the sofa, her head in her hands.

"You've had a really shitty day. I'm sorry."

"Now I've got to get that damned fingerprint powder off of everything."

"Why don't we just leave all this here for tonight. You come back to my place."

She looked up and Hanson saw her getting ready to argue. Maybe she was thinking about Quinn, needing to grieve for him in private.

"We're both exhausted," she said, brushing the hair from her face. "And I have another appointment early in the morning."

He'd been right about her absence that morning. She'd had a session with a paying client.

"Early morning is a popular playtime?" he asked, trying to keep his voice light.

"For this particular client, yes." She got to her feet and went over to her desk, picking up scattered mail, bills and such. "It's the only time he can squeeze our sessions into his schedule."

"But this is a regular client, right?"

"Yeah. Why?"

"You know him real well? You trust him?"

"What are you getting at?" That annoyed line showed between her eyebrows.

"Has it occurred to you that you might be on the killer's list? I mean, shit, Gee—"

She smiled. She was too goddamned cocky for her own good, he thought.

"Get serious, Gee! Someone is killing your kinky friends and now somebody's broken into your house."

"You really think there's a connection?"

"I dunno," he said. "But I don't like it."

She said nothing for a moment.

"You're overreacting. I don't think . . ."

She stopped, looked at the papers in her hands, and then dropped them. She pawed through the other stuff on the desktop.

"What?"

She said nothing for a moment, then looked at him oddly.

"My day-planner is missing. Why would anyone take my day-planner? There's nothing in there . . ."

"Nothing," he said, "except your schedule."

In the end, he helped her clean up, and they fell into bed sometime after two a.m. The issue of sex never even came up, because both were out almost as soon as their heads hit the pillow.

He didn't mind. He hoped God would forgive him for being just a little bit happy about the break-in. He had been afraid she would send him home, alone and aching, to his empty bed.

It was frightening how quickly he had gotten used to having her back in his life, and he would have contentedly slept at the foot of her bed if she said that's where he belonged.

Chapter 28

The end is the beginning of all things,
Suppressed and hidden,
Awaiting to be released through the rhythm
Of pain and pleasure.

— JIDDU KRISHNAMURTI

"Your clients don't come here, do they?"

"No. I keep a separate place." Gina spooned up Special K and crunched. "It's easier that way."

"Safer, too."

"Yeah, that's true"—she shrugged—"but mainly I worry about drunks banging on the door at three in the morning. I've never had any real problems, just minor annoyances."

"Like when they call you twenty times a day?"

"Hey." She laughed. "Not *all* those calls are from him."

Hanson wanted to ask who "he" was—badly—but knew he shouldn't.

"So where *does* a hip young professional dominatrix keep a dungeon these days?" he asked instead, using humor to cover his discomfort.

"I have a studio loft in an old warehouse. It's low-rent, mostly a lot of artists and musicians."

"And nobody knows what you do there?"

She shrugged and carried the empty bowls to the sink.

"I don't think anybody cares."

"I really don't think you should go alone," he said, trying to sound like the very soul of reason.

"I may not carry a badge anymore, but I still carry a gun and I'm still a damned good shot."

"You can't always count on a gun to protect you."

"Then I'll have to rely on my good looks and kick-box-ing skills."

He followed her anyway. If she spotted him tailing her, she didn't try to shake him. Hanson wondered what the starving artists and musicians made of her shiny BMW parked in front of the run-down building.

Hanson watched her go in. He sat there for a good five minutes, wondering if he should stay. Someone had stolen her day-planner, for Christ's sake. What little crap they had pocketed could be just a smoke screen for their real prize.

Horses, Hanson, he told himself. *Horses, not zebras. You're just being paranoid.*

He put the car in drive and headed for the office.

Griggs was already at his desk with a donut and huge cup of over-priced coffee.

"What? No donut for me?"

"Nah. I don't bring extra donuts for guys getting pre-mium ass while I'm jerking the chicken all by my lone-some."

He told Griggs about the break-in at Gina's.

"You think we oughta put some guys on her?"

"She'd kill you and me both. What about your theory that she's the perp?"

"Well, you gotta admit, she's got motive," Griggs an-swered. "At least for Cassandra and Quinn—"

"Oh, come on—"

"But we got a solid lead now, and it was always a long-shot that Gee was involved."

"Nice that you admit it," Hanson grunted.

"You think it could be our guy?"

"I don't know. I don't like it. I'm hoping CSU found some prints."

Hanson sat down and shuffled through reports, looking for the final on Quinn's autopsy.

"It ain't in yet," Griggs said, reading his mind. "Miles got pretty pissy when I asked him ten minutes ago."

They had preliminary results, but the final report might take days to be finished, waiting for final blood tests and such, before it was transcribed and signed-off on. There really wasn't much else the final report would tell them, but harassing Miles was a favorite pastime.

The lieutenant appeared in the door of his office. He glared at them.

"Shouldn't you two be out doing some kind of police work or something?"

"I was just about to call the DMV," Hanson explained. "We're looking for a white van that was seen in the area, maybe registered to a service company of some kind—"

"I'll get some rookie to do that," the lieutenant said. "Get out of here so I can tell Daubs I haven't seen you."

"Thanks." Hanson stood quickly and grabbed his jacket.

"Don't thank me," the lieutenant said. "The sound of that bastard's voice gives me a migraine, and I don't need that shit this morning."

"Come on," Hanson said to Griggs. "Let's go back to the Madison and see if we can find out anything about our mystery repairman."

The day was heating up, and the air conditioner in the car didn't seem to be blowing any cool air.

"You oughta get that fixed," Griggs said. He drained the last of his giant coffee and threw the cup into the backseat.

"Do you have to be such a slob?"

"Yep. It's in my job description. Gina too good to go slumming with us today?"

"You're the one who keeps reminding me she's not a cop anymore."

"She's kinda growing on me. Like mold. And she *is* sexier than you."

The Madison was surprisingly busy for noon, but then they probably got a lot of lunch-hour quickies.

The motel manager, Mr. Patel, gave Hanson a blank look when he asked about a repairman.

"I do most of the work around here myself. If it is something I cannot fix, I will call someone, but I have not had anyone out in the last two months."

He didn't recall seeing anyone in dark blue coveralls, or a beat-up white van in the parking lot.

"I do not usually leave the office here," Patel said. "Many of our customers are not very nice people."

His wife and daughters had already cleaned the rooms on the morning of the murder, and spent the rest of that afternoon at the local mall.

They walked back across the broken asphalt of the parking lot to the car.

"I get the feeling that Daddy prefers they keep away from the guests," Hanson said. "Can't say that I'd want my teenage daughters wandering around here."

"Every time we talk to that guy, I wanna start talking like Gandhi."

Hanson's phone vibrated against his chest. He dug it out and looked at the incoming number.

"Shit," he groaned. "It's Daubs."

He flipped it open. Before he could even say hello, Daubs began to yell.

"Where the blazes *are* you? You're *supposed* to keep me informed *daily* on this case!"

"We're out working it, sir—"

He held the phone away from his ear while Daubs carried on with his usual administrative rant.

Griggs grinned and made yakking motions with his hand.

When Daubs paused, Hanson brought the phone back to his ear.

"Yes, sir . . . Yes, sir . . . I understand."

He flipped the phone shut and put it back in his inside pocket.

"Are we in for an ass-chewing?" Griggs asked.

"Bright and early tomorrow morning. . . .

"All we gotta do," he said with a grin, "is arrest somebody tonight. No problem."

Chapter 29

In matters of sexuality we are at present, every one of us,
ill or well, nothing but hypocrites.

—SIGMUND FREUD

Griggs didn't ask why they were parked in front of the
old warehouse. He didn't even bitch about turning
off the engine and the air conditioner.

The two of them watched as a young man came out of
the building and walked up the block. He turned the corner and passed out of their view.

"He look familiar to you?" Griggs asked.

"It's the kid we saw at the club."

It was Gina's admirer, the pretty boy toy with pierced
nipples. *Damn it.*

"Are you two spying on me, now?" Gina's voice star-
tled them both. She leaned into the open window, and she
did not look happy.

"Just watching out for you," Hanson muttered. "Sorry."

"You got a boy toy, Gee?" Griggs grinned.

"Shut up, Griggs."

"Was it him yesterday morning, too?" Hanson asked.
Damn it. The question just popped out, and her icy glare
told him she didn't care for it at all.

"Where are you going?" she asked.

"Back to Cassandra Lee's neighborhood."

"Why? I thought the uniforms already canvassed the
area?"

"Yeah, but there was no one home at the house directly

behind Cassandra's. Besides, we've got something specific to ask the neighbors now."

"You wanna come along, Gee?" Griggs asked.

She hesitated for a moment, then got in the backseat.

"Your car gonna be okay in this neighborhood?" Hanson asked.

"It'll be fine," Gina muttered. "Just like me. Stop worrying."

As it turned out, the resident of the house behind Cassandra's—Hal Grooms—had been at his doctor's that day. He was not happy to have missed all the commotion at the Lee house.

"I coulda told you some stuff about that woman! All those damned dogs. I couldn't even go out onto my back porch if they were out in the yard! I had to take out my hearing aid just to get a little peace and quiet.

"They weren't happy just tearing up her yard, oh no! The little devils kept trying to dig under the fence to get into *my* yard. Probably because they ran out of places to do their business. That woman never cleaned it up. Just let the doggy doo lie in the yard. When it rained, you could smell it from my back door. You'd think after thirty-four years driving a garbage truck, I'd have lost my sense of smell, but I just can't abide the stink of doggy doo."

"What about the neighbors on your street?" Hanson asked. "You see a lot of what goes on out in front of your house?"

" 'Course I do. I'm retired." Grooms kept stealing little glances at Gina, though he never spoke directly to her. Hanson wondered if he was reacting to her as a woman police officer, or just as a good-looking woman in his living room. "Ain't got much to do but sit here and watch the History Channel and what goes on outside that big window."

He complained about the "hoodlum kids" two houses

down; he was sure they were the ones who kept dumping over his trash cans. The woman next door was having an affair; they should take a look at the sleazy guy she had over there whenever her husband was on the road in his eighteen-wheeler.

"But did you see a white van or a guy in a maintenance suit in the neighborhood about two weeks ago?" Griggs asked impatiently.

"No, not a white van," Grooms grunted, not even pausing. "There was a black one, though."

The hairs on the back of Hanson's neck stood up.

"A black van?" Hanson repeated.

"I ain't color blind," Grooms grumbled. "I can tell the difference between black and white. Lousy paint job, too. Idiot had spray-painted the whole thing, like he was too stupid to know that ain't a proper way to paint a vehicle."

"Did you get a look at the license plate?" Griggs asked.

"I was going to. Moron was parked in front of my mailbox. Mailman won't stop if someone's blocking the box, too damned lazy to get out of his little truck—"

"I'm sure that's a great inconvenience," Hanson said, trying to pacify the old man. "So why didn't you—"

" 'Cause I'm an old man with an irritable bowel! When I come out of the john, the van was gone. And good riddance to it."

"Did you see who was driving it?"

"Nah. If I'd seen him, I'd have given him a piece of my mind, bowel movement be damned."

They listened to another round of Mr. Grooms's complaints and observations about his neighbors until they were sure he had nothing more of value to add. Hanson almost regretting leaving his card behind, sure that he'd be getting calls about trash cans and drug trafficking neighbors for months to come.

"A quickie paint job," Gina said as they walked back to

the car. "After the first two murders, he was getting worried someone might have seen him."

"Or he's just being careful," Griggs said. "If Grooms weren't such an asshole, we might never have made the connection."

"Let's hope the bastard doesn't decide to change vehicles completely," Gina said. "That van is the only real lead we've got."

Chapter 30

"Sex" is as important as eating or drinking and we
ought to allow the one appetite to be satisfied with as
little restraint or false modesty as the other.
—MARQUIS DE SADE

Hanson sent Griggs back to the office to deal with
changing the APB to a black van, while he and Gina
followed up on Quinn's late-night rendezvous. They might
not have Quinn's phone, but they did have the name and
number of his last coffee date.

"Stands to reason," Hanson said, "that the next step
would be a trip to his studio, right?"

"That's how he usually worked," Gina admitted.

Hanson had to hand it to her. Except for the occasional
puckering of her brow and a slightly sour twist to her lips,
Gina acted as if Quinn was just another case. She seemed
utterly unfazed by either Maggie or the woman who now
came scurrying into Starbucks like an amateur spy.

"Are you trying to ruin my life?" Angela Sabatta asked
in an urgent whisper as she leaned across the table. "What
do you want *now?*"

Her question was directed at Hanson, but it was Gina
who responded.

"Tell us about meeting Quinn Lee at his studio last Sunday night."

Her mouth fell open. She gaped at Gina, finally recov-
ering enough to bristle.

"How did you know about that? And who the hell are
you, anyway?"

"This is Ms. Larsen," Hanson said. "She's assisting the police in our investigation."

Hanson wanted to tell Angela that she'd attract less attention if she'd stop glancing around the place like a crack addict looking for a dealer.

"So, you were there?" Gina asked, stirring sugar into her coffee.

"Yes," she admitted sullenly. "It's not illegal, is it?"

"You didn't see it on the news?" Gina raised the cup to her lips and blew on it.

"See what?" Angela was annoyed. "I've been working twelve-hour shifts the last four days—"

"Quinn Lee was murdered."

Angela stared first at Hanson, then at Gina.

"Murdered?" She paled. "He was the one—"

"So you did hear about it?" Gina asked.

"I heard there was another murder, but I didn't realize— Oh, shit!"

Angela admitted that she'd gone to Quinn's studio at eight o'clock that night to "play."

"But that was it! We did *not* have sex—"

"Look," Hanson said. "We don't care whether you fucked him or not, but we've got three used condoms with your DNA on them. Don't bother lying."

They didn't actually know if it was Angela's DNA, but she didn't know that.

"It insults our intelligence," Gina said. "We don't like being insulted, Angela."

"All right, all right! We had sex. But I don't know what happened to him after I left, and I don't know who he was talking to on the phone—"

"He had a phone call?" Gina leaned forward, suddenly intent. "What did he say?"

Angela crossed her arms over her chest.

"I don't know," she whined, then glanced at the ceiling

as if trying to remember. "He said hello . . . Then nice to hear from you, or something like that."

Angela rolled her eyes.

"I figured it was some woman."

"What made you think that?" Hanson asked.

"Just the tone in his voice." Angela shrugged. "You know. All charming and shit."

"What else did he say?" Hanson asked.

"He said he would be there for a little while longer. Then he listened, then he said yes, and then he hung up."

"Did he say anything after he hung up?" Gina asked, staring into Angela's face. "Anything about who he was talking to?"

"No. I was in a hurry to get out of there. I had to be at work for my shift at eleven."

"All right," Hanson said. "If you think of anything else, call us."

Angela practically ran out of the coffee shop.

"Jesus," he said, swigging the last of his latte. "Is everybody cheating?"

"Most of my clients are married men. They feel they can't share that part of themselves with their wives. They're too embarrassed. Some women feel the same way. It's hard to admit to anyone that you want . . . what you want."

Hanson felt a prickle of guilt but swallowed it away. Had Gina gone to Quinn in the same way as Angela Sabatta? Yearning for things she was afraid to ask for? But she had asked him. And he hadn't been able to handle it.

He had to focus. He couldn't let his brain go down these side roads.

"Miles put Quinn's time of death between midnight and three a.m.," he said. "It's possible he's off by an hour, but I don't see Angela as a killer."

"She feels too guilty over her cheating," Gina said. "She

couldn't handle murder. She's gonna spill her guts to her husband by the weekend."

"So that still leaves us with a big question. Who the hell was he talking to?"

"It could be something totally unrelated. Quinn was always getting phone calls."

Again, there was that missed beat between them, both of them intensely aware that she spoke from experience.

"I don't know." Hanson picked up the crumpled sweetener packets and shoved them into his empty cup. "I wish we had his phone."

"Come on, Angela said he was talking to a woman. You already said women don't kill that way."

Hanson's phone began vibrating. He answered it.

"Hanson . . . Yeah? Shit. Okay. Be there in fifteen."

"What's up?" Gina asked.

"A break-in at the lake house."

"Where is she?" Hanson asked.

"She's in the patrol car, sir."

Hanson squinted at his badge. Officer Hill looked fresh out of the academy.

Then he turned and stared at the long wall that ran from the front door, past the kitchen, into the living room.

MINE was written in letters about a foot high, in what appeared to be blood.

"Surprisingly neat lettering," Gina commented. "Not exactly the usual Helter-Skelter penmanship."

"It's the cat's," the other uniform—Officer Bowers, older and rounder than his partner—explained. "The blood, I mean."

The cat was lying on the floor beneath the message.

Hanson hunkered down to get a better look.

"Looks like its throat was cut. Did anybody touch anything?"

Officer Hill looked uncomfortable.

"We came in first, you know, to check the house—"

"What do you mean, 'first'?" Hanson demanded. "She left the house?"

"She had a doctor's appointment," Officer Bowers said, hitching his belt up onto his hips. "She's under protection, not a prisoner."

Hanson sighed.

"We followed her downtown," Bowers continued. "Everything was fine until we got back here—"

Griggs appeared in the doorway.

"Shit!" He looked down at the matted lump of fur on the floor. "Goddamn it!"

"It's just a cat," Hanson reminded him.

"I happen to like cats more than I like most people," Griggs shot back. He looked down at the cat again. "Aw, what kind of fucker kills a poor little animal like this?"

"A sadistic sociopath," Gina murmured. "Did Cherry see this?"

"We told her to stay in the car, but she kept asking what was wrong—" Hill looked miserable.

"I told her it was just a break-in, that she shouldn't go in until the crime scene unit got here," Officer Bowers said. "But she insisted she had to find Gunther—"

"Gunther?" Hanson asked.

"The cat!" Officer Hill and Griggs shouted at him in unison.

"Man, you are one cold son of a bitch sometimes," Griggs said.

"Hanson's more of a dog person," Gina said, looking at Griggs.

"What you're telling me is that she came in here and picked up the damned cat. Am I right?"

"Yeah," Bowers admitted.

"But CSU is on the way, correct?"

Bowers nodded.

Hanson noticed the smears on Hill's uniform.

"Shit," Hanson groaned. "How did you get blood on you? Did you pick up the cat, too?"

"I had to get it away from her," Hill said, shamefaced. "She was hysterical! I thought we were gonna have to call an ambulance, you know, to give her something."

"You guys can explain it to Fortner. She's gonna be pissed that you contaminated the scene."

Hanson walked around the outside of the house. The back door had a window in it, and one of the panes was broken.

"Nothing else seems to be disturbed," Gina said, coming to stand beside him. "Just the door, the wall, and the cat."

From inside the house, Hanson could hear Fortner's voice.

"All I ask you people to do is protect the integrity of my crime scene. Is that too much to ask?"

They went back in and found Fortner putting Officer Hill's shirt into a brown paper sack.

"Nice abs," Gina said, winking at him.

The boy flushed pink.

Fortner threw a scrub top at him.

"That's sexual harassment," Griggs put in.

"Shut up, Griggs," Gina said.

"So what are we gonna do with her?" Hanson nodded his head in the direction of the patrol car out front.

"Cherry?" Gina shrugged. "We have to find someplace else to put her."

"Whatever you do," Fortner called over her shoulder, "I need her clothes!"

"Nazi," Griggs muttered.

"Moron," Fortner snorted.

Chapter 31

What I need is someone who will make me do what I can.
—RALPH WALDO EMERSON

Cherry's parents were in Spring Hill, which was only half an hour down I-65, but Cherry refused to go there.

"I can't tell them what's happening! They would be so disappointed in me! I just can't deal with that on top of everything else."

Finally they settled Cherry into Gina's place with two officers—Jamison and Silvy this time—parked out front.

Hanson was actually relieved. Protecting Cherry also meant Gina was protected, whether she wanted it or not.

"I'm really sorry about Gunther," Griggs told Cherry. "He was a good cat."

"Thank you." Cherry nodded, still dabbing at her eyes. "I just can't think why he had to hurt Gunther—Oh, God!"

She began sobbing again, and it was several minutes before they could pull the words from her.

"I just remembered!" she choked. "His last e-mail. He said I still hadn't done something he'd asked me to . . . When we first talked, I told him I had a cat, and he said he was allergic and Gunther would have to go—"

Hanson expected Gina would put the girl in the little guest room downstairs, but she led them upstairs to the master suite.

The bungalow's second story was just one room of slanted walls and a couple of dormer windows. But it was big enough for a small sofa as well as the usual bedroom furnishings, and it had a private bathroom.

Gina quickly stripped the bed, tossing the sheets soiled with her and Hanson's bodily fluids into the overflowing hamper. She motioned to Hanson.

"Get me the other sheets out of the closet behind you, will you?"

Cherry looked around the room, blinking swollen eyes. "But this is your room—I can't take your room!"

"I'm not home that much," Gina insisted, "and this will give you some privacy."

"Really, I can sleep on the sofa downstairs—"

"You'll have a bathroom to yourself," Gina continued, gathering up a handful of her own essentials—some underwear, a few toiletries, and a paperback from the night-stand. "And I think you'll feel safer up here."

Cherry stopped resisting and crawled gratefully between the fresh sheets.

"Get some sleep," Gina told her. "We'll be downstairs if you need us."

"So where are we going to sleep?" Hanson whispered as he followed Gina back down the stairs.

"I'll be sleeping in the guest room," she said. "You'll be sleeping at your place."

She must have heard his sigh, for she turned and pressed against him, kissing him hard on the mouth.

"Maybe some forced celibacy will do you good," she said. "But there will be no more hot sex for us for a while, not here at least, not with a witness upstairs and uniforms outside."

Hanson didn't like it, but he thought a few cold showers were a small price to pay for keeping Gina safe.

When they reached the bottom step and turned the

corner into the living room, Griggs was just flicking his cell phone shut.

"They found it."

"The van?" Gina asked, instantly alert.

"Yeah, the van," Griggs said. "Come on—No, not you, Gee. You ain't going this time—"

"The hell I'm not!"

"No, you're not," Hanson said, pushing past her out the door. "Don't be stupid, Gee—"

Griggs was already starting the engine, and Hanson had to physically block her as he opened the passenger-side door.

"You don't have a badge," he told her. "If we do catch this guy, I can't let you fuck it up with some half-assed citizen's arrest! You know I'm right."

"Goddamn it!" She stepped back from the car, but her eyes were blazing. She slammed her fist on the hood before stalking away, still swearing.

"She's pissed," Griggs said, pulling away from the curb. "You ain't getting none tonight."

"She can be pissed all she wants, but she knows we can't risk taking her along on this one. There's no way I could trust her to just stay out of the way and let us handle it."

"Yeah, she runs faster than either of us," Griggs said, just as the radio crackled to life. "A patrol car spotted the van crossing Division Street on Twenty-first. Talk to them—"

Hanson snatched up the radio and identified himself.

"Don't stop him yet, don't approach in any way, understood?"

"Um, well, sir," came a hesitant voice on the other end. "We already got the van, but . . ."

"Aw, shit," Hanson groaned.

Griggs turned the car onto Twenty-first and they both saw it at the same time.

Grooms had been right: it was a crappy paint job. The

van was sitting in a fast-food parking lot, with two un-happy uniforms standing beside it.

"You were supposed to wait 'til we got here," Griggs yelled, exploding from the driver's seat. "What the fuck?"

Hanson's stomach sank into his shoes.

"We didn't do anything," the shorter of the two said de-fensively. "We were staying a couple of cars back, and sud-denly he turned into the lot, parked it, and walked away."

By the time they'd gotten through the crawling traffic, there'd been no sign of him.

"Shit, shit, shit!" Griggs was shouting.

"Come on," Hanson said to him. "We don't know for sure this was our guy."

"It was him, damn it!" Griggs snapped. He gestured at the van. "Look at this piece of crap. You can still make out 'repair' under the paint on this side. You think there are two like this in Metro?"

"You think he saw you?" Hanson asked the patrol cops.

"I don't know," the taller uni said, shaking his head. "We saw him just park, easy as pie, and walk away. He looked like he had someplace to go, yeah, but he wasn't running."

"You forgot about the bag," the other uni said.

"What bag?" Hanson demanded.

"He was carrying a duffel bag when he got out," the tall one said.

"Shit." Hanson groaned again, and his hands ran through his hair in sheer frustration. The evidence they needed was probably in that bag.

"What'd he look like?" Griggs demanded. He jerked his thumb at the restaurant. "You check inside?"

The driver had been of average—damn that word!—build, wearing a dark blue baseball cap, jeans, and a not-quite-white T-shirt with some kind of logo or picture on

the front. Caucasian and clean-shaven, they said, but neither had gotten a good look at his face or hair.

The four of them spread out, checking the restaurant
and the alley behind it, but there were so many businesses
and restaurants jammed into this block of Twenty-first
Avenue, their suspect could have slipped away without
even trying.

"Maybe we should leave it here," Hanson said, coming
back to the van. "Maybe he just happened to be going
someplace, and he'll come back——"

"Yeah," Griggs snarled, coming up in the other direction and peering into the van's open window. "That's why
he left the keys in the ignition, along with a vanilla milk
shake and a half-eaten Big Mac in the passenger seat——"

They called in backup, and sent twelve uniforms out in
a four-block radius looking for anybody that fit their too-
vague description.

"Fuckin' waste of time," Griggs grumbled. "We had
him! We fuckin' had him and we lost him!"

"Let's tow it in." Hanson sighed, staring at the van's in-
terior. "Maybe we'll get something off it."

Chapter 32

Many men are deeply moved by the mere semblance of
suffering in a woman; they take the look of pain for a
sign of constancy or of love.

—HONORÉ DE BALZAC

The van, now sitting in the impound lot, was registered
in the name of Barnard Wesley.

"Looks like we're driving to Chattanooga," Hanson said.

Griggs groaned. "Can we at least stop for coffee on the
way?"

What they found at Barnard Wesley's address in Chattanooga was a retired sixty-seven-year-old black man who
had, until eight years ago, run his own HVAC service.

Barnard was a talker.

"Arthritis got so bad, I had to sell the business and re-
tire," Barnard told them. "Couldn't hardly even hold a
pair of pliers anymore."

Barnard held out his hands to display joints that looked
like walnuts.

"I'm sorry to hear that," Hanson said. "Did you sell the
van, too?"

"Lord have mercy, no! What I mean is, I had two vans
then—the other one was a pretty thing, only five years old
with a real nice logo on the sides.

"I sold *that* one, even though the fella only offered me
fifteen hundred for it. I shoulda held out for more, but he
was buying the rest of the stuff so I figured—"

"The other van?" Griggs interrupted. "That's the one
we're interested in."

"That one wasn't even running—it needed a new radiator—and I just couldn't see any point in putting more money into it at the time, you see."

The van in question sat in his driveway for three years until his seventeen-year-old grandson fixed it.

"That boy is good with anything mechanical." Barnard beamed proudly. "He gets that from me, I guess. It just skipped a generation,'cause his daddy, Devon, my youngest boy, can't even change a fuse without hurtin' hisself."

"The van, Mr. Wesley. Did you sell it then?"

"Oh, no. Not *then*. I told my grandson if he could get it running, he could drive it. You know how kids is, they gotta have wheels to get around in—"

"Mr. Wesley, we just need to know when the van left your possession," Hanson said.

"Let me think." Barnard scratched his ear. "Petey was still driving it until he left for college, that must have been three years ago.

"Dang thing sat in my driveway for another couple of years," he continued. "I wanted to hang on to it, you know, for hauling stuff, but my wife just kept on about how it made the house look trashy, having that van rusting away out there."

"So the wife finally made you get rid of it," Griggs said. "Who'd you sell it to?"

"Shoot, I don't remember his name," Barnard said, waving a hand. "I just put an ad in the *Penny Saver*. Them classified ads in the regular paper, Lord have mercy, they sure are expensive! Highway robbery, if you ask me."

"When was this?"

"It was a couple of months ago, back in May. I just planted my tomatoes, you see—"

"You don't have the man's name, maybe written down somewhere?"

"Now why would I write it down?" Barnard scowled at

Hanson. "It ain't like I was giving him no warranty or something.

"This fella gave me a hundred dollars in cash and I gave him the keys and the registration. I told him he was gonna have to transfer the title to get a new tag, 'cause the one on the van expired two years back. It ain't my fault if he didn't do right."

"Do you remember anything about him?" Hanson fought the urge to bang his head against something.

"Cain't rightly recall nothing. Average fella, I guess."

"Mr. Average," Griggs muttered. "That's just great."

"Age? Hair color? Anything at all? What was he wearing?"

"I couldn't see his hair, 'cause he was wearing a ball cap. He wasn't young, but he wasn't that old, either."

"Christ," Griggs breathed, getting up from the table.

"No need to take the Lord's name in vain," Barnard said, bristling. "I'd sure like to help you, if this fella is doing bad with my old van, but he just wasn't nothing special to remember."

They thanked him for his time and turned down the offer of his wife's icebox lemon pie for the second time.

Back in the car, Griggs called in and had them run a search through tickets for expired tags. Twenty minutes later, his phone rang with the bad news.

"If I drove two days with expired tags, I'd get a freakin' ticket," Griggs muttered. "Mr. Average Psycho drives around two months with expired tags on a POS, nobody pulls him over. Christ!"

This time it was Hanson's phone that vibrated. It was Fortner at CSU, and Hanson put her on speaker so Griggs could hear as well.

"Tell me you love me," she said. "Tell me I'm the most amazing, beautiful, talented CSU you have ever known—"

Griggs hooted.

"You are all that and more," Hanson said. "What have you got?"

"One big juicy fingerprint—"

"On the van?"

"No, the van is so clean it's spooky. Your perp is being really careful about wearing gloves."

"So where did you find—"

"At the cat house. On the laundry hamper in the bathroom."

"Seriously?" Griggs asked.

"I thought he might be a panty-sniffer," Fortner said. "He'd want to touch those with his own hands."

"Bastard was too excited to be careful."

"We're running it through AFIS now," Fortner said. "I'll call you if we get a hit."

"I owe you a drink for this."

"Drink, hell! You owe me a bottle of nice wine. Something with a cork."

Chapter 33

They also serve who only stand and wait.
—JOHN MILTON

It was three in the afternoon, and Griggs and Hanson were back in the office under the pretense of catching up on paperwork. In reality, they were waiting for a hit on that fingerprint.

It was stupid, and they knew it. It could take days for a print to run through all the channels, and a match in AFIS wasn't guaranteed.

"Come on," Griggs said. "You know a guy who'd kill a cat must have some kinda jacket. No way he's kept it clean until now."

Gina insisted on keeping a regular appointment—one that had been penciled in on her day-planner.

"I'm not letting you go alone," Hanson insisted. "We'll just tail you, whether you want us to or not."

She agreed to let Griggs lurk in the hallway outside the front door, while Hanson sat in the tiny kitchenette, separated from the main space by a counter with shutters. The door to the fire escape, beside the refrigerator, had three deadbolts, but he wasn't taking any chances.

Gina's dungeon was spacious, but the big windows along one wall were painted over, then covered in thick wine-colored drapes, until no natural light entered. There was little conventional furniture: a mostly empty bookcase with a few bits of erotic sculpture, including a crystal phallus; a chair; a large plush rug over the hardwood floor; and a table on which stood a row of candles.

The first thing that caught Hanson's eye, though, was a huge painting, maybe six or seven feet tall and at least five feet wide.

"It's beautiful," he said.

The painting showed a woman hanging upside down from a tree in a complicated harness of rope. The sky behind her was nearly black but for swirling snowflakes, and snow was mounded on the ground beneath the tree and on its branches. The woman had the rapturous expression of an early saint.

He was just glad there were no photographs.

But the rest of it looked like the things he'd seen at the Inferno. A St. Andrew's cross; a padded table hanging by chains from the exposed metal beams of the ceiling; a spanking bench. There was even a rolling, multi-drawer toolbox, like a mechanic would have in his garage, which he could only assume was filled with toys.

"Isn't that . . . ?" He nodded to the far corner, suddenly feeling uneasy.

"A modified electric chair?" She smiled. "Yes, it is."

There was also a small bed with a scrolled brass headboard, already draped in chains and cuffs.

"Maybe it's better that you came," Gina said. "I know you're dying to know just what it is I do here, and we might as well get it over with."

She allowed him to help her dress in clothes from a large armoire. He laced her into a black and red leather corset, and felt his dick twitch as her breasts were pushed up into that stunning cleavage.

"This looks really uncomfortable." He tugged the laces tighter. "How can you do anything in this?"

He was trying to ignore that she wore nothing else except a tiny black thong, garters, black-seamed stockings, and four-inch stilettos.

"This is what a paying client expects. Stereotypical, I know, but part of what they are paying for is the fantasy. It's not really submission, to me, when they're paying for it."

He suddenly noticed that her throat was bare.

"You're not wearing your medallion."

"No." She leaned in and kissed him hard on the mouth. "Maybe you can buy me another one sometime."

The recessed lights around the room were on a dimmer switch, and she turned it down until they barely glowed. She lit a row of candles, then went to a mini-stereo system in the bookcase and switched it on.

Deep throbbing music—instrumental, full of soft drumbeats and chimes—came from speakers around the room.

"You make a sound, or you stick so much as your nose out of those shutters, I swear to God, I'll hurt you."

"Promises, promises." He grinned.

She glared.

He made a zipping motion over his mouth. At that moment, he meant to keep his promise.

But later, he did look. He couldn't stop himself.

When she opened the door, it wasn't some balding, paunchy old guy, but the same multi-pierced man-child who had approached her at the Inferno.

Jason: that was his name. Did he really want to see this?

Want to? No, he told himself. He didn't want to. But he had to.

"Get undressed," she said.

She turned her back to Jason and walked to the lone chair.

She turned again, sat down, and crossed those long, long legs. Wordlessly, without any expression, she watched him take his clothes off until he stood naked in front of her.

"On your knees, boy. Get on your knees and crawl to me."

Her voice was low, firm, and oddly detached. From the moment Jason entered the room, some other woman had taken over Gina's body. Similar, yes, but colder. Crueler, even, though she hadn't touched him yet.

Jason crawled the ten feet without once looking up at her. When he reached her feet, he knelt there, motionless, his forehead pressed to the floor.

"My boots are dirty."

He put his mouth to the toe of one boot and began to lick them. Not timidly, but enthusiastically, with long wet swipes of his tongue.

"Enough." She stood up.

He remained crouched on all fours until she snapped her fingers. Then he shot bolt upright, still on his knees with his hands clasped behind him. He still did not look her in the face, but kept the unfocused gaze of a soldier at attention.

And he stayed that way as Gina slowly walked around him. Once. Then twice.

When she was behind him once more, she grabbed his hair and pulled him backward.

She smiled down at him, but it was not a kind expression.

"Do you think you deserve to serve me, boy? Do you think you have earned the right to call me Mistress?"

Hanson saw him struggle with the strained position, saw the pulse beating in his throat as he swallowed.

"No, ma'am," he whispered. "This boy is worthy of nothing until my lady says it is so."

"Damned right." She gave his head a shake. "I am still considering whether an infant like you could ever be worthy to serve me."

She let go of his hair, pushing him forward hard enough that only his quick hands kept him from hitting the floor face first.

"You were exceptionally rude and disobedient when you saw me last." She placed one foot on his bare ass cheeks and pressed the stiletto heel into his flesh. "I should simply send you away now as punishment."

At this, he raised his head and almost looked around at her, but she pushed harder.

"Down!"

He dropped his head to the floor, but his voice trembled.

"Please, my lady. Have mercy on this boy."

"Stand up."

He got to his feet and stood at attention, hands again clasped behind his back.

He was slender but athletically built. Hanson guessed early twenties. A college student, perhaps? One of the rich frat boys from the university? Maybe Dad's credit card was paying for this session.

Hanson noticed, then, that his nipples were not the only things pierced. A stud of some kind glinted from his limp cock.

She reached both hands around him, found both nipple rings, and tugged upward.

He strained, rising up on his toes, as a strangled sound came from his lips.

She let go and stepped back, circling him again.

"You know where to go."

He walked quickly to the cross and pressed himself, face first, against it. His hands reached up to grasp a rope woven around the upper arms of the X.

Gina ran a hand along his back, a long sensual trailing of fingertips, and Hanson saw him shiver.

She went to a rack on the wall and selected a small black instrument, the size and shape of a ruler, maybe a little longer.

"Spread your legs, boy. Wider."

When she brought the instrument down on his ass, it made a loud slapping sound.

Jason inhaled quickly, but made no sound.

He remained still and silent, until about twenty licks in. Gina began to swing wider, harder, and faster, moving the impact around his butt cheeks until they glowed red from waist to thighs.

God, she was beautiful to watch. She moved smoothly and precisely, a look on her face that was impossible to read. Her hair bounced around her shoulders with each stroke.

Hanson knew she was hitting harder because Jason began to twist up on his toes again, his hands flexing convulsively on the rope. When Hanson got a glimpse of the boy's face, his lips were pressed together in a tight line of pain.

She thrust the slapper between his thighs and brought it up against his exposed balls. Little more than taps at first, but faster and faster until he cried out.

She threw the slapper to the floor and leaned against him.

She bit him hard on the shoulder and he moaned.

"Get on the table, boy," she whispered in his ear. "On your back."

"Yes, Lady."

He scrambled onto the table, breathing heavily. Knees bent, he let his thighs fall open, as his hands curled onto the sides of the table.

Gina reached between his legs and grabbed his cock in

one hand, while the other reached up to the line of small metal clothespins clipped to the supporting chain.

One by one, she attached ten of them all over his cock and balls, until his crotch looked like a porcupine had nested there. With each addition, Jason sucked in his breath and pressed his lips together.

Damn. Hanson fought the urge to clamp his own legs together. But then he had an image of Gina's tits, bitten by tiny clothespin teeth, and felt his cock stiffen.

She surveyed her work with a pleased little smile and then flicked one of the clothespins, making it bob. Jason gasped again.

She laughed—a full, throaty sound. Some of her reserve seemed to fall away as she flicked again, nearly giggling like a child with a new toy.

She climbed onto the table and positioned her cunt directly above his face, holding on to the support chains.

Her cunt, separated from his mouth and nose by only the thinnest slip of satin, came down on him, letting her full weight rest over his face. It took a moment before Hanson realized she wasn't inviting him to eat her pussy, she was *smothering* him.

She raised her crotch an inch or so, and Jason wheezed.

"Do you smell my cunt, boy?" she asked silkily. "My hot, wet pussy? I bet you'd like to taste it, wouldn't you?"

"Yes—" Jason began, but she pressed herself down on him again.

At the same time, she reached for one of the pins and yanked it away.

His scream was only a little muffled with Gina sitting on his face. His legs jerked and his body spasmed.

Her smile was gleeful, and Hanson found it both fascinating and a little frightening, how much she was enjoying this.

Again and again, she lowered herself and removed a pin. Again and again, Jason screamed into her cunt.

When only two pins remained, she ground her snatch into his face, dry-humping him. She was breathing heavily, and Hanson realized that she was about to cum.

"Do you like this?" she panted. "Do you like me humping your face?"

Jason began to thrash, his hands beating frantically on the table, but making no move to push her off.

He can't breathe, Hanson thought, feeling a touch of panic. Gina seemed lost, intent on her own pleasure; had she lost track of how long he'd gone without air?

She ground wildly, hips jutting, and reached for the last two pins. As she ripped them both from his balls, she threw her head back and came.

"Oh, fuck *yes!*"

Jason made horrible strangling sounds, his body arching until only his heels and head were still touching the table.

Then she was grabbing the chains, lifting herself off of him.

He lay there coughing, gasping. His face was wet with her juices.

She leaned over the table, looking down into his face, and stroked his matted hair.

"That's a good boy," she whispered.

Incredibly, he smiled up at her, meeting her eyes for the first time.

"May I, Lady?"

"Yes, you may."

He was a little unsteady on his feet, and she led him back toward the chair, picking up a large cushion along the way.

She dropped the cushion in front of the chair and sat down.

Jason wobbled to his knees and curled up in a tight little ball around her feet.

Hanson didn't know which frightened him more: how much she had enjoyed hurting this boy, or the way she stroked his hair now with such tenderness.

That's when she looked up, directly at Hanson, with a sly little smile. He knew then that she'd known he was watching all along.

"I thought you didn't fuck your clients."

"I didn't fuck him," she said, stretching like a cat. "I dry-humped his face. But Jason's not a client anymore, and I do fuck him."

Hanson felt a flicker of anger.

"You dragged us down here for this? Just so you could get off?"

"Please." She sounded bored.

"You wanted me to see that. Why?"

"Because before we get any further into whatever the hell it is between us," she said in a hard voice, "I had to make sure you knew who I am, and what I am."

"I know—"

"You know who I used to be."

"And that changes what, exactly?" Hanson jammed his hands into his pockets.

"I'm not hiding anything, not anymore." Her chin tilted forward ever so slightly. "From anybody. And I'm not changing; not for you, not for anybody."

He knew she meant more than just the pro-domme work.

"So no matter what happens between you and me," he said slowly, "Jason stays? Is that what you're telling me?"

"Jason, or somebody like him. Unless you want to let me beat the crap out of you on a regular basis?"

"No, thanks," he said with sarcasm.

"Well, then. There we are." She turned her back to him and lifted her hair. "Would you mind unlacing me?"

Hanson turned and stalked out the door, letting it slam shut behind him. He took the stairs two at a time until he saw Griggs at the bottom.

"Whoa," Griggs said when he saw Hanson's face. "What happened in there?"

"Nothing," Hanson muttered.

"Is that the green-eyed monster I see—"

"Shut up. We're waiting for her in the car."

Griggs had parked up the street. Hanson was grateful that for once, Griggs kept his mouth shut as they walked toward it.

Movement across the street caught his eye. A figure had stepped out of an alley between buildings, but then stepped back in. Was it because he'd seen them?

Hanson glanced at Griggs, who nodded slightly. He'd seen it, too. Together they jogged across the street. Hanson was more curious than concerned, until he saw a man running full-throttle down the alley.

"Stop!" Hanson yelled. "Police!"

"Come back here, dickhead!" Griggs shouted.

The man didn't slow, didn't even look back. He just kept running until he reached the end of the shadowed alley.

"Damn it," Griggs swore.

Hanson spotted their quarry ducking into the doorway of a convenience mart. He motioned for Griggs to follow and slammed through the door, pausing just long enough for the clerk to simply point to the back of the store.

The back door was still swinging as Hanson shot through it. His foot came down awkwardly on an unexpected step, making him swear in pain.

By the time Hanson had regained his footing, Griggs already had the runner up against a brick wall.

"Don't move, asshole," Griggs growled, pulling a wallet from the man's back pocket with one hand while the other pressed against his back. "Don't even breathe."

"I didn't do nothing, I swear!"

Griggs was looking at the wallet with a frown.

"Elliot McKanney?" Griggs handed Hanson the wallet. "Turn around, slowly."

Hanson knew immediately that this was not the man they were looking for. For one thing, Elliot McKanney was scared shitless.

"What the hell did you run for?" Hanson asked, bending over with his hands on his knees.

"You were chasing me!"

"We identified ourselves as police! Jesus!"

"You coulda been lying," Elliot stammered. "How was I to know? I been mugged twice in this neighborhood."

Griggs had pulled up Elliot's T-shirt to expose a bulge in the waistband of his camouflage pants.

"Oh, I get it," Griggs said, rolling his eyes at Hanson as he pulled out a freezer bag of marijuana and swung it by two fingers. "What, we look like *narcs* to you?"

"Christ. Let him go, Griggs."

"Oh, no! Little bastard makes me break a sweat in ninety-degree weather, he's going in."

"Come on, man," Elliot moaned. "Gimme a break, will ya?"

"You really want to do the paperwork?" Hanson asked. "For a baggie of pot?"

"Shit," Griggs said, glaring at Elliot. "Get out of here before I change my mind."

"Um . . ." Elliot hesitated. "Can I have my weed back?"

"Are you *shitting* me?" Griggs bellowed. "You better run, asshole!"

Elliot took off.

Chapter 34

And Elena was thinking how she would have liked to change places with Bijou, for the many times when men grew tired of courting and wanted sex without it, bestial and direct. Elena pined to be raped anew each day, without regard for her feelings; Bijou pined to be idealized.

—ANAIS NIN, *Delta of Venus*

"Superfreak" blared again.

In the rearview mirror, he watched Gina look at the number and then flick open the phone.

"Yes? . . . Slow down—"

Griggs and Hanson exchanged glances and waited.

"No, I didn't know anything about it . . . I swear to you, no."

Gina listened again.

"Whatdaya mean, why? Because he's a prude with a stick up his ass."

Another long pause.

"I don't know," Gina said into the phone. "Let me find out what I can and I'll get back to you."

"Fuck!" Gina clicked the phone closed and threw it at the back of Griggs's seat.

"Hey, watch it!" Griggs grunted.

"That was Dante." Gina was seething. "The city codes examiner padlocked the Inferno this morning. Some crap about the wheelchair ramp being two degrees out of ADA guidelines—"

"What's ADA?" Griggs asked.

"Americans with Disabilities Act," Gina snapped. "It's bullshit."

"What does that mean, exactly?" Hanson asked.

"It means that until Dante can redo the wheelchair ramp, the Inferno is closed. And if he doesn't do it within ninety days, the club loses its license to operate."

"So they'll have to fix it." Griggs shrugged.

"And then it will be something else! Goddamn it! Did you tell Daubs about going to the club?"

"Me? Hell, no!"

"Don't look at me!" Griggs raised both palms. "I ain't even allowed to talk to the chief anymore."

"City codes are a crock of shit anyway," Gina muttered. "They only use them to get rid of people they don't like."

"I'm sorry, Gee. This isn't anything new. Daubs has always been a hard ass on anything not rated PG."

"These murders just reminded him we perverts still exist," Gina said. "Bastard."

Griggs's phone went off.

But this time the news was much better.

They had a match.

Kerberos's real name was William "Billy" Harold Knoll.

"Two domestics," Hanson said, flipping through his jacket. "Two DUIs, and one stalking charge."

"That's our boy, all right," Gina said.

"Asshole did more time for the second DUI than he did for beating up his girlfriend," Griggs grunted. "Fuckin' cat killer."

The photo showed an average guy, all right. He stood an average five feet seven inches, and weighed an average one hundred ninety pounds. His thin blond hair was receding, but it was cut neatly, and his face was clean-shaven.

Except for the eyes that glared coldly out of the photo, and a twist to his lips that hinted at a general contempt for the world, Billy didn't stand out in any way.

The phone on the desk rang, and Griggs and Hanson looked at each other.

"It's Daubs," Griggs said. "Bastard already knows."

"How the fuck can he know already? We just got this."

"He's got his little birdies all over the place," Griggs hissed. As the phone rang a second time, he gave it the finger.

Hanson grabbed up the receiver. He didn't even have the chance to identify himself before the chief's voice drilled into his ear.

"So you know *who* you're looking for," Daubs said. "Now *find* him."

And then the line went dead. Hanson put the receiver back into the cradle and sighed.

"It's creepy how he does that," Griggs said, staring at the phone. "Makes the hair on the back of my neck stand up."

Chapter 35

Maids' nays are nothing, they are shy
But to desire what they deny . . .
—ROBERT HERRICK,
"Maids' Nays Are Nothing"

"A waste of Kevlar and adrenaline, Hanson." Jimmy Swails, the lead on the entry team, removed his vest to reveal a T-shirt sticking to his abdomen. "Sorry, but your boy ain't home."

Billy Knoll lived in a loft in one of the trendy revamped warehouses downtown. As soon as the SWAT boys had verified that no one was in the apartment, they filed out— arguing over where to go for dinner before heading back to the office—and left the others to do their search.

Two CSUs—Fortner and Lenny—came in with their cases. Bingham and Mercer had come along, presumably as backup, but really in hopes of cashing in on what should have been a headline arrest.

"You know she ain't supposed to be here." Bingham's eyes narrowed as he watched Gina edge past him into the loft.

"Don't tell Daubs about this, or I'll—"

"You'll what?" Bingham stepped closer and stared into his eyes.

Hanson stared right back, not moving.

"Or I'll let Gina bust your other kneecap," Hanson said quietly.

Bingham glared at Hanson and sauntered out of the apartment.

"Daubs finds out about her being here," Mercer said, "he's gonna rip you a new one. You know that, right?"

"You gonna tell him?" Hanson asked.

Mercer shrugged.

"I'm staying out of it," he said, following his partner down the hallway.

"Nice to see ya, Bingham," Gina called over her shoulder. "Hope the knee hurts like a bastard when it rains."

"Don't provoke him," Hanson muttered, turning back into the apartment.

"Blow me," Gina said absently, looking around.

The loft had twelve-foot ceilings of glossy timber and three walls of exposed red brick. The remaining wall was all glass, and would have enjoyed a fabulous view of the skyline if only it were on the opposite side of the building. Instead, the window looked out onto a motley assortment of roofs and alleys.

It was small, barely a thousand square feet, Hanson guessed, though the high ceilings kept it from feeling claustrophobic. There were only three rooms: a living room/kitchen combination, a bedroom, and a single bath.

"You know, for a sadistic serial killer, the guy keeps a nice house," Griggs said, surveying the living room with hands on his hips.

"Place looks more like a hotel room than an apartment," Hanson observed, walking across the hardwood floor to the tiny kitchen, which was separated from the living area only by a granite countertop with a couple of stools in front of it.

A large carpet of geometric patterns in warm browns, reds, and oranges was in the center of the floor, flanked by a simple brown sofa and a single chair, obviously second-hand. The flat screen on the wall reflected the window's glare, making it look like a big square dead eye.

"Not much personal here," Gina said, standing in front

of a mostly empty bookshelf. "Except for a few CDs and books—and they're alphabetized."

"Can you say anal-retentive?" Griggs asked.

"It makes sense, actually." Hanson opened a cabinet door and was surprised to find there was actually food inside. "He's a control-freak, anal, methodical—"

"Oh, Christ," Gina groaned, pulling out a thick and well-worn paperback. "He's got the entire Gor series."

"What's Gor?" Hanson asked.

"Garbage," she said, sliding the book back into place. "Don't even get me started."

Griggs whistled from the bedroom. "We got his stalker shrine in here."

The room was barely big enough for the double bed, a small dresser, and a desk. But photos of Cherry were plastered all over the walls.

"Christ." Griggs surveyed the walls. "He musta spent a fortune on enlargements. That one is almost life-size."

"Bastard has pictures of her in the grocery store." Gina looked at the collection of cameras and lenses on the dresser. "He's even got a tiny video recorder here."

"Got some boots." Lenny, the CSU, bent over, reaching into the floor of the closet, and held up a pair of scuffed Dickies.

"No computer, no laptop," Hanson said. "He must have it with him."

"We're gonna take these in, right?" Lenny asked, waving at the photos.

"Take it all," Hanson told him.

"Can you say DNA?" Fortner came out of the bathroom holding up a toothbrush, making it do a little happy dance. "Got hair, too."

"Great." Hanson frowned. "We got evidence, now we just need the damned suspect."

Chapter 36

She would have been so glad if she could have been cut
to pieces, body and soul, to show what joy this pain
caused her. What torments could have been set before
her at such a time which she would not have found it
delectable to endure for her Lord's sake?
— SANTA TERESA DE JESÚS,
The Life of Saint Teresa of Ávila by Herself

The bathroom, with its sunken whirlpool tub, was separated from the rest of the room by a Chinese screen.
But Cherry had discovered that if she adjusted the screen,
she could watch the TV while she took a bubble bath.

She felt incredibly decadent, soaking in lavender-scented
foam while watching *Weeds*.

There was little enough to do besides sleep, read, or
watch TV, and at least the bubble bath component was a
novelty.

The sunlight in the dormer window was fading. The
sky was streaked with crimson and pale blue as indigo
crept in.

Cherry was grateful to have the upstairs room for another reason; she was terrified of windows on the first floor.
It didn't matter if the shades or curtains were drawn—
Kerberos could be standing right on the other side of the
glass, his eye pressed close to peek into the smallest opening.

Even if he couldn't see her, she could imagine him listening to every movement.

Up here, she didn't have to be afraid of the windows.
She could watch the sky turn colors as the sun faded away.

Cherry wasn't sure what to think about Gina. As a
woman detective, she was formidable enough, but Cherry

remembered her as *bella rosso*—had seen her at the club with Quinn, doing hard, edgy play that scared the bejesus out of her even as it made her wet to watch. They did the kinds of things she fantasized about but would never have the courage to actually do.

She wasn't sure which of them scared her more: the man who could do such things, or the slave who would willingly allow him to do them to her.

Cherry had never seen her as Lady Gee, but she'd heard about her, of course. Jason actually played with Lady Gee, and he worshipped her. He would talk about her for hours if you didn't shut him up. Robyn used to tease him about "Lady Gee Whiz."

Now she was hiding in Lady Gee's house from a man who had raped her and murdered two of her best friends. Three, if you counted Gunther. God, she just wanted all of this to be over, to get back some semblance of a normal life.

Weeds was over. She turned the TV off with the remote.

She pulled the drain in the tub and got out as suds began to swirl downward.

She missed her own towels at home; these were scratchy on her skin. She wanted her own towels, her own bed, her own kitchen—

She heard a door open downstairs and was glad she hadn't eaten yet. Maybe Gina would order pizza again. She'd had cereal for dinner last night. She didn't think Gina realized just how little food there was in the house.

She slipped into a clean pair of pajama pants and a T-shirt. Barefoot, she padded down the stairs.

"Gina, have you had dinner yet?"

The downstairs was dark but for the light over the kitchen sink.

Something in the stillness made her heart slip in its

rhythm. She stopped on the bottom step and peered into the dim light.

"Gina?"

When there was no answer, she moved back up another step.

Somewhere down there in the shadows, a board creaked.

The bungalow, built in the forties, was full of creaks, but this hadn't sounded like *that* kind of creak. This had sounded like a person walking over a loose board.

Stop being stupid. There are policemen just outside, watching the house.

She was safe . . . wasn't she?

But she was sure she'd heard someone coming in the back door.

If it were Gina, she'd have answered, wouldn't she?

Gina would have turned a light on, wouldn't she?

Cold fear flooded her body, and she couldn't decide whether to go forward or back.

I should run. Run for the front door as fast as I can and down the steps and even if it's nothing and I look like an idiot, it's still okay, because I'll be safe . . .

Yet the urge to turn and run back up the stairs was stronger. She knew there was no one up *there*. She wouldn't have to run through shadows and darkness in which anything might be waiting.

She was afraid to move. Afraid of making any sound that would give her away. It was as if a cowardly little voice in her head was pleading with her not to do anything, anything at all.

If you just stand here very, very still, you'll be all right.

He can't chase you if you don't run.

There it was again. That creak. Such a small sound became a shout in the silence closing around her—

She jumped the two bottom steps and ran—

Her hip banged against a heavy piece of furniture. She yelped, spun, and then slammed into the front door, fumbling for the knob.

Why wouldn't it open?!

The deadbolt, you idiot! Open the deadbolt!

Her hand fell on it, turning it until it clicked. She pulled the door open—

Someone fell into her back, slamming the door shut with a sharp crack.

She screamed as fingers snarled into her hair, yanking her backward with enough force to make her lose her footing.

"No! No! No!"

She nearly went down, but he had an arm around her throat now. He was pulling her backward, away from the door.

She beat against his arm with a fist, then sank her fingernails into his flesh. When she felt something warm and slippery, she screamed wordlessly with a savage joy.

"Bad girl!" he shouted. "Very, very bad girl!"

His other arm went around her waist and lifted her off the floor. Her legs kicked wildly as she twisted.

She reached behind her, felt his ear under her fingers, and grabbed it. She twisted viciously, and he howled.

Suddenly he stumbled. As he fell, she found her feet again and jerked free.

She ran the only way she could—away from him.

Up the stairs, some of them two at a time, every step pounding as loudly as her heart in her ears.

She heard him running up the steps behind her, but she was faster. She reached the top of the stairs and slammed the heavy oak door shut.

She turned the lock and the deadbolt just seconds before he began pounding on it.

"Open the door!" His voice was deep, breathless, and angry, though he didn't shout. "You know I can break it down if I have to."

She dragged a bookcase across the room until it was blocking the door, while all the time he pounded his fist hard enough to shake the door frame.

Then the pounding stopped.

"You've disappointed me so badly," he said. She could tell he was breathing hard. "Come out and take your punishment like a good girl."

She snatched her cell phone from the bedside table, clutching it to her chest as she stared at the door.

How long would it hold? How long until he was in here, with her?

He hit the door again.

"I'm tired of playing games with you! Open the goddamned door, girl!"

Her eyes scanned the room desperately for something to defend herself with, but there was nothing—

She stumbled to the closet and crawled inside, as far back under the slanting roof as she could, pushing clothes and shoe boxes out of her way.

Her hands were shaking so bad she had to try twice to dial 911.

"Please," she told the dispatcher on the other end. "Someone is trying to kill me; he's in the house—"

"What is your address?"

Cherry began to cry hysterically.

"It's on Holly Street—but I don't remember the number! There are supposed to be police outside watching the house, it belongs to a detective named Gina Larsen—"

Outside, he hit the door again, and this time she thought she heard wood splintering.

"Call Detective Tom Hanson! He knows where I am—"

In the light from the cell phone, she could see a shoe box that had fallen open near her feet, exposing a pair of flat sandals.

"Calm down and tell me your name."

"Cheryl Gavin—Please hurry!"

She tore open another box, praying for a pair of stilettos, but it was only a pair of Nikes.

"We're tracing your call now, just hang on. Can you get to a safe place?"

"I locked myself in the upstairs bedroom—oh, my God, he's breaking through the door!"

She grabbed wildly at boxes with one hand, not looking now, only feeling for anything sharp and pointed.

Her hand fell on something harder and colder than a shoe. She held it up to the cell phone—

A gun.

The car skidded to a stop, the front tires hitting the curb just inches from the parked cruiser where Officers Jamison and Silvy sat, looking bored.

"What the fuck are you two doing?" Hanson slammed his hand against the window, making the younger uniform spill a Coke down his shirtfront. He hissed rather than yelled, not wanting to give warning to Billy Knolls inside the house. "She just called nine-one-one saying the bastard is in there with her!"

Officers Jamison and Silvy stared at him, slack-jawed.

"That ain't possible—" Silvy began.

Hanson ran past the cruiser, toward the house, his gun unholstered, as Silvy and Jamison scrambled out of the cruiser and nearly collided with Griggs and Gina.

"Did you leave your post?" Griggs whispered violently. "Goddamn it, you did, didn't you?"

"We just drove around the block to Subway—"

"Oh, fuck me!" Griggs swore.

"It ain't our fault!" Officer Silvy's face was red. "We been here since six a.m., and our relief never showed. We just went to get something to—"

"Griggs, you take the back, I'll go in the front," Hanson directed. "You two assholes stay out here and if someone comes out that ain't us, shoot him!"

Griggs slipped around the side of the house as Hanson moved cautiously up the front steps.

"You can't come in here," Hanson hissed at Gina as she crept up behind him with her Beretta in both hands.

"The fuck I can't! It's my house."

The door was unlocked. He turned the knob and pushed the door gently.

The door swung wide with an ominous creak.

"Billy?" Hanson yelled, edging through the door. "Billy Knolls? This is the police. Come out where we can see you."

Gina hit the switch by the door, and the room burst into light.

"Cherry?" Hanson called. "Where are you?"

He heard muffled sounds from the back of the house.

"Billy," he called again, trying to keep his voice calm. "Come out with your hands up."

"This doesn't concern you!" a male voice shouted. "Get out!"

"Cherry?" Gina called. "Are you all right?"

"He's got your gun." Cherry's voice, high and terrified, shaking like something about to shatter, answered. "The one from your closet—"

Cherry screamed in pain.

"I told you to keep your mouth shut!" Billy hissed, then raised his voice. "Yes, I have your gun! The girl was gonna shoot me with it, but she didn't know how to take the safety off."

"Fuck," Gina hissed. "He's got my backup."

"Is it loaded?"

She grimaced and nodded.

"It sounds like they're in the downstairs bedroom," she said. "I think he's trying to get her out the back door."

He felt his stomach lurch, thinking that guys like Billy Knoll often opted for the murder-suicide option when cornered.

"Hey, Billy," Hanson called. "Any chance you want to talk about this? We don't want anybody to get hurt here."

"I'm only here taking what's mine! Why don't you and your girlfriend just leave us alone!"

"Keep him talking," Gina whispered, and before he could say anything, she had slipped around the corner and back out the front door.

"You know we got people outside, right, Billy?"

Hanson slipped into the bathroom and picked up a handheld mirror from the vanity. "My partner's at the back door, and a tactical team is gonna be here any minute—"

"Is that supposed to scare me? I've got a hostage here, so you better keep away from me!"

"I was just telling you the situation."

Hanson walked back into the hallway on the balls of his feet, edging closer to Billy's voice. "You're in control right now, we all know that."

"Damned right."

"Just tell me what you want, Billy."

Hanson pressed himself up against the wall and held out the mirror. He angled it, hoping to get a glimpse of Billy's position in the room.

"What the fuck are you doing?" Billy shouted.

"I'm just trying to see if Cherry is okay—"

He could see one wall . . . the edge of the bed . . .

And, finally, Cherry's terrified face as Billy Knoll stood behind her with an arm around her throat.

Then he saw the faint ghost of Gina's face in the window behind Billy just as a gun blasted and glass shattered.

Cherry screamed, and she kept screaming as Hanson stepped into the room. Bits of brain and bone were clinging to her face and hair.

Billy Knoll lay in a heap on the floor.

Half of his head was blown away, but one eye stared up malevolently, then began to twitch. Gurgling sounds came from deep in his throat.

Hanson kicked the gun away from the body, and took Cherry by the shoulders.

"It's all over. Come on. Don't look at him, just come on out of here . . ."

Griggs was in the doorway.

"Jesus Christ," he breathed. "He dead?"

"RFD," Hanson said, steering Cherry through the door. "Real fuckin' dead."

Officer Jamison was on the front porch, looking so scared that Hanson almost felt sorry for him. But any sympathy for the young officer was short-lived. It was partly his fault that a man was dead and that Cherry was covered in his blood. He hoped that Jamison had pissed himself.

"Take her down to the ambulance, will you?" Hanson said, pushing Cherry gently in his direction. "If you think you can do that without losing her."

Cherry moved like a sleepwalker down the front steps, clutching Officer Jamison's arm. The paramedics were already running toward the house with a gurney.

Gina came around the corner of the house.

"Christ," Hanson said, wiping his mouth and beginning to feel slightly sick as the adrenaline began to fade. "Goddamn it! Did you have to blow his head off?"

"I had a shot," she said evenly. "I took it."

"You coulda killed Cherry! Or me!" Hanson wanted to shake her.

"But I didn't."

How could she stand there looking so goddamned calm? She had broken basic rules of procedure, specifically the one that said you didn't shoot when another officer was in your line of fire. *Goddamnit!* The bullet could very easily have gone through Knoll and into him. And a shot through a window? She was too smart to have taken such a risk.

Hanson held out his hand and she laid the gun in it.

"Shit," he muttered. "How am I gonna explain this to Daubs?"

Chapter 37

The motive forces of phantasies are unsatisfied wishes,
and every single phantasy is the fulfillment of a wish, a
correction of unsatisfying reality.
—SIGMUND FREUD

Daubs got there just behind the ambulance, before the
CSU or coroner showed up. Damn, Hanson thought.
What was he doing, monitoring dispatch?

The chief looked like hell. He needed a shave for one
thing, and a couple of breath mints wouldn't have hurt,
either. But he seemed oddly energized, and Hanson was
wary.

He paced down the sidewalk, away from the ambulance, motioning Hanson to follow.

"What in *blazes* was *she* doing here in the first place?"

"It's her house."

"You *deliberately* ignored a direct order that she stay *out*
of this!"

"What I *did* was close the case. Sir."

Not to mention saving the taxpayers the cost of a trial,
Hanson thought.

Daubs slumped against the hood of the cruiser and
stared at the crime tape being strung around the bungalow.
At both ends of the street, cruisers were blocking access,
but neighbors stood on the sidewalk, gawking.

Hanson had a whole speech prepared about how they'd
never have broken the case without Gina, how she'd put
in countless hours to bring a serial killer to justice without
even getting paid for it—

But what Daubs said next made Hanson's brain freeze.

"It would be best if we finesse the story a bit. *She* didn't do the shooting. It would be better if Griggs took the credit."

Did he really mean credit, or blame?

It wouldn't be the first time the department bent the truth a little. Usually for a good cause. And this was a good cause, wasn't it? Rewriting history would uncomplicate things, keep Gina out of a sticky investigation, maybe even jail time. She was a civilian who'd blown a suspect's head off.

Still, it made Hanson queasy.

"Sometimes it's better," Daubs continued, "not to ask too many questions, *understand*?"

Hanson nodded cautiously.

"I'm not *entirely* unhappy that we'll be spared a potentially embarrassing public trial dragging *innocent* people through the mud."

Innocent people meant Roger and Marla Banks. Daubs didn't give a damn about Robyn, Quinn, Cassandra, or Randall Heeler.

"*Nobody* talks to the press. I want this to go away as quickly as possible. Do *whatever* you need to do to make it happen. Whatever it takes."

He locked eyes with Hanson, and Hanson knew this wasn't just the chief's usual bluster. He meant it.

What exactly did he mean, *Whatever it takes*?

Hanson thought he knew. Daubs was telling him to make sure everyone had their stories straight. Putting Gina's Beretta in Griggs's hand, and finding a credible way of explaining why he hadn't used his usual sidearm. And doing it fast, before CSU arrived.

He meant convincing Gina that she'd merely been an observer with no knowledge of what had gone down.

"There's a lot of glory to be had here," Daubs said. "And personal credit in the favor bank. *Don't* screw it up."

He looked up as Louise Fortner dropped a report on the desk in front of him.

"You're here early," he said. It was six a.m. Griggs had only left a few hours before, and Gina was at her house, probably trying to get the bloodstains out of her nice oak floorboards. "Or are you on nights, now?"

Hanson was still at his desk, going through his notes and reports for the thousandth time, wondering if the story they'd pieced together would hold.

"I don't even know what shift I'm on," Fortner said, frowning. "Or what day it is. Daubs told me not to go home until I processed all the stuff from your shitstorm last night. He said nobody but me should handle anything."

"That's job security, at least."

"It's too early for jokes. Or too late. But the next time Griggs blows the head off a high-profile suspect, tell him to do it earlier in the day."

The lies were already making their way through the system. Hanson couldn't meet her eyes.

"So, what have you got for me?" he asked instead. He picked up the report—marked PRELIMINARY in big capital letters—and tried to read the first page. His eyes didn't want to focus.

"What *you've* got are problems, Hanson."

"What kind of problems?" His body tensed.

"We found some trace at the other scenes," she said, sitting on the corner of the desk. "You know, blood that didn't belong to the victim—"

"Right. We just never had anything to match it to."

It was hard to butcher someone while they struggled,

even weakly, without nicking oneself in the process. He knew CSU had DNA from blood—and sweat—from some of the crime scenes. Not much, but then it didn't take much.

"We still don't have anything to match it to," Fortner said.

Hanson's chest constricted. He shook his head, certain he must have misheard her.

"Knoll's DNA doesn't match," Fortner repeated. "He didn't do the murders. At least, not the first two. Not Banks or Macy."

"Double check it." Hanson rubbed his palm over his heart, feeling the band around his chest tightening.

"I did. Three times. And it gets worse."

"Fuck!" Hanson's voice came out in a hoarse whisper. "How can it possibly get any worse?"

Hanson stared at her, realized that Fortner looked almost as miserable as he felt, and wondered why. She hadn't just told fifty lies to tidy up the death of a man who was now no longer their prime suspect.

"The boots we took from Knoll's place?" Fortner continued. "Wrong size, and the tread pattern doesn't match."

They both sat there, saying nothing for a seemingly endless moment.

"So you're telling me there's nothing to put Knoll at the scene on any of the murders?" Hanson said finally.

"Nada. But he wasn't totally innocent," she said. "I mean, he did rape that girl and he was probably going to kill her, right?"

"We still have a serial killer out there." Hanson cradled his head in his hands. "Oh, fuck, fuck, fuck, fuck . . ."

He ran his hands through his hair and straightened.

"Don't mention this to anybody yet," he said. "Please."

"I can give you twenty-four hours, no problem. I

rushed this because I knew you'd want it for the press release."

"Aw, shit," Hanson groaned. "The press."

"And I'll try to hide it from Creepy."

"Creepy? Why?"

"You didn't know?" Fortner gave a bitter little bark of laughter. "He's in Daubs's pocket. That's why he's always creeping around the lab, messing with stuff that isn't any of his business."

"The DNA," Hanson said in desperation. "You found it in all the crime scenes?"

"Well, no. Just on Banks and Robyn Macy. You saw the mess. I was lucky to find anything."

"So it's possible that it could be a fluke? The DNA wasn't from the killer at all?"

Fortner frowned.

"Yeah, and it's possible there really is a Santa Claus. But I wouldn't bet on it."

"Look at everything again, will you? Please? *Please?*"

"Hanson, there isn't anything else—"

"Please, I'm begging you."

"All right." She sighed. "I'll look."

Hanson's eyes were burning and his head hurt like a mother, so he took a half hour nap in the bunkroom before going back to his desk.

He had to find something that would link Knoll to the murders before breaking the news to Daubs. But he could find nothing new in his notes.

Then again, he was so tired he wasn't sure he'd see a giant pink elephant if it stood on his desk.

He pulled the stack of phone records in front of him. He did have one thing now they hadn't had before—Knoll's cell phone number. He and Griggs had looked for duplications, and there were some numbers that had crossed over. Marla had talked to her husband, of course, but she'd also talked to Cherry and Cassandra. Cassandra had talked to Quinn. Robyn had talked to Roger and Cherry. Hell, Roger and Cassandra both had calls to Daubs, for Christ's sake—

555-7286.

He looked down and realized he was looking at Robyn Macy's LUDs.

555-7286.

He took out his phone and punched in the number.

Just to be sure.

"This is Milton Daubs. I'm not available to take your call but if you—"

Chapter 38

I am ashamed that women are so simple
To offer war where they should kneel for peace;
Or seek for rule, supremacy and sway,
When they are bound to serve, love and obey . . .
And place your hands below your husband's foot:
In token of which duty, if he please,
My hand is ready; may it do him ease.

—WILLIAM SHAKESPEARE,
The Taming of the Shrew

He went to Daubs's office on the fourth floor with the LUD printout still in his fist.

"I need to see the chief."

"He's not in right now," Sandy, his secretary, said without looking up from her computer screen.

"He was here thirty minutes ago," Hanson said, wiping his mouth in frustration.

Daubs had stalked into Hanson's office around 8:30 a.m., demanding to see Hanson's report. Hanson was on his third draft by then, but Daubs had taken a pencil, crossed out a line or two, and handed it back to him.

"He went across the street for a bagel," Sandy said, looking over the top of her bifocals. "You can wait in his office if you want. He should be right back."

There had to be a rational explanation for Daubs's phone number appearing on Robyn Macy's LUDs. But Hanson was damned if he could come up with a single one that made any sense.

He collapsed in one of the chairs facing the chief's desk and looked at the printout again, as if the numbers would suddenly rearrange themselves.

An affair? Even if Daubs, Mr. Morality himself, was

cheating on his wife, the odds of his other woman being one of the murder victims were astronomical.

"You want some coffee while you wait?" Sandy called.

"No, thanks." He'd had too much coffee already, and his stomach was awash in acid.

The wall behind Daubs's desk was devoted to professional vanity. Plaques for service and honors from local charities were interspersed with photos. Hanson had seen them all before, but now they annoyed him more than ever.

Daubs shaking hands with the mayor; Daubs at a charity golf event with several gray-haired titans of local commerce; Daubs with the fire chief, Floyd Haggard; Daubs with the Honorable William H. Denton, his father-in-law . . .

Hanson stood up and moved closer for a better look at the man responsible for Gina's fall from grace.

In the photo, the governor had one arm around Daubs and another around a matronly brunette. Hanson recognized Daubs's wife, Linda.

Linda had her hand resting on the shoulder of a teenage boy.

It was Jason.

Jason . . . *Daubs?*

Shit—

"Do you want me to give him a message?" Sandy called as Hanson jogged past.

He didn't bother to answer.

Damn it, damn it, damn it! Hanson castigated himself mentally as he drove, too fast, to Daubs's house.

The clues that somehow Daubs was linked to this mess had been there since the beginning, but he'd been too distracted by his personal demons to pay attention. And he'd been too jealous of Gina's boy toy to even consider that Jason might have anything to do with the case.

Linda Daubs opened the front door.

Hanson pulled his face into what he hoped was an easy smile and tried to sound as if his own pulse wasn't galloping full speed.

"Mrs. Daubs? I'm Detective Tom Hanson—"

"Of course. I remember you from the Christmas party." Linda smiled. "Are you looking for my husband? I'm afraid he's not here—"

Hanson threw the dice and prayed that this wasn't going to blow up in his face. But there was nothing else to do, consequences be damned.

"Actually, I was hoping I could talk to your son."

"Jason? Why do you want to talk to Jason?"

He noticed, too late, that Linda's eyes were red, her face puffy as if she'd been crying.

"Are you all right?"

"I'm fine. Just allergies." The smile was brittle and didn't reach her eyes.

"I really need to speak with Jason," Hanson repeated.

"He's not here." The smile faltered and crumpled.

"I recognize his Jeep in the driveway, ma'am. This is really important—"

Linda tried to shut the door, but he pushed his way in.

"What do you think you're doing? You can't come in here!"

Jason was coming down the stairs, struggling with a big duffel bag over one shoulder. He saw Hanson and stopped.

Jason's left eye was swollen almost shut, and there was an enormous bruise on the other cheek as well. His lip was split, and his right arm was in a cast.

"Did your father do that to you?" Hanson asked quietly.

Jason came to the bottom of the steps.

"You can't be here!" Linda's voice became a desperate whisper. "My husband won't like you being here!"

"Does he beat you, too? Or just your son?"

"Jason had an accident." Linda's voice trembled with the lie. "It was just an accident, that's all."

"Mom, I'm not covering for him anymore," Jason said. "I'm done, and I'm out of here."

The boy's eyes swiveled from his mother to Hanson.

"If you wanna talk, you better make it fast," he said. "I don't wanna be here when that bastard comes home."

"When did you get that beating?" Hanson asked.

"Yesterday. Could you give me a hand with this?"

Hanson took the bag and followed Jason to the Jeep in the driveway. Jason wasn't moving very fast, and Hanson wondered what other injuries were hidden under his T-shirt and jeans.

There were already boxes and another suitcase in the back of the Jeep.

"Was this the first time?" Hanson hefted the duffel bag into the passenger seat.

"No." Jason's voice was flat with the faintest edge of bitterness. "My dad is a firm believer in corporal punishment, which makes all this pretty fuckin' ironic."

"So it's about the kink stuff." It was more statement than question.

"Bingo." Jason leaned against the Jeep with a deep sigh. "When I was little, it was just hand spanking for breaking any of his ten thousand rules.

"As I got older, he switched to a belt and then his fraternity paddle." Jason gave a brittle laugh. "He's been trying to beat the pervert out of me since I was twelve, and he found me tying shoelaces around my dick."

Hanson tried to imagine what it had been like for Jason. Hell, most likely, but then it had to have been hell for

Daubs as well. His only son was what Daubs hated most: a pervert.

"Why didn't you leave before now?"

"I have left," Jason said. "He always bribed me to come home. Bribes or blackmail. The last time I moved out and stayed with Kitty for about six months. But he refused to pay my college tuition until I came back. I've only got a semester left. I thought I could get through it. But the past couple of months, he's just gone crazy. He's lost it."

"How crazy is he, Jason?"

Jason looked at his feet.

Hanson could hardly think it, let alone say it. God only knew how hard it was for Jason.

"Were you close to Roger Banks?" Hanson asked.

"He was my godfather," Jason said dully.

"And Roger knew about you and the kinky stuff?"

Jason nodded, then hastily wiped eyes that had grown suspiciously bright.

"Uncle Roger probably saved my life. You know what autoerotic asphyxia is?"

"It's hanging yourself to get off, isn't it? People die that way."

"Uncle Roger caught me doing it in his garage when I was fifteen. He sat me down and talked to me. He understood."

Jason sucked in a shaky breath.

"I thought I was defective, sick. If I hadn't killed myself accidentally with the hanging, I might have killed myself deliberately without Uncle Roger."

Hanson could almost hear the clicks as, one by one, pieces fell into place. All the murders had begun with this one miserable boy and his fucked-up father.

"Roger Banks introduced you to the community, didn't he?"

"Yeah. First, just Lady Cassandra. She knew about the autoerotic stuff that Uncle Roger didn't. When I was legal age, he and Aunt Marla took me to the club with them—"

"When did your father find this out?"

Jason's eyes were wet and pleading: *Don't make me say it.*

"About two months ago," Jason said softly. "Christ, I can't even think about it without wanting to throw up. It's all my fault. My father found out about Lady Cassandra. He had hired a private detective to follow me because he'd found some books hidden under my mattress.

"He made me stop seeing Lady Cassandra. I think he threatened to arrest her if she came near me again. I stayed away for a while, from her and the club. I didn't want to get anybody else into trouble. But Lady Gee—"

Jason broke off, as if suddenly realizing who he was talking to. His face flushed with color and he shook his head miserably.

"I couldn't stay away from her. She's in my head and my heart and I didn't want to stay away from her. You understand that, right? You understand what that's like?"

Hanson opened his mouth, intending to explain that his relationship with Gina wasn't like that . . . But who was he kidding? In his own way, Hanson was as much Gina's slave as this beautiful, bruised boy was.

Again Jason swiped a hand over his eyes. He sniffed, then squared his shoulders, and when he spoke again, his voice was harder.

"That was the first time my father didn't use the paddle. He used his fists. Uncle Roger was furious, said he had to put a stop to it."

"Do you know *when* he talked to your dad?"

Hanson knew what Jason was going to say, but he still couldn't believe it. Hanson could hardly breathe, terrified of hearing the words that would change everything.

"The day before Uncle Roger was killed." Jason broke, sobbing. "Oh, Christ, I think that bastard killed him."

Hanson called Gina first, but her phone rolled over to voice mail immediately. He turned the car toward her house and then punched speed dial for Griggs.

"Where are you?"

"Hello and good day to you, too, buddy," Griggs drawled. "Where the hell are——"

"No time for bullshit. Where's Gee?"

"What's wrong?"

"Where's Gee, damn it?"

"I don't know! Tell me what's——"

"We got it all wrong. Knoll was not our guy. It's Daubs!"

"Right. You almost had me, you asshole——"

"Shut up and listen to me! Jason, the boy toy? That's Jason Daubs! He's the chief's son."

"Holy shit." Griggs's voice was hushed and strained.

"The kid's on his way to the coffee shop around the corner right now. I told him you'd meet him there——"

"Okay——"

"You need to get a statement from him, but keep Daubs away from him! Get to a judge for a restraining order, but mostly don't let him out of your sight. It sounds like Daubs has snapped, and who knows what the fuck he might do."

"What are you gonna do?" Griggs asked.

"I gotta find Gee first and make sure she's all right. Then we need to get a warrant to arrest Daubs and search his house."

"Oh, fuck, this is gonna be a cluster-fuck. Are you sure about this?"

"Yes!"

"All right. I'm on my way now. I'll take care of Jason, you just find Gee."

★ ★ ★

Gina's BMW was in the driveway.

"Gee?" Hanson called as he walked through the front door. "Are you here?"

He heard Gina's voice coming from somewhere in back of the house.

"Watch it, Hanson! He's—"

Something hit the back of his head with enough force to make his vision dance with white static.

Then pain exploded in his knee. Hanson felt the sickeningly wrong sensation of a leg bending in a way nature never intended. He hit the floor, fighting the urge to vomit.

For a second, he saw Daubs clearly. The chief's face was pale but for the hectic blotches of color on his cheeks.

He swung the tire thumper again and made contact with Hanson's left ear.

The thumper clattered to the floor as Daubs fell on top of him. One of Daubs's knees landed in his groin as his hand fumbled for the gun in Hanson's shoulder holster.

Hanson grabbed for Daubs's hand and caught his thumb, twisting it hard enough to make him drop the gun, sending it clattering across the wooden floor, as Daubs's other hand flew into his face.

Blood burst from Hanson's nose, into his eyes. He groped blindly, praying to feel the cold steel under his fingers.

Hanson brought his head up sharply into Daubs's chin. The chief gave a cry of outrage as he reeled backward just enough for Hanson to push his weight off and send him crashing into the coffee table.

Hanson dimly saw the flash of shiny metal as Daubs's arm cut through the air, then felt the thin, burning sensation of flesh slicing open along the side of his neck and chest.

The blade was inches from Hanson's face. He grabbed

Daubs's wrist with both hands and brought his good knee up into the chief's groin.

Hanson was still hanging on to the hand that held the knife with all his strength, pushing it and twisting it. But Daubs wouldn't let go, wouldn't stop.

He's going to kill me. This is how it all ends. He's going to kill me.

Hanson's legs thrashed wildly in spite of the agony every movement brought to his shattered knee. He kicked at Daubs's shins again and again.

Daubs was kicking, too, and when his foot finally connected with Hanson's busted knee, Hanson screamed in pain. White static danced around the edges of his vision again.

I cannot pass out. I cannot die like this.

The knife came closer and closer, until all that filled Hanson's vision was the flashing edge of the blade and Daubs's eyes behind it.

What Hanson saw in the man's eyes scared the hell out of him. They were enormous and black and bottomless. To see such madness, such consuming hatred, in a face he thought he knew was somehow more terrifying than any physical pain.

Hanson threw his upper body forward and clamped down on Daubs's hand with his teeth. Even as Hanson felt the sting of the blade against his cheek, he bit down hard.

Hanson tasted copper in his mouth as Daubs shrieked, a high keening sound like an animal. The knife fell with a single hollow *plink* to the floor.

Daubs was on top of him again, this time pressing the bulk of his weight against Hanson's chest. Hanson fought to draw air into his burning lungs as he bucked and twisted.

Daubs grabbed his ears, pulled his head forward, then slammed it back against the floor.

Hanson's world was reduced to pain and desperation.

His arm reached outward, palm and fingers beating in a frantic search.

The gun! The gun! Gotta find the gun!

Daubs slammed his head down again, and suddenly Hanson felt as if he were falling . . .

Then blackness slid over him and consumed him.

Hanson didn't know how long he'd lost consciousness, but the sound of wood splintering brought him struggling back up from the depths of pain.

"Open the door!" Daubs was shouting. "This has been coming for a long, long time, and I'm not waiting any longer!"

Another splintering sound, and for a moment Hanson fought the urge to just fall back into the blackness until he realized the sound was coming from the direction of the bathroom.

Gina must have locked herself in. He couldn't remember: was there a window in there?

Her gun? Where was her gun?

Her gun was in the evidence room at the station.

Shit, shit, shit!

He couldn't figure out where all the blood was coming from, or why his eyes kept trying to close. He just knew he had to get up. *Gina—*

There was a crash, then breaking glass and Gina's guttural curses.

Gotta get up. Gotta get up . . . He'll kill her!

Daubs dragged Gina into the room by her hair as she screamed like a wild thing. Her fingers clawed at his arm and he punched her in the face twice, his fist pistoning like a machine.

"Get away from her!" Hanson tried to scream, but his voice came out in a croak. He kept trying to lift his head, but every movement was agony. It was all he could do to hang on to consciousness.

Gina slumped and Daubs let her fall to the floor. When she curled onto her side, he kicked her in the stomach, then stood there looking down at her, breathing heavily.

"Whore," he said, wiping a trickle of blood from the corner of his mouth. He watched her pull herself across the floor, leaving a bloody smear on the hardwood.

"Come'n, Daubs," she said in a slurred voice that still carried biting condescension. "This how you get off, issst? Beatin' up on w'men?"

She raised a foot, but Hanson saw, with a sinking heart, that she was in only panties and a T-shirt, her feet bare. Even if she summoned enough strength, a barefoot kick probably wouldn't be enough to bring Daubs down.

"First, you make my department look ridiculous." Daubs reached for the thumper he'd dropped and brought it down on her.

She screamed, and he struck her again.

"Do you have any idea what my father-in-law said to me when they arrested you? Do you have any idea what I have to put up with from that smug, corrupt worm of a man?"

Hanson screamed, too, in rage and frustration. *I will kill him, I will fuckin' kill him . . .*

Blinking blood from his eyes, Hanson spied a glint of metal under the sofa. He tried to sit up, failed, and then began to crawl toward it. He paid for every inch with a sickening dizziness.

So much blood . . . He couldn't tell how much of it was his anymore. Gina was bleeding; a pool of darkness was spreading from underneath her head, matting her curls.

Daubs literally fell onto Gina, straddling her chest.

"Time to still that vile tongue of yours," Daubs said. "No more lies or profanity—"

He pulled a pair of pliers from his shirt pocket.

"Fuck 'ou!" she screamed.

Suddenly he howled, a sound full of rage and pain. When he fell over onto his side, Hanson could see that she'd managed to get a grip on either his cock or balls through the loose khaki of his trousers. Daubs kicked at her, but she wouldn't let go, just kept twisting viciously.

Then Gina was scrambling up onto her feet. Daubs was still holding his crotch with one hand, rocking on the floor, but he grabbed at her ankle.

She went down, and Hanson heard her skull make a horrible crack against the floor.

She didn't move. He couldn't even tell if she was breathing.

The gun was so close now . . . Hanson could almost touch it—

Please, God, please . . . Just let me have the gun, let me kill this bastard, and then I'll die if you want me to . . .

Daubs must have seen Hanson's movement, for he lunged at Hanson just as his fingers grasped the barrel—

There was no time to fumble the gun around into a firing position. Hanson brought the gun down hard against the side of Daubs's skull.

Daubs slid sideways and his hand touched his head. When it came back bloody, he simply stared as if surprised he was capable of bleeding.

Hanson scuttled backward, struggling to sit up and holding the gun steady.

"You son of a bitch," Hanson gasped. "You fuckin' son of a bitch—"

"You're a better detective than I gave you credit for," Daubs panted.

Hanson half-slid, half-crawled to Gina's still body, feeling for a pulse.

Oh, God, don't be dead . . . don't be dead . . .

She had a pulse, but she was bleeding badly.

"You might have gotten away with it, you dumb fuck!" Hanson fumbled for his phone with one clumsy hand. "We even gave you the perfect scapegoat for all of it, but you just couldn't let Gina slip away, could you?"

"You kept getting in the way!"

"So you stole her day-planner to figure out where she'd be and when—"

"I've thought about putting a bullet in her brain since the night she was arrested," Daubs sneered.

"How were you gonna explain it?" Hanson asked. But suddenly he knew. Daubs had been planning to kill him and Gina both. He would make it look like a murder-suicide, a lover's quarrel.

Daubs laughed at the expression on Hanson's face. He started to rise.

"Don't you fuckin' move!" Hanson screamed. The phone slipped from his blood-slick hand and clattered to the floor.

"You're all *perverts,*" Daubs said, still crouching. "Larsen was the worst—with my *son!* She did all those filthy things with *my son!*"

"I said *sit down!*"

Hanson fired a shot into the wall just behind the chief, and Daubs froze. Hanson, not taking his eyes off him, fumbled for the phone.

"Officer down! This is Detective Tom Hanson, at four-fifty-one Holly Street, I need a bus and backup right away—"

Hanson let the phone drop into his lap. He needed both hands to steady the gun.

Don't pass out . . . Don't you dare fuckin' pass out now . . .

"Roger was your friend, you crazy bastard! All your talk about fraternities and Christmas cards—"

"He was a *pervert!*" Daubs shouted, flecks of blood and

spittle flying from his lips. "He seduced my *son* with his lurid lifestyle and had the *gall* to tell me to accept it! *To accept it!*"

"So you killed him?"

Hanson needed to hear him say it.

"I did what *any* father would do to protect his child."

"How were you protecting Jason when you butchered Robyn Macy?" Hanson demanded. "She was somebody's child, for Christ's sake!"

"She was another Jezebel!" He pounded his fist against the wall beside him. "Jason kept running to her for sympathy, hiding from his own father!"

"And Cassandra Lee?"

"She was the lowest form of garbage, manipulating his lust for *money*—"

"Who the fuck are you to be judge and jury?" Hanson leaned back against the edge of the sofa, feeling the room slide dangerously.

"I am a *righteous* man! Like Lot was in the days of Sodom—!"

"You're fuckin' nuts, is what you are."

As Hanson's speech became slower and thicker, Daubs's only became more agitated.

"There are *rules*!" Daubs babbled wildly. "People cannot just do whatever they please, spitting in the face of *God*! If God won't punish them I *will*!"

Hanson couldn't bear to listen to him any longer. The gun in his hand was so heavy, and his arms so weak. Was he shaking? He wasn't sure.

"You butchered five people, you sick fuck." Hanson spit out a mouthful of blood and saw, with an oddly detached sense of wonder, one of his teeth land on the floor.

"Oh, no," Daubs said, smiling crazily and wagging a finger as if admonishing a naughty child. "Only four. Quinn

Lee wasn't *my* doing, though he certainly *deserved* to be put down like a dog."

"You killed him. You'll get Death Row for five just the same as four. Why bother denying it?"

"Because it wouldn't be true," Daubs said. "Lying is a sin. Quinn wasn't mine."

Hanson looked at the gun in his hand and then back at Daubs as the full impact of the chief's words hit him.

Daubs just kept smiling.

Hanson lifted the gun, took aim, and shot him in the head.

Chapter 39

God is a dominant sadist. Look at Job, look at Abraham and Isaac, look at what he did to his own son. God is all about making us suffer to prove our devotion and obedience.

—JADE ADDISON, *Waiting for God*

Gina's body was dotted with curling snakes of stitches where the skin had to be sewn back together. She bloomed black and purple in twice as many places, bruised right down to the bone.

Every time he looked at her, he was amazed and grateful that she was alive. Daubs had begun working her over even before Hanson had interrupted them, and she had gotten far worse than he had.

He didn't want to think about what might have happened if he hadn't seen that photo of Jason Daubs when he did.

Aside from the bruises, a slight concussion, a dislocated shoulder, a broken arm, and two broken ribs, her most serious injuries were internal. It took two emergency surgeries to find and repair them all.

She'd been in and out of consciousness for two days before Hanson could talk to her. Then he waited another day until he thought she was strong enough to have the conversation they had to have.

"Why didn't you tell me who Jason was?"

She closed her eyes and sighed.

"I didn't think it mattered. I swear to God, Hanson, I knew Daubs was a bastard and an abuser, but I never dreamed he was the guy we were looking for."

"You should have been honest with me, Gee."

She reached for his hand, and he let her hold on to it.

"I care about Jason. A lot. Not the way I care for you, but he is important to me."

"So you were trying to protect him?"

"Yes. I didn't even know that Daubs knew I was Jason's mistress. I just wanted to keep him out of all this."

Hanson could understand that now. He had come too close to losing her forever to hold a grudge, and he knew he would do whatever it took to hold on to her.

"We would have caught Daubs sooner if all you people weren't so damned secretive."

"Most people feel the world doesn't give them a choice." She smiled at him wanly. "And I don't think you can say 'you people' anymore. You're a pervert, too."

Daubs had cut him clean through his shirt but had managed to miss anything important. The doctor in the ER told Hanson that another half-inch to the left, and Daubs would have cut his jugular.

His kneecap, he was glad to find out, was not shattered to hell and back—that's what it had felt like—but only dislocated. Once the headaches from the concussion had faded, and his broken nose had been set, the knee was the most annoying injury Hanson had to deal with. He'd be on crutches for at least a month, and physical therapy for even longer.

"I think my therapist is one of you," he told Gina after his first visit. "Woman is a freakin' sadist."

"Did she make you cry?" Gina grinned from her little nest on the sofa.

"I tried hollering 'Red,' but she wouldn't stop."

Even with his bad knee, Hanson was up and around before Gina could do more than hobble from the couch to the bathroom. He was back at his desk dealing with the reports, paperwork, and internal affairs crap within a week.

"Shouldn't you be resting?" Griggs had asked. "Take your ass home and watch the soap operas or something."

Hanson wasn't sure if Griggs was angry because he'd missed the chance to arrest Milton Daubs, or because he felt bad about the beating Hanson had taken.

"I shoulda been with you," was all he said. "Son of a bitch coulda killed you both."

"I didn't know you cared." Hanson grinned.

"I'd have to break in a new partner," Griggs grunted. "I don't have time for that shit."

Instead, he nearly smothered them with his attention. He came over to Gina's house every day, always bringing something: donuts, DVDs, magazines, Chinese food.

He offered to do laundry, but Gina wouldn't hear of it.

"He's just trying to get his hands on my panties," Gina complained.

Jason's statement had been enough to get a search warrant for Daubs's house, and by the time Daubs's body was at the morgue, Griggs had found a pair of work boots in his garage. They were stained with blood that turned out to belong to Cassandra Lee.

Griggs also found Gina's day-planner in Daubs's car, along with photos from a private detective showing Jason with Cassandra Lee, Robyn Macy, and Gina. The duffel bag that the traffic cops had seen was discovered in the garage, too, containing a dark blue jumpsuit, stained with Cassandra Lee's blood.

It was lucky for all of them that they had a mountain of evidence to confirm Daubs's guilt.

Daubs's DNA was found to match traces taken from Roger Banks and Robyn Macy. No semen—even in his murders, Daubs had been a prude—but his blood and sweat were on the bodies, and their DNA on the tire thumper.

It was an ugly, sensational case, all the way around. No one, including Internal Affairs, was happy that Hanson had shot and killed the Chief of Police, but the extent of his and Gina's injuries proved he'd been fighting for his life.

Chapter 40

I feel a little like the moon who took possession of you
for a moment and then returned your soul to you. You
should not love me. One ought not to love the moon. If
you come too near me, I will hurt you.

—ANAIS NIN, *Delta of Venus*

There had been no commitments made, but most of his
clothes were now in Gina's closet and his toothbrush
snuggled up to hers in the bathroom.

Hanson was pretty damned happy about that.

She was on the sofa, with a pillow behind her head and
a blanket tucked around her. She was watching *The Usual
Suspects* again, one of the DVDs that Griggs had brought
over.

Hanson stumped over to the chair and fell into it, letting his crutches clatter to the floor.

"It's late," she said, turning down the volume. "Bad day
at the office, honey?"

"Something like that."

"Griggs brought over pizza. There's plenty left. You
want a beer?"

"No, thanks. And you can't have one, either. Not with
the meds."

He watched her move toward the kitchen. She was still
slow, but she didn't suck in her breath every time she
moved now. She had told him to stop fetching and carrying for her, or she'd never improve.

"I know. I'm getting another glass of tea."

Hanson stared at the television until she'd come back
and resettled herself.

"So?" she asked. "Are you gonna tell me what kept you so late?"

He looked at her, feeling very tired.

She was so beautiful, even with the ring of fading green around her eyes.

He pulled a plastic bag from his coat and tossed it onto the coffee table.

Inside the bag was a tire thumper.

She looked at him, and neither spoke for a very long minute.

"Imagine you've got a string of murders, victims all linked together in a tidy little package," Hanson said softly. "And there's somebody else who could be made to fit into that package with very little effort. If you hated that person, it might be tempting to slip in a murder of your own, don't you think?"

"Some things," she said carefully, "are better not to think too much about."

"Funny, Daubs said something like that to me after you shot Knoll.

"I can't help thinking, you took an awful big risk shooting him like that. You broke every rule in the book about dealing with a hostage situation."

"I just reacted. I told you, I had a shot and I took it."

"Still, we never got to question him, did we?"

Hanson nodded toward the thumper. "You didn't even bother to clean it very well. You just dumped it back into Quinn's toy bag after you'd used it to bash his brains in. You knew we'd already tested it, so we wouldn't even look at it again. Lucky for you, no one noticed that the evidence seal on the bag had been broken."

He waited for her to say something. Anything.

"So why *did* you look at it again?" she asked.

Hanson shrugged. Suddenly he felt very weary.

"Daubs claimed he didn't kill Quinn." And there was

something in his face when he said it. Like he was enjoying a private joke. He knew you'd done it, somehow he had guessed, and he thought it was funnier than shit."

"So you checked the thumper in Quinn's bag," she said, not meeting his eyes. "Did you tell anybody else?"

"You know I didn't."

"I didn't go there to kill him," she said, so softly he could barely hear.

"So you were the one that called him that night?" Hanson asked.

She ducked her head into her hands, then took a deep breath and looked up again. But she still did not meet his eyes.

"He left a message for me—"

"Can I hear it?"

"Don't be stupid," she said wearily. "I deleted it, naturally."

Hanson felt the muscles in his chest clench. He could still check the phone records, to see if she were telling the truth . . . If he wanted to.

"He said he had things to tell me—"

All day he'd been imagining how it might have happened. How Quinn had lured her to his studio, how that smug little bastard had tried to get under her skin with more of his mind games. Or had Quinn gotten physical with her?

"He said he would tell me what he knew, but only . . . Only if I let him use me, one more time.

"Don't you understand?" she begged, tears unshed along her lower lashes. "I hit him, I pushed him away—"

"And he got angry." It was more a statement than question. Hanson shut his eyes, trying not to let the images form in his mind.

"I got angry," Gina snapped. "I was so . . . Goddamned

furious! That he thought I was just this, this . . . *thing* he could take like he always did!

"The thumper was there, and I grabbed it, and I hit him. I hit him again and again, and then when I realized he wasn't breathing anymore . . ."

Now she was crying, silently with tears slipping down her cheeks. She brushed them away angrily.

"I thought I could make it look like just another victim. But I had to . . . to do all the things that the killer did.

"It was . . . unimaginable."

Both were silent as time crawled by. Hanson watched her wipe her face with the bottom hem of her T-shirt, and saw the fading bruises across her stomach. Finally she looked at him, and she must have seen the struggle in his expression, for she got up and crawled into his lap, bringing her face close to his.

"Please believe me." Her lips were close enough to his ear for her breath to tickle. "'I didn't know what else to do."

She took his face in her hands and kissed him on the mouth; a deep, soft kiss that tasted faintly of lemons.

"I love you," she continued, clutching his shoulders so hard it hurt, rubbing her still-damp face across his chest. "I don't want to lose you. Please . . . tell me you understand why I had to do it. Tell me that you don't hate me now."

But he couldn't find the words. His heart twisted, aching, rising into his throat and robbing him of speech.

She slid from his lap and stood up, wincing briefly before her expression went slack and dead. Her shoulders slumped, and she looked like a child: defeated, lost, abandoned.

He watched her shamble toward the bedroom with an odd kind of grace in spite of her awkwardness. Watched the shape of her ass stretching the satin of her panties, the way her breasts strained against the too-small T-shirt.

How could he still be so stirred by her, even now, after hearing her awful confession? He wanted her still. Not just her body, but her mind and soul.

He understood now. Whatever hold Quinn once had on her soul . . . she now had on *his*.

He wanted so badly to tell her what he'd done for her. That he'd committed cold-blooded murder to protect her. *Because I couldn't risk Daubs talking, and neither could she.*

In the doorway, she turned one final time, those amazing eyes pleading with a kind of naked need he had never seen there before.

"Please," she said again in a small voice. "Come to bed."

And, with one small prayer of contrition to whatever God might be listening, he did.

KATE KINSEY is a lifelong writer who has been very involved in the BDSM community on both local and national levels. Education within the community is one of her passions

"Sex," says Kinsey, "is one of the most powerful forces in our lives. It affects who we are and how we feel about ourselves. When that drive carries shame and repression, it cripples us in a very real and pervasive way.

"The stereotype that people who embrace BDSM—or indeed, any kink considered outside the mainstream of 'normal'—are somehow sick or damaged could not be further from the truth. It takes courage and self-awareness to seek out the things that fulfill and satisfy us. People who do what we do are among the healthiest and happiest people I know."

To learn more about Kate and BDSM, visit her at www.katekinsey.weebly.com.

Adrienne Basso

His Noble Promise

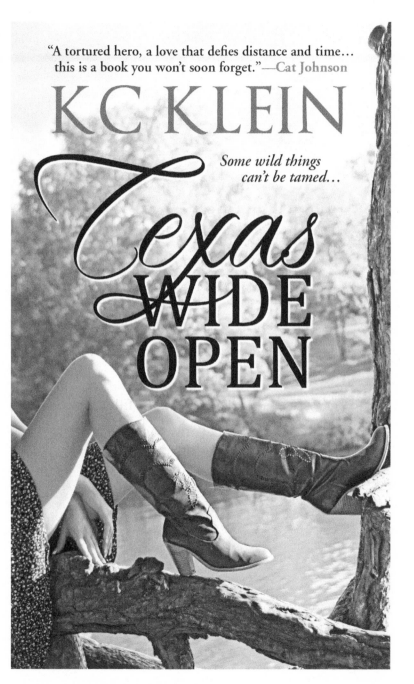

"A tortured hero, a love that defies distance and time…
this is a book you won't soon forget."—Cat Johnson

KC KLEIN

*Some wild things
can't be tamed…*

Texas
WIDE
OPEN